LAYING DOWN THE LAW

BY
DELORES FOSSEN

First Published in Great Britain 2016
By Mills & Boon, an imprint of HarperCollins*Publishers*
1 London Bridge Street, London, SE1 9GF

© 2016 Delores Fossen

ISBN: 978-0-263-91915-8

46-0916

Our policy is to use papers that are natural, renewable and recyclable products and made from wood grown in sustainable forests. The logging and manufacturing processes conform to the legal environmental regulations of the country of origin.

Printed and bound in Spain
by CPI, Barcelona

Delores Fossen, a *USA TODAY* bestselling author, has sold over fifty novels with millions of copies of her books in print worldwide. She's received a Booksellers' Best Award and an RT Reviewers' Choice Best Book Award. She was also a finalist for a prestigious RITA® Award. You can contact the author through her website at www.deloresfossen.com.

Chapter One

Blood.

Special Agent Cord Granger's stomach tightened into a knot.

Since he'd worked for the Drug Enforcement Administration for the past nine years now, he'd seen plenty of blood before at various crime scenes. And a lot more of it than the drops that were here on the floor of the barn.

But this wasn't any ordinary crime scene.

There shouldn't be blood here because there shouldn't be a victim.

Cord cursed under his breath and caught the eye of Sheriff Jericho Crockett, no doubt one of the first responders to the small ranch in Appaloosa Pass. This was the sheriff's jurisdiction. Jericho normally doled out glares and hard looks to Cord, but tonight he just lifted an eyebrow.

Cord lifted one of his own and felt that knot tighten even more.

"Miss Southerland insisted on seeing you," Jericho told Cord. "Said she wouldn't get in the ambulance until you got here."

Yeah, Jericho had relayed something similar about Karina Southerland when he'd phoned Cord about twenty minutes earlier. Jericho had asked him to come to the rental house on a local ranch and had rattled off the address. As an agent, Cord got plenty of bad calls in the middle of the night, some even from local sheriffs, but this one wasn't DEA-related.

This one was, well, personal.

"Karina said it was the Moonlight Strangler who attacked her?" Cord asked the sheriff.

Jericho nodded. "The guy had on a ski mask, came at her from behind. It fits the MO, too." He glanced up at the night sky, where there was a full moon.

The glancing hadn't been necessary, though. A full moon was always a reminder of murder. That could happen when a person had a personal connection to a vicious serial killer known as the Moonlight Strangler.

And when the killer was Cord's biological father.

It didn't matter that Cord didn't personally know the man. Though they had met. In a way. When Cord had been on the receiving end of the Moonlight Strangler's knife only a month ago. But because the Moonlight Strangler had pumped him full of drugs, Cord didn't have many memories of the incident at all.

Only the scars.

And while Cord would never—*never*—think of that snake as his father, they would always share the same blood.

"How bad is Karina hurt?" Cord added.

Jericho hitched his thumb to the rear of the barn. "See for yourself. It's not nearly as bad as it could have been."

True. She could be dead. "Did she say how she got away from…her attacker?"

"Oh, she's got plenty to say. Thought you'd want to hear it for yourself so you can try to make sense of it." Jericho paused. "Is there any sense to be made from this?"

Cord hoped there was. But he wasn't seeing it so far.

"The sooner you talk to her," Jericho continued, "the

sooner she'll be in that ambulance so I can get the CSIs in here to examine the place."

Cord wanted that, as well. Because the CSIs had to find something, *anything*.

Making sure he didn't step on the blood or any other item that could possibly be evidence, Cord made his way toward the two paramedics who weren't looking any happier about this situation than Jericho or him. The ambulance was parked at the front of the barn, the red lights still on and slashing through the night. That alone spiked his adrenaline and so did the fear of what he might see when he spotted the woman on the floor by some stacked hay bales.

Karina Southerland.

Over the past month he'd met with her at least a dozen times. In those confrontations—and they were confrontations, all right—she'd been intense but composed.

There wasn't much left of that composure now.

Her dark brown hair was a tangled mess, strands of it sticking to the perspiration on her face. No jeans and working cowboy boots as she'd worn during their previous meetings. Tonight, she had on just an oversize plain white T-shirt that she was obviously using as a nightgown. It was cut low enough at the neck that he could see the bruises there. She had bruises on her knees, too, and scrapes and nicks on her hands that looked like defensive wounds.

And there was the blood, of course.

A smear of it was still on her left cheek, which one of the paramedics was tending. Another cut on her left arm. She had yet another small one near her shoulder.

Along with the two paramedics, there was a third guy with graying brown hair. Lanky to the point of being scrawny, he was pacing just outside the rear entrance of the barn. The guy was chewing on his left thumbnail, had a cell phone gripped in his right hand and was tossing some very concerned glances at Karina. He was in his fifties, and it looked as if he'd dressed in a hurry. No boots, just his socks. But there was a gun tucked at an angle in the waist of his baggy jeans.

"Who are you?" Cord asked the guy right off.

He stopped chewing on his thumbnail long enough to answer. "Rocky Finney. I'm a ranch hand here. You need to help Karina."

"He works for me," Karina volunteered. "And he saved my life."

Cord stared at Rocky to let him know he wanted a lot more details than the ranch hand had just doled out to him.

"I was sleeping in the bunkhouse." Rocky glanced at the small barn-shaped building about twenty yards from the main house. Such that it was. The *main house* was small, too. "I heard Karina scream, and when I came out, this man wearing a mask was choking her. I shot at him. I think I hit him in the shoulder. And he ran off."

Maybe some of the blood belonged to the attacker. If Rocky was telling the truth, that is.

"Where did the man run?" Cord continued.

Rocky pointed in the direction of a heavily wooded area. Which was also the direction of the road since it was just on the other side of all those trees.

"There's no blood trail immediately around the barn," Jericho quickly informed Cord. "But the CSIs will look. I don't want anyone in that area until they've searched it."

Neither did Cord. Because blood could give them the DNA of the person responsible for this.

"She needs stitches," the paramedic said when he snared Cord's gaze.

The bulky, bald paramedic looked at Cord as if he could magically make Karina get in that ambulance and head to the hospital. But Cord had less influence on her than anyone else in this barn.

"I told you Willie Lee was innocent," Karina said, her mouth tight, "that he wasn't the Moonlight Strangler." Her voice was raspy but clear enough for Cord to hear the accusation in there.

The Moonlight Strangler had been a source of contention between Karina and him after Willie Lee Samuels was identified as the serial killer. And then captured. That had happened a month ago, after he'd attacked Cord.

Of course, Willie Lee didn't know about the multiple murder charges against him yet because he'd sustained a gunshot wound and been in a coma ever since being taken into custody.

And Cord had been the one to shoot him.

Willie Lee hadn't been able to confess. Hadn't been able to confirm anything related to the dozens of murders he'd committed as the Moonlight Strangler. Or any of the other crimes for that matter. Still, Cord had been sure Willie Lee was the right man.

Until tonight.

If the Moonlight Strangler was in a coma, then who the heck had attacked Karina?

"He's your father," Karina added. "Don't you feel in your bones that he's innocent?"

"No. I don't feel anything about him one way or another."

It was a lie. Cord felt plenty. Plenty that he didn't intend to share with her or anyone else for that matter.

Cord knelt down to make better eye contact with Karina. "Why don't you go ahead and get in the ambulance? We can talk this out on the way to the hospital."

She didn't budge, probably because she didn't trust him. She'd wanted him here only so she could say that she had told him so, that the cops had the wrong man in custody. But he glanced around at the signs of the struggle to remind her what'd gone on here. The toppled bales of hay and feed. The scattered tools and tack.

And the blood.

"You don't want to stay here," Cord reminded her.

He motioned for the paramedics to come closer and do their job, and Cord breathed a little easier when Karina didn't resist. Once she was on the stretcher, they started toward the ambulance. Cord followed right along beside them.

Rocky didn't attempt to go with them, probably because Jericho ordered him to stay put. No doubt so he could question the ranch hand and begin this investigation. Well, unless…

Cord stopped that thought. He didn't want to go there yet.

Because the real Moonlight Strangler hadn't done this.

"Make sure the horses are okay," Karina called out to Rocky.

Rocky assured her that he would.

"I'll meet you at the hospital as soon as the CSIs get here and I take Rocky to the station," Jericho said to Cord. "Anything Karina says to you will need to go in the report."

That last part wasn't exactly a request, but Cord had already known it would need to happen. Whether he wanted this or not, he was officially involved. Partly because Karina had insisted on calling him. Also in part because anything that had to do with the Moonlight Strangler automatically had to do with Cord.

"You'll need to drop the charges against Willie Lee," Karina insisted.

Cord had been stunned with the news of this attack on

Karina, but he was a lawman above all else. And a born skeptic. Being abandoned at a gas station when he was just a toddler could do that. Hard to grow up trusting people when most people he met weren't trustworthy.

Karina just might fall into that category.

And that was just one of the many, many reasons he wouldn't even consider trying to get those charges dropped against Willie Lee.

"Did you set all of this up to make Willie Lee look innocent?" Cord came right out and asked her.

She didn't exactly look outraged by the question. Just disgusted. "You think I had this done to myself?" Her breath shattered, and the tears came while her gaze skirted across the two cuts she could see.

There was another one, on her cheek, that she couldn't see.

The bald paramedic scowled at Cord, probably because he thought Cord was being too hard on her. If he was, he'd apologize later. For now, he needed to get to the truth, and the fastest way to do that was by not pulling any punches.

"Did you set this all up?" Cord persisted.

The glare she gave him could have frozen a pot of boiling water. "No."

Cord didn't want to believe her—it would be easier if he didn't. Easier because it would mean there wasn't a killer out there. But even if she hadn't done this to herself and there was another killer, it didn't mean Willie Lee was innocent.

One of the paramedics got in the driver's seat. The other got into the back with Cord and Karina, and they finally started the drive to the hospital.

"This attack could have been done by a copycat," Cord suggested to her. "Maybe someone who wanted to get back at you?"

If this had been a regular interrogation, this was the point where Cord would have asked Karina if she had any enemies. But he already knew the answer.

She did.

And Cord was one of them.

It was hard not to be enemies with a woman who was defending and praising a serial killer. But that's exactly what Karina had done.

"You don't know Willie Lee," she said. "And if you did, you'd know he wasn't capable of murder."

It was the same argument he'd heard from her too many times to count. She considered herself a good judge of Willie Lee's character because the man had worked on her family's ranch in Comal County for the past fifteen years. A ranch she still owned now that her folks had passed, but she'd rented this place near Appaloosa Pass so she could be near Willie Lee while he recovered.

If he recovered, that is.

After all, the man had been in a coma for over a month.

"Willie Lee's DNA was found at the scene of a woman he murdered," he reminded her, though it was something she already knew. That DNA match had been confirmed shortly after he was caught. Since it was a verbal jab, Cord waited for her to get her usual jab back.

"It could have been planted, and you know it."

Yes, he did. But there was the other match. "My own DNA is a familial match to Willie Lee's. No one planted that. I had three labs repeat the test." And each time Cord had hoped the results would be different. "How do you explain that?"

She huffed. "Willie Lee might be your father, but that still doesn't mean he's a killer."

Again, it was an argument they'd already hashed and rehashed. "Willie Lee also matches the height and weight descriptions that witnesses of the Moonlight Strangler have given over the years."

Many witnesses. Cord didn't bother to remind her of that, too. She knew. She also knew none of those witnesses had gotten a look at his face.

But that didn't explain who'd done this to her.

"Serial killers often develop a following," Cord said, going for a different angle. One that might put an end to this conversation sooner rather than later. "Groupies. Has anyone like that contacted you? Maybe someone calling themselves a fan who wanted you to get a photo or some other personal item of Willie Lee's?"

Karina shook her head after each of the questions and then winced. The paramedic moved quickly to examine her, and that's when Cord noticed that she had another cut that her hair was covering.

"He clubbed me on the head." Karina's voice was trembling again. No doubt from the fear and adrenaline. None of her injuries appeared to be serious, but the memories would be with her for a lifetime.

"Start from the beginning," Cord insisted. Because that hit on the head was a game changer. She couldn't have done that to herself. "Tell me everything that happened."

Karina flinched again when the paramedic dabbed at the head wound. "I woke up when I heard the horses. I thought maybe they were just spooked because it was a new place. I'd just moved them out here this week."

Yes, he'd known about that. Karina was setting up a temporary operation here for training her cutting horses. Ironically, the name for that kind of trainer was a cutter. A sick joke now considering her injuries.

"I went outside to check on the horses," Karina continued after she'd gathered her breath. "When I stepped into the barn, he hit me over the head. I didn't even see him. Didn't know he was there until it was too late."

Cord jumped right on that. "But you could tell for sure that it was a man?"

"Yes," she said without hesitation.

Damn. He hoped that meant the guy hadn't sexually assaulted her in some way. But if this piece of dirt had done that, it would definitely break from the MO of the Moonlight Strangler, who'd never sexually assaulted any of his victims.

"What happened next?" he persisted when she didn't continue.

Karina closed her eyes a moment. Shuddered. "I screamed as I was falling, and he cut my face." She reached to put her fingers there, but the paramedic moved them away.

It was the slice on her cheekbone. And the signature of the Moonlight Strangler.

Or rather the signature of his copycat.

"Did your attacker say anything to you?" Cord asked.

She swallowed hard. "He laughed and said, 'This will show them.' It wasn't in a regular voice. He was whispering as if his throat was raspy."

Perhaps just someone who wanted to clear Willie Lee's name. Of course, to the best of his knowledge, there was still only one person who fell into that particular name-clearing category.

Karina herself.

Cord studied her injuries, trying to look at the pattern to see what they could tell him. Karina didn't seem like the vain type, but he had a hard time believing that any woman would allow her face to be cut so she could try to prove someone's innocence. If she'd set this up, she could have merely had the person hit her on the head and leave bruises on her neck.

Cord's phone buzzed, and when he saw Jericho's name on the screen, he answered it right away. "Did you send that ranch hand, Rocky, off to do something?" Jericho asked.

"No. Why?"

"Because he's not here. The CSIs finally made it so I started looking for him to take him to the office, but he's not in the house or bunkhouse."

Hell. "You don't think he went looking for the attacker?"

Jericho cursed, too. "If he did, I don't need this now. If Karina has his number, try to call him."

Cord assured him that he'd try, but he figured since she didn't have her phone with her, there was little chance Karina would remember the ranch hand's number.

But she surprised Cord when she rattled it off.

"I have a good memory," she mumbled. A comment that snagged his attention because there seemed to be something else, something that she wasn't saying.

Something that she *remembered*.

"What is it?" Cord asked, staring at her.

She didn't get a chance to respond. Didn't get a chance to explain, either. The driver hit his brakes, bringing the ambulance to a jarring stop.

"Draw your gun," the driver told Cord.

Cord did. And he soon saw why they'd stopped and why the driver had given that order.

It certainly wasn't what Cord had expected to see.

There. In the middle of the dark country road. A man. He was wearing a ski mask.

And he had a gun pointed right at them.

Chapter Two

Karina lifted her head to see what had caused the ambulance driver to give that order to Cord.

Draw your gun.

Not exactly an order to steady her racing heart. But then, seeing the man in the ski mask didn't help with that, either.

Oh, God.

He'd found her.

Cord did indeed draw his gun. Fast. "Call for backup and get down," he told the paramedic beside her.

While the paramedic did that, Cord maneuvered himself in front of her, and the driver got down onto the seat. But the man on the road did some maneuvering, too. With his weapon still aimed at them, he ducked behind a tree, probably so that Cord wouldn't just shoot him.

"Don't try to drive off, Agent Granger," the man shouted. "Wouldn't be good for your health right now if you tried to do that. We need to have a little chat first."

There were no side windows on the back of the ambulance, and with Cord in front of her, she couldn't see much through the windshield. However, it sounded as if this monster had some kind of backup. Or maybe he was just bluffing and wanted them to be like sitting ducks while he fired shots at them.

"The ambulance is bullet-resistant," Cord said, as if reading her mind. "And I want to catch this sick bastard."

So did Karina. More than anything. Not only could catching him clear Willie Lee's name, but it would also get this killer behind bars, where he belonged. She'd known in her heart that Willie Lee wasn't the Moonlight Strangler, and arresting this man would prove it.

She hoped.

Of course, Cord might continue to believe this was a copycat. He might not want to admit they'd charged the wrong man with multiple murders. Because in this case the wrong man was his biological father and he wanted to see him punished.

"There are explosives in the ditches on both sides of the road," the man shouted. "If you shoot at me or do anything else to otherwise rile me, the explosives will go off."

Karina gasped, and the paramedic didn't fare much better. He dropped down to the floor.

"Explosives?" Cord asked, glancing around. He spoke in a loud enough voice that the guy outside would have no trouble hearing him. "That's not the MO of the Moonlight Strangler."

"You're right, but sometimes a man's gotta get creative. The explosives might not kill you. *Might* not. But it's a big ol' risk to take with such fragile cargo inside, isn't it?"

That got Karina snapping to a sitting position. Or rather she tried to do that. She was strapped to the gurney that was locked in place on the floor, but she still lifted her torso as much as she could.

"I'm not that fragile," she insisted. However, the dizziness hit her, and almost immediately she had no choice but to drop back down.

Karina cursed the dizziness. The pain. Cursed the fact

that this idiot was taunting her after he'd come so close to killing her.

She could still feel his hands around her neck. Could still smell his stench on her skin. Could still hear his gravelly voice as he'd cut her.

This will show them.

But he'd whispered something else to her, too. Something she hadn't been able to catch because by then the pain and the panic had been screaming through her head.

What had he said to her? *What?*

Knowing that might help them if she could somehow use those words to figure out who was behind that mask.

He'd seemed…familiar. Or something.

"Do you see any explosives?" the driver asked Cord. Unlike Cord, his voice was trembling. Probably the rest of him, too.

Cord shook his head. "It's too dark to see much of anything out there."

No doubt part of this killer's plan. There might not be any explosives at all. But Karina rethought that. The attack at her place had happened nearly an hour ago. That was plenty of time for the killer to get out here and set up an ambush, especially since this was the only road leading into town.

It was also the same road that the backup lawmen would be taking.

Karina prayed their arrival wouldn't make this situation worse than it already was. Maybe the deputies or whoever responded would be able to sneak up on the man and capture him. Alive. That way, he could answer questions and clear Willie Lee's name for good.

"What do you want?" Cord shouted to the man.

"The woman," he readily answered.

Had her heart skipped a beat or two? It certainly felt like it.

Cord glanced back at her, probably trying to reassure her that he wouldn't just hand her over to a killer. And he wouldn't. She'd only known him a month, but he wasn't a coward or a dirty lawman. He didn't like her. Possibly even hated her. But he would protect her with his life.

But that wasn't comforting.

Karina didn't want anyone dying to save her. Still, she wasn't exactly in a position to defend herself.

"Why do you want her?" Cord called out to him.

"Because I'd like to finish what I started." Another fast answer. Whether it was true or not, she didn't know.

Was something else going on here?

"We should have started with introductions first," Cord said. He moved to the front seat, probably so he could be in a better position to return fire. "Who are you?"

The man laughed. "And here I thought you were smarter than that. After all, we do share the same DNA."

She could only see the side of Cord's face, but she saw a muscle flicker in his jaw. "So, you're saying you're the Moonlight Strangler? Because you can't be. He's in a coma."

"I'm not just saying it. I *am* the Moonlight Strangler."

"Right," Cord grumbled under his breath. Karina had no trouble hearing his skepticism.

"Though I gotta tell you, I never liked that name," the man continued. "Moonlight Slasher would have been a whole lot better, don't you think?"

"Haven't given it much thought. A killer's a killer no matter what he's called. But I'm not convinced you're who you're saying you are. Convince me," Cord insisted.

The guy laughed. "Boy, you got a smart mouth. I like that. It's something we have in common."

"I have nothing in common with you," Cord snapped.

Karina figured that Cord didn't want her to be part of this conversation. Correction: a part of this taunting. But this might be the only chance she got to ask the question she needed her attacker to answer.

"Why do you want me dead?" Karina shouted to the man.

That earned her a glare from Cord, and he motioned for her to get back down. She didn't.

"Tell me why!" Karina said in an even louder voice when the man didn't answer.

"You're not gonna like the answer, sweetheart," the man finally said.

The *sweetheart* turned her stomach. He'd used that same syrupy tone when he'd been attacking her.

Except he had used a different tone when he'd mumbled those handful of words that she hadn't understood.

"Besides," the man went on, "talking time is over now. I figure Sheriff Jericho Crockett or his lawmen brothers are trying to sneak up on me right about now. Hope they don't step on anything that'll make 'em go ka-boom." He laughed. "Oh, wait. I do hope that happens. Crockett blood spilled all over these woods. What a nice way to end the night."

Oh, mercy. "You have to warn Jericho," she told Cord.

Cord motioned for the ambulance driver to make another call. The man did, and he told whoever answered that there might be explosives not just in the ditches, but also in the woods. Hopefully, the lawmen would get the word in time.

"Time's up," the man yelled. "Hate to sound all dramatic, but hand her over or else."

"She's hurt," Cord answered. "And I'm sure you know why since you're the one who hurt her. She can't walk."

"Liar. I didn't do a damn thing to her legs."

"It's her head," Cord explained. "You hit her hard enough that you might have fractured her skull. That's why she's in an ambulance on the way to the hospital."

Silence.

For a long time.

So long that Karina got a really bad feeling. A feeling that went all the way to her bones. If she didn't do something fast, he was either going to kill them all or get away.

"Cord can carry me to you," she told the man.

As expected, that really didn't go over very well with Cord. "Have you lost your mind?" he snarled.

Possibly. She didn't have a fractured skull, as Cord had told her attacker, but she was dizzy and in pain. Still, this might be their only shot at catching the man. After all, he'd have to come out of his hiding place to get to her.

"He doesn't want to shoot me," she whispered to Cord. "If he did, he would have done that in the barn."

Cord's eyes narrowed. "A bullet isn't the only way to kill you."

She was well aware of it and touched her fingers to her neck to let him know that. "If you're carrying me, he won't shoot. And once you're close enough to him, you can drop me and grab him."

Cord cursed. "There are about a dozen things that could go wrong with a stupid plan like that—including he could kill us both and then come after the paramedics to kill them, too. Is that what you want?"

Karina didn't get a chance to answer that because her attacker ducked out of sight behind the tree.

"Too late," the man shouted.

"Get down!" Cord warned them, and he moved back to the gurney to cover her body with his.

Not a second too soon.

The blast tore through the ambulance, tossing it and shaking the ground beneath them.

It was deafening.

And then everything happened much too fast for Karina to process a lot of it. They were moving, tumbling. Crashing into things.

Debris, flying everywhere.

Somehow, Cord managed to keep hold of her, and since the gurney was anchored to the floor, he was toppled around with her. No way to brace herself, no way to do anything but wait for this nightmare to end and pray they stayed alive.

There was the sound of metal screeching against the pavement, and the ambulance finally stopped with a jolting thud.

What had happened now?

And was everyone okay?

The ambulance was a jumbled mess, and it took her a moment to realize it was on its side. That was likely where the impact had landed him.

"He set off the explosives," she said. Though Cord had obviously already figured that out.

There was a cut on his forehead and some blood in his light brown hair. Heaven knew where else he was hurt, but at least he wasn't moaning in pain like the bald paramedic crumpled next to them.

"Are you all right?" Cord asked her.

No. Not by a long shot. But Karina didn't think she'd gotten any other injuries, probably because she'd been held in place on the gurney. And because of Cord.

"I'm not hurt," she responded. Maybe that was true, but everything inside her felt bruised and raw.

Cord pulled the straps off her and eased her sideways off the gurney and onto the floor. "Help him," Cord told her.

That's when she saw the angry gash on the bald paramedic's head. Not a simple cut like the one on Cord's, either. This one was deep, and he was losing a lot of blood.

It was hard to find anything in the debris, so she used the cotton blanket that'd been covering her and pressed it to his wound. While she did that, Cord checked on the paramedic in the front seat. It didn't help her nerves any when he pressed his fingers to the guy's neck.

"Is he dead?" she asked hesitantly.

Cord shook his head. "Just unconscious." He used the radio in the front to call for assistance. "Stay put," he warned her.

Despite the debris and clutter everywhere, Cord managed to make his way to the back of the ambulance. He had his gun ready when he tried the door handle. It took several pushes, but he finally got it open.

Karina couldn't see anything outside because Cord was blocking the way. He didn't go outside. He stayed there, his gaze firing around and his head raised. Listening.

She heard the moan coming from the front seat, and several moments later, the paramedic in the front lifted his head. "What the heck happened?" he grumbled.

"An explosion." Cord didn't even glance back at the guy. He kept his focus outside. No doubt in case the killer came after them again.

That gave her a fresh jolt of adrenaline.

They were stuck here. Right where the killer could get them. And this time, he just might succeed.

This nightmare wasn't over. It was just beginning.

"Try to level your breathing," Cord told her. "I don't want you to hyperventilate."

Since she was very close to doing just that, Karina tried to slow down her breathing. Tried to steady her heartbeat, too. She wasn't very successful at doing either.

"Jericho should be here any minute," Cord assured her.

She wasn't sure if that was wishful thinking or if he'd gotten confirmation of that when he'd used the ambulance's radio. Karina certainly didn't hear any sirens.

But then she also didn't hear their attacker taunting them.

"Is he still out there?" she asked, and wasn't aware she was holding her breath until her lungs started to ache.

Cord didn't jump to answer her. He continued to look around. "I don't see him. That doesn't mean he's not there."

True. "You'll have to warn Jericho." She didn't want the sheriff driving into a trap.

"He knows," Cord assured her. He shifted his position, lifting his head.

And then he cursed.

He drew in several more breaths and cursed again.

"Can you walk?" Cord looked at her first for an answer, then at the bleeding paramedic.

"Yes," Karina answered at the same time the paramedic mumbled a not so convincing "yeah."

"Why?" she asked.

But it wasn't necessary for Cord to answer her because she smelled two things that she didn't want to smell.

Gasoline.

And smoke.

"Did he set a fire?" she blurted out.

Cord didn't answer her question. "We're getting out of here now. Now!" he ordered, glancing back at the paramedic in front.

"What's going on?" the paramedic asked, but despite being dazed and injured, he started climbing over the seat toward them.

Now, Cord made eye contact with Karina. Their gazes held for a few intense seconds. "When you get out, start running as fast as you can and don't look back."

Chapter Three

Their situation had gone from bad to much, much worse.

Cord wasn't sure if he could get Karina and the paramedics out of there alive. Still, he had to try because he didn't have many options here.

"Stay out of the ditches," Cord reminded them.

Maybe their attacker had lied about putting explosives on both sides of the road, but it was too big of a risk to take. Especially since there had indeed been explosives somewhere near the ambulance. Where exactly those explosives had been placed, Cord still didn't know, and he didn't have time to find out if there were others.

Cord stepped out of the ambulance. Not easily. He'd been banged up when they'd been tossed around. No broken bones, thank God, but he'd have bruises, and he was still recovering from injuries he'd gotten last month, thanks to the Moonlight Strangler. Those bruises and injuries made themselves known when he pivoted, looking for the idiot who'd done this to them.

No sign of anyone.

But at the moment the bomber wasn't even his main concern. It was the thin line of fire snaking its way from the side of the road toward the ambulance. The fire line was too narrow and straight to have been spilled randomly or have leaked out from the ambulance.

Which meant their attacker had set it.

Probably before they'd even arrived at this point on the road.

In addition to the smoke from the fire trail, there was white steam spewing from what was left of the ambulance engine. Normally, he wouldn't have considered that a good thing, but he did now. Because the steam and the smoke just might conceal them enough so their attacker wouldn't be able to gun them down when they made a run for it.

"Stay low and move fast," Cord told them, doubting either of the paramedics could do that last part.

He had to keep watch, but he reached behind him, and with his left hand, he hauled out Karina. The paramedics followed after her, and once they all had their feet on the ground, Cord got them moving.

Away from the spot where he'd last seen the man in the ski mask.

Away from the ambulance.

That meant jumping the ditch. Again, it wasn't easy. Everyone was limping, hurt, struggling. But Karina and the paramedics all had a clear sense of how critical it was to put some distance between them and the fire.

Cord sure had a clear sense of it.

"Try to make sure the ambulance and steam hide you as much as possible," Cord added.

They each crossed the ditch while Cord kept watch. Still no signs of their mask guy or of Jericho. Cord figured both were out there, though. The trick would be to avoid another attack before backup arrived and not hit Jericho or one of the deputies with friendly fire.

He braced himself for shots to come right at them. After all, their attacker was armed. But no shots came. Nor were there any sounds that the man was about to launch another attack. Just the stench of the smoking rubber tires and the gasoline.

Cord was the last to jump the ditch, and as soon as he was on the other side, he hurried the others into a cluster of trees. Not ideal cover since someone could sneak up on them, but if the ambulance did explode, then they'd at least stand a chance of being protected from flying debris.

"Get down on the ground," he told them. "And stay low."

Again, not easy. The paramedic with the head wound tried to muffle his groans of pain, but he didn't quite manage it. Worse, he was still bleeding, and even though Karina was trying to add some pressure to the gash, he was losing a lot of blood.

"The killer wants me," Karina whispered. "If he has me, you and the paramedics might be safe."

Hell, no. Cord knew where this conversation was about to go, and he nipped it in the bud. "You're not going out there. He wants us all dead. That's why he set those explosives."

That was possibly true anyway. Obviously, the blast hadn't killed them, so maybe this was all part of some sick plan to get them in the open.

If so, it'd worked.

They were indeed in the open with only one gun among them and a likely copycat killer ready, willing and able to do them all in.

"Just stay down," Cord snapped to Karina when she lifted her head. "I don't have time to watch you and everything else."

Yeah, it was a jab that she probably didn't deserve, since she'd certainly pulled her own weight getting out of the ambulance. But maybe it was enough of a jab to keep her head out of the path of a bullet.

Or an explosion.

Even though he'd tried to brace himself for it, the blast jolted through his body, shaking him to the core.

The debris came bursting out from the fireball, all that was left of the ambulance. The trickle of flames had obviously made its way to the engine and heated it enough to cause the blast.

That was probably what their attacker intended.

A chunk of metal flew into the tree, inches from where Cord was standing, and he felt a sharp tug on the leg of his jeans. Karina pulled him to the ground next to her.

"It won't help us if you get yourself killed," she warned, sounding a lot tougher than she probably felt right now.

But she was right. Cord had to stay alive.

The wave of smoke came at them. It was mixed with the stench of the burning rubber, and Cord had to cover his mouth to keep from coughing.

"Y'all okay?" their attacker called out.

Cord wished he could do something about that smug tone. Like beat the guy senseless. What Cord couldn't do was answer him. It was possible the question was meant to help the fool pinpoint their location.

"Because I'd hate to think I gave any of you more boo-boos," the man added. Then, he laughed. He was still somewhere on the other side of the road.

That was the good news.

It meant he wasn't sneaking up behind them.

But he could have hired guns. And probably did. It would have been hard for him to pull this off by himself unless he'd set the explosives before attacking Karina, and those hired guns could be anywhere.

"What? Cats got your tongues?" the man asked.

His taunts made Cord's blood run cold. And made his temper run hot.

"Being quiet won't help," he taunted. "I'll find you."

"His voice," Karina whispered.

Even though he hated to risk looking at her, Cord did, to see what the heck she was talking about. "What about his voice?"

She opened her mouth. Closed it. Shook her head. "It's the same man who attacked me in the barn."

Of course it was. There'd been no doubt about that. So, what exactly had Karina meant to say?

Or rather what was she trying to keep from him?

Well, whatever the heck it was, Cord would find out. As soon as they got out of this mess.

The seconds crawled by, turning into minutes. Cord forced himself to listen through the crashing of his heartbeat in his ears. Each tiny sound put him on full alert.

Until one sound caused him to pivot in that direction.

Footsteps.

"It's me," someone said. Jericho.

Cord didn't ease the grip on his gun, though, until he actually spotted the sheriff. He was weaving his way through the trees, coming toward them.

"He's over there," Cord informed him right off, and he tipped his head in the direction where he'd last heard the guy. "Did you bring backup?"

Jericho nodded and glanced at Karina and the paramedics, before focusing on the area Cord had pointed out. "My brother Jax is somewhere nearby." He motioned toward the area just south of the attacker. "My other brother, Levi, is on the way."

So, maybe Jax was already close enough to stop him. Cord didn't know Jericho's brothers that well, but Jax had been a deputy sheriff for years. Hopefully, that was enough experience so he wouldn't walk into a trap.

"There might be other explosives," Cord pointed out.

Another nod from Jericho. "We got your warning and then heard the blast. Jax will be watching for anything suspicious. If Jax gets a shot, though, he'll take it."

Cord knew what that meant—they might not be able to take this guy alive. Part of him wanted the moron alive. Because he wanted answers. But since he was convinced this was a copycat, they could perhaps get those answers even if the man was dead. Besides, if he stayed alive and managed to get away, he'd likely just come after Karina again.

"I can't stop the bleeding," Karina mumbled.

Her hands were covered with blood now, and the paramedic was barely conscious. They needed an ambulance and needed one fast. It was time to try to end this stalemate and maybe distract the man so that he wouldn't hear Jax approaching him.

"Just how long do you think you can stay out here like this?" Cord shouted.

The guy laughed. "Well, you're alive after all. And to answer your question, I can wait as long as it takes. But I'm guessing that's not true for you, huh? Just how bad are Karina-girl and the others hurt? I didn't get a good enough look to know when y'all ran like rats."

Cord had to get his teeth unclenched before he could answer. "If you're so concerned about them, why don't you surrender and find out for yourself how they're doing? We can have a chat about them after they're on the way to the hospital."

Silence. It went on way too long. "Nope. Not in a chatting mood right now. I'm thinking it's time for me to get myself out of here. Another time, another place, Agent Granger."

And almost immediately Cord heard some footsteps. Not the light treading ones as Jericho's had been. Someone was running.

Karina would have gotten to her feet if Cord hadn't pushed her back down. "He's getting away," she argued.

Not if Cord had something to do about it. "Wait here with them," Cord told the sheriff.

He was about to bolt after the man when Jericho moved in front of him. "I'll go. My brothers and I have signals already worked out. Keep watch, though, because this could be a trick."

True. The man could be pretending to leave so he could ambush them. With Jax already out there somewhere, Cord didn't want him to get caught in friendly fire.

Jericho headed out, hurrying but threading his way through the trees to keep his cover. Cord figured Jericho wouldn't cross the road until he was clear of all the debris from the burning ambulance. Or until he was sure this clown wouldn't spot him and shoot him.

All Cord could do was wait.

The paramedic who'd been driving took off his shirt and moved closer to Karina so he could help with his bleeding partner. Cord tuned them out and listened. No more running footsteps, but he did hear something. A sort of loud pop.

Karina obviously heard it, too, because her gaze slashed in the direction of the sound. "Did he hit someone?"

Cord shook his head. Too bad he knew from a case he'd worked the sound a hammer made when hitting a human body.

The next sound was one he had no trouble recognizing.

A shot.

It cracked through the air in the same general area where their attacker had been. And it was soon followed by another bullet.

Damn. He hoped Jericho and his brother hadn't become this snake's next targets.

Waiting had never been Cord's strong suit, and it didn't help that he had a guy literally bleeding to death next to his feet and a would-be killer was out there who thought this was a sick game.

Finally, he heard another sound that wasn't more shots. It was footsteps, and they were heading right in Cord's direction.

"It's me," Jericho called out again. He wasn't running exactly, but it was close. And the lawman was all in one piece.

The breath Karina blew out was loaded with relief. Relief that Cord shared. Jericho hadn't been shot. But that didn't mean all was well.

"Your brothers?" Cord asked.

"Are in pursuit of the guy in the ski mask." Jericho looked up the road. "An ambulance will be here in just a few minutes."

Good. That was a start.

"You can't let that man get away," Karina said, standing and meeting Jericho's gaze.

"We'll do our best. In the meantime, there's a note for you nailed to a tree over there."

That explained the sound of the hammer Cord had heard. This guy had taken the time to leave a note. Why?

"A note for me?" Karina asked.

Jericho nodded. Frowned. Or maybe that was a scowl. "I didn't touch it because it might have prints or traces on it. It's handwritten. Or I should probably say it was handscrawled, as if he'd written it in a hurry. Which is a given, I suppose."

"And?" Cord persisted when Jericho didn't continue.

The sheriff stared at Karina. "It said, 'Remember what I told you, Karina-girl.'"

Her shoulders snapped back, and she shook her head.

But a head shake wasn't the answer Cord wanted. "What did he tell you?" Cord demanded.

"'This will show them,'" she said. "He repeated that a couple of times."

Cord stepped closer to her, getting right in her face. "And that's it?"

Karina looked ready to give him a resounding yes. But then she paused. "No. He said something else." Now, she shook her head again. "But it doesn't make sense."

Or maybe it was something she didn't want to make sense. "What did he say?" Cord asked.

"He said, 'You know exactly who I am, Karina-girl, don't you?'"

Chapter Four

Karina was hurting in nearly every part of her body. She felt like one giant bruise, probably looked it, too, judging from the glances Cord kept giving her from across the hospital treatment room that they were sharing. Sympathy mixed with plenty of frustration.

She understood both.

The bald paramedic was in another room getting stitched up and also receiving a transfusion since he'd lost so much blood. The second paramedic had two broken ribs, one of which had punctured his lung. He'd already been admitted to the hospital.

And then there was Cord.

Karina wasn't exactly sure what his injuries were because he had refused medical attention and had instead been making a string of phone calls. However, he looked as banged up as she did. Maybe more. Because she knew he was still recovering from the injuries he'd gotten last month.

Stab wounds.

And he'd gotten them when the Moonlight Strangler had taken him hostage.

Of course, Cord and everybody else on the planet believed that Willie Lee had been the one to do those horrible things to him, along with killing all those women. Despite the latest attack, Cord was still convinced that Willie Lee was the Moonlight Strangler. But Karina knew differently. The only thing that made sense to her was that the Moonlight Strangler had set up Willie Lee to take the blame not just for that attack on Cord, but for all the other murders.

She'd had zero luck proving it so far.

The nurse finally finished with the last of the stitches. "Wait here," she said.

She glanced down at Karina's bare legs and the blue paper examining gown she was wearing. Her bloodstained T-shirt had already been bagged for evidence.

"I'll see about getting you a pair of scrubs, and I'll talk to the doctor about releasing you," the nurse added and left the room.

"Good," Karina said before she thought it through. She didn't want to spend the rest of the night in the hospital, but she wasn't sure where she could go.

Certainly not back home.

That thought alone caused her to curse this monster. Her horses were there. Her things. Her life. Well, her temporary life anyway. And now she might not ever feel safe there again.

Cord finished his latest call and made his way to her. She was surprised he wasn't limping. Or maybe he just didn't want her to see that.

She'd only known him a month and couldn't quite figure him out. Hurt and bitter. Determined to put his biological father away for the rest of his life.

Drop-dead hot.

Yes, she'd noticed that, too, and hated that she'd noticed.

"After you're released, I'll drive you to the sheriff's office so Jericho can take your statement," he explained. "Then, we can arrange for you to go into protective custody."

Karina nodded. This was going to be a very long night,

and while she just wanted it to end, she wasn't stupid. She wouldn't refuse protective custody.

"Certainly, this attack must make you doubt that Willie Lee is really the Moonlight Strangler?" she asked.

Cord shook his head. "It only convinces me that we have a copycat or else a groupie who wants to pretend he's a serial killer."

She didn't bother with a sigh, though it was frustrating that Cord wouldn't even consider his father's innocence. "Then at least tell me they found the man responsible for this latest attack."

Cord shook his head. "Nothing. So far. But Jericho's got a CSI team out there now. One out at your place, too. They're going through every inch of it so something might turn up. After that, they'll go through your house to make sure your attacker didn't stash something inside."

He didn't sound very hopeful, though, that they'd find anything. Neither was Karina. Mainly because she didn't believe the attacker had actually been in the house.

Oh, God.

Had he gone inside?

Just the thought of that required a deep breath. It was bad enough that he'd been in her barn.

"Are you remembering something else?" Cord asked.

He'd no doubt noticed the hard breath she'd taken. Heck, she could have even gone pale, too. But she didn't want to spell out her fears to him. Especially since what was done was done. If the killer had been in her house, if he'd watched her, stalked her, she couldn't undo that. No. It was best to move on and try to work through this.

She looked up at Cord and caught him in mid-grimace. So, he wasn't perfect at masking his pain after all.

"You really should let the doctor check you out," Karina suggested.

Cord must have considered that a closed and shut argument since he didn't even address it. He dragged over a chair and sank down on it so they were facing each other. She braced herself for another round of "blame this all on Willie Lee," but it surprised her when he reached out and lightly touched his fingers to her cheek.

To the cut that was there.

Karina hadn't seen it yet. No mirrors in the treatment room. She figured that was intentional since all kinds of injuries were treated here.

"How bad is it?" she asked, though she wasn't sure she wanted to know the answer. Especially since just looking at her had caused Cord's forehead to bunch up.

"It'll heal," he said, obviously dodging her question. "You're the third woman I know who has that scar. My sister, Addie, and her sister-in-law, Paige. Of course, plenty of other women had it, too, but they're not alive."

Karina knew about the other women. About Paige, as well. She was the deputy's wife and had been left for dead by the Moonlight Strangler. However, the other person was a shock. "I didn't realize your sister had been cut."

He nodded, leaned back in the chair and scrubbed his hand over his face. "When she was three, Addie was found wandering around the woods near the Crockett ranch. Jericho's dad found her, and she had the cut then. Of course, nobody knew what it meant at the time."

No. But Karina knew the rest of this particular story. The Crocketts had adopted Addie and raised her along with their four sons: Jericho, Jax, Chase and Levi. Because the Crocketts had wanted to find Addie's birth parents, they'd entered her DNA into the databases, and there'd been no match until a year ago, when Addie had learned she was the daughter of the Moonlight Strangler. Cord had been matched a short time later and was Addie's fraternal twin brother.

Ever since then Cord had made it his mission to find the killer. Which would mean also finding his father. And Cord was certain he'd managed to do that now that Willie Lee was in custody.

"Did you ever find a birth certificate for Addie or you?" she asked, not sure he would even answer. They'd had so many uncivil discussions about his paternity. Well, his insistence that Willie Lee was a killer anyway, and Karina thought he might just blow her off.

Much to her surprise, he didn't.

"No. And believe me, I looked. The county clerk said that some home births don't get registered."

Neither would someone wanting to hide those babies. But why would Willie Lee have done that?

No answer for that, either. No answer for a lot of things, but Karina was certain she could get to the bottom of it if she could just talk to Willie Lee. He'd have to come out of the coma first, and there were no indications when or if that would ever happen.

"Addie's scar is barely visible," Cord went on. "Yours will fade, too."

All in all, it was a kind thing to say. And a surprising one since it took this civil conversation to a different level.

"I must really look bad for you to be so nice to me." Karina was only partly joking. She was dead certain she looked bad.

The corner of his mouth lifted. Almost a smile. Almost. But it was gone as quickly as it came. He leaned forward, his gaze connecting with hers, and she could see that he was all lawman again. Not that he slipped out of that mode for more than a second or two.

However, the brief change in his demeanor gave her another reminder of that drop-dead-hot thought she'd shoved aside earlier. And continued to shove aside now. Hard to do, though, with him right in front of her.

He was pure cowboy with that tousled hair and those bad-boy eyes. Sadly, he was her type, and her body just wouldn't let her forget that wherever she saw him. Thankfully, Cord didn't seem to notice.

Or maybe he did.

He gave her a look. The kind of look a man would give a woman who was hands-off. Which described how he felt about her to a T.

He cleared his throat, looked disgusted with himself. "I keep going back to that note found on the tree."

Good. A change of subject. Exactly what she needed to get her mind back on track.

"The note said, 'Remember what I told you, Karina-girl,'" Cord continued. Not that he had to say the words aloud. They were etched permanently in her mind. "And you did remember."

She nodded. "'You know exactly who I am, Karina-girl, don't you?'" she repeated. "But here's the problem with that. I don't know who he is. I really don't."

"Then why would he say that? He could have put a lot of things in that note, but he didn't." Cord paused, apparently waiting for her to will the memory into her consciousness.

When she didn't come up with anything, he huffed. "All right. Let's try a different angle. Who would want to kill you? An ex-boyfriend, maybe? A stalker?"

Karina didn't get a chance to answer because the sound of footsteps had Cord springing to his feet and drawing his gun.

However, it was only Rocky.

Her ranch hand was all right. The killer hadn't taken him after all. He looked a little disheveled, but that was it.

The relief she felt didn't last long, though, because of Cord's reaction. She was usually the one to get his jaw muscles stirring, but they were stirring like crazy now. Ditto for the glare he shot Rocky.

"Where were you?" Cord snapped. Definitely the lawman now.

Rocky pulled back his shoulders. "Out looking for the guy who attacked Karina, of course."

"You were supposed to go with the sheriff. I heard him tell you that."

Rocky's gaze shifted to her, and he looked as if he wanted her to defend him. But she couldn't. "Going out there on your own was dangerous," she reminded him. And stupid. "You could have been killed."

He threw his hands up in the air in an I-give-up gesture. "I just wanted to find him before his trail turned cold."

"And did you find him?" Cord challenged.

Rocky's jaw muscles tightened, too. "No. But I did see him. After I heard the explosion."

That got her attention. Cord's, as well. Cord made a circling motion with his finger for Rocky to keep going with the details.

"I'm pretty sure it was him," Rocky went on. "I mean, how many men are running around the woods this time of night?"

Maybe plenty since the guy had almost certainly had help in blowing up the ambulance. "Did you actually see his face?" Karina asked.

Another "no." Rocky made a sound of frustration. "He was wearing dark clothes, though, just like that man who attacked you in the barn. I know it was him, Karina." He turned to Cord. "I followed him all the way to a farm road before I lost sight of him. I think that's the direction of the Appaloosa Pass Ranch, the one the Crocketts own."

Cord didn't waste a second. He took out his phone and fired off a text. Probably to Jericho.

Karina touched her fingers to her mouth. "You don't think the killer will go after your sister?"

Cord didn't answer right away. "I don't know. I don't know who or what we're dealing with here."

"We're dealing with the Moonlight Strangler," Rocky said as if it was gospel.

That earned him another glare from Cord. "You need to go to the sheriff's office and give your statement. *Now.*"

Rocky looked ready to argue with that, but Karina nodded. "Go ahead. I'll be there as soon as the doctor releases me."

It still took Rocky several long moments and a few volleyed glances before he huffed, mumbled something she didn't catch and headed out. Cord followed him, stopping in the door to watch him leave.

"How well do you know Rocky?" Cord asked with his back still to her.

Karina wanted to be upset with his tone and the question itself, but it was something a lawman would want to know. "Not long. I just hired him earlier this week. But his references checked out," she quickly added. "He hadn't worked with cutting horses in a while, but I decided to give him a chance."

Mainly because he'd been the only one who had applied for the job.

"References can be faked." Cord made a sound that could have meant anything and sent another text. "I told the Crocketts it would be a good idea to lock down the ranch." He finally turned, walked back to her. "You trust Rocky? Any gut feelings about him?"

"Yes, I trust him. No reason not to."

Was there? Maybe it was because of the frayed nerves,

but Karina mentally went through the handful of interactions she'd had with the man.

"He works well with the horses, but the truth is, I don't know much about him," she admitted.

That was partly her fault. She'd been so preoccupied with Willie Lee and staying in business that she hadn't even bothered to get to really know the man she'd hired. A man who was living just yards from her.

"I'll have a thorough background check done on him," Cord said. He walked closer, standing over her and looking down at her. "Now, back to the question I asked before Rocky came in. Is there anyone who would want to do you harm?"

Karina didn't even have to think about this. "DeWayne Stringer." Just saying his name aloud caused her stomach to churn. "He's a wealthy cattle broker over in Comal County and lives near my ranch. I've had run-ins with him for nearly a year now since he bought the property next to mine. He wants me to sell him my land so he can expand and isn't very happy that I won't do that."

A huge understatement. DeWayne had done everything in his power to pressure her into selling. Plain and simple, he was a bully.

"Over the past couple of months, I've had livestock go missing," she went on. "Some vandalism. I'm sure it's his doing. Or else he hired someone to do it. He doesn't seem the sort to get his hands dirty."

"And what have the local cops done about it?" Cord asked. He used the note function on his phone to type in DeWayne's name.

"Nothing because there's never any proof. DeWayne always covers his tracks."

Cord stared at her. "You think he's capable of murder or attempted murder?"

Now, she had to pause. "Maybe." Then she shook her head. "But I heard my attacker speak, and it wasn't De-Wayne's voice."

"He could have disguised it," Cord suggested. "Or else hired someone to do the job. You said he didn't like to get his hands dirty."

That was true, but there was still something that didn't make sense. "Why would DeWayne come after me here in Appaloosa Pass?"

"Because you're more vulnerable here," Cord answered without hesitating. "You have six hands at your place in Comal County, but here it's only Rocky and you. Plus, you're distracted, worried about Willie Lee. That made you an easier target."

The word—*target*—made her want to throw up. "I was distracted at my house, too, after I heard about Willie Lee," she pointed out. "I was there for several days before I made arrangements to come here."

Cord didn't miss a beat. "And it would be far easier to get onto the place here sight unseen than it would be to get on your ranch in Comal County. I've seen pictures of your ranch. There, the house is in the center of acres of pasture. No trees, no place for a would-be killer to hide while sneaking onto the grounds."

Karina couldn't argue with any of that, and she could go even one step further with it. "I think it might have been DeWayne who planted Willie Lee's DNA at that crime scene."

Cord stared at her, not exactly rolling his eyes but almost.

"Willie Lee stood up to DeWayne, and DeWayne hates him. They've had plenty of verbal run-ins. And one not so verbal," she added in a mumble.

She hated to explain this because it might make Cord

believe Willie Lee was a violent man. He wasn't. Not normally anyway.

"I'm listening," Cord said when she hesitated.

Best just to tell him because Cord would find out anyway now that he was going to have DeWayne investigated. "Willie Lee punched DeWayne after DeWayne insulted me. Please don't make me repeat the names DeWayne called me. Anyway, it was only about a week later when Willie Lee's DNA was found at the crime scene."

"Now exactly how would DeWayne have managed to do that?" There was so much skepticism in Cord's voice.

But maybe she could do something to remove a bit of that doubt. At least she could try. "The DNA found at the crime scene was in some chewing gum. Willie Lee quit smoking a few years ago, and he's been a gum chewer ever since. It wouldn't have been hard for DeWayne to get a piece that Willie Lee had spit out on the ground."

Cord's eyebrow rose more than a fraction. "And then what? DeWayne happened to find a crime scene so he could plant the gum?"

It did sound far-fetched when Cord put it that way. Still, it was possible. "Maybe DeWayne held on to the gum for a while until he could plant it. And then perhaps DeWayne just happened to find that scene. I mean, it wasn't that far from my ranch and his land."

"Ten miles," Cord quickly declared, which meant he'd memorized all the details. With reason. It was the first time DNA had been recovered from the crime scene of the Moonlight Strangler.

Cord leaned in closer again. Too close. Probably a lawman's ploy to violate her personal space and make her uneasy so she'd spill any secrets she was hiding. Sadly, it would have worked if she'd had secrets.

She didn't.

But it also worked in a different way, too. For a man who hated her, her body certainly didn't let her forget that she was a woman. And that he was a man.

"I've been looking into Willie Lee's life," Cord went on. "He was in the area at the time of that murder because his signature is on a feed purchase in town."

She knew all about Cord's efforts to seal the deal and pin these murders, all of them, on Willie Lee. And Cord had indeed managed to place Willie Lee in the areas of several of the murders. That still didn't convince her.

Karina leaned in closer to him, too. "You're asking me to believe that a man I've known for fifteen years, half of my life, murdered women and then calmly went on as if nothing had happened. A man I trust—"

"A man you don't really know," Cord interrupted. "According to your own statement, he just showed up one day, and your father hired him. Willie Lee had no references. No past. He just materialized out of thin air fifteen years ago."

Karina knew there was an explanation for that. One that Willie Lee could give her if he ever came out of that coma.

Especially since Cord's DNA had proved that he was Willie Lee's son.

"Do you have any childhood memories whatsoever of Willie Lee?" she suddenly asked.

"None. Neither does Addie." He moved away from her. Fast. "I'll have Jericho get DeWayne in for questioning," Cord said, and he sent another text. Apparently ending their conversation about his *father*.

Karina wanted to press him on the subject. Actually, what she wanted Cord to do was remember that Willie Lee was the same loving, caring man that he'd been to her over the years. He wasn't just her hired hand. He'd become a father figure to her after her own dad had died of lung cancer when Karina was just seventeen. Her mother had never been the same after that. Had never really been part of Karina's life, or even her own life. Her mom had finally ended it all with sleeping pills.

And Willie Lee had been there to help Karina get through that, too.

"Anyone else other than DeWayne who might want to hurt you?" Cord persisted. "An ex-boyfriend, maybe?" he repeated. "Or a current boyfriend?"

She seriously doubted he was fishing to find out if she was romantically involved with anyone. "No current boyfriend. No recent ex, either. The ranch keeps me busy," Karina added because she felt she had to add something so Cord wouldn't think she was a loser.

Though he probably thought that anyway. A loser and very gullible to believe in Willie Lee's innocence.

"How about any disgruntled employees?" Cord asked a moment later. "Or just someone you got a bad vibe about?"

She opened her mouth to say no, but that wasn't true. "There might be someone else. *Might.* A couple of days after Willie Lee was captured, a man showed up at the ranch. Harley Kramer. He said he was an old friend of Willie Lee's, of my mother's, too. But I'd never heard either of them mention him."

"What'd he want?" Cord asked.

"He said he wanted to look through Willie Lee's things, that Willie Lee had some old photos he wanted. I told him that wouldn't be possible, not without Willie Lee's permission. He left, and I thought that was the end of it." She paused. "I definitely got bad vibes from him, and it wasn't just because of his scars."

"Scars?"

She motioned to her face. "He'd been burned and had obviously had a skin graft. And I know that sounds shallow to be creeped out by a guy with a scarred face, but it wasn't just that. It was the way he looked at me. Then, I caught him sneaking into the cabin where Willie Lee lived. I called the sheriff, and he arrested him for trespassing and breaking and entering. Needless to say, Harley wasn't happy about that."

Cord added Harley's name to the note on his phone. "Did this guy threaten you?"

"Not exactly, but he was furious. His trial date will be coming up soon, and he might have to do some jail time." Probably not much, though, since the sheriff had told her that Harley didn't have any priors and would likely get probation.

Still, it must have been enough motive for Cord because he typed something else in his notes. He was still typing when his phone rang.

"Jax," Cord said, glancing at the screen.

One of the deputies. This was no doubt about the investigation. "Put the call on speaker, please," she said.

Karina wasn't sure Cord would do that, and judging from the way the muscles in his face stirred, Cord wasn't sure of it, either. However, he did press the speaker button when he answered it.

"This is a heads-up," Jax informed Cord. "You need to keep that ranch hand, Rocky, away from Karina."

Her heart went to her throat. "Why?" Cord and she asked in unison.

"Because you're not going to believe what we found in the bunkhouse where he was staying. I just called Jericho to have him take Rocky into custody."

Chapter Five

Cord didn't know what Jax had seen that'd caused him to make that call, but he figured he wasn't going to like it.

Karina certainly wouldn't, either.

She'd practically jumped to defend her ranch hand, but judging from Jax's tone, she wouldn't be defending Rocky after she saw the photos that Jax had sent to the sheriff's office.

Jax hadn't wanted to describe them over the phone, only adding that the pictures would be worth a million words. Cord only hoped whatever they were, it would be enough to pin attempted murder charges on the man so he could end Karina's doubts about Willie Lee not being the Moonlight Strangler. That way, Cord could walk away from this, from her, and know that they had the right man in custody.

Then, maybe he could start dealing with the feelings that he'd buried deep within him.

Of course, first they had to find Rocky.

Despite being told by both Cord and Jericho to go to the sheriff's office, the ranch hand had yet to show up. Cord figured that wasn't a good sign.

"Are you okay?" Cord asked her.

Karina gave a heavy sigh and tore her gaze from the cruiser window, where she was looking at the shops on Main Street as they rode past them. She was pretending to look at them at least. He figured her mind was really on her ranch hand and the fact that she'd nearly died tonight.

"Every inch of me is hurting," she admitted. "And I'm upset about Rocky. How about you?"

Cord went with the lie. "I'm fine."

But every inch of him was hurting, as well. Man, he needed a long soak in the tub and a handful of aspirin. He wasn't counting on getting either anytime soon.

"Move fast when we get out of the cruiser," Cord instructed Karina when the sheriff's office came into view.

Jericho had sent the vehicle to the hospital to pick them up, and Cord was thankful for not only the ride—his truck was still back at Karina's—but also for the deputy driving. With Karina's attacker still out there, he didn't want to be without some kind of backup. And he didn't want her in the open any longer than necessary.

The deputy stopped by the front door, and Cord hurried her in. Jericho and Levi were there, both talking on their phones, but Jericho motioned for them to follow him into his office. Judging from what part of the conversation he could hear, Jericho was having a chat with one of his other deputies, and once they were in his office, he motioned for them to sit.

Jericho cursed and ended the call. He looked at both of them and mumbled yet more profanity. Probably because they both looked like hell, but Cord knew the cursing wasn't all for them.

"Still no sign of Rocky, but Jax is staying at Karina's place a while longer to see if he shows up there. Any idea where he'd go?" Jericho asked her.

Karina shook her head, winced a little. No doubt from the pain. Jericho noticed, and that prompted him to take out a huge bottle of ibuprofen from his desk and two bottles of water from the small fridge in the corner.

"Help yourself," Jericho offered.

Well, it wasn't aspirin and a bath, but it would do for now. Cord exceeded the recommended dose by a lot and hoped that the pain in his head faded to at least a tolerable throb before long.

"I don't know where Rocky would go," Karina said, gulping down two of the pills. "On his references he said he didn't have any family, that he'd been raised in foster care." She lifted her shoulder. "I'm not sure if that's even true."

"It's not," Jericho quickly responded. He turned his laptop in their direction so they could see the screen.

Not photos of the bunkhouse but rather a mug shot. Of Rocky.

"He was arrested for stealing a car," Jericho went on.

Karina was shaking her head before he even finished. "I did a computer check, and a record didn't come up."

"Because he was arrested when he was a juvie, and it was sealed. But he has parents, all right. They adopted him from foster care when he was a kid. They're in their eighties now, and they basically disowned him when he was in his twenties and haven't seen him since. They don't want to see him, either, and said they'd call the cops in a heartbeat if he showed up at their house."

Jericho clicked to the next picture. Or rather the next pictures. There were a series of shots that filled up the whole screen. "This is what Jax found in the bunkhouse. It was all in a box beneath Rocky's bed."

Karina stood, probably so she could have a better look. Then, she gasped.

Damn.

There were newspaper clippings. Dozens of them from the looks of it. With headlines detailing everything about the Moonlight Strangler. Including Willie Lee's capture.

"Rocky clearly has a disturbing *hobby*," Jericho explained. "I just had a quick chat with his parents—he's not there, by the way—and they said for most of his life Rocky's been obsessed with serial killers. And that they've heard through acquaintances that he idolizes the Moonlight Strangler."

"Oh, God," Karina whispered, sinking back into the chair.

"He had other pictures in that box." Jericho clicked to the next screen. Not newspaper clippings.

But rather photos of Karina.

In them, she wasn't doing anything special. Just errands, grocery shopping, that sort of thing. However, there were dozens of them. Including some of her in the interior of the barn.

Cord could have sworn that with each one she studied more and more color drained from her face. With reason. Most of the photos were grainy, as if they'd been taken with a long-range lens. And that meant Rocky had probably been spying on Karina for days or even weeks.

There were also shots of the Appaloosa Pass Hospital, where Willie Lee had stayed two days before being transported to the hospital at the prison. There were photos of the exterior of the prison, too.

"Rocky's a groupie," Cord concluded. If there hadn't already been a knot in his stomach, that would have done it. It was hard to understand why anyone would attach themselves to a serial killer.

But it did give Rocky a motive for what'd gone on tonight.

Cord made eye contact with Karina before he said anything. "It's possible Rocky was responsible for the attack. He might have believed this was the way to get Willie Lee released from jail."

He gave her some time to let that sink in and saw her trying to process it. At first, Cord saw a lot of doubt in her chocolate-brown eyes. Then, the realization that it could be true.

"So, you're thinking he hired someone to attack me," she added a moment later.

Cord shrugged and glanced at Jericho to see if they were on the same page. Judging from the look they shared, they were.

"Could Rocky have attacked on his own?" Cord asked. "Think it through. Did you actually see two men?"

Karina paused a moment, glanced at the photos on the laptop and then turned her head away from them. "I'm not sure. I'm not sure of anything right now."

Well, Cord was. They had a bona fide suspect. Now, they just had to find him.

Jericho's phone buzzed. "I gotta take this call," he said when he glanced at the screen. He headed for the door but then came back to turn his laptop around, no doubt so that the pictures wouldn't be right in Karina's face.

That might help steady her nerves, but Cord figured the images were already fixed in her mind. The photos weren't gruesome, and there'd been none of her undressing or sleeping. But it had to get to her that someone had been stalking her and violating her privacy.

"You must think I'm stupid," she said. "Stupid to hire someone like Rocky."

"Not stupid. It's just your trust was misplaced."

Her gaze whipped around, snaring his. "Now we're talking about Willie Lee."

Yeah. No need to spell it out for her, though. Plus, footsteps got Cord's attention. Even though they were in the sheriff's office, he still slid his hand over the gun in his holster. But it wasn't a threat.

It was Addie.

Since his sister was the last person he expected to see come through that door, he immediately got to his feet. So did Karina. Clearly, she was uncomfortable with this face-to-face encounter, since she started rubbing her hands down the sides of the scrubs the nurse had given her.

"I heard what happened." Addie went straight to Cord and hugged him.

Addie had hugged him before, but it always gave him a jolt. He wasn't usually a hugging sort, but it felt right when Addie did it. Maybe there was some truth to that saying about twins being connected subconsciously, because he'd loved her, and wanted to protect her, from the moment he'd laid eyes on her.

Cord didn't need to do introductions since Karina and Addie had met shortly after Willie Lee's arrest. Or rather they'd seen each other at the hospital. Addie had been there visiting Cord. Karina had been checking on Willie Lee, and there had been that strained awkwardness that was still there between them.

"Please tell me you didn't drive here alone," Cord said to his sister.

"No. Chase is with me. Weston is home with the baby."

Weston was her husband. And Chase, her adopted brother. Cord was glad Chase had come with her because he was a lawman, too. He didn't want Addie out on the roads alone until Rocky, or whoever was behind this, was caught. After all, Rocky had said he'd spotted Karina's attacker heading in the general direction of the Appaloosa Pass Ranch, and while Rocky could be lying through his pearly whites, Cord didn't want to take any unnecessary risks when it came to Addie.

"Are you all right?" Addie asked, the question meant for Karina and him because she glanced at both of them.

Karina kept her response to a nod, and Cord could see her trying to steel herself up. Probably because she believed Addie was about to blast her for defending Willie Lee.

Addie's gaze went from the cut on Karina's face to the bruises on her neck. Addie shuddered. "Who did this to you?"

Karina shook her head. "We're still trying to figure that out. Maybe a ranch hand I recently hired. Maybe someone else."

"A copycat," Cord added.

Oh, no. He could see the argument brewing in his sister's eyes. "Or the real deal," Addie mumbled.

Karina blinked, her gaze shifting to him. That gaze demanded an explanation. An explanation Cord didn't want to get into. Because his sister had her own doubts about Willie Lee's guilt. Doubts that Addie had expressed during several heated discussions.

Addie made a vague motion toward her stomach. "It's just a gut feeling. And it might be nothing. But I'm not sure…"

"You think Willie Lee might not be the Moonlight Strangler," Karina said, finishing for her.

Addie gave a heavy sigh. Nodded. Then, shrugged. "Some things just don't add up, that's all. Months ago, not long after I found out about the DNA match, the Moonlight Strangler called me. He said he wouldn't come after me because I was blood. Well, Cord's his blood, too, and Willie Lee took him hostage and cut him. Have you seen the scars on his chest?"

This wasn't any more comfortable than discussing Willie Lee's serial-killer label. "I'm fine," Cord assured her. "And in that call, the Moonlight Strangler never said he wouldn't come after me."

There was plenty more to this argument, too.

"Besides," Cord went on, "even if your gut won't let you believe Willie Lee is the Moonlight Strangler, then he's still a violent man. And I have the scars to prove it."

He hadn't meant to include that last part. It just flew out of his mouth, and it caused Addie's eyes to fill with yet more concern.

"What if it wasn't Willie Lee who kidnapped you?" Karina suggested. "What if it was someone setting up Willie Lee?"

Again, not a new argument. He could have repeated the facts to her, that there'd been no other DNA or evidence found at the crime scene to indicate Willie Lee had been set up. But Karina was as familiar with the evidence as he was.

Addie reached out, touched his arm and rubbed it gently. Probably trying to soothe that anger inside him. It was a lost cause, but Cord welcomed it anyway.

"Cord told me that Willie Lee worked for you and your family for a long time," Addie said to Karina. "Would you mind if I asked you some questions about him?"

"I don't mind." But Karina didn't sound so certain of that. Probably because she'd already been grilled six ways to Sunday about the man.

"Was Willie Lee ever mean or violent with you?" Addie continued.

Karina didn't hesitate. "Never. He did punch a man once, but that was to defend my honor." Then, she paused. "Willie Lee became like a father to me after my parents died."

That had Addie tensing a little, and she dropped back a step. "Did he ever say anything about having children?"

"No." Again, no hesitation. Probably because the FBI, and Cord, had asked Karina that multiple times. "But Willie Lee didn't share a lot about himself. Never talked about his past, and whenever it would come up in a general sort of way, he'd get this sad look in his eyes."

Maybe because he'd abandoned his two kids and murdered their mother. But there was enough salt in Karina's wounds without Cord stating the obvious. Still, it could be true. During that phone conversation with Addie, the Moonlight Strangler had told her that he'd killed their mother.

Something that still felt like a cut to the heart.

It didn't matter that Cord couldn't remember anything about his mother, the Moonlight Strangler had taken her from Addie and him. And he was going to pay for that.

Cord heard more footsteps, and a moment later Jericho came back in. "Everything okay?" he asked, caution in his voice and expression.

"Fine," Addie assured him. As she'd done with Cord, she went to Jericho and hugged him. "Karina and I were just talking."

Jericho seemed as uncomfortable with that as Cord. But there was something else in Jericho's body language, and since he had stepped out to take the call, maybe there was bad news.

"I'll just be going," Addie said, likely sensing that something was going on. She kissed both Cord and Jericho on their cheeks and added a whispered goodbye. She even gave Karina's hand a gentle squeeze.

Which Cord wished she hadn't done.

He didn't want Karina having any more encouragement for believing Willie Lee was innocent, and even something like a hand squeeze from Addie could do that.

Jericho didn't say anything until Addie was out of the room. "The CSIs found some blood about thirty yards from your barn, where the attack occurred," he explained.

Since the layout of the crime scene was still fresh in his mind, Cord knew that could mean trouble.

"Did you go out there in that area before the ambulance or I got there?" Jericho asked Karina.

"No. Heavens, no. I couldn't even stand up my legs were so shaky. And Rocky wasn't hurt. I didn't see any injuries on him anyway."

Neither had Cord.

Damn.

This wasn't good because it could mean Rocky was telling the truth about having injured Karina's attacker. Or it could mean he had a partner who had simply gotten hurt in the fray. And if so, there could be at least two thugs out there ready to come after Karina again.

"There's more," Jericho went on. "After I got your text about DeWayne Stringer, I had one of the deputies make some calls. He did indeed have a run-in with Willie Lee, and he apparently isn't a fan of Karina's."

That meshed with what Karina had told him. "Are you bringing him in for questioning?" Cord asked.

Jericho nodded. "He'll be here first thing in the morning." He paused. "Did you know the Comal County sheriff is investigating him?"

"For what?" Karina took the question right out of Cord's mouth.

Jericho drew in a long, frustrated breath. "For murder."

Chapter Six

Karina's eyes flew open, and her heart jolted when she glanced around at the unfamiliar surroundings. She fought through the haze in her mind and the fresh round of panic and remembered where she was.

In Cord's bed.

And she had apparently managed to sleep there, something she hadn't thought possible. Not after the attack and all the other things they'd learned. Still, she'd clearly done more than just take a catnap because the sunlight was peeking through the edge of the blinds.

After they'd left the sheriff's office in the wee hours of the morning, Cord had brought her to his place. Or rather to the guesthouse on the grounds of the Appaloosa Pass Ranch, where he'd been staying since his attack the previous month. His stay there probably wouldn't last much longer, though, because she figured he'd soon be cleared for duty and go back to his apartment in San Antonio.

From the moment Cord had mentioned where he'd be taking her, she hadn't thought it was a good idea for her to come here.

Karina still didn't.

And now she needed to do something about that and make arrangements for another safe place to stay.

If a safe place was possible, that is.

In addition to Rocky, she had to worry about DeWayne. Now that Jericho had dropped that bombshell about the county sheriff investigating the man.

For murder, no less.

Jericho hadn't gotten all the details, but apparently the county sheriff had found something to make him suspicious of DeWayne, and the sheriff was looking to tie him to the murder of a woman over in Comal County where DeWayne and Karina both lived.

Part of her almost wished that DeWayne had done it. And better yet, that the county sheriff could prove it. That way, DeWayne would be behind bars and not a possible threat to her. Of course, that didn't solve her problem with Rocky unless, during the past hours, Jericho and the deputies had managed to find him.

She got up. Too fast. And had to sit right back down.

That's when she noticed the clothes on the foot of the bed. Jeans, a blue top, some underwear and flip-flops. There was also a handwritten note on top of the neatly folded stack of clothes.

"'Addie sent these over,'" she said, reading the note. "'There are toiletries in the bathroom.'"

Cord had no doubt written the note and left the clothes, but it was a little unnerving to know she'd been so sacked out that she hadn't noticed a man coming into the bedroom. Especially *that* man. It wasn't as if Cord was a wallflower, and he always seemed to get her attention whenever he was around.

Disgusted with that thought, and with herself, Karina forced herself to stand. She scooped up the clothes and went into the adjoining bathroom.

Karina got another jolt, a really bad one, when she caught a glimpse of herself in the mirror and was glad to see that the toiletries mentioned in the note also included some makeup. Including a tube of concealer. She didn't normally wear much makeup, but she would today, though she probably didn't stand much of a chance of covering up the stitches on her cheek or the other bruises.

The one on her forehead was purple.

Since this was the only bathroom in the small guesthouse, she hurried with her shower. She definitely didn't want Cord walking in on her. She hurriedly dressed, too, and even though she did try with the makeup, she finally just gave up. Looking at that god-awful cut on her face turned her stomach, and she already felt lousy enough without seeing it.

Karina made her way to the kitchen. Not that she had to go far. The guesthouse was simply the bedroom suite and an open space area for the kitchen, dining and living room. There were pillows and covers on the sofa, where Cord had spent the night.

Maybe.

But it was just as likely he hadn't slept at all judging from the fatigued look on his face. He was at the window, drinking coffee from a large mug. Since the pot was nearly empty, she figured he'd already had several cups, so she started a fresh pot.

"I need to check on my horses," she said right off the bat.

"Already taken care of. Jericho sent one of the hands over there this morning."

Okay. At least that was one thing she could tick off her list. Still, she'd want to personally check on them soon.

"I'll also want to thank your sister for the clothes," she added. They didn't fit exactly, but it was better than wearing the borrowed scrubs and no underwear.

"Maybe we can stop by your place later so you can get

your own things," Cord suggested. "But the CSIs are still out there now so we'll have to wait until they leave."

Of course. And even then Karina wasn't sure she would feel comfortable in the house. And especially not alone. Then again, judging from the *we* that Cord had used, he would be going with her.

"Thank you for putting the clothes in the bedroom," Karina said. "I'm not sure exactly when you did that because I didn't hear you come in."

Not very subtle of her, and he picked up on what she didn't say. "I did knock on the door, but when you didn't answer, I went in to check on you. Just to make sure."

To make sure someone hadn't broken in and tried to murder her again. Karina certainly hadn't forgotten that. Or maybe Cord had just wanted to make sure she hadn't crawled into a corner and gone catatonic.

"Another thanks for doing that," she added. "And for saving my life last night. And for this." She motioned around the guesthouse.

"But?" He stared at her from over the rim of his cup.

For a man he was darn perceptive. She hadn't met many men in her life like that. "*But* I can't stay here. It feels a little like the enemy camp."

"And I'm the enemy." Not exactly a question.

And Karina didn't address it head-on, either. "You don't want me here, and I'm also sure you don't want me in your protective custody any longer than necessary." Too bad she wasn't sure just how much longer that would be.

Cord took his time, had another sip of coffee. "I want you safe, and right now Jericho's got every available deputy tied up with this investigation. I'm on a leave of absence and volunteered to do it."

The corner of her mouth lifted, but it wasn't a smile from humor. "Did Jericho blackmail you or something?"

No mouth lift for him. "It was the only way he would agree to let me be part of the investigation."

Ah. That made sense. No way would Cord want to back away from making sure a copycat had done this. Still, it stung a little. What with arranging for a safe place to stay—and keeping her alive—she had thought maybe he was doing this because…well, it didn't matter what she thought.

She'd been wrong.

"Any breaks in the case?" she asked. Best to keep this conversation professional. Even if he did look hot with his stubble and rumpled hair.

Get a grip.

And some coffee. That might get her mind off Cord. The caffeine might help with the dull throb in her head, too.

Karina went to the counter and poured herself a cup, but she was shaking, and she ended up spilling some of it on her fingers. She barely had time to jerk back her hand and make a small yelp of pain before Cord was there.

He cursed, took the coffee cup from her and pulled her hand beneath the faucet, turning on the cold water. "Just how much are you hurting?"

Now, that was a question she didn't want to answer. And it wasn't just limited to her hand. From the corner of his eye, he glanced at her face. Then, the rest of her body.

Cord looked disgusted with himself again.

"Like you, I'm not hurting at all," she said.

Now, that got a smile tugging at his mouth. She was glad he appreciated her lame attempt at a joke. Glad they could share that smile, too.

Karina was surprised just how much she needed it.

Because while she was indeed hurting in too many places to name, that was only the tip of the iceberg. It felt as if she had a crushing weight on her heart and chest. Her mind, too.

The tears came again, burning her eyes, and she tried to blink them back. She already felt like a basket case. No sense acting like one.

"Crying's a normal reaction after everything you've been through," Cord said. He kept hold of her hand while the water spilled over it.

"You're not crying," she pointed out, hoping it would get him to smile again. It didn't.

But his gaze did meet hers. "It's a man thing. A couple of my foster fathers taught me that."

That didn't help the crushing feeling in her heart. She'd known Cord had been placed in the system after being abandoned, and unlike his sister, he hadn't been adopted by a loving family. He had been raised in foster care. And not good foster care, from the sound of it.

"I'm sorry you've had such a rough life," she whispered.

Big mistake. He let go of her as if she'd scalded him and took a towel from the drawer so she could dry herself. He would have gone back to the window, but Karina didn't let him get away that easily. She took hold of his arm.

"I shouldn't have brought it up," she told him. "But the apology's still there. I know what it's like to be raised without parents."

Their gazes came together again. And held. Until Cord finally nodded. Maybe that nod was his way of accepting her apology or maybe they had simply reached a truce. Either way, he didn't pull his gaze from her, and she didn't take her hand off him.

There it was.

That tug she felt deep within her belly. And lower. The tug that reminded her of just how attracted she was to him.

He put his hand over hers, keeping it there a moment.

Then, two. At first, she thought he might kiss her. Because his attention slid from her eyes to her mouth. That lasted several moments, too.

Before he stepped away from her.

"I can't get involved with you," he said as if that would make this heat all go away. "I can't lose focus. Not while I'm protecting you."

Until he'd added that last part, Karina had thought maybe he was just blowing her off, but that last part made it sound as if one day she might get that kiss after all. Even if it was the last thing she needed from Cord Granger.

He poured her a cup of coffee and went back to his spot at the window. "Talk to me about Mona Wallace," Cord said.

Karina was very familiar with the name, but she hadn't expected Cord to bring up the woman now. "What about her? You know as well as I do that she was murdered and that Willie Lee's DNA was found at the crime scene."

It had been the start of this current nightmare since that DNA meant the cops believed Willie Lee was the Moonlight Strangler.

"Did you know that Mona had a connection to De-Wayne?" he asked.

Karina couldn't shake her head fast enough. "No. I mean, I knew Mona and DeWayne lived in the same county, but I didn't realize there was a connection." She froze, and it hit her then. "Does the county sheriff believe DeWayne was the one who killed Mona?"

"He does."

Oh, mercy. This could be the break she'd been looking for. Because if DeWayne had murdered Mona, then it meant DeWayne could have also been the one to plant Willie Lee's DNA at the scene.

"Don't get your hopes up," Cord went on. "The sheriff only has circumstantial evidence. Mona was a married woman, and DeWayne and she had had an affair. But there's no evidence or eyewitnesses to put DeWayne at the crime scene."

It was too late. She had already gotten her hopes up, and Cord had dashed them just as quickly with that reminder.

"Then, why does the county sheriff suspect him?" she asked.

"Because Mona's husband was pushing for DeWayne's arrest. He claims Mona had broken off the affair and that DeWayne was furious, that he'd even threatened her."

Since Karina had been on the receiving end of many of DeWayne's threats, she knew all about his hot temper. "Is there any way to have the evidence from the scene reexamined or—"

"I'm already working on that," Cord interrupted. "I called the FBI this morning to get them started on it. But again, don't get your hopes up. The county CSIs didn't cover that crime scene. The Texas Rangers did, and I'd be surprised if they missed anything."

So would she, but at this point she was simply grasping at straws. If Willie Lee ever came out of that coma, she wanted to be able to tell him that he was a free man. This was the first step in making that happen. Because if DeWayne did kill Mona, then he could have easily planted Willie Lee's DNA at the scene.

Of course, that didn't explain the attack last night.

She was certain, though, that Jericho would ask DeWayne about an alibi when the man came in for questioning. If it was DeWayne, then he would probably find a way to wiggle out of this—alibi included.

"Has Rocky turned up?" she asked. Karina was certain they could get more answers from him, especially after all those photos and news articles that Jax had found in the bunkhouse.

"No sign of him yet. But we did find out that the blood outside the barn isn't the same type as yours. That means it's probably the blood of the person who attacked you, so the lab will put a rush on processing it." He paused. "Now, you *can* get your hopes up about that because both Rocky's and DeWayne's DNA are in the system."

She had to shake her head. "I figured Rocky's would be there because of his record, but DeWayne's, too?"

"He voluntarily gave a sample to the county sheriff when the sheriff started investigating him for murder."

Oh. Karina didn't have to think too long on why he'd agreed to that. DeWayne wouldn't have done it if he'd known there was any chance whatsoever that his DNA would turn up anywhere near Mona's body.

Still, it might be a match to her attacker.

Which brought Karina to her next concern. "That wasn't Rocky talking to us right after the ambulance blew up. I would have recognized his voice."

Cord nodded fast, which meant he'd been thinking about it, too. "Like I said earlier, he could have disguised his voice. Or maybe that was Rocky's partner in crime." He pointed to the laptop on the table.

Karina went closer and saw the webpage for a site called Bloody Murder. Not exactly the sort of site she would surf. Especially since the home page was covered with photos of famous serial killers.

"There are sixty-two members," Cord explained. "They apparently don't consider themselves groupies but rather amateur sleuths. They look through the clues of old cases and try to solve them. Sometimes, they even go so far as to get close to the victim's friends and families."

Sweet heaven. Karina felt violated all over again. Even

if Rocky wasn't behind the attack, he'd lied to her, had pretended to be something he wasn't.

"According to their site," Cord went on, "they're convinced Willie Lee is innocent. That he was framed."

She didn't have to think too long about why Cord had mentioned that. "And you believe that's why Rocky attacked me. To make Willie Lee look innocent."

He nodded. "San Antonio PD will be handling this since the club is based there, but they'll take a close look at each member to see if one of them knows where Rocky is. Or if one of them was Rocky's accomplice. I'm betting at least some of them have criminal records, too, so once the CSIs have a DNA profile, they can start comparing it to the club members."

Karina doubted all of that would happen overnight, and that meant she really did have to come up with a different place to stay. However, before she could even bring up the subject, Cord continued.

"I also made a call about Harley Kramer, the guy you had arrested. He's on bail right now, and his trial date is in five days." Cord paused and made eye contact with her again. "And you're the only person scheduled to testify against him."

Karina stopped and gave that some more thought. "At most Harley's only looking at a year or two in jail if he's found guilty. That's not much of a motive for wanting me dead."

"It's a motive, though," Cord concluded. "He's got a very wealthy wife and some in-laws who want all this to go away so he won't muddy their name. And that alone makes him a person of interest in the attack."

Cord didn't add more because his phone rang, and he held it up for her to see.

Jericho's name was on the screen.

When Cord answered it, he put it on speaker, and even though she shouldn't read too much into that, Karina thought maybe he'd done that so she wouldn't go closer to him so she could hear. She definitely got the feeling that he wanted to keep some distance between them.

"A problem?" Cord asked.

"Maybe," Jericho readily admitted. "DeWayne just came in, and let's just say, he's not a happy camper. He's lawyered up already and insists the only person he'll talk to is Karina. If she's up to it, you should get her down here right away."

Chapter Seven

Cord wasn't sure Karina was actually *up to* this visit with DeWayne, but she had insisted on coming anyway.

He had to hand it to her. Most people who'd just survived two murder attempts probably wouldn't want to face their possible attacker. But she hadn't backed down an inch.

Maybe not a good thing.

After all, if DeWayne was indeed the one who'd tried to kill her, then it could antagonize the man even more if she went toe-to-toe with him. Still, Cord had no intentions of trying to rein her in. If he'd been in her situation, he would have wanted to do the same thing.

As they'd done the night before, Cord parked his truck in front of the sheriff's offices. Jax had been good enough to bring it to the ranch. Good enough to have been pleasant about dropping it off, too.

Cord's relationship with Addie's adopted brothers wasn't picture-perfect, but since Willie Lee's capture, it'd gotten a little better. At least Cord didn't feel as if they were ready to slug him anytime they saw him. Cord blamed those earlier reactions on his obsession to capture the Moonlight Strangler. An obsession that the Crockett lawmen believed might put Addie in danger.

Thankfully, it hadn't.

Well, not so far anyway.

"Remember, don't let DeWayne get to you," Karina whispered to herself.

Cord figured she'd been giving herself that pep talk since they'd left the ranch. It seemed to be working. She marched into the sheriff's office just ahead of him and made a beeline to the tall, dark-haired man who was standing across from Jericho.

It was DeWayne, all right.

Cord had never met the man, but he had pulled up his DMV photo, and it was a match. However, the photo hadn't shown that smug expression that DeWayne aimed at Karina. Cord couldn't be sure, but he thought maybe the smugness went up when the man looked at her cuts and bruises.

DeWayne wasn't alone. There was a man about the same age—late fifties—wearing a suit, and he was right by De-Wayne's side. His lawyer, no doubt.

"Karina," DeWayne said, smiling. "You came."

Oh, man. With just that handful of words and sick smile, he pissed off Cord. Talk about pompous, and Cord wished he could take him down a notch.

Jericho didn't seem any more pleased with the man than Cord did. "We can take this to the interview room now."

So, DeWayne was waiting on Karina after all. Too bad he hadn't made a confession or two. Of course, his lawyer probably wasn't going to let him say much of anything. That's where some button-pushing came in. Cord was banking on DeWayne's nasty temper that Karina had told him about. If Cord could get the man riled up enough, he might spill all sorts of secrets.

Of course, one of those secrets could topple the case against Willie Lee. But that was a bridge Cord would cross if he came to it.

"I have an alibi for last night," DeWayne said without any prompting. He strolled into the interview room, hands stuffed into the pockets of his overpriced designer jeans, and he sank down into one of the chairs.

Cord looked at Jericho to see if he knew anything about that so-called alibi. "He says he was with a friend. I'm having Levi check it out now."

"Oh, I was with her, all right," DeWayne insisted. "And I didn't leave her place until this morning. She'll vouch for me."

"Or lie for you," Cord said. He couldn't help himself.

No flash of temper, but DeWayne did turn that sickening smile on Karina. "Of course, my lawyer could have handled all these false accusations that you're making, but I wanted to see you. Did you do something different with your hair?" And he laughed.

Cord was certain he had his own flash of temper.

Karina, however, hardly reacted. Which meant she'd likely been on the receiving end of this idiot's bull way too often.

"I'd like to talk about Mona," Karina said, her voice as calm as she was trying to look.

That's when Cord realized she had her hands clenched into fists and that her knuckles were turning white. He ushered her to the chair across the table from DeWayne and had her sit down. At least that way DeWayne couldn't see her hands and the effect he was having on her.

But Karina also had an effect on DeWayne.

"Mona," DeWayne repeated, his eyes narrowing for just a split second. "What about her?"

"Did you kill her?" Cord asked.

That had an effect, too. Cord got a dose of those narrowed eyes. Maybe DeWayne hadn't thought they would discuss the woman, that this chat would be solely about alibis and attacks. But DeWayne was wrong.

The narrowed eyes went away, but DeWayne huffed, the sort of huff a man might make if he was bored with the subject. "You've been talking to Sheriff Ezell over in Comal County. Wouldn't put much stock into what he's saying. He's basing everything on what he heard from a jealous man."

"Mona's husband," Cord said. "The sheriff doesn't think it's just the jealousy talking."

"Well, he's wrong." Now, there was some temper. A tightening of the mouth. The sharp tone. There was just a glimpse of it before he pulled back his claws. "I've already admitted to having an affair with Mona. Plenty of men had affairs with her. I hope you and the sheriff are pestering them as much as you're pestering me."

Karina rolled her eyes. "If you're just going to rehash what we already know, then why ask me to come here?"

Cord figured DeWayne would dole out another smart-mouthed answer, but he didn't. He sat there, his face muscles stirring, before he looked at Karina again.

"Because I don't want you thinking I did this to you," DeWayne finally said. But he said it through clenched teeth. "I have enough legal battles dealing with Sheriff Ezell without you adding this to it. The man's like a dog with a bone. He won't let go of this Mona thing."

Cord liked the sheriff already, and he hadn't even met him. "I guess you have something to convince us that you didn't attack Karina?" he said to DeWayne.

"Maybe. Someone broke into my house a few days ago. I thought it was a kid since they didn't take anything, but then I had a PI look at the security feed. He managed to ID the intruder. A guy named Scott Chaplin. He belongs to some stupid club called Bloody Murder."

Well, that got Cord's attention. "Have you spoken to this guy?"

DeWayne shook his head. "My PIs haven't been able to find him, but I found out a lot about him. The club is a group of losers trying to prove Willie Lee isn't the Moonlight Strangler." He paused. "I'm worried that he might have planted some kind of evidence in my house."

"Evidence?" Jericho challenged.

DeWayne reached into his shirt pocket. And Cord automatically slid his hand over his gun. Jericho would have searched DeWayne when he first came in and disarmed him if necessary, but Cord didn't want to take any chances that the guy might have sneaked in a knife.

However, it wasn't a weapon that DeWayne pulled out. It was a small plastic bag containing what appeared to be a note.

"I found this on the desk in my home office." DeWayne put the bag on the table, and Karina, Jericho and Cord had a closer look.

"'You'll pay for planting that DNA at the crime scene,'" Jericho said, reading aloud. He huffed and looked at DeWayne. "Please tell me you gave this to Sheriff Ezell."

Judging from DeWayne's scowl, the answer to that was no. "He's already trying to railroad me for murder. This wouldn't have helped."

"And it won't help now," Cord assured him. Which brought him to his next question. "Why bring it to us?"

DeWayne stayed quiet a moment. "Because I thought it would convince you that I'm in danger, too. That I'm not the one after Karina. I think we're both in danger from the idiots in that club."

Karina leaned in, staring at DeWayne. "I didn't set up Willie Lee," she said.

"Neither did I!" DeWayne snapped. "But these dimwits think I did. Hell, like I said, they could have planted something in my house."

"Like what?" Cord pressed.

"I don't know," DeWayne shouted, but he stopped, paused, regrouped. "Something to do with Mona maybe. They could have perhaps stolen some evidence. And Sheriff Ezell might have stood back and watched them do it. Anyway, I figure the same person after Karina is after me, too."

His concern seemed genuine. *Seemed.* But Cord wasn't about to buy in to this. Judging from Jericho's huff, neither was he.

"I'll have the note sent to the lab so it can be checked for prints and trace," Jericho said. "I'll also want that security footage of this Scott Chaplin guy in your house. But I'm keeping Sheriff Ezell in the loop. Save your breath and don't bother to argue about that. I'll call you when and if I want to talk to you again. In the meantime, you stay away from Karina."

Jericho picked up the note and started out of the room.

"That's it?" DeWayne practically jumped to his feet. "You're not going to arrest every single member in that stupid club right now?"

"No," Jericho said from over his shoulder as he walked away.

DeWayne's temper flared again, and his face was turning red when he shifted his attention to Karina. "You believe me, don't you?"

"You've never cared what I thought of you before," she growled.

DeWayne pointed his finger at her. "I won't let you and these local yokels try to pin this on me. If I'd wanted you dead, you would be."

Oh, hell. That was the wrong thing to say, and Cord felt

himself moving before he even knew he was going to do it. He got right in DeWayne's face.

"Is that a threat?" Cord didn't wait for him to answer. "Because as a local yokel, it sounded like a threat to me."

DeWayne looked plenty ready to return verbal fire, but the sound of voices stopped him. Jericho's was one of those voices, but Cord didn't recognize the man Jericho seemed to be arguing with.

But Karina and DeWayne appeared to know who it was.

Karina got to her feet, and both DeWayne and she left the room and went into the hall. Cord didn't think it was his imagination that Karina suddenly looked less steady than she had just seconds earlier.

Their visitor was likely the reason for that.

While Cord hadn't recognized his voice, it was a face he recognized because he'd checked out all their suspects' driver's license photos. And this was definitely one of their suspects.

Harley Kramer.

No visible weapon. Harley had just a phone in his hand.

One thing was for sure—Karina was right about the scars. Very noticeable. But he didn't look like a B and E suspect. He was wearing a suit. A nice one, too. Probably the result of his wife's money. However, a suit couldn't smooth away his craggy face and the lines around his eyes. Harley looked every one of his fifty-nine years and then some.

"You weren't supposed to be here for another hour," Jericho said, checking the time.

"I came early. Good thing, too." His attention zoomed right to Karina. Then, to DeWayne. Judging from the glare he gave DeWayne, Harley wasn't a fan, either. "Because I'm betting that SOB is telling lies about me."

"I didn't mention you," DeWayne fired back.

"How do these two know each other?" Cord asked Karina.

"Harley came to me and accused me of setting up Willie Lee," DeWayne snarled. "I'd never even met this joker, and he starts spreading lies about me. About how I want to get back at Willie Lee and Karina."

"I don't have a beef with you," Harley argued. "Other than I want you to tell the truth. I know Willie Lee, and he's not a killer."

Apparently, Willie Lee had someone else in his corner. Interesting. But then again, Harley had already admitted that he knew Willie Lee. Cord would press him about that first chance he got.

"I want Harley arrested," DeWayne went on. "I want him grilled like you just grilled me."

"That wasn't a grilling," Cord assured him. "When it happens, you'll know."

That put some fire in DeWayne's eyes. Enough fire that his lawyer noticed and took his client by the arm. "We should be going," DeWayne's attorney said to him.

Cord agreed with the lawyer. He needed some time to check out whatever was going on between Harley and DeWayne. Needed to find Scott Chaplin, too. First, though, he had to finish up here so he could get Karina far away from both of these clowns. She was trembling again, and that steel she'd fought so hard to maintain in the interview room was melting away fast.

"Leave," Jericho told DeWayne when he just stood there and glared at Harley. "Unless you'd rather I put you in a holding cell for forty-eight hours?"

DeWayne turned his glare on Jericho. Then, on Karina and Cord before he stormed out with his lawyer.

Harley kept his attention on the man until he got into his car and drove off. Only then did Harley open his mouth to continue, but Jericho stopped that by frisking him. Even though Harley had to know it was standard procedure for anyone entering the sheriff's office, he still managed to look insulted.

"I'm here to help you," Harley snarled at Karina. "But you treat me like a criminal."

"Help me?" Karina questioned. "And how exactly do you want to do that?"

"By giving you information that could save your life." He made an uneasy glance over his shoulder.

Cord hated to look a gift horse in the mouth, but he wasn't sure he could trust anything Harley gave them. He also hated those glances that the man kept making. It was as if he was waiting for a killer to jump out at him.

"Before we continue this little chat," Jericho interrupted, "tell me where you were last night."

Harley huffed, no doubt because he thought he was still being treated unfairly. The treatment wouldn't get any better unless he had an alibi.

"I was at my house in San Antonio, and I was alone all night because my wife's out of town. I thought it might be a good time for her to take a long trip to Europe." Harley cursed. "If I'd known I was going to need an alibi, I would have gone out with friends or something. But that doesn't make me guilty of hurting Karina. It just makes me a loner."

Maybe it made him a would-be killer, too.

"Did you make any calls while you were home?" Jericho persisted.

Harley paused as if giving that some thought and shook his head. "No."

"Well, then, it won't take long to go through your phone records." Jericho motioned for Harley to hand him the phone.

"I'll give it to you in a minute," Harley said. "First,

though, I have to show Karina a picture I took. I think it's the guy who tried to hurt her last night."

She didn't react to it as if it was a bombshell. Probably because she didn't trust or believe Harley, either. But Harley seemed convinced he had something.

"I need to tell you about him first," Harley explained, looking not at Karina but Cord then Jericho. "Because I don't want you two arresting me or anything."

"Do we have reason to arrest you?" Cord challenged.

That put some anger in his eyes, and he turned to Karina to continue. "I stumbled onto this by accident when I was at a bar in San Antonio the night before last. I heard two guys talking. Nut jobs. They were saying how they thought the cops had framed Willie Lee and that they should do something about it."

"Do what exactly?" Karina asked when Harley didn't continue.

Harley shook his head and took a deep breath. "Kill somebody and make it look like the Moonlight Strangler."

Everything inside Cord went on alert. Because if this was true, then Harley had been in the right place at exactly the right time to hear just what they needed to hear to solve this.

Well, maybe.

If Harley had been the one to attack Karina, he could be using this as a way to deflect the guilt off him. It wouldn't work unless there was a whole lot of evidence to back it up.

"Did you get their names?" Cord asked.

"No. I didn't exactly feel good about going to two morons who were just talking about murder." Harley held up his phone again. "But I took their picture."

All right. So maybe that was evidence.

"Any reason you didn't tell us about this two nights

ago?" Jericho demanded before he even looked at the photo.

"I thought…hoped that it was just talk. And then I heard about the attack and knew they'd done it."

Cord snatched the phone from Harley then, and he expected to see an out-of-focus shot. It wasn't. The image was crystal clear.

Clear enough to cause Karina to gasp.

Because the man in the picture was someone they both recognized.

Chapter Eight

Rocky.

Karina knew she shouldn't be shocked at seeing his picture on Harley's phone, but it still hit her hard. For days, Rocky had been right by her side, helping her with the horses, and all that time he'd wanted her dead.

If Harley was telling the truth, that is.

She reminded herself that Harley did indeed hate her, and he could want her out of the way so she couldn't testify against him at his trial. Somehow, that was easier to accept than Rocky choosing her as some random victim to copycat the Moonlight Strangler.

"We need to find Rocky," she said under her breath.

Until she heard her own words spoken aloud, Karina hadn't realized just how shaky she was. But Cord must have because he took hold of her arm and led her back toward Jericho's office.

"That's it?" Harley called out to her. "I give you picture proof, and you just walk away?"

Karina stopped. "Thank you," she managed to say, but it was hollow. Maybe not even deserved. Harley could be playing some kind of sick game with her. "But you broke into Willie Lee's cabin. Someone who does that isn't exactly trustworthy."

"Willie Lee would want me to have those pictures,"

Harley insisted. Something he'd said, and repeated, right from the start.

And he didn't stop there.

"Just pictures," he added. "I wasn't after anything of value. I only wanted mementos from an old friend. And now I'm facing charges for that. Any idea what this is doing to my wife and her family?"

She nodded. Karina did know. Harley's wife, Miriam, was a socialite. An apparently beloved one. And people had praised her for marrying a disfigured man. Well, Karina wasn't going to let Harley's wife, or his scars, keep her from getting to the truth.

Harley demanded that she come back and talk to him face-to-face and was still essentially calling her out when Cord and she went into the office. Cord shut the door, and Harley instantly went quiet. It was possible Jericho had threatened the man, or perhaps it wasn't any fun to torment her if she wasn't around to listen.

"I don't even know what Harley was really looking for in Willie Lee's cabin," she admitted. "And yes, I searched the place. No pictures. I'm talking zero. In fact, Willie Lee had nothing personal in there."

That had to interest a lawman, and Cord no doubt believed that meant Willie Lee was leading some kind of secret life.

The life of a serial killer.

"Let's assume for a second that Harley was indeed an old friend," Cord mused. "Maybe he's looking for something Willie Lee hid away. Nothing to do with the Moonlight Strangler," Cord quickly added when she opened her mouth to object. "But maybe they committed some other crime. Something that Harley wanted to make sure didn't come back to bite him."

"Like what?" she asked, caution in her voice.

Cord lifted his shoulder. "There was a big money-laundering operation going on at the time the murders started over thirty years ago. Willie Lee and Harley would have been in their midtwenties then. Someone died as a result of that operation. Again, I'm not saying that Willie Lee did it, but there's no statute of limitations on murder. That would be a good reason for Harley to break into the cabin."

It would be. And she wasn't naive enough to believe Willie Lee had a perfect past. Still, it was hard to think of him as a criminal. Any kind of criminal.

"We'll leave as soon as Harley's out of here," Cord added, checking his watch. "I just want to make sure neither he nor DeWayne follows us."

Mercy, she hadn't even thought of that, but she wouldn't put it past either of them. Plus, she wasn't exactly thrilled with the idea of going back to the Appaloosa Pass Ranch.

Cord went to Jericho's computer, and after he pulled up the results of his search, he showed it to her. "That's Scott Chaplin's DMV photo. Do you recognize him?"

Karina shook her head. That was something at least. She wasn't sure she could have stomached knowing that both Rocky and Scott had somehow insinuated themselves into her life.

She leaned against the back of the door, looked at Cord and saw something she didn't usually see in his eyes. Sympathy. As someone who'd always had to stand on her own two feet, it stung to have someone feel sorry for her.

Karina tried to put on a much stronger face. "I need a place to stay. And it's not as if I have a lot of options. I'm guessing my ranch in Comal County is out." She didn't wait for Cord to confirm that.

It was out.

All three of their suspects would look for her there. And besides, going there could endanger the six ranch hands who worked for her. No way did she want to bring this to their doorstep.

"I'm not exactly close to my friends these days," she went on. "Because of Willie Lee. They think I'm crazy to believe he's innocent."

And mercy, could she sound any more miserable?

She wouldn't have been surprised if Cord had just groaned and walked out. But he didn't. He just stood there, staring at her, as if he was waiting for her to quit whining and do something.

So she did do something.

Karina kissed him.

It was barely a brush of her mouth to his, but she still felt it in every inch of her. She snapped away from him, ready to apologize and promise that it wouldn't happen again. But the words died on her lips when Cord slid his hand around the back of her neck.

"If we're going to make a mistake, it might as well be a good one," he drawled.

And he kissed her.

Not some brief little peck, either. This was a real kiss, and Karina could have sworn she lost every bit of her breath. It just vanished, and for those moments he was kissing her, all the pain and the flashbacks vanished, too.

She heard herself make a sound, a mixture of relief and pleasure. Mostly pleasure. From practically the moment Karina had first laid eyes on Cord, she'd wondered what it would be like to kiss him.

And now she knew.

He eased back from her, slowly, meeting her eye to eye. "Was that a big enough mistake for you?"

She couldn't help it. Karina smiled.

Cord didn't smile, though. He apparently wasn't feeling any relief, but she was certain that she saw the heat in his eyes that was mirrored in her own. He stepped away, turning his back to her for a moment as if he was trying to regain control. Or maybe he was just cursing himself for that lapse in judgment.

"I need you to stay at the Appaloosa Pass Ranch just one more day," he said.

Karina hadn't been sure what he was about to tell her, but she certainly hadn't expected that. And then something occurred to her.

"You didn't kiss me just so I'd cooperate with you, did you?" she asked.

He angled his head, looking back at her, and she had her answer with just that one glance.

No.

That wasn't the reason he'd kissed her.

Well, good. Her state of mind was already eggshell-thin, and she didn't want another hit. Especially since she wasn't so sure that kiss was indeed a mistake.

"The Appaloosa Pass Ranch has security already in place," Cord said a few seconds later. "A day will give Jericho and his deputies time to find Rocky, and it'll give me time to figure out where to take you."

"I'm staying in your protective custody?" she asked. Karina hadn't added *after that kiss*, but she figured Cord understood the full question.

"Yeah. For the time being anyway. I'll work on that, too."

But he might not be able to get everything in place in twenty-four hours. And Jericho certainly might not be able to find Rocky by then.

"I need some things at my rental house. Clothes, for one thing," she said, motioning toward the borrowed items Addie had lent her. "Plus, I take meds for my thyroid.

When will I be able to get back into the house to get those things?"

Cord took out his phone, sent a text and thankfully got a response almost right away. "Jax said you can stop by now," he answered after reading the text. "The CSIs are still there, but they can escort us in and out."

He got her moving out of the office, and Karina braced herself for another round with Harley.

"He's gone," Jericho volunteered. "I had nothing I could use to hold him."

Karina had been afraid of that. Yes, Harley hadn't shown them that picture sooner, but it would be hard to pin withholding-evidence charges on him when they weren't even sure Rocky was the one who'd tried to kill her.

"But I did just get an interesting phone call," Jericho added. "A woman named Taryn Wellman."

"I know her. She's DeWayne's current girlfriend." Karina had to shake her head. "But why would she call you?"

"Because she's apparently worried about lover boy. She says he's been acting suspicious and that she's afraid someone's blackmailing him or something."

"Blackmail?" Cord questioned.

"She didn't have a lick of proof. No other details, either. Hell, maybe because there aren't any details to have. I'll check it out, of course, but DeWayne could just be fooling around with another woman, that's all."

Yes. That sounded like DeWayne. According to the rumor mill, he'd had several lovers in the short time since he'd moved near her, one during the same time as Taryn.

"I'm taking Karina to her place and then back to the ranch," Cord told Jericho. "I'll work from there with the SAPD on contacting the members of the Bloody Murder club. One of them has to know where Rocky is."

Jericho nodded, and Cord and she headed out toward his truck. As he'd done earlier, he got her inside fast, and they sped away from the sheriff's office. Karina glanced around to make sure no one was following them. Cord did the same.

"I've been thinking about Harley just showing up at your ranch," Cord said. "Jericho and I discussed it earlier, but I forgot to ask Harley about this particular point. Did Harley happen to tell you how he knew Willie Lee and your mother?"

It took her a moment to switch mental gears. Partly because her mind was still hazy from that kiss. And also because there seemed to be some kind of accusation in his tone. Probably because she'd said Harley gave her the creeps.

"Harley was short on specifics, but he said Willie Lee and he were old army buddies." She paused. "And that he'd met my mother after my father died."

Cord didn't say anything. Probably because he was waiting for more. But Karina figured this wasn't going to make sense to him.

"I don't know if my mother and Harley actually met," she went on. "I certainly never saw him around the ranch. But my mother suffered from depression, and Harley knew all about that. He said he was trying to help her, but that clearly didn't work. She finally overdosed on pills one night."

Of course, Harley could have gotten those details from the same gossip mill where she'd gotten dirt about De-Wayne's affair.

"Did Harley talk to you about your mother's suicide?" Cord asked.

Karina had to shake her head. "No, only that he knew

my mother was dead and that he was sorry about that because he loved her."

And she could say the same for herself. Karina had indeed loved her mother. Once. But after the woman had fallen apart and quit living, she had become a hard woman to love.

There was a lesson in that for Karina.

She couldn't let all of what happened break her. She had to keep fighting, not only to find the person who'd attacked her, but also to figure out a way to prove Willie Lee's innocence.

Cord didn't ask her anything else. He drove in silence, but it wasn't a peaceful drive. He kept watch all around them, and he didn't seem to relax one bit when he finally pulled up in front of her rental place. But then neither did she.

There was yellow crime-scene tape on the barn and the area around it, and a CSI van was parked next to the house. Both reminders of the attack.

"Let's make this fast," he insisted. Cord reached to open his door, but then stopped. He stopped her, too.

Karina wasn't sure why he'd done that, but she followed his gaze. He was looking at the barn, specifically at the opened door, where the wind was rattling the yellow tape.

"What's wrong?" she asked.

He only shook his head and kept his attention pinned there.

She wasn't touching Cord, but Karina knew the exact moment that his muscles tightened. And he pulled his gun.

That put her heart in her throat, and she was about to ask him again what was going on. But she saw it for herself.

Someone was moving inside the barn.

"It's probably one of the CSIs," she said, hoping that was true.

It wasn't.

The person moved again, and for just a split second, Karina got a good look at him.

It was Rocky.

CORD COULDN'T TELL if Rocky had a gun, but he couldn't risk it. Nor could he take the chance of having Karina run into the house with the CSIs.

"Get down on the seat," Cord told Karina, and he threw open the door.

"You can't go out there." She caught on to his arm.

Cord shook off her grip and maneuvered himself into a position to take aim while still using the door as cover. Not that it would be much cover if Rocky did indeed have a weapon, but it was better than nothing.

He tossed Karina his phone. "Text Jax and tell him what's going on. I don't want the CSIs walking out of the house and getting caught in gunfire. I also want somebody out here to take Rocky into custody." Cord didn't want to do that himself, not with Karina with him.

She nodded, and despite the fact that Karina had to be shaken up by this, she got busy with the text. And Cord got busy with their suspect.

"Rocky?" Cord called out. "I need you to come out of the barn with your hands up."

No answer.

Damn.

Cord was hoping Rocky would make this easy. But apparently no such luck.

"We know about the Bloody Murder club," Cord tried again. "We also know you discussed a copycat killing so you could clear Willie Lee. I'm not just going to let you walk away from this."

Especially since he could return to have another go at Karina.

If that's what he'd done.

The seconds crawled by and Cord glanced at the house when he saw some movement there. One of the CSIs was looking out the window. He didn't recognize the guy, but he had his creds clipped to his shirt pocket. Cord motioned for him to move back. The county CSIs weren't issued guns as part of their jobs, but many carried their personal weapons. He hoped that was the case here because he might need backup before this was over.

Thankfully, Cord could see both of the barn doors, so it would be easy to spot Rocky if he tried to escape. However, there were trees, fences and watering troughs nearby. Plenty of places for someone to hide and wait for an ambush. That was even more reason to hurry this along.

"Rocky, get out here now!" Cord shouted, though he didn't hold out much hope the man would answer. That's why Cord was so surprised when he did.

"I can't do this," Rocky said. Not a shout like Cord's. He seemed to be arguing with someone. Or maybe himself.

"Yes, you can come out," Cord insisted. "Because if you don't, I have to come in there after you."

It wasn't a bluff. Not exactly. Eventually, Cord would have to go inside the barn, but that wouldn't happen until he had backup in place and someone to help him protect Karina.

"I need to end this," Rocky added. Cord couldn't be sure, but it sounded as if he was crying. Or else pretending to cry.

"Maybe I should try?" Karina asked. "I might be able to talk him into surrendering."

Cord was about to tell her no, that he wanted her down

on the seat. However, before he could even get out a single word, there was a sound. A really bad one.

A shot blasted through the air.

And it was quickly followed by another one. Both bullets slammed into the bed of his truck, just inches from where Cord was standing.

Cord jumped back in the truck, slamming the door and trying to position himself in front of Karina. The sides of the truck were reinforced—a modification he'd made after being attacked by the Moonlight Strangler—but the bullets could still tear their way through.

"Backup will be here soon," she told him.

That was good, but soon might not be soon enough, though.

The bullets just kept coming, and Cord tried to pinpoint Rocky's position. But the shots weren't coming from the barn. They were coming from the direction of the bunkhouse.

Hell.

Rocky wasn't alone.

"It's Scott Chaplin," Karina said. "I recognize him from the photo you showed me."

And that's when Cord realized she was peering over the dash and at the doorway of the bunkhouse, where the man was standing. Cord pushed her back down on the seat and hoped she would stay put so he could figure out what the devil was going on.

He looked at the man again. Yeah, it was Scott.

But something wasn't right.

Cord didn't actually see a gun in Scott's hand, and the man darted out of sight before he could get a better look. He couldn't see Rocky any longer, either.

However, the shots continued.

All coming from the side of the bunkhouse. Did that

mean Scott and Rocky had brought another member of the group with them?

The CSI that Cord had spotted from the window opened the front door of the house. He was armed, and even though he took aim in the direction of the bunkhouse, he didn't fire. Probably because he didn't know if this was a hostage situation or not.

Cord didn't know, either.

But he had to put a stop to the shooter. Cord hit the button to lower the window, and he levered himself up so he could get the guy in his sights.

And Cord fired.

The shooter scrambled back, but Cord sent another shot his way. Then, a third.

With the sounds of the blasts still ringing in his ears, it took Cord a moment to hear the other sounds. An ax or something striking against the wood in the barn.

Great. Now, Rocky could be trying to escape.

"Cover me," Cord called out to the CSI who had now made his way onto the porch. He took a backup gun from the glove compartment and handed it to Karina. "Stay down but try to keep your eye on him."

"On the CSI?" she asked, her eyes widening.

"Yeah." Cord hated that he'd just caused her fear to soar even higher, but he didn't know the CSI and wasn't ready to completely trust him with his and Karina's lives.

Cord climbed over her and got out through the passenger's door so he could hurry to the rear of his truck. The CSI reacted, too, moving to the end of the porch and aiming his gun at the bunkhouse.

The sounds of the chopping continued. And it was coming from the side nearest the truck.

What the hell was Rocky thinking?

Cord would still be able to gun him down, but if he did

that, the man wouldn't be able to give them answers. Cord preferred that not to happen.

Another shot came from the bunkhouse. This one was aimed at the CSI. The CSI dropped back a step, using the house for cover, but he didn't stay there. The CSI fired into the bunkhouse.

And this time, he hit something.

Or rather someone.

Scott came staggering out the front door. He was clutching his chest, and there was blood all over his shirt. He said something, or rather he tried, but Cord didn't catch a word of it before Scott collapsed onto the ground.

"No!" Rocky yelled.

Repeating that shout, Rocky tore through the rest of the wood and crawled out. He dropped onto his knees, his attention staying on Scott. That's when Cord spotted the gun in Rocky's right hand. His phone was in his left.

"Don't die. Don't be dead," Rocky said. He tossed both the gun and phone at Cord, got to his feet and started running.

But so did Cord.

He hurried toward Rocky, blocking his path and pointing his gun right in the man's face.

"Move one inch," Cord warned Rocky, "and you're a dead man."

Chapter Nine

Karina knew she couldn't ever come back to this place. The attack on her alone would have made her feel that way, but now she was certain of it. There'd been more blood spilled.

And there was a dead man lying in front of the bunkhouse.

The CSI had confirmed that fact not long after he'd shot him and while Cord was putting a pair of plastic cuffs on Rocky. Rocky wasn't looking at Cord, her or the body. He was staring blankly at the ground. Probably because he'd just seen his friend and fellow club member die right in front of him.

"You should stay in the truck a while longer," the CSI said, making his way toward her.

According to his name tag, he was Mitchell Durst, and the woman who had come out of the house shortly afterward was Helen Krauss, another CSI. Even though they both often dealt with violent crime scenes, they were visibly shaken.

Karina was, as well.

Before Cord had even gotten out of the truck, he'd given her a gun and told her to keep an eye on the CSI. Karina still had the gun gripped in her hand, but she was fairly sure the CSI wasn't a threat. However, it suddenly felt as if anyone and anything could be.

All except Cord.

He'd saved her life, again.

Karina heard the sirens on the cruisers long before they pulled into her driveway. Jax and the other deputy, Dexter, got out of the first cruiser. Jax hurried toward Cord, while Dexter headed for the dead body.

Scott Chaplin.

Karina wanted to believe this was the end of it now that Scott was dead and Rocky was in custody, but there were other club members out there.

And so was the real Moonlight Strangler.

She wasn't safe, and thanks to her getting Cord involved, neither was he. Any one of those bullets could have killed him.

Jax took over with Rocky, and the two deputies who pulled up in the other cruiser went to help Jax with the arrest. Cord kicked aside Rocky's gun, probably so that it would be well out of the man's reach, and he picked up Rocky's phone. Cord looked at her, but he had a short conversation with Jax and then made a call with his own phone before he started toward her.

"The horses are all okay," Cord said. "Jericho's hand had moved them to the back pasture early this morning. Neither the ranch hand nor the horses were anywhere near those shots."

In the grand scheme of things, most people might not have considered it important for her to know that. But it was.

"Thank you for checking," she said, finally managing to get out the words. "Did Rocky say anything about why he was here?"

Cord shook his head and opened the door to help her

out. "But he probably realized he was in a lot of trouble and needed a lawyer before he started talking. We can wait inside until the scene's cleared enough for us to leave."

He didn't say how long that would be, and Karina wasn't sure she wanted to hear the answer anyway.

While Cord led her up the porch, she glanced back at Rocky. The deputies were hauling him to the second cruiser. No doubt taking him to the sheriff's office so he could be jailed. Jax joined Dexter by the body.

Both of the CSIs were outside, so that's probably why Cord locked the door. However, it was a reminder that there could be others out there. Not exactly a thought to steady her nerves.

"Go ahead and gather up the things you wanted to get," Cord added. "That way, when Jax gives us the green light, we can leave right away."

Good. Even though the alternative wasn't much better.

"What if someone comes after me at the Appaloosa Pass Ranch?" she asked, going straight to her bedroom.

Cord followed her but didn't answer until she looked back at him. "I can't give guarantees this won't happen again. Hell, it happened right under my nose. But I can make the guesthouse at the ranch as safe as I can make any place."

Which wasn't 100 percent. Nothing was at this point.

Since she felt she had to keep moving or else she would collapse, Karina went to the closet, took out a suitcase and started shoving clothes into it. She knew she was moving too fast, that she probably looked like a malfunctioning windup toy, but she couldn't stop herself.

She hurried to the dresser and grabbed some underwear, tossing them into the suitcase, too. Karina would have done the same to her toiletries in the bathroom, but Cord took her by the hand to stop her in her tracks.

"I'm not going to cry," she insisted. "I can be as strong as you."

"You already are."

Damn him. It was the right thing to say. Perfect, in fact. And that's why she didn't listen to her common sense and back away from him when he pulled her into his arms. Besides, she wanted to be in his arms. Being there took the edge off the nerves, and it got her mind off the fact that she'd just seen a man die.

"Most people have a meltdown, a major one, when violence happens around them," Cord went on. His voice was as soothing as his arms.

"The meltdown still might happen," Karina mumbled. "Especially when I run out of things to pack."

She certainly hadn't meant to make that sound like a joke, but Cord smiled. It was lazy and slow like the long look he gave her before he lowered his head and did something she hadn't seen coming.

He kissed her.

Judging from the soft sound he made, he wasn't sure who was more surprised by that—him or her. Karina was thinking he'd won on that count. She'd dreamed of doing this since that kiss in Jericho's office, but she was betting Cord had been spending his mental energy on making sure it didn't happen again.

But here it was. Another kiss. And it was a good one.

Being in his arms had been incredible, but this took things up a mile-high notch. How could someone taste that good? And make her forget, for a few seconds anyway, about the nightmare that'd just happened.

Karina got lost in the kiss. Cord did, too. And while she figured he hadn't wanted this to go much further, it did. He lowered his hands to her waist, pulling her closer. And closer. Until they were plastered right against each other.

Mercy.

It'd been a long time since she'd felt this kind of fire. And never like this. Karina found herself wanting more, and she was the one who deepened the kiss. The one who pulled him even closer. Until she couldn't breathe. Couldn't think.

But Cord could apparently hear, because he stopped.

"My phone," he said, breaking away from her and taking out his cell.

Great day. She hadn't even heard the ringing sound, but sure enough it was Jax. No doubt important. And she'd been so lost in that kiss, she hadn't even heard it. So much for the vigilance she needed to make sure they weren't attacked again.

"You still got Rocky's phone?" Jax asked when Cord answered the call and put it on speaker.

"Yeah. You need it?"

"Not yet, but if what he says is true, I will. Rocky claims he's been getting texts from the Moonlight Strangler. Check and see if there are any messages from God. And yeah, you heard that right."

Cord scowled, maybe at the name or maybe because he thought this was part of the game that Rocky and his club buddies were playing. He took out Rocky's phone, scrolled through the messages and then stopped.

"God," Cord repeated, "texted Rocky three times, and Rocky answered two of them."

Jax cursed. "Is there anything in the messages that jumps out at you?"

"Not really." He glanced through all the messages. "But they need to be analyzed, of course. There might be something important in them." He didn't sound very hopeful, though. "Did Rocky say anything else?" Cord asked. "Like maybe something about there being a third shooter?"

Karina's stomach dropped. A third one? Good grief, how many people wanted her dead?

"Rocky didn't mention anything about a third guy, but he said he's innocent. And that Scott was, too."

Of course, he would say that. "Then why was he here with a gun?" Karina asked. "And why didn't he just turn himself in to the cops?"

"He claims he wanted to get his stuff. By that, I'm guessing he wanted all those photos and newspaper clippings. You know, the very things that will incriminate him when he's arrested?"

"He was trying to cover his tracks," Cord said as if giving that some thought. "But it was pretty gutsy of him and his buddies to come here with the CSIs still around."

Jax made a sound to indicate he was giving it some thought, too. "It doesn't add up. He's hiding something. Or maybe he thought he could hide out until he got another shot at Karina."

The chill came so fast that Karina had to fight off a shudder. Had that been it? Had Rocky been waiting to kill her?

"Jericho will grill him during interrogation," Jax added. "Dexter and the other deputy, Mack, are taking Rocky to the sheriff's office now. Once the ME gets here, I can follow Karina and you back, too, so you can listen to what Rocky has to say."

That meant she wouldn't be going to the ranch. Not right away. It also meant she'd have to give yet another statement of yet another attack. Her third one in less than twenty-four hours.

Cord ended the call and sank down on the foot of her bed. His attention went straight back to Rocky's phone, and she sat down next to him so she could go through the messages with him.

There were five in total—three from "God" and two responses from Rocky. The first was by far the longest, and it had been sent nearly five weeks earlier, right before Willie Lee had been captured. Karina read it word for word.

"'I saw your website, and I thought you might like to chat with me instead of just collecting pictures and doing all that blogging. I'm the Moonlight Strangler, aka the object of your affection. Since you seem like the sort who needs proof that I'm really him, here you go—I took a necklace from Gracie Hernandez. The cops didn't put that in the reports, but if you dig, you'll find out it's true. Bye for now.'"

She looked at Cord, and he nodded. "The Moonlight Strangler did take the woman's necklace. She was photographed wearing it just an hour or so before she was murdered, and it wasn't on her body when the cops found her. Her family said she never took the necklace off."

That twisted at her stomach, but Karina reminded herself that someone in law enforcement could have leaked the info. Still, why go to the trouble of pretending to be the Moonlight Strangler? It wasn't a smart thing to do since the serial killer had gone after those impersonating him.

"Here's Rocky's response," Cord continued. According to the time, he'd sent the text later that same day.

"'I can't confirm about the necklace, the cops won't talk to me, but I do believe you're the Moonlight Strangler. Can you *please* call me?'" *Please* was all in caps and underlined.

It sickened Karina to think that someone—anyone—would actually want to talk to a serial killer, but judging from Rocky's interest in the Bloody Murder club, this wasn't a surprise.

"'No calls.'" Cord said, reading God's answer aloud. "'But we can chat here. I'll answer your questions, give you stuff to put in that blog of yours, and in turn you'll help me.'"

"'Help you how?'" This was Rocky's return text.

"'I need to switch to a different phone,'" Cord said, reading the killer's response. "'I'm ditching this one so don't text this number. You'll get another message soon.'"

There were no other messages from God, but Cord went through the cache. There were literally dozens of them, some even to Karina when she'd been in the process of hiring Rocky.

And then she saw the message from an unknown caller. It was buried in the middle of plenty of others, but the first line caused Cord to stop.

"'It's me, again. God. And I have a problem. I'd wanted you to help me with someone playing around with my name, but there's something bigger for you to do right now. The cops think they have the Moonlight Strangler. They don't, and I don't want anyone getting credit for my handiwork. Have one of your club buddies fix that, now, or the next woman I kill will be somebody you know and love.'"

Karina froze. Cord didn't, though. He read through it again. Then, again, before he cursed and leaned in to have a closer look at the small print with the date and time the message had been sent.

"Hell," Cord said, passing the phone to her.

Her heart thumped in her chest. Because the date of the message was two days after Willie Lee's capture. While Willie Lee had been in a coma.

"This is the proof that he's innocent," Karina insisted.

"No," Cord insisted right back. "It could be just another groupie or club member pretending to be the Moonlight Strangler."

She wanted to remind Cord that he'd known about the

necklace, but she herself had already dismissed it as proof positive. Still, Karina wanted to believe it.

"The texts will be analyzed," Cord reminded her. He looked at her then. "If the FBI finds something and it turns out that Willie Lee is innocent, then we'll deal with it."

Coming from him that was a huge concession. Huge. "You're having doubts about his guilt?" she asked.

"No. But I want to have doubts." He cursed again, and scrubbed his hand over his face. "And that's why I shouldn't be backing you against a wall and kissing you."

It was true. It was clouding both their minds at a time when cloudy thinking could get them killed.

Especially with the Moonlight Strangler still out there.

Cord's phone rang, the sound slicing through the room and causing her to gasp. She hated the nerves, hated that they almost certainly wouldn't be going away until this was all settled.

Whenever that would be.

"It's Jax," Cord informed her, and he answered the call.

"We got a big problem," Jax said the moment he came on the line. "Two of them, actually. Rocky escaped."

Sweet heaven. That was not what she wanted to hear. Ditto for Cord.

"How the hell did that happen?" Cord snapped.

"The cruiser was attacked on the way into town. Someone shot out the tires, tossed in some tear gas. When Dexter and Mack were coughing their heads off, the attackers rushed in and took Rocky at gunpoint."

Cord shook his head. "Someone *kidnapped* Rocky?"

"Or else someone wanted to make it look that way."

Yes, that was possible, but it didn't matter about the why. Rocky was on the loose again.

However, Karina also thought about what else Jax had

told them at the beginning of the call. "You said there were two problems?"

"Yeah." That's all Jax said for several long seconds. "The sheriff over in Comal County just found another body. A woman. She'd been strangled and had a crescent-shaped cut on her cheek. And there was a message from her killer." Jax paused again. "A message left for Karina and you."

Chapter Ten

Cord hated that he had to drag Karina back to the sheriff's office. Hated even more that she was going through this and had that troubled look in her eyes again. But this latest murder had made it necessary.

That, and the fact that whoever had killed the woman apparently had something he wanted to say to Karina and him.

Cord and Karina, I'm still here.

Considering the words had been cut into the dead woman's body, it was obvious the killer wanted to send them a message.

Message received.

The Moonlight Strangler—or more likely someone pretending to be him—had wanted them to know he wasn't in a coma in a prison hospital, that he was free and killing again. If it was a copycat, it was too bad that the woman had paid for that with her life.

By now, Karina knew the drill about not being out in the open any longer than necessary, and she moved fast when Cord parked in front of the sheriff's office. The moment she was inside, her gaze zoomed around the room until she spotted Jericho. He wasn't hard to find because it was only him and one of the reserve deputies in the squad room. All the others were no doubt tied up with the various legs of this investigation.

"Who's the murdered woman?" she asked right away.

Jericho answered right away, too. "Taryn Wellman."

"Oh, God." She didn't stagger, but it was close.

"Yeah, DeWayne's lover," Jericho added. "I haven't had a chance to follow up on the call Taryn made to me. And I obviously won't be able to talk to her about it now. But DeWayne's on his way here, and judging from the way he carried on when I spoke to him, he's not in a good mood. He thinks this is somehow all our fault."

Cord was so not in the mood to deal with DeWayne. "How the heck is this our fault?"

"Yours," Jericho amended, pointing at Cord. "He's blaming you specifically for this."

Karina shook her head and sank down into the nearest chair. "DeWayne and Taryn are lovers. And I guess he blames us for the Moonlight Strangler still being out there."

Twenty-four hours ago, Cord would have verbally blasted anyone who accused him of that. But now he was rethinking every single second of the attack a month earlier, where he'd been hit with a stun gun, drugged and then cut. All by the man he believed to be his father and the Moonlight Strangler.

However, there was a problem.

Cord hadn't seen Willie Lee's face, something he'd repeatedly told Jericho and the FBI.

"Hell," Cord said, sitting down beside Karina. "Maybe this is all my fault."

He expected her to give you an I-told-you-so look. But she didn't. Karina simply put her arm around him.

"If the Moonlight Strangler really did set all of this up," she said, "then he set up Willie Lee, too. And he would have made sure that you believed Willie Lee was responsible."

Cord had considered all of that before, but for the first time, it really sank in. He blamed the kisses in part for that. However, that had only brought down a few barriers. The facts stayed the same.

"The FBI had one of their so-called memory recovery experts talk to me," Cord explained to her. "It didn't work, but I think I should try it again."

"I can get that started for you," Jericho offered.

But Cord waved him off. "You've got enough to do." Including yet another death and an escaped prisoner. "I'll take care of it when we're done there." Which hopefully would be soon, but there were still plenty of things he needed to discuss with Jericho.

"Anything on Rocky yet?" Cord asked.

Jericho shook his head. "But the so-called kidnapping was captured on the police camera that was in the cruiser. The two thugs were wearing gas masks and gloves, so there's no visual ID, and they didn't leave any prints behind." Jericho turned the computer screen so they could see it. "And then we have this. I'm not sure what to make of it."

That got Cord moving toward the computer. Karina, too, and the first thing Cord saw was Rocky on the screen. It was a clear shot, the image paused in mid-action and what appeared to be mid-cough. There was one gas-masked guy in front of him. Another behind him. The one behind had a gun aimed at Rocky's head. There was a white cloud of tear gas misting all around them and the cruiser.

"Keep watching and listening," Jericho instructed, and he hit the play button.

Since only Rocky's face was visible, it was easy to focus just on him, but Cord tried to take in the whole picture as the two men moved and shoved Rocky away from the cruiser. They were rough with them, but it could be all for show to make it look convincing.

Which it did.

Because the deputies and Rocky were coughing almost violently, it was hard to hear what else was being said, but Cord hit Pause when Rocky looked directly in the camera and said something. Cord replayed it three times.

"He said, 'Help me,'" Karina said and Cord agreed.

Jericho nodded. "And he really looked as if he means it. I'm thinking Rocky might have gotten in over his head in this murder club. Maybe because he didn't manage to kill Karina like they wanted. If he really did go off searching for her attacker last night like he said, then he could have been going after one of his fellow club members."

Definitely, and that wouldn't have set well with the group.

"I haven't made much progress finding out the names of the other members," Cord explained. "What about the FBI? Can they go after the IP addresses and try to find these idiots?"

"Already put in the request," Jericho assured him, and he reached for the desk phone when it rang.

Cord figured with all that was going on, the call could have been about plenty of things, but then Jericho pulled back his shoulders.

"Really?" he said to the caller, and he pressed the button to put it on speaker. "You're the Moonlight Strangler?"

It was probably a crank call. The FBI had been getting hundreds of them, but Cord still found himself moving closer to the phone. Karina, too. Jericho also hit the record button just in case this turned out to be something more than just a poser out for publicity.

For instance, one of their suspects. Or even someone

in the Bloody Murder club. At least now, they'd have the guy's voice on tape so it could be analyzed.

"Cord, you listening?" the caller asked. His voice was a raspy whisper. Barely audible, but Cord had no trouble hearing his own name. However, he couldn't hear anything in the background to give him a clue as to where the guy was.

"I'm here. Now, who the hell are you?" Cord snapped.

"Don't you know?" That voice was a taunt, laced with a mock sweetness that stirred something inside Cord.

Cord shook his head. It didn't matter what he felt. He needed to focus on the man doing this.

"Well, I know you're calling yourself the Moonlight Strangler." Cord added some mock sweetness to his tone, too. "But you can't be him because we already have him in custody."

"No, you don't," the man quickly answered. "You have a moron in that prison hospital. Willie Lee Samuels hasn't got the guts to kill. Didn't Karina tell you that?" He didn't wait for an answer. "Of course she did. But you didn't believe her."

"I don't believe you, either," Cord assured him.

"But you will." The caller let that hang in the air for several long moments. "Let's play a little memory game. When you were three years old, you were abandoned at a gas station, and your sister, Addie, was found near the Appaloosa Pass Ranch—"

Cord huffed. "Everybody knows that."

"True. But not everybody knows that Addie was wearing a yellow dress with little flowers on it. And you had on blue overalls and a white shirt. There was a stain on the left sleeve."

Cord felt as if someone had punched him.

Because it was true.

"They didn't put that in the newspapers, did they?" the caller went on, and he gave Cord another dose of that taunting tone. "I know what you were wearing because I was there that day. With you, Addie and your mama. You looked me straight in the eyes, boy, and you saw what I did. Yet you still think Willie Lee is the Moonlight Strangler?"

"Are you okay?" Karina whispered to him, and she took hold of his hand.

No, he wasn't okay. Not by a long shot. The flashback came, staying right at the fringes of his memory. And maybe not a real memory at all. Cord had gone over all the details so many times that maybe he was imagining that day.

But the caller certainly wasn't.

Had Cord really looked into his eyes that day?

"What did I see you do?" Cord heard himself ask.

"Think. It'll all come back to you."

Cord repeated his question, shouting this time, and he hated that this monster had caused him to lose control. The laugh didn't help, either. It was as sickening as the rest of this conversation.

"I'm sending you a gift," the man continued without addressing Cord's question. Or his outburst. "It should be there real soon. After you've had a chance to look at it, we'll talk again."

And with that, he hung up.

Cord sat there, trying to pull himself back together. Hard to do, though. Because if the caller was telling the truth about those clothes—and he was—then, was the other thing the truth, too?

Had Cord really looked him in the eyes?

Maybe, but that wasn't even the worst of it.

"I'm guessing you have no idea what he claims that you saw?" Jericho asked.

"No." And Cord had undergone all kinds of treatments to recover those memories, as well. Including some drug that a behavioral scientist had given him. A drug meant to pull out those memories of a three-year-old boy, and he'd remembered nothing except a white teddy bear and some Christmas lights.

Hardly a revelation.

But it had been an actual memory because Addie had recalled the same thing. Maybe that meant more memories would come. Even the ones that Cord wasn't sure he wanted to remember.

Had the Moonlight Strangler murdered someone while Cord watched?

As a lawman, he cursed that. And the memories that were so close to the surface, but not clear enough for him to recall them. They could put an end to all his questions. But then, they could also give him plenty of doubts about Willie Lee's guilt.

Hell.

Would this never end?

Jericho gave a heavy sigh and took out his phone. "I'll get someone from the bomb squad down here ASAP. If this clown is really sending you something, I want to make sure it doesn't blow up in our faces."

Cord agreed, and he stood, easing Karina to her feet next to him. "While we're waiting, I'll take Karina to the break room and maybe find her something to eat."

Cord knew he couldn't put anything in his stomach, but maybe he could convince her that she needed to keep up her strength. While he was at it, maybe he could also convince her that he was okay.

He wasn't.

And she knew it.

"There are some sandwiches in the fridge back there,"

Jericho told them. "Help yourself," he added before he went back to his call.

"Just try taking deep breaths or something," Karina whispered to him. "It won't stop whatever's going on in your head right now, but it'll make you feel as if you're doing something to get past it."

He nodded, and managed to mumble a "thanks."

"But you're going to be all right," she said. "Aren't you?"

Cord stopped, looked at her and was about to give her a reassurance that he darn sure didn't feel. But it seemed stupid to lie to her. They weren't lovers, but they'd been through hell and back together, and if there were any barriers still left between them, it wouldn't be long before they were shot to hell, too.

"What if I was wrong about Willie Lee?" he asked her. A simple question, but he was afraid there were no simple answers.

But somehow Karina managed to find one. "Then, we'll fix it. And then we'll find the real killer." She brushed a kiss on his mouth, slipped her arm around his waist and got them moving toward the break room.

They didn't get far.

The front door opened, and Cord heard a voice he didn't want to hear.

"I told you this would happen," Harley called out to them. "I warned you that somebody would try to kill you again."

Karina turned around to face him. The breath she took was a weary one. "So you did. Why are you here, Harley?"

"Because I don't want to die." His attention shifted to Cord. "And I want you to do something to find this snake that keeps killing people. Why would you let your number one suspect escape like that?"

"Rocky's just one of our suspects," Cord said to clarify. "But then so are you."

Harley practically snapped to attention. "Me? How do you figure that?"

"Karina's going to testify against you," Cord quickly explained. "You could want her out of the way. Plus, there's that history you say you have with Willie Lee. Any chance you two were involved in money laundering back in the day?"

With all the scars on Harley's face, it was hard to see much change in his expression. But Cord saw it in his eyes. He'd struck a nerve.

"Money laundering?" Harley challenged.

"Don't play innocent," Cord warned him. "It was all over the news recently. No way that you could have missed it."

Of course, it was possible that neither Harley nor Willie Lee truly had anything to do with that operation, but Harley had been looking for something in Willie Lee's cabin. And in Cord's experience, when a man was willing to commit a crime to find something, it was because he was covering up something.

Jericho hit another nerve with Harley, too.

"I just got your background check," Jericho said to Harley. "You were a demolitions expert in the army. Considering that someone blew up an ambulance last night, I have to wonder if you had anything to do with it."

Yeah, definitely a nerve.

"Anything else you have to say to me, you say through my lawyer. My wife and I keep several on retainer." Harley didn't spare any of them even a glance. He stormed out.

Karina shook her head. "Did he get those scars in the army?"

Jericho shrugged. "I don't know, yet. The army hasn't

sent his full military service record, only his career field. In fact, I don't have much more on him at all."

Cord recognized that tone. A suspicious lawman. And it occurred to him that while they knew quite a bit about Rocky and DeWayne, they knew very little about Harley.

"He has a degree in psychology," Jericho said. "He used his GI Bill to go to college at A and M. After that, he dropped off the radar for a while. That's about the same time that big money-laundering scheme was going on."

Too bad the records for that were sketchy at best. "Does he actually have a job now?" Cord asked.

"No. Doesn't need it what with his wife's money. But that money comes with strings attached. There's a prenup, and if she divorces Harley over this B and E scandal, he won't get a penny. Plus, it'd be an even bigger scandal if he's linked to the money-laundering scheme."

Jericho was about to say more, but he reached for his gun. Cord and the deputy went for theirs, too, and Cord pivoted in the direction of the door. But it wasn't the threat his body had prepared him for.

It was a kid.

A girl, no more than eleven or twelve years old.

The guns nearly had her bolting, but Jericho, the deputy and Cord quickly reholstered. Jericho motioned for her to come in. She did, but she took her time with her gaze firing at all of them.

"It's okay," Jericho assured them. "That's Annabeth, and her dad's the cook at the diner."

"Someone left this on one of the tables," she said, holding up an envelope. "It's addressed to the Appaloosa Pass sheriff's office, and my dad told me to bring it right over."

Cord doubted this was a coincidence. It had to be from the caller who'd shaken him to the core. He figured that was just the beginning, though.

"We didn't see who left it there," the girl went on. "We've had a lot of customers in and out all morning, and someone had stuck it between the salt and pepper shakers. Not exactly hidden, you know, but not right out in the open, either."

Because whoever had left it had wanted it to be found. Just not while he was there. Cord made a note to check the security cameras in the area to see if they could spot the person. Again, though, the person had likely covered their tracks.

Jericho put on some latex gloves that he grabbed from a desk drawer, went closer and took it from the girl, but he only touched the edges of the envelope. He was trying to preserve any evidence that might be on it.

Cord figured there wouldn't be any. Not if this guy was the real Moonlight Strangler. Other than that DNA—which was now under suspicion—he'd left no part of himself behind.

Jericho thanked the girl, and she took off, clearly ready to get out of there, and the three of them looked at the envelope. It was indeed addressed to the sheriff's office. No return address. No stamp. And it wasn't sealed.

Cord could see the edges of a photograph, and Jericho took out a note. It had been typed and was only one sentence.

"'Cord, everything you need to know about yourself, and me, is right here.'"

Chapter Eleven

Karina held her breath while Jericho eased the first of the three photos from the envelope. She could practically feel Cord trying to bolster himself for whatever he was about to see. Unfortunately, he might need some bolstering.

"Remember," Karina whispered to him, "anything the person says or gives you could be a lie. We're not dealing with a sane, normal person here."

But she had no idea exactly who they were dealing with, and she doubted anything in that envelope would tell them, either. If the real Moonlight Strangler had indeed sent this, then she figured there would be nothing to incriminate him.

So, why had he sent it?

Jericho carefully placed the photo on the desk, and Karina got a good look at the one on top. It was an old Polaroid, yellow with age and worn in spots, but the image was still fairly clear. It wasn't a posed shot. There was a woman on a porch. Her head was down so it was hard to see much of her face, but she had her hand on her throat and was looking down at two children.

A boy and a girl.

Cord jerked back his shoulders. And Karina knew why. The children were wearing clothes exactly like the ones the caller had described. The clothes that Cord and Addie had been wearing the day they disappeared.

Someone had written "Mom" at the bottom of the photo. Oh, God.

Was that actually Cord's mother?

Jericho took out another pair of gloves when Cord reached for it, and Cord put them on without taking his attention off the photo.

"That's Addie," Jericho concluded. "I was eight years old the day they found her wandering around the woods near the ranch, and she looked exactly like that. Well, except when they found her, she had a cut on her cheek. She doesn't have one in the photo."

Not yet. Karina had the sickening feeling that it'd come shortly thereafter. And the cut had been the crescent shape that the Moonlight Strangler had given all his victims.

Or in the cases of Addie and herself, his near victims.

Cord picked up the picture and brought it closer, his eyes combing over every inch of it. Especially the woman's face. "I don't remember this. I don't remember *her*."

Since there was nothing she could say to make this better for him, Karina simply put her arm around him and hoped that helped. It did.

Until Jericho went to the second photo.

Cord actually staggered back a step, and it took him a second to regain his composure. Karina didn't even try to regain hers. Because the photo turned her stomach.

It was the same woman who'd been in the previous shot, but she wasn't on the porch with the kids in this one.

She was dead.

Karina didn't have a lot of experience looking at dead bodies, but the woman was ashen, not a drop of color on her face. Except for that obscene cut on her face and the bruises on her neck.

"It could have been faked," Jericho quickly pointed out. "I'll have the crime lab examine it, but that could be makeup."

Yes, it could be, but Karina doubted it. Judging from the profanity Cord said under his breath, so did he. Like her, he believed he was looking at the face of his dead mother.

"The Moonlight Strangler told Addie that our mother was dead," Cord added.

Karina looked at Jericho to see if he knew about that, and he nodded. "The snake called her months ago to tell her that he wasn't going after her, that she was safe. But he also said her mom was dead."

"Did he kill her?" Karina blurted out before she could stop herself. She wished she had stopped herself because she wasn't sure it was an answer Cord would want to hear.

Jericho shrugged. "He mentioned something about spilling blood."

She was glad she hadn't been around for that call, and even though Cord and Addie had had months now to come to terms with it and everything else they'd learned, they must have had their doubts that the killer was telling them the truth. Or rather their hopes that he was lying.

And maybe he still was.

Karina was going to hang on to that, and she prayed Cord would do the same. They were dealing with a serial killer here, and if he could murder all those women, it wouldn't be much of a stretch for him to lie.

After looking at the first two photos, Karina wasn't sure she wanted to see the third one. Mercy, she hoped it wasn't one of the kids being harmed.

But it wasn't.

The third photo was nothing like the other two. It was a man. And it was someone she instantly recognized.

Willie Lee.

Now, it was Karina's turn to feel as if someone had put a knife in her.

He was young, probably still in his late twenties, but Karina had no doubts that it was Willie Lee. None.

It appeared to be a selfie shot. The lens was close to his face. No smile. His mouth was set in a tight line, and he was holding up something next to his cheek.

A knife.

Oh, God.

A knife!

Karina heard the hoarse groan tear from her throat, and she fumbled around behind her until she found a chair. Cord was right there, helping her sit, and despite the jolt he'd just gotten from his mother's photo, he managed to look a lot steadier than she felt.

"Again, the photo could be fake or doctored," Jericho reminded them both. "Or Willie Lee could have been forced to pose like that."

It was the first time Jericho had even hinted that Willie Lee might be innocent, and if this had been any other time, Karina would have considered it a victory. Not now, though.

Not after seeing that knife.

"I think I should go ahead and take Karina back to the ranch," Cord said.

She didn't argue. Couldn't. It felt as if someone had taken hold of her heart and was crushing it. Besides, the person who'd sent those photos could still be nearby. Just the thought of that was too much for her to handle.

Cord helped her to her feet, but before they could make it to the door, she saw someone else she didn't want to see.

DeWayne.

No. Cord and she had been through enough today without adding this.

Of course, Jericho had said DeWayne was on his way to the sheriff's office, but what with the phone call and those photos, she'd forgotten all about it. And she didn't have the energy to deal with DeWayne right now.

"On second thought, I'll take Karina to the break room," Cord said. Probably because his truck was parked right out front. Exactly where DeWayne was walking. That would mean running right into the man.

Jericho gathered up the photos, note and envelope and put them in a clear plastic bag that he then placed in the desk drawer. No doubt so that DeWayne wouldn't see them. But then it occurred to her that DeWayne might have known all about them because he could have been the one who sent them.

Heck, she was latching on to Jericho's theory that the photos could have been faked. DeWayne could have done that.

That gave her some much-needed strength, and she didn't go running to the break room when DeWayne walked in. Even though judging from the scowl Cord gave her, that's exactly what he had wanted her to do.

"Taryn's dead," DeWayne snapped, and he looked directly at Karina as if she was the one responsible.

"Yes, I heard. And I'm sorry." She meant that. Karina was indeed sorry about the woman's murder, but that's where her sympathy ended. "Were you the one who killed her?"

"Kill her?" DeWayne asked, his voice practically a shout. "She was my lover. Why would I want her dead?"

Karina could think of several reasons, but Cord spoke before she could voice them.

"Because you want to make yourself look innocent of being the real Moonlight Strangler," Cord said. "Or maybe because Taryn learned something about you and you wanted to silence her."

The anger shot through DeWayne's eyes. And not just ordinary anger. Rage. "You have no proof of any of that, and you're grasping at straws." He jabbed his index finger at Karina. "And it's because of her. Because you're sleeping with her, and she's been feeding you lies."

"No, it's because I'm a lawman, and I can see there's a problem here. You're covering up something. It could be your involvement in that old money-laundering operation—"

"I don't have to listen to this," DeWayne interrupted, throwing his hands in the air. "I came here to find out what she knows about Taryn's murder." Karina got another finger jab in her direction.

Karina didn't even pause. "I don't know anything about it. Well, nothing except that it appears she was either murdered by the Moonlight Strangler or by someone who wants us to believe she was. Since you believe Willie Lee is the serial killer, then maybe you just lost your temper with Taryn, killed her and then decided to go with the copycat buzz that's all over town."

"I know something," Jericho volunteered. "Taryn called me earlier to say you'd been acting suspicious and that she thought you were being blackmailed or *something*. Want to talk about that?"

The question clearly threw DeWayne. No rage this time. He seemed to be sizing up Jericho to see if he was telling the truth. He must have decided he was because his shoulders dropped.

"Taryn was wrong," DeWayne finally said, "and she shouldn't have talked to you." But then, his head snapped up, his attention going back to Karina. "Did you say anything about Taryn to those Bloody Murder club guys? Because one of them could have killed her."

"I haven't spoken to any of them," Karina answered. But then she rethought that. Maybe she had. Maybe she was talking to one of them now. Or Harley could be a member, too.

DeWayne made a sound of outrage. "I don't know how you did it, but you're responsible for this."

"Enough," Cord declared. He took hold of her arm and led her toward Jericho's office.

She expected DeWayne to follow them. And he tried. But Jericho stepped in front of him. "Let's have a discussion about Taryn's call. I want your statement on the record."

Karina didn't wait to see how DeWayne would react to that. Cord didn't let her. He took her into Jericho's office and shut the door.

"I'm sorry," she said at the same moment Cord said it, too.

Despite the hellish things they'd just seen in those photos, he smiled. Not for long, though. "I need to talk to Addie," Cord said. "And tell her about the pictures."

He was obviously dreading it. With good reason. It wouldn't be an easy conversation, especially when he told her about the dead woman in the photo.

"Addie will probably want to see the pictures for herself," Karina suggested. She would want to see them if she was in Addie's shoes. Karina only hoped Addie could "unsee" them after that.

Cord nodded. "Maybe the photos will trigger something in her memory."

Though he didn't sound pleased about that. Still, Addie might be able to tell them something about the photos that they didn't know. Since Addie and Cord were twins and had therefore been the same age, maybe Addie could remember some fragments of that day.

Cord pulled her to him, bringing her right into his arms. Not for a kiss this time. He just held her.

Like the other times she'd been close to him like this, the heat came. Slowly consumed her. But there was more to it now. The heat didn't cloud her mind. It gave her some clarity.

She was falling hard for him.

Not exactly something that she should be doing, but Karina didn't know how to stop it. Oh, mercy. It wouldn't be long before she would have to deal with a broken heart in addition to all these other memories from the attacks and the deaths.

Cord pulled back, their gazes connecting. For a moment, she thought that kiss might happen after all. But it didn't.

"Why did he send us those pictures?" he asked.

Because of the sheer shock of seeing the photos, Karina hadn't questioned it. She should have, though. "To shake us up, to keep us off balance?"

Cord gave another nod. "And that must mean we're getting close. Too close." He glanced between them, and she didn't think he was just talking about a serial killer now.

Was he talking about them?

Karina didn't get a chance to find out because there was a knock at the door, and a split second later, Jericho opened it. Cord and she stepped apart, as if they'd been caught doing something wrong.

However, Jericho didn't even seem to have noticed, and if he did, he didn't mention the close contact between Cord and her.

"DeWayne's gone," Jericho explained. "I threatened again to put him in a holding cell, and that got him moving." He held up a notepad. "I just got a call from a military record's rep, and he gave me some more info about Harley."

That got her mind off the broken-heart possibility. It got Cord's attention, too.

"Harley's scars are from an accident. A live explosive that he mishandled. This happened forty years ago when he was just nineteen. After his injuries healed, he failed a psych exam and was discharged from the army."

A failed psych exam wasn't good, but then maybe it didn't mean anything. After all, Harley was just a teenager then, and anyone who'd gone through that would have been altered for life.

"Is there a record of Willie Lee ever being in the army with him?" Karina asked.

"Well, Willie Lee was in the army, only for six months, though, before he was given a medical discharge for bad knees. Harley and he were in training at the same time in South Carolina."

So, maybe that's how they'd met. Karina carried that one step further. Harley and he could have reconnected after Harley's discharge. Maybe even gotten involved with money laundering. But there was still no proof of that.

Or was there?

The memory came to her in a flash. "Years ago, I remember seeing Willie Lee burning something. He had an old oil barrel outside his cabin, and he would sometimes burn paid bills and such. He said it was better than buying a shredder. But that time, it looked as if he was burning a book."

"A book?" Cord questioned.

"Not a regular book. Smaller. Like maybe a journal or something."

Cord stayed quiet a moment. "Did you ask him about it?"

"No." And Karina remembered why. "Willie Lee always got this look on his face when he didn't want to talk about something. And he had that look then, so I didn't say anything about it."

But she certainly thought about it now. Had it really been a journal? With perhaps something in it about the money laundering?

Jericho's phone rang, and he was cursing the interruption before he took out his phone. However, the cursing stopped when he looked at the screen.

"It's the prison," Jericho said.

He didn't put the call on speaker, and Karina wasn't close enough to him to hear what the caller was saying. However, she could tell something had happened.

Probably something bad.

That's the way their luck had been running since this whole ordeal had started.

Karina tried to rein in her fears, but she failed. Thankfully, the conversation didn't last long, only a few seconds, but even after he pressed the button to end the call, Jericho continued to stare at his phone.

"That was the prison hospital," Jericho finally said. "Willie Lee just came out of his coma."

Chapter Twelve

Cord still wasn't sure that coming to the prison hospital was the right thing to do. Not with Karina anyway. But he hadn't been able to talk her, or himself, out of letting Jericho handle this.

He had to face his birth father. And get some answers to all those questions that'd been haunting him for years.

Well, he'd get answers anyway. But Cord wasn't sure he could believe anything Willie Lee told him.

Of course, Willie Lee wasn't the only elephant in the room. There was the question of Karina's safety. That's why Jericho had told Mack to follow them in a cruiser. It was broad daylight so maybe they wouldn't be ambushed, but the earlier attack had happened in broad daylight, too. Better to be safe than sorry, so Mack was waiting outside in the prison parking lot and would follow them back to Appaloosa Pass when they were done.

Without saying a word to each other, Karina and he made their way through security and the maze of corridors, each closed off with its own bars. An in-the-face reminder that this was maximum security. And that Willie Lee was here for a darn good reason.

They made it all the way to the hospital section before Karina stepped in front of him, stopping Cord in his tracks. Cord had been waiting for this, waiting for her to say that no matter what happened, they'd get through this. Or else she'd put a different spin on that pep talk.

But she didn't.

She just leaned in and kissed him. "I think we should sleep together."

All right. Well, he sure as heck hadn't seen that coming. "Now? Here?"

Karina smiled, making him smile, too. Though there really wasn't anything to smile about. Except for her. For some reason, she just kept making him smile.

Kept distracting him, too.

"Well, I was thinking later would be better timing," she answered. "You know, after we've survived this."

Survived. That was a good word for it. She'd survived three physical attacks, a whole host of verbal ones, too. Now, this chat with Willie Lee. If the man confessed to being the Moonlight Strangler, it would tear her world apart.

"We're still not on the same side here," Cord reminded her.

She kissed him again. "We don't have to be. We just have to get through this." She slipped her hand in his.

And Cord knew she was right. One step at a time. Get through this. Put an end to the danger. Then, he'd definitely haul her off to bed. Even if it meant complicating the hell out of things.

Which it would.

Maybe this fire he felt for her would cool some after their chat with Willie Lee. Or not, Cord amended when he glanced at her.

He finally got them moving again, and when they reached the next security checkpoint, a woman wearing green scrubs was there to greet them. According to her name tag, she was Dr. Dana Kenney.

"I wasn't sure you would come," the doctor said to Cord. "I understand you're his son?"

"Biological son," Cord automatically amended. He tipped his head to Karina. "And Willie Lee has worked for Karina for years."

"He's a friend," Karina said. An automatic correction for her as well that had the doctor staring at them and then clearing her throat.

"Well, I have good news and bad," the doctor continued. "Yes, Willie Lee is awake, and he's nearly healed from the gunshot wounds to his chest."

Wounds that Cord had given him. The doctor didn't mention that, but she likely knew. If they wanted to swap stories, Cord could have shown her his own scars from that day.

"And the bad news?" Karina prompted when the doctor paused.

"His blood pressure is way too high, and his memory is all muddled. The medical term for it is dissociative amnesia, probably brought on by the trauma of being shot."

Cord cursed. "Or he could be faking it."

The doctor didn't hesitate before she nodded. "And it's also possible the medications he's been receiving are contributing to the problem. We're weaning him off the meds now so we might see an improvement in a day or two."

Cord could see the frustration in Karina's eyes. "Please tell me we don't have to wait that long to see him," Karina said.

"No. You can see him. This way." The doctor began to lead them down yet another corridor. "Just don't expect too much. And you can always come back later this week."

Cord didn't want to wait another second, much less days. Willie Lee had to give them something to stop these attacks. They might not get so lucky if there was another one.

"Has Willie Lee said anything to you?" Karina asked the doctor.

"Nothing about his arrest if that's what you want to know. But then he just started talking right before you got here. He's had a tube down his throat so he might be still experiencing some pain when he moves any of the muscles required for speech."

Cord felt the anger swell inside him. Each thing the doctor said sounded like some kind of excuse. Of course, his anger was mixed with a whole laundry list of other things that Cord wished he didn't feel.

The doctor took them into a large room. Not a usual hospital room, either. This one had multiple beds, all empty, and along with some cameras, there was also a guard. Standing right over the sole prisoner in the room.

Willie Lee.

"I'll wait here," the doctor said, motioning for them to go closer. "Don't touch him and keep at least two feet away from the bed."

Rules. But Willie Lee didn't look in any shape to attack anyone. Of course, maybe the doctor was worried about Cord doing the attacking.

Willie Lee was in the bed, machines all around him, covered from neck to toes in bleached white sheets. The man didn't have much more color in his face, either.

Cord had never actually gotten a good look at him. When he'd shot Willie Lee a month ago, it had been from a distance while Cord had been drugged and bleeding. After the shooting, Cord had been whisked away in one ambulance, Willie Lee in another.

But Cord sure saw him now when he went closer to the bed.

His first thought was the man looked a lot older than

fifty-nine. His hair was threaded with gray, and his face was hollow. Cord couldn't see a bit of himself in the man.

Until Willie Lee opened his eyes.

Ah, hell. There it was—that punch of recognition. Because both Addie's and his eyes were a genetic copy of Willie Lee's.

Willie Lee blinked several times as if trying to focus, and his attention landed on Karina. He smiled. Tried to speak. But it was definitely recognition that Cord saw in those troublesome eyes. If Willie Lee did indeed have amnesia, then it was pretty darn selective.

"Karina," the man finally said. He winced, maybe in pain. Maybe pretending.

Cord wasn't giving him the benefit of the doubt just yet, though there were times when Cord's wounds still gave him more than a twinge or two.

Willie Lee's wincing turned to a frown, and he reached out toward her as if to touch her cheek. He didn't make it far because his hands were in restraints. Puzzled, he looked at those, too.

"What happened to you?" Willie Lee asked. "Who hurt you?"

"I'm fine. It's just a scratch. How are you?"

That last part was the usual question someone would ask when visiting a friend in the hospital, but she was blinking, too. Not to get her focus but to fight back the tears.

Willie Lee shook his head. "Why am I here?"

"You were shot. Do you remember?"

"No," he answered after a long pause. "Are the horses okay? Did something happen to them? You look really sad."

Karina moistened her lips before she said anything.

"I'm sad because you were hurt. And because you're here. You're in a prison hospital," she added a heartbeat later.

His forehead bunched up. Willie Lee glanced around the room as if seeing it for the first time, and then his gaze finally settled on Cord. "Who are you?"

Easy question. Tough answer. Especially now that Cord had a blasted lump in his throat. Best not to sugarcoat this. Cord just put it out there. "According to a DNA test, you're my biological father."

Willie Lee shook his head again, his stare never leaving Cord. Then, the head shaking stopped. Like Karina, his eyes filled with tears. "You're actually my son?"

Best to add this, as well. "Yeah, and you have a daughter. Her name is Addie, and someone—probably you—abandoned us when we were only three years old. But I guess you're going to say you don't remember her, either?"

Willie Lee didn't jump to respond, but he did close his eyes, and he groaned. Even Cord had to admit it was a pitiful sound. However, he didn't let it get to him. He needed to ask some questions.

Well, one big question anyway, but Willie Lee spoke before Cord could even continue.

"Your mother," Willie Lee said. Not a question. And the tears weren't just in his eyes now. They were streaming down his cheeks. "She's dead?"

Now, that last part was definitely a question.

"I believe she could be," Cord answered. If those photos weren't fake, that is. "Did you kill her?"

"No." Willie Lee's chest dropped with a heavy sigh, and he repeated, "No."

He made another sound. Pain mixed with grief. Maybe the real deal since it seemed like something too intense to be faked. Of course, the grief could be there because Willie Lee regretted murdering her.

"I loved her," Willie Lee said a moment later. "She was a good woman. Her name was Sarah."

Cord latched on to the name as if it was a lifeline. He knew so little about her, and other than her name and those two pictures, he still didn't know much. Later, there'd be time to question the man about that.

"Are you the Moonlight Strangler?" Cord asked.

Willie Lee's eyes widened. "I don't think so. Am I?"

"I'm the one asking you," Cord returned.

But if the comment even got through to him, Willie Lee showed no signs of it. "Your mother was murdered, wasn't she?" he went on. A sob tore from his mouth, and he broke down, crying.

Since the man's memory seemed to be pretty good on the subject of his dead wife, Cord figured it was time to repeat the real question.

Are you the Moonlight Strangler?

The words seemed to freeze in his mind, though, when Willie Lee opened his eyes and looked at him. "You're the one who shot me," he said. "I remember that now. But why?"

Cord decided to show him. He unbuttoned his shirt but didn't need to look down to know what Willie Lee—and Karina—was seeing. The two scars. Nowhere near healed, but they weren't the raw mess they had been. Still, he'd carry them for life.

"Mercy," Karina whispered, and she'd gone almost as pale as Willie Lee.

Cord hadn't intended to shock her like that. Heck, he hadn't intended for her to see them, period, and he gave her a whispered apology.

However, he had no apology for Willie Lee.

"You did that to me," Cord snapped, yanking the sides of his shirt back together with far more force than necessary. "And now you say you don't remember cutting me and tying my leg with a rope?"

"I don't think he's lying about that," the doctor interrupted. She walked toward them. "According to the tox screen sent from the Appaloosa Pass Hospital, Willie Lee had been pumped full of barbiturates when he was admitted."

Cord dropped back a mental step. He hadn't known that about Willie Lee. Hadn't bothered to ask once he found out that the man hadn't regained consciousness before he was taken into custody.

"That could affect his memory?" Karina asked.

The doctor nodded. "Especially with the large amount he had in his system."

Yeah, it could. And Cord knew that firsthand because his captor had dosed him with barbiturates, too. A boatload of them. It'd been a miracle that Cord had managed to take aim at, much less shoot Willie Lee.

Karina looked at Cord. "You said you had broken memories of that day, too."

"Yes," he admitted. "There aren't many details between being hit with a stun gun and then turning up by the old church where I shot Willie Lee."

"And you don't think it's strange that both of you were drugged?" Karina queried.

"Of course I do, but Willie Lee could have drugged himself when he realized he was about to be captured."

Or maybe someone else had done that to him. There was only one way to find out.

Cord didn't hesitate with the question this time. "Are you the Moonlight Strangler?"

It was as if the world exploded. The machines started beeping like crazy, and Willie Lee threw back his head, his body going stiff and his face stretching like some kind of sick death mask.

"He's having a seizure," the doctor said, urgency in her voice and movements. She shoved Cord and Karina to the side so she could get to her patient. "You two need to wait in the hall. Go, now!"

But Cord's feet seemed glued to the floor. Was Willie Lee faking this? If so, it looked darn real.

"Come on." Karina took his hand and got them moving out of there.

They went back into the hall, and Cord hoped he didn't do something wussy, like lose his lunch. He could feel every nerve inside him, and even though he'd never remembered having his mother in his life, her loss had hit him hard. Much as it had done to Willie Lee.

Cord hadn't forgotten that all of this had to be affecting Karina, but he didn't realize just how much until their gazes met. Hell. She was crying and no doubt on the verge of losing more than her lunch. She loved Willie Lee, and it must have cut her to the core to see, and hear, all of that.

"I'm sorry," Cord said, pulling her into his arms.

She didn't break down exactly, but she made some hiccupping sounds when she tried to gather her breath. "If he's the one who cut you like that…"

Karina didn't finish. No need. But it did let him know just how much his scars had affected her. He'd curse himself for that later, but for now he just held her and tried to undo the damage.

"I'm fine," he assured her. And that was only a partial lie. "I'll be returning to duty in a week." Once he cleared the Justice Department shrink who'd be assigned to evaluate him. "They wouldn't let me go back to work if I wasn't a hundred percent."

She pulled back, looked at him again. There was a new

set of trouble in her eyes. "I didn't realize you'd be leaving so soon."

Ah, that. And here just minutes earlier they'd discussed having sex. Judging from that look in her eyes, she was thinking he'd meant for their theoretical lovemaking to be a one-night stand.

And hell, it might be.

But Cord wasn't even ready to go there yet.

"I won't be leaving the area," he explained. "Well, I will be given a desk job somewhere, but I won't be going back in the field."

Karina stared at him, probably waiting for more. Or maybe she just wanted something else to fill her mind so she wouldn't have to think about what was going on in the room behind them.

Willie Lee could be dying. Or already dead.

"I was a Joe," Cord went on. "A deep cover operative. Once I stayed undercover on the same assignment for two years." A drug-dealing operation that he wouldn't discuss with her. Not with anyone. He'd been lucky not to get PTSD, but those were memories he didn't want to poke, either.

"I just thought, well, I thought you'd want to be closer to Addie."

"I do." And he did. Close to his nephew, too. Heck, after this ordeal, he was starting to feel as if Jericho and he had forged some kind of peace treaty.

The door behind them opened, and after Cord got one glimpse of the doctor's face, he figured it was time for him to put his arm around Karina again.

"This could take a while," Dr. Kenney said, making some notes in a chart. "He had a grand mal seizure, and his blood pressure hasn't stabilized. There's a café just up the road next to a big gas station," she added. "If you don't want to drive home, you can wait there for a while, and I'll call you if there's any news. The guards have your cell phone number, I'm sure."

Karina caught on to the doctor's arm before she could leave. "How bad is it?" she asked.

"Bad," Dr. Kenney admitted. "I hope you got everything you needed from him because Willie Lee might not make it."

Chapter Thirteen

The chicken club sandwich tasted like dust, but Karina forced herself to eat it anyway. She couldn't make herself sick with worry over Willie Lee. Even though that's exactly what she was doing.

Cord wasn't faring so well, either.

He was on the phone again, something he'd been doing practically since they'd left the jail and had driven to the diner the doctor had recommended. He had hardly more than a bite of his cheeseburger and fries before sliding his plate to Mack. The deputy had his own meal but had mumbled something about getting a to-go box.

Karina thought maybe Cord's latest call was to Jericho, though she couldn't tell much of what was going on since Cord was doing a lot more listening than talking. Of course, he had already told Jericho about the prison visit. Had then called Addie and told her what was going on. That had required him to talk his sister out of making a trip there.

Karina was glad he'd managed to do that.

Even though Addie wanted to see Willie Lee, that wasn't going to happen until the doctor called them. It was best if Addie was at the ranch, safe with her son and husband. Karina had known from the start that just being out on the road had been a risk, and she didn't want Addie taking that risk, too.

Cord was already dealing with enough without adding his sister's safety to his worries.

"So, Willie Lee never made an actual confession?" Mack asked.

Mack didn't just blurt it out, though. He sounded as if he'd chosen his words carefully and probably had. Had no doubt even debated asking it since they'd been at the diner for nearly a half hour, and he'd only listened to the summary she'd given him of their visit with Willie Lee.

"No confession about the Moonlight Strangler," she confirmed. "But he did admit to being Cord and Addie's father."

Karina had purposely kept her voice to a whisper because the three of them were all together in a booth, but Cord likely heard her because he looked up from his phone conversation and caught her gaze.

"*Biological* father," Karina amended as Cord had done at the hospital.

In her fantasy world, she'd hoped that Willie Lee could resolve everything for all of them. She'd hoped that he could somehow clear his name. Give them the identity of the real killer. And that the real killer could already be behind bars.

But it'd been just that—a fantasy.

Now, Willie Lee could be dead, and any information could die with him. Along with her losing a friend. A man she loved and thought of as family.

"Hey, it's okay." Mack patted her hand. "We're going to work all of this out somehow."

It took a moment for Karina to realize why Mack had done that. It was because she was crying. Again. She wiped away the tears, cursing them, and told herself that they wouldn't return. Tears wouldn't help Willie Lee.

Prayers might, though, and that's why she'd said a few for him.

The fresh round of tears seemed to do the trick for getting Cord off the phone, and he handed her a paper napkin from the metal dispenser.

"No sign of Rocky yet," Cord said right away, and while he kept his attention on her, he gulped down some more coffee. "Two of the reserve deputies are still looking, though."

So, he had been talking to Jericho. "Anything on Taryn's murder?"

He shook his head. "But there's a connection between Rocky and DeWayne. Rocky's father, Frank, and DeWayne were once in business together, and Frank apparently doesn't have good things to say about DeWayne. He said DeWayne got drunk one night and rattled on about an old business deal gone bad with Willie Lee." Cord lifted his shoulder. "It could mean nothing."

And it could be connected to that money-laundering scheme. In fact, Karina wondered if they'd all been involved in some way—DeWayne, Harley. Heck, even Willie Lee. Maybe that's what'd prompted Harley to break into Willie Lee's cabin.

Cord drank some more coffee and downed a couple of ibuprofen that he'd bought at the counter.

Karina wanted to ask if it was his chest or head hurting. Maybe both. But she doubted he'd tell her the truth. Doubted even more that he'd want to discuss those scars on his chest.

However, they didn't need to discuss it for her to know it was something she'd never forget. God. He'd been through so much. Being abandoned, the attacks, learning that his mother was almost certainly dead. And it wasn't even over.

It might never be over.

"Don't look at me like that," Cord said.

Karina knew what he meant. She was feeling sorry for him, and it showed. She quickly tried to change her expression, but it was too late.

Mack picked up on it, too. "I got to take a trip to the men's room. I won't be long."

But Mack probably would stay away from the booth to give Cord and her a chance to talk. However, Cord didn't say anything. He clammed up after the deputy scurried away.

"I'm okay, really," Cord insisted.

As Mack had done to her, she slid her hand over his. "Liar." She'd hoped that would make him smile, but it didn't work.

"I should have gotten right in Willie Lee's face until he gave me a straight answer about being the Moonlight Strangler." Cord cursed himself. "I'm a federal agent, and I know how to interrogate someone."

"Willie Lee wasn't just *someone*," Karina reminded him. "And besides, even if you had repeated the question, he might not have been able to answer. Something was clearly wrong with him."

Cord stayed quiet a moment, nodded. "Has he ever had a seizure before?"

"Not that I know of. But that doesn't mean it never happened. Like I said, Willie Lee could be secretive." She paused. "He did seem to love your mother, though."

The muscles in his jaw went to war with each other. "Yeah. Maybe if he comes out of this, he can tell us where her body is. I'd like to give her a proper burial. And no, she wasn't any of the other known victims. All of their DNA is in the system now, and it would have hit as a match to Addie and me."

True. But there was also someone else in the DNA pool. Karina had never met him, but it was a man named Lonny Ogden, who was now confined to a psychiatric facility. Months ago, the cops had learned about Ogden, and since he was a match to Cord and Addie, it also meant he was a match to Willie Lee. That meant Willie Lee had three children.

Karina was about to bring that up to Cord, but she could see that he was shutting down again. Already looking at his phone for somebody to call so he wouldn't have to discuss this with her. But his phone rang before he could punch in a number.

"Jericho," he said, and he answered it immediately, probably because the sheriff had gotten some big news to call back so soon.

Cord didn't put it on speaker. There were people eating nearby, but Karina moved closer to him so she could hear.

"The photo is a selfie," Jericho said without even saying a greeting. "Or whatever they called them back when it was taken."

It took Karina a moment to realize what he was talking about. The picture that'd been left in the diner and brought to the sheriff's office.

The picture of Willie Lee.

"He took it himself," Jericho went on. "I faxed the photos to the FBI lab, and they did a rush job. They enhanced the image, and Willie Lee is definitely holding the camera. And the knife. Of course, that doesn't mean someone wasn't there in the room forcing him to do it."

No, but it didn't make him look innocent, either.

"What about the other photos?" Cord asked.

She didn't like Jericho's hesitation that followed. "They

did age progression for the one on the porch. It's you and Addie all right, but there was a problem with the woman. They used some kind of facial composite program, and the woman's features didn't match yours and Addie's."

Karina hadn't expected that. Judging from Cord's deep breath, neither had he. "So, she's not our mother?" Cord asked.

"Doesn't appear to be. But of course, that leaves us with the question of who is she. You think Willie Lee could or would tell us?"

"Maybe," Cord said as if going over that in his mind. He didn't look relieved exactly, but he had to be. Because there was the possibility his mother was still alive. After all, Willie Lee didn't seem as if he knew for sure.

"And as for the final one," Jericho went on, "well, they're pretty sure the woman in the photo—whoever she is—is dead, that it wasn't faked. Are you okay?" he added a moment later.

"I'm fine," Cord answered, after a short hesitation. "How would they know it wasn't faked?"

"It hadn't been doctored. They could tell that, too, because it was a Polaroid, and they're hard to alter without leaving lots of signs. And the woman had classic petechia in her eyes, a sign of strangulation. Plus, she'd been strangled with some kind of wire that had apparently cut through her skin. A deep enough cut that her hyoid bone was likely broken."

So, there it was, all spelled out for them. A woman who'd been in an earlier photo with them had been murdered.

"Still okay?" Jericho asked Cord.

"Does Addie know?" Cord obviously didn't want to answer Jericho's question.

"Not yet. Maybe you two can talk about it soon. I wasn't

sure if this would get up her hopes or not about your birth mother, and I thought you might want to wait to tell her until you knew for sure."

Of course, they might never know for sure.

Cord's phone beeped to indicate he had another call coming in. "The prison," Cord said, glancing at the screen. "Jericho, I'll have to call you back."

Cord ended the call with Jericho and took the one from the prison. This time, he did put the call on speaker.

"This is Dr. Kenney," the woman said when Cord greeted her. "Willie Lee's stabilized for now."

Karina's breath rushed out. From the relief. However, Cord wasn't sharing that relief with her. "Good. I need to finish the interrogation—"

"Sorry," the doctor interrupted, "but I'm not allowing him any other visitors today."

"I need to talk to him," Cord snapped.

"I know. And I know he's been accused of some horrible crimes, but he's also my patient. I'm sorry, Agent Granger, but you'll have to wait. I'll give you a call in the morning." The woman hung up so that Cord didn't even get a chance to pressure her.

Cord immediately stood up, finishing off the rest of the coffee and dropping some money on the table. "I'll get Mack," he said.

But the words seemed to die on his lips, and Cord reached for his gun.

Karina whirled around to see what had caused him to do that. And her heart went to her knees.

No.

This couldn't be happening again.

Mack was there all right, but standing behind him was a man wearing a ski mask. He had Mack in a choke hold and held a gun to the deputy's head.

"Everybody out!" the man shouted. "Everybody but you two," he added to Cord and her.

Karina didn't recognize his voice, but there was something familiar about his size and stance. This was almost certainly one of the men who'd taken Rocky at gunpoint.

The diners immediately started to scatter, all running for the door. Cord moved, too, putting himself in front of her and taking aim at the man. However, he didn't have a clean shot.

"I'm sorry," Mack said. "I didn't see him in the bathroom until it was too late. I think he came in through a window."

Which meant he'd probably been watching them, waiting for the right time for this. Whatever *this* was. Did he want her dead?

Karina figured she'd soon find out.

The thug waited, his back against the wall so that no one could sneak up on him. And he watched as the last of the diners hurried out. At least one of them would call the cops if they hadn't already. The thug must have known that so that meant he might start shooting.

"Stay down and behind me," Cord told her without taking his attention off the man.

But Cord wouldn't do that. Again, he would be the one in the direct line of fire. Maybe, just maybe, this snake hadn't been sent there to kill him.

"This all has to happen fast," the man finally said. "I leave with the woman, and both of you get to live."

"No deal," Cord answered without hesitating. "Who sent you to do this?"

The guy actually chuckled. "That kind of information is well above my pay grade. I just do what I'm told, and I expect you to do the same. Let's go. Follow me."

And he started dragging Mack toward the kitchen.

The diner wasn't that large, and the staff had obviously fled. Good. Because Karina didn't want anyone hit by friendly fire.

Especially since she was the target.

God, who wanted her? Maybe she'd find out before this jerk managed to hurt or kill her.

"Move faster," the guy barked.

Cord and she did, and she stayed behind him, looking over her shoulder to make sure no one came in through the front. However, once they got into the kitchen, she saw something else she didn't want to see.

Another hired gun in a ski mask.

He was by the back door and already had it open. She could see a car parked just outside, and that door was also open. They were ready for her.

Her heart was already pounding, but it raced even more. And her breath became so thin that it felt as if she was about to hyperventilate. But she couldn't. If she did, Mack or Cord could die.

She didn't have a weapon, but Karina glanced around for anything she could use. The only thing nearby was a paring knife, but she snatched it up, holding it by her side so that hopefully the thugs wouldn't see it.

"Now, for the tricky part," the first man said. "Karina, come here, and I'll let the deputy go. Scout's honor."

She doubted she could believe anything he said, and Cord must have agreed because he kept in front of her.

"I'll go with you instead," Cord offered.

The guy shook his head. "Sorry, but I've heard about you. You're a big-shot DEA agent. You could probably kick my butt into the next county with some fancy martial arts. No, thanks. If the woman doesn't come over here now, the deputy gets a bullet."

Karina only hesitated a second, but it was obviously too long because the shot blasted through the kitchen.

And Mack yelled out in pain.

The thug had shot him in the arm.

"The next one goes in his belly," the man growled. "Then, his heart. After that, your precious DEA agent takes a bullet to the head and all because you're too stubborn to follow orders."

"I'll go with you," she said, earning her a sharp glare from Cord.

She wasn't sure if he saw the knife she was holding. Or maybe he had and knew it wouldn't be much of a weapon against two armed men. If they got her in that car, they would take her somewhere and kill her.

Maybe even take her to the Moonlight Strangler.

"Don't do this, Karina," Cord insisted. He was volleying glances from Mack, who was grimacing in pain, to the men and then to her.

She connected gazes with the man who was holding Mack, and she could tell from his eyes that he was about to pull the trigger again. This wasn't a bluff, and it didn't help when she heard the police sirens approaching. The thugs were running out of time.

And so was she.

Karina started walking. Not slowly, either. She didn't want to give them a chance to see the knife. The moment she was near the thug, he shoved Mack forward, the deputy falling onto the floor, and he grabbed Karina.

That's when she made her own move.

She brought up the knife, aiming for his neck. But he saw her and tried to knock her hand away. Karina came right back at him, and this time she jammed the knife in his throat. He yelled out, cursing her, and with the blood gushing from his neck, he fell to his knees.

The other man brought up his gun, but it was too late. Cord fired. Two shots. Both of them slamming into the man's chest. He dropped to the floor next to his partner while Mack scrambled away from them.

Karina moved, too, thanks to Cord. Her legs seemed to have stopped working, but he maneuvered her to the other side of the room behind a stainless prep table. That's when Karina looked at her hand. She still held the knife.

And now she had his blood on her.

As horrifying of a sight as that was, she wasn't the only one with blood. Mack had the gunshot wound to his arm, and Karina dropped the knife so she could grab a dish towel and apply some pressure to it. The wound didn't look that bad, but he would need a doctor soon.

There were some sounds in the diner. Then, hurried footsteps. Several seconds later, two uniformed officers came running to the door to peer into the kitchen. Both had their weapons drawn.

"I'm Cord Granger, DEA," he said, taking his badge from his pocket to show them. "We need an ambulance."

"Already on the way," one of the officers assured him. One of the uniforms went toward the thugs. The other stayed near Cord, Mack and her.

"Who are these guys?" the officer asked.

"Hired killers," Cord answered. Good thing because Karina wasn't sure she could speak yet. Cord went to the men, yanking off their ski masks. "Strangers," he added.

That didn't make it any easier to stomach. They'd come close to dying. And now Mack was hurt. All because of her. And Karina still didn't know why.

"Is it clear back there?" someone called out. Another officer probably, because one of the uniforms responded right away.

"It's clear. And there's a DEA agent on scene. Two injuries, though."

Karina shook her head when she realized he was adding her to the injured list. Probably because of her bloody hands and the cuts and bruises she already had.

"I'm not hurt," she said.

"How many dead bodies you got?" the cop in the diner called out. He came into the doorway of the kitchen. Not a uniform this time. He was in khakis and a white shirt. Probably a detective.

"Two," the officer next to her answered.

The cop in the doorway mumbled something she didn't catch, and he looked around the room until his gaze connected with Cord. "You're the DEA agent?" he asked.

Cord nodded.

The cop hitched his thumb toward the diner. "A woman's out front, and she says she needs to speak to you immediately, that it's important." The cop paused. "She says she's your mother."

Chapter Fourteen

Cord stood there a moment, trying to process what the cop had just told him. He couldn't.

"My mother?" he questioned.

After his conversation with Jericho about the photos, Cord was just coming to terms with the notion that his mother might not be dead. But he sure as heck hadn't expected her to show up at a crime scene.

And maybe she hadn't.

This could be another part of some sick hoax. Or else the woman could be working for the person who'd hired these now-dead thugs. Because her timing was certainly suspicious, and she could be here to make sure she finished the job that her hired guns had started.

"Did the woman give you her name?" Karina asked.

Good question. One that Cord should have already asked. He needed to collect himself. Hard to do, though, with the adrenaline still pumping through him, and his body primed for the fight.

The cop shook his head. "I figured if she was your mother, that you'd know her name. I also figured she had come here with you." He did another thumb hitch. "You want me to get her ID and question her?"

"No. I'll do it." In fact, Cord didn't want anyone else

talking to her yet. After they were done, it was possible these uniforms would be arresting her.

"I'll clean up," Karina said, looking at the blood on her hands. "I'll be out there in a minute."

"Stay back here until I know what we're dealing with."

That clearly didn't do anything to put Karina at ease. But then nothing would at this point.

Cord didn't holster his gun when he went into the diner, and he spotted the woman right away. Not inside but rather standing at the glass door. He couldn't see much of her face because the diner's name, Tasty Eats, was etched on it, so he went closer.

She stood there wearing a dark blue dress, her nearly white hair pulled back. Not in a fashionable style, either. She looked old.

No, he corrected. She looked weary.

An emotion he completely understood, but Cord pushed it aside. He didn't want to feel any connection with this woman until he found out exactly who she was and why she was there.

With his gun still ready, he opened the door. She was looking down at the ground and was holding a purse in front of her like a shield. Cord snatched it from her, causing her to gasp in surprise, and he rummaged through it.

No gun.

Wallet, keys, tissues and some papers, all neatly arranged.

"Who are you?" he demanded, handing her back the purse.

The woman lifted her head then, their eyes connecting. He didn't see the resemblance as he'd done with Willie Lee, but he did *feel* something.

Hell.

He couldn't trust a gut feeling on something like this.

"You don't remember me," she said, sounding a little hurt by that. "Of course you wouldn't. You were hardly more than a baby. Your name was Courtland then, but we called you Court."

Court. No doubt what he'd been trying to say when the person found him in that gas station. His name had gone down on record as Cord. No last name because Cord hadn't remembered one.

"And your sister was Gabrielle," Sarah added in a whisper. "I didn't think you would remember me, but I'd hoped…"

Each word put him through an emotional wringer. Because they could be true. He cursed that feeling again. The tug deep within him that told him that this could indeed be his mother.

"I'm Sarah Prior," she said, extending her hand for him to shake.

He put out his left hand, without even thinking about it. Mainly because he couldn't take his attention off her. Then, he fired off a text to Jericho, asking for the sheriff to run a quick background check on the woman's name.

"May we sit down and talk?" she asked. "I have some things to tell you."

"And I have some things to tell you." Of course, he didn't sound anywhere near as friendly, and frail, as she did.

Cord got another look at that frailness when he stepped back, and she came inside. She was limping, and judging from the way she maneuvered herself, the limp had been with her for a long time. Maybe an old injury.

She sat down at one of the tables, glancing over at the detective who was watching them. "Will he arrest me?" she asked. "Will *you* arrest me?"

Cord had to relax his jaw muscles before he could speak.

"What have you done to warrant an arrest? Did you hire those two armed men in the kitchen?" He didn't tell her they were dead. Because if she was behind this, she might think they were in there spilling their guts to the cops.

Her eyes widened, and her hand went to her mouth, muffling yet another gasp of surprise. "No. Of course not. I wouldn't do anything to hurt you. I love you."

A burst of air came from his mouth. Definitely not humor. "If you're really my mother, then you abandoned me at a gas station. That doesn't sound like love to me."

That put some tears in her eyes, and even though what he'd said was the truth, Cord suddenly felt bad about it.

There was some movement to the side. Karina. She stepped around the officer in the doorway, but she didn't come closer. Not until Cord motioned for her.

"Is she your mother?" Karina asked.

"The jury's still out on that. This is Karina Souther-land," he said. Great. He was making introductions now. If this kept up, he'd be hugging the woman.

Much to his disgust, it was something he wanted to do.

"I'm Sarah." The woman shook Karina's hand, too. "Willie Lee works...worked for you."

"He did. And I don't think he's the Moonlight Strangler. I don't believe he could hurt anyone, and I've known him for years."

Well, since Sarah and Karina had brought it up, it was time to get this conversation moving. The cops likely wanted to start processing the scene and get them out of there for statements.

"Start from the beginning," Cord ordered her. And it was an order. "Tell me what happened. If you lie, or even if I think you're lying, you will be arrested." He had no idea what the charges would be, but he'd come up with something.

Sarah nodded, nodded again and then took a deep breath. "Willie Lee and I got married thirty-four years ago when I was pregnant with you and your sister. Samuels wasn't his last name then. It was Joyner. Willie Joyner. He didn't start using Willie Lee Samuels until, well, later."

That explained why no one had been able to find birth certificates for Addie and him, but there was no official name change on record for Willie Lee. However, he could have just started using the name without making it legal.

Cord would want to know all about that *later* part she'd mentioned, but he wanted to hear more of the beginning. He motioned for her to keep going.

"We were happy, for a while anyway," she finally continued. "Money was tight so Willie Lee took a lot of jobs. Sometimes, he had two or three at once. I complained about never seeing him, and I think that's what made him desperate. Because he got mixed up in something with some bad men."

"Money laundering?" Cord asked.

"Yes. I don't think he knew what was going on. Not at first. And then it was too late." She pulled one of those tissues from her purse and dabbed her eyes. "Things got bad. One of the men involved in that mess took Addie. He kidnapped her, and he did that to keep Willie Lee quiet."

That meshed with some of the things Addie had learned and remembered about some man taking her to a woman's house. Obviously, Addie hadn't been hurt, but she darn well could have been. It sickened him to think of that even now.

"How did you get Addie back?" Cord asked.

She tucked a strand of her hair behind her ear, twisted the tissue in her hand. "I'm not sure. Willie Lee worked that out. And we moved, he changed our last name and started a new life. Things were better for a while. And then *he* came."

"He?" Cord persisted.

Another breath. "I don't know who he was. A stalker. It started with hang-up calls and…escalated. He started leaving pictures of your sister, you and me. Pictures I didn't know he was taking. Some of them were taken from my bedroom window when I was dressing."

Karina winced a little. Probably because she had her own version of a stalker with Rocky and his club friends.

"And you never saw this man?" Karina asked.

"No. Not once. But I always got the feeling he was there, nearby. Once I even stood out in the yard and yelled for him to tell me why he was doing this. He didn't answer, and the following day he sent me some photos of mutilated animals."

Even though Cord didn't want to believe her, he did. About that part anyway. Cord could practically see her reliving what must have been a frightening time for her.

"Someone claiming to be the Moonlight Strangler sent me photos," Cord said. "One was of Addie and me on the porch with a woman."

"Yes, she was a neighbor lady, Ida Kincaid, who babysat the two of you sometimes. She was watching you while I had a doctor's appointment." Sarah shuddered, touched her mouth again. "When I came home, I found Ida's body in my bedroom. It was obvious someone had murdered her."

Cord didn't bother holding back the profanity, and he was about to jump down Sarah's throat about why she hadn't reported it to the cops. And he knew she hadn't because Cord had all the names of the Moonlight Strangler's known victims and even those who had similar MO's.

Karina shook her head, silently begging him to pull back on the anger, and she moved closer to Sarah and slipped her arm around her shoulders. That's when Cord realized Sarah was crying again.

"What did you do after you found the body?" Karina continued, and her voice was a lot calmer than Cord's would have been.

"The twins were outside playing, and I was afraid he was still in the house. So, I gathered up the children and drove off as fast as I could."

Cord didn't hold back this time. "Why didn't you go straight to the police station or call them before you left the house?"

"He'd cut my phone line, and I didn't have a cell phone in those days. And he'd left me a message. A note that said he'd kill me next…after he killed my kids."

Cord would have needed a heart of ice not to react to that. It felt like a sucker punch. Because Addie and he were those kids.

"I went to look for Willie Lee," Sarah explained after wiping away more tears. "But he wasn't at work, where he was supposed to be."

Maybe because he'd been back at the house taking that selfie and the photo of the dead woman.

But why would Willie Lee have pretended to be a stalker? If he wanted to torment his wife, it would have been much more effective if Sarah knew she was living under the same roof with a deranged man.

"I kept driving," Sarah went on. "Kept looking for him, and you had to go to the bathroom. It was dark by then, and I stopped at a gas station. You were too young to go into the men's room by yourself, so I took you in the women's bathroom. That's when he attacked me."

Sarah didn't jump right into the rest of that in part because the detective motioned for them to hurry things along. Probably because the crime-scene photographer had arrived and wanted to get started. Cord would have to take the woman to the local police station, but he had to hear the rest of this first.

"How did he attack you?" he asked.

"He turned off the lights and just came crashing through the door. He punched me hard. Both you and your sister started crying. But he kept punching me until he had me on the floor, and then he got me outside. I don't remember how. I was fading in and out of consciousness and terrified he was going to hurt my kids."

Yeah, that fear was real, too, and Cord got just a shimmer of a memory. Of the violence. But the images were gone before he could latch on to them.

"What happened then?" Karina prompted.

"I woke up in the trunk of his car. I could still hear my kids crying. Well, one of the kids anyway. My daughter. I couldn't hear Court...Cord," she amended, "and I thought the worst. God, I thought the worst."

So, maybe that's when Cord had been abandoned. That felt like the truth, too, and he caught another image of him crying in the corner of the dirty bathroom. A roach had crawled across his shoes, and he'd been too scared and numb to react to it.

"I kept banging on the trunk," Sarah explained. "Kept trying to get out so I could help my kids. The man finally stopped out in the middle of nowhere. It was dark, no moon that night, and he was wearing some kind of mask. Like a stocking maybe. He dragged me from the trunk, and that's when I saw the blood on my baby girl's cheek. The bastard had cut her face."

Cord wished he'd been there. Yes, he was just a kid, three years old, but maybe he could have stopped it.

"I told my daughter to run. And she did. Thank God, she did. Because the man stabbed me, and he ran after her.

I crawled into a ditch, trying to get up enough strength to help my baby. But the man didn't find her because she wasn't with him when he came back. I stayed hidden, and he finally drove off."

"And you survived," he concluded for her.

She nodded. "I got to a hospital eventually and gave them a fake name so he wouldn't find me. When I was back on my feet, I went looking for you."

No way could he keep the anger out of his voice. "You should have told the cops I was in that bathroom and that Addie was in the woods."

"I was stupid. The man had warned me he'd kill us all if I went to the cops. And by then, I'd read in the newspapers about you and your sister being found. Not together, of course. But you were safe. So, I pretended to be dead so that he wouldn't try to use you to get to me."

Cord sat there, trying to process it, but he couldn't. However, he could see that this was ripping Sarah to pieces.

"I haven't seen you, your sister or Willie Lee since," Sarah added. Her gaze came to Cord's. "Has Willie Lee said anything about me?"

"He thinks you're dead, that you were murdered."

She didn't seem surprised by that. Probably because she'd just said she faked her death.

Karina leaned in, and she gave the woman one of the napkins from the table so Sarah could dry her eyes again. "Why didn't Willie Lee go to the cops with all of this?"

"I'm not sure. But it must have been something big to make him turn away from you. He loved you. Loved all of us." Sarah paused. "I want to see him. Do you think you can arrange that?"

Cord's first reaction was to say no, but he might learn a lot watching the two interact. "I'll work on it."

Sarah nodded, then stood, glancing around. "I need to use the ladies' room, and then I guess you'll be taking me to talk to the cops?"

"Yes," Cord answered without hesitation. All of this had to go on the record.

And then he had to call Addie.

"But you won't be able to use the bathroom here. Everything in the building will have to be processed."

Sarah eyed the gas station next door. "I'll have to go there, then."

When Sarah stepped outside, Cord got the attention of one of the uniforms. "Could you go with her and keep an eye on her?"

"Sure, but we're kind of busy here." It was obvious that the officer had more important things to do, but he did follow her and then stood by the door when Sarah went inside.

"You believe her?" Karina asked right off.

"Yeah." Cord thought Sarah was the real deal, and judging from the sound Karina made, so did she.

Cord's phone rang. Jericho, again. So he answered it right away.

"When were you going to tell me that someone tried to kill Karina and you again?" Jericho began.

It wasn't that Cord had forgotten about it. But meeting Sarah had pushed the attack to the back burner. "We're okay. I'll tell you about it when we make it back to Appaloosa Pass. In the meantime, did you find out anything about Sarah Prior?"

"Yeah," Jericho said. "Who the hell is she?"

It took Cord a moment to get out the answer. "I think she's my mother. Why? What'd you find out about her?"

"Not nearly enough. No records on her until twenty-nine years ago, so I'm betting that's not her real name. Or else she made sure not to leave any trace of herself so there'd be a paper trail. She's had various retail and clerical jobs. Nothing that stands out. But something must have stood out for you."

"It did. She's got a story to tell, and after Karina and I are back, you'll get to hear it, too."

Jericho stayed quiet a moment. "Does Addie know?"

"Not yet. Soon. Karina and I need to give our statements first. There are two deaths so that might take some time." It'd take more than *some time* to get that look out of Karina's eyes.

"Let me know if there's anything I can do," Jericho added, and he hung up.

Cord stood, helping Karina to her feet, and he went to the gas station bathroom to speak with the officer who was standing guard outside the door.

"The woman inside will need to go to your police station," Cord told him. "She has key information about an old murder investigation." Or soon it would be an investigation anyway. "Can you make sure someone gives her a ride there?"

Of course, he could have offered for Sarah to ride with Karina and him, but Cord really needed some time to try to make sense of this and clear his head. It wouldn't be long before Karina would be facing a serious adrenaline crash, and he needed to save some energy for that.

"I'll get somebody out here to give her a ride," the officer assured him.

Cord took a step, then stopped. He felt that too familiar feeling go down his spine. It was a feeling that he'd learned not to ignore.

Because it had saved him a time or two.

"What's wrong?" Karina asked.

Cord didn't answer. Instead, he hurried to the ladies' room, and he threw open the door. It wasn't a large space, just two stalls, two sinks and a window, so it didn't take him long to see who was there.

Or rather who wasn't.

Hell.

Sarah was gone.

Chapter Fifteen

Sarah.

The woman's name and her story kept going through Cord's head, and the hot shower wasn't helping. Wasn't helping with the images, either. Images of those two thugs who'd tried to kidnap Karina.

Who were they?

That was still the million-dollar question, and in a perfect world, the cops would be able to pin this on someone in that stupid Bloody Murder club. But so far, there'd been no arrests, and both of the hired guns were not only unidentified, but they were also dead, so they obviously weren't talking.

That's why Cord and Jericho had beefed up security once again at the ranch. And it was the reason he kept his shower short. Karina had been asleep when he'd gotten up from the sofa, walked through the bedroom and gone into the bathroom, but he wanted to be there when she woke up.

In case she fell apart.

She had to be on the edge, especially after dealing with an adrenaline crash. When they'd finished giving their statements to the cops, they'd returned to the guesthouse. She'd showered, to get that blood off her hands, and had fallen right into bed. He'd checked on her several times throughout the night, but she hadn't moved from the spot where she'd landed.

But she had moved now.

Cord saw that the moment he stepped into the bedroom. Good thing he'd gotten some clean clothes from the closet before he'd hit the shower, or he would have walked in there stark naked.

Just the thought of it seemed to give his body some bad ideas.

Of course, seeing Karina gave him even worse ideas.

She was sitting up as if waiting for him. Her hair was tumbled all around her face and shoulders. And she was looking at him as if he might have the answers to the universe.

"I didn't hear you when you went into the bathroom," she said.

Cord shrugged. "You're a very deep sleeper."

"Yes." She flexed her eyebrows, repeated that *yes*. "Please don't tell me you watched me drool or anything."

"No drool." But then he thought they could use some lightness. "All right. Minimal drool."

It worked. She laughed. And it was so good to hear that. In fact, a first, and he hoped he got to hear her laugh and see her smile again.

The laughter didn't last long, though, and she studied him. "Bad news?"

"No. More like no news." Which some might say was a good thing. "There's still no sign of Sarah. No change in Willie Lee's condition. Mack's good to go, though. He's already home since the bullet went straight through and didn't hit anything vital. His girlfriend is giving him some TLC."

"That's good."

It was, but he could still hear the sadness in her voice.

Mack had been shot by the men who wanted to get to her. Karina would see that as her fault.

It wasn't.

Maybe he'd be able to make her understand that.

"The San Antonio cops are going through Sarah's place," Cord continued. "They're hoping to find out where she could be hiding. And why."

He especially wanted to know the why.

He shook his head. "I don't understand it. Sarah came there to that diner. She spilled all those details of what'd happened to Addie and me. So, why did she just run off like that?" Climbing out of a window, no less.

"Maybe something spooked her," Karina suggested. "If you want to know what I think, though, I believe she's telling the truth. If you want to know for sure, I stole the tissue she'd used and put it in the pocket of my jeans. You can use it to do a DNA test."

"You did what?" But he waved off his question. He'd understood just fine. "I didn't see you take her tissue."

"I have sneaky fingers." With that, her gaze dropped down to her hands. They were spotless, but she could no doubt still see the blood that'd been there.

"I killed a man," she whispered.

"You killed a *bad* man. That doesn't count." But he knew it counted. Knew that it would stay with her for the rest of her life.

Because he'd killed several bad men, too. He remembered each one of them. Their faces. The blood. And even now, it twisted his gut.

She reached for him, motioning for him to come closer.

Uh-oh. Cord figured he should just turn around and walk out. With the morning light slipping through the edges around the blinds, he had no trouble seeing every one of Karina's bruises. That cut, too. No trouble seeing the worry still in her eyes, either. The energy was practically zinging between them.

She was in no shape for what he was thinking about doing. Which meant he should leave her alone so she could try to get some more rest. Then he could fix her some breakfast and pretend that all was right with the world.

But he didn't walk out.

Instead, he gave trouble an engraved invitation and sank down onto the bed next to her.

Karina seemed to know exactly what that *invitation* meant because she reached out, pulled him closer and kissed him. It was a tentative kiss, not much of a real one.

So, Cord made it real.

Mindful of her bruises—but just as mindful of the need he felt in her—he dragged her to him and kissed her until there was no turning back.

She made a sound of pleasure. He'd heard it when he'd kissed her before, but it was lot hotter now than then. His body seemed to take that as a challenge, to make that sound even louder.

Stupid, yes. But it worked.

It felt as if Karina melted in his arms, and for the first time in ages, the flashbacks weren't in his head. Nor the images he wanted to forget. The only thing in his head was her.

He kept kissing her until they both needed more. It was easy to give more since she was half dressed. Wearing his T-shirt. He pushed it up and found a naked woman beneath.

Oh, man.

Just the sight of her nearly had him rushing this. His body was pushing him to take her now. But he could also see bruises on her rib cage and stomach.

Cord kissed each one. Softly. Gently. Then, he went lower and planted some not-so-gentle kisses there.

He heard her make that sound again. Louder. Much more urgently. Something he understood, but he wanted to linger a few moments longer. Wanted this to last a lot longer than his body was urging.

But Karina had a different notion about that.

She caught on to his arm, pulling him back up, his body sliding over hers to create some interesting friction. Yeah, this had to happen soon.

Karina must have thought so, too, because she yanked off his shirt. Cord went stiff for a second, bracing himself in case the scars killed the mood. They didn't. With her gaze connected to his, she lowered her head and kissed the scars, the way he'd kissed her bruises.

That did it. No more foreplay.

Karina and he were clearly on the same page about that because she went after his zipper. He was barefoot, so that made it easier to get his jeans off. Well, it would have been easier if she hadn't kept kissing him the whole time.

"Condom," he growled. He sat up, fumbling around to locate one in the nightstand drawer.

Later, he'd tell her that he hadn't put them there, that they'd been in the drawer when he first started staying at the guesthouse.

Later, he'd tell her a lot of things.

For now, though, he just managed to get on the condom, and he pulled her onto his lap so that his weight wouldn't put pressure on her bruises. She lowered herself, easing her body onto him until she took him inside her.

Cord had to take a second to catch his breath.

He'd known it would be special with Karina, but he hadn't expected to feel this. And he didn't have that thought for long. Every logical thought in his head vanished when they started to move together.

The face-to-face position was right for him to kiss her,

so that's what he did. He took her mouth, touching her, moving her harder and faster against him. Time seemed to stop and yet speed up, too.

Until he felt her climax ripple through her body.

Cord hadn't needed much more incentive to finish this, but that was it. He gathered Karina into his arms, pulling her to him, and he let himself go right along with her.

IT WAS SILLY, but Karina kept smiling.

It'd been a long time since she'd been with a man, and never like that. Never. Which didn't make it just silly, it made her stupid.

Mercy.

She'd fallen in love with Cord.

How the heck could she have let herself do that? The answer didn't come even when Karina held her head under the shower for so long that her lungs started to ache for air. She'd hoped if she could just clear her mind, she might be able to get a handle on this.

But no handle.

Just some really great sex with a hot guy whom she loved.

Of course, he didn't feel the same way about her. How could he? Cord still thought she was defending a serial killer. Plus, many would say they didn't even know each other that well. They'd only met a month ago.

However, even after spelling all of that out, her feelings hadn't changed. And wouldn't. Yes, that broken heart was breathing down her neck now.

She finished her shower and dressed in yet more of Addie's borrowed clothes. After packing the things at her place, Karina had ended up leaving them behind when Cord and she had rushed out of there. Thankfully, someone had dropped off her meds, so at least she had those, but it was too bad she couldn't feel just a little bit normal in her own things. But after what'd happened the last time she was at her rental house, she wasn't eager to go back.

Karina made her way toward the kitchen, following the scent of coffee. And eggs. Cord was at the stove, cooking, while he had his phone sandwiched between his shoulder and ear.

"Yeah, I'll tell her," he said to the caller, and as if he'd known all along she was there, he glanced back at her. "Hungry?"

Not even close, but she nodded, smiled. Hoped that she looked seminormal. "What are you supposed to tell me?" she asked, motioning toward the phone that he was in the process of putting away.

"That was the ranch hand out at your place. Your horses are fine."

It was the second time he'd checked on them for her. Something she greatly appreciated. But when he turned, she saw something else in his eyes. Something she didn't believe had anything to do with what had just happened between them in the bedroom.

"Is something wrong with Willie Lee?" she asked, trying to tamp down her fears. Hard to do that, though, after everything that had happened.

"No word from the doctor yet." He paused, dished her up some scrambled eggs. "This isn't exactly a good conversation to have over breakfast, but Jericho called. Harley's missing."

Well, wasn't what she'd been expecting, and at first, she thought maybe it was a good thing. Especially after they'd learned about what had gone on with him in the army. But Cord's face told a different, less-than-happy story.

"When Jericho sent a deputy over to question Harley,"

Cord continued, "they found blood on the floor and no sign of him."

She thought about that for a second while she poured herself some coffee. "What about DeWayne? Is he okay?"

It was a reasonable question considering that two of their suspects, and his *mother*, were now missing.

"I don't know about okay," Cord answered. "DeWayne's alive, but he's talking to the press and bad-mouthing you, me, Jericho and anybody else who had anything to do with Taryn, the Moonlight Strangler or Willie Lee."

That was a long list of people, but it did lead her to a strong possibility. "You think DeWayne could have done something to Harley?"

Cord shrugged, and they sat down to eat. "I think anything's possible when it comes to those two. But it's also equally possible that the Bloody Murder club is behind this. Maybe they think I'm not working hard enough to clear Willie Lee's name, and if they give us enough copycat kills, I'll start to believe them."

Karina didn't get a chance to respond to that because his phone rang, and she saw the caller ID on the screen.

The prison.

Karina automatically moved closer. Not that it was necessary, though. Like before, Cord put the call on speaker.

It was Dr. Kenney.

"Willie Lee is stabilized now," the doctor immediately told them. "And while I still don't think it's a good idea for him to have visitors, he's insisting on seeing you two right away."

"Why?" Cord asked. "Did he get his memory back?"

"Yes. And he has something important to tell you."

That brought Karina to her feet. "What?"

"I wrote down the message word for word," Dr. Kenney continued. "Willie Lee says, 'I'm not the Moonlight Strangler, but I believe I know who is. I think it could be my brother.'"

Chapter Sixteen

Cord was a thousand percent sure that returning to the prison was a bad idea, but there was no way he was going to pass up the chance to question Willie Lee about this latest bombshell.

Or maybe it was just a lie.

After all, Willie Lee clearly loved Karina, and maybe this was his way of saving face with her by trying to make her believe he was innocent.

Of course, that meant bringing Karina with him, since she wanted to hear what Willie Lee had to say, as well. With the memory of the attack still so fresh in her mind, Cord had hoped she would stay at the ranch.

No such luck, though.

She was right by his side again as they started the process to get them through security.

"You're sure Willie Lee never mentioned anything about having a brother?" It wasn't the first time he'd asked Karina that. The first time had come shortly after the doctor's call, but Cord was hoping that the thirty-minute drive out to the prison had jogged her memory.

But just like before, she shook her head. "Then again, he didn't mention having kids, either," she reminded him.

Yeah, failing to tell anyone about a brother wouldn't have been much of a stretch after that. The man could have a dozen siblings for all Cord knew. Plus, there were plenty of other things that Willie Lee had omitted. Maybe he would blame that on his fuzzy memory, but he'd clearly remembered something.

I'm not the Moonlight Strangler, but I believe I know who is. I think it could be my brother.

Cord hoped Willie Lee had a name to go along with the accusation. And while he was hoping, maybe this mystery brother would be someone the cops could arrest before Karina and he even finished this visit.

"We should ask Willie Lee about Lonny Ogden, too," Karina added as they made their way through the second checkpoint. "I'm sure it's something Addie would want to know."

Cord certainly hadn't forgotten that name. Hadn't forgotten that he had another half sibling out there.

Well, maybe he did.

Lonny Ogden was flat-out crazy, and that wasn't just Cord's opinion. Ogden had been committed to a mental hospital, where he would likely spend the rest of his life, and he didn't know any more about his birth parents than Cord did. However, Cord, Addie and Willie Lee all shared DNA with Ogden. That was a fact. And it was enough DNA that it was possible Ogden was Cord and Addie's half brother.

Once they made it all the way back to the hospital section, there was a guard there who motioned for them to take a seat by the nurses' station. "Dr. Kenney said for you two to wait here, that she'll be out soon to take you in to see the inmate."

Hell. Cord didn't want to wait. Or sit. He had way too much restless energy inside him so he started to pace. Karina paced with him.

"If you want to get your mind off this," she proposed, "we could talk about what happened this morning."

He doubted she was referring to the phone calls now. No. One look at her, and he knew this was *the talk*.

Of course, he'd expected it. Cord seriously doubted Karina was the sleeping-around type. Neither was he. But despite that, they'd landed in bed for exactly what he'd known it would be—great sex.

"Or maybe we won't talk about it," Karina added when she studied his face. "What, did you think I was expecting some kind of commitment? Because I'm not." She suddenly got very interested in looking at her fingernails. "I just wanted to make sure you're, well, okay with it?"

"Are you?" he asked.

She nodded. Patted his arm. The gesture was a little too quick, her smile a little too thin, which meant she wasn't okay with it. However, that wasn't what she said.

"It worked." She gave him another thin smile. "I got your mind off the rest of this mess."

He flinched a little at having sex lumped into *this mess*, but she was right. Just the mention of the talk that he wasn't ready to have had gotten his mind off Willie Lee. But it didn't take long for the thoughts and questions to creep right back in.

So much to consider.

"What if Willie Lee really does have a brother?" Cord decided to say that out loud, hoping it would help him work through it. "And what if the brother was the stalker Sarah told us about?"

The one who'd cut Addie's face.

Something that still turned Cord's stomach. That ate away at him even more than Sarah or him being in danger when that stalker had taken them. Of course, now he had a new reason for his stomach to twist and knot because every time he looked at Karina, it was yet another reminder that he hadn't been able to stop this monster.

Heck, he didn't even know if they were dealing with two killers or one.

Karina nodded, and made a sound of agreement after she gave what he said some thought. "You're thinking this brother could also be the Moonlight Strangler? If it's not Willie Lee, that is," Karina quickly added.

It was exactly what he was thinking. And that took Cord back to their three suspects. "All of them, Harley, Rocky and DeWayne, are the right age to be Willie Lee's brother."

Maybe even Ogden's father.

And that meant they were all the right age to be the Moonlight Strangler.

"All of them have sketchy pasts," Cord went on. "Harley failed that psych eval. Rocky is a serial-killer groupie. And DeWayne had a personal connection to at least two of the murder victims. Any of them could have started killing back when all that happened with Sarah."

And just kept on killing.

However, Karina must have seen a flaw in his theory right away because she shook her head. "Wouldn't Sarah have known if her own brother-in-law was the one stalking her and attacking her?"

"Maybe not. She said he wore a stocking mask. And besides, maybe Willie Lee and he were estranged."

There was another possibility, though. Perhaps Willie Lee knew exactly who—and what—his brother was and had maybe tried to keep him away from his family. After all these weeks of hating him, it was hard to paint Willie Lee in that kind of positive light, but it was something Cord had to consider.

"I should also have Jericho look in to Rocky's adoption.

And have him check deeper into Harley and DeWayne, too. It's possible their birth records are fake."

Having that information would help to prove or disprove what Willie Lee would tell them, but it was also info that could be needed when they made an arrest.

Which would perhaps happen today.

Cord reached for his phone to make that call, only to remember that he didn't have his phone. Or his gun. It was prison policy that all electronics and weapons be left with the guards at the front entrance.

The door to the hospital room opened, and Dr. Kenney finally stepped out. She looked exhausted, probably because she'd been nursing her patient back to health.

Cord skipped the usual greeting. "Can we see him now?"

"Yes." The doctor motioned for them to come in.

Cord stepped inside, his attention going straight to the bed where he'd last seen Willie Lee. He was still there.

But he wasn't alone.

There was someone standing right beside him.

Sarah.

KARINA CERTAINLY HADN'T expected to see Sarah Prior at the prison. Not after she'd sneaked out of the bathroom. But here she was.

And she was holding Willie Lee's hand.

Normally, Karina would have been pleased to see someone showing affection to a man she cared about, but she wasn't sure she could trust Sarah. Even if everything the woman had told them was true, that didn't mean she hadn't come here to try to hurt Willie Lee.

Still, that hand-holding had Karina rethinking that particular worry.

"I was going to have you wait until his other visitor

left," Dr. Kenney explained, "but Willie Lee said he'd like to see all of you. She can't stay much longer, though. Personal visits are limited to an hour, and she's been here longer than that."

"Why are you here?" Cord's eyes were narrowed and fixed on Sarah.

Dr. Kenney, however, answered before Sarah could say anything. "She's been trying to see him for a while, but it took several weeks to get the paperwork approved for a visit."

"And who exactly did she say she was?" he asked the doctor.

That put some alarm on Dr. Kenney's face. "His wife. Is that not right? Did they make a mistake with the paperwork?"

"She's my wife," Willie Lee insisted. He sounded a lot stronger than he had the day before.

Good.

Because he needed to answer some questions. So did Sarah.

"No touching," the doctor said when she noticed the hand-holding. She aimed a look at the guard, no doubt a reminder for him to do his job and reinforce the rules.

Sarah eased back her hand, slowly, and Karina couldn't be sure, but it seemed as if both Willie Lee and the woman hated the loss of physical contact. Heck, maybe they were in love. Or at least had been at one time.

As the doctor had done with their other visit, she stepped to the back of the room and got busy writing on a chart. The guard, a huge bald guy, didn't budge, but he didn't especially seem interested in what was playing out in front of him, either.

"You sneaked off yesterday," Cord said, walking closer to the bed and with his attention still on Sarah. "Why?"

"The photographer was snapping all those pictures in and around the diner," Sarah answered without hesitation. "I was afraid my photo would turn up in the papers, and he's still out there. I didn't want him to see me."

He.

The stalker.

And maybe the killer, too.

Sarah's excuse was pretty weak, considering she was at the prison now, where lots of people could see her, but Karina would give her the benefit of the doubt. If Sarah had told them the truth, she'd lived her life on the run and in hiding for the past three decades. She probably didn't trust easily and didn't take many risks. Having her picture in the paper would have been a risk.

Besides, it wasn't Sarah she wanted to talk to today. That could come later. For now, both Cord and Karina turned to Willie Lee.

"Start talking," Cord insisted. "And this time, no memory lapses. I want a name and details."

Willie Lee nodded. "My brother's name is…was," he amended, "Nicky Burnell. I don't know what name he's using these days, but I'm betting it's not his real one."

Karina silently repeated the name, and she figured Cord was doing the same thing. But it wasn't a name that had come up in the investigations.

"Where is he?" Cord snapped.

"I don't know. That's the truth," Willie Lee added when Cord gave him a hard look. "My parents divorced when Nicky and I were just six. We're fraternal twins. Nicky went to live with my father—I never saw or heard from either of them again—and when my mother remarried, my stepfather adopted me, and I took his surname."

Cord huffed. "So, let me get this straight. You haven't seen or heard from your brother in fifty or more years, but yet you believe he's the Moonlight Strangler? And even though you've been struggling to remember things, you just happen to remember that?"

"I didn't piece it together until Sarah told me what went on that night you and Addie were taken, and it triggered the rest of the memories. I'm not sure why Sarah would have helped with that, but she did. Maybe because this is the first time I've seen her since all of that happened."

"Because I thought it best if I stayed away," Sarah whispered. "I didn't want to get him killed, and I didn't want that monster going after my babies again. I figured if I started looking for you, that it would make waves. And that he would find out about it."

She'd been crying again. Or maybe she'd never stopped. Her eyes were red and swollen, but even with that and this awful situation, every time her gaze landed on Willie Lee, Karina saw the love Sarah had for him.

Cord obviously didn't see the love, though. Or if he did, it didn't play in to his emotions right now. He was all lawman and looked ready to pick Willie Lee's story apart word for word.

"What did you piece together?" Cord asked him.

"That day he took Sarah and you kids, he left a dead woman at our house."

Cord nodded. "I saw the picture. There was a picture of you, too, and you were holding a knife. Want to explain that?"

The sigh Willie Lee exhaled was a weary one. "He made me pose for it. Held a gun to my spine and said if I didn't take it, he wouldn't tell me where Sarah and my kids were. Of course, at the time I didn't know that you'd been abandoned and that Addie and Sarah had escaped."

Cord's hands went on his hips. "You're still not giving me what I want here. Why would you think that was your brother?"

"Because of something he said to me when he was cutting me," Sarah explained. "He said this was to settle an old score with his brother. I wasn't sure what it meant at the time. Truth is, I tried to forget what he'd said. And what he'd done."

Even now, after all this time, Karina could see that just repeating those words shook Sarah to the core.

"What old score did he have to settle?" Cord asked, glancing at both Willie Lee and Sarah.

It was Willie Lee who answered. "I'm the one who told my mother about Nicky. He wasn't right in the head. He liked to torture and kill animals, and one night I woke up, and he was standing over me with a knife. I rolled away from him just as he stabbed the blade into my pillow. He was trying to kill me."

Like Sarah, there was plenty of emotion in Willie Lee's eyes and voice. Mercy. He'd lived with a nightmare, and it crushed her heart to think he'd held all of this inside.

"After that, my dad and mom divorced, and my dad took Nicky away," Willie Lee continued. "He was going to have Nicky admitted to some mental hospital in Mexico. He wanted to go where no one knew them, where they could get a fresh start."

And that could have happened. But she also knew that torturing animals was a red-flag warning.

"You know DeWayne," Cord said. "Wouldn't you be able to tell if he was your brother?"

Willie Lee shook his head. "I haven't seen my brother in twenty-nine years. People change. And Nicky and I were only six when he was taken away."

True. And the problem with Harley was that even if there'd been a brotherly resemblance, his scars would have hidden it. Besides, she wasn't even sure Willie Lee had ever actually met Harley or Rocky. Harley and Willie Lee had been at the same army training base, but that didn't mean they knew each other.

"Sarah had nothing to do with any of this," Willie Lee added. "She told me what happened that night. How he took her. How he hurt all of you. She was just trying to save you."

Since that no-touching rule didn't apply to Cord and her, and because Karina was pretty sure they could both use it, she took Cord's hand in hers. Their gazes met. Held. And she saw it all sink in.

Willie Lee and Sarah were telling the truth. They were his parents.

That meant the real Moonlight Strangler was still out there. Plus, he might not even be one of their suspects. Nicky Burnell could be anyone now.

And could be anywhere.

Cord used his free hand to scrub it over his face. "What about Lonny Ogden?"

Sarah and Willie Lee exchanged glances. "Wasn't he the man arrested for trying to hurt Addie?" Sarah asked.

"He was," Cord confirmed. "But Addie, he and I have enough DNA in common that he could be my half brother or some other close relative."

"Or Nicky's son," Willie Lee suggested. "I don't have any other siblings. No other children, either. And, yes, I'm sure."

Even though Willie Lee seemed so certain of that, Karina knew that Cord would check it out. He'd check out a lot of things. Hopefully, somewhere during that, maybe he'd be able to catch his monster and make peace with his parents.

And himself.

"Mrs. Samuels," Dr. Kenney said to Sarah. "You really do have to go now."

Sarah nodded, reached out as if to touch Willie Lee, but then she pulled back her hand at the last second. "I'll be back as soon as they let me see you again."

"Be careful." Willie Lee then looked at Cord and Karina and he repeated what he'd said.

Sarah started for the door, but Cord didn't budge. Clearly, he had some other questions on his mind. Ones that maybe he didn't want to ask in from of Sarah.

However, before Cord could say anything else, the overhead lights flickered. And then went out.

Just like that, they were plunged into total darkness.

Chapter Seventeen

"What the heck is going on?" the guard grumbled.

Cord was wondering the same thing. He automatically reached for Karina, pulling her closer to him, and he waited.

"The generator should kick in," Cord told her.

"It should have already kicked in," the guard said.

That sped up Cord's heart rate. Here he was with Karina in a prison, and he had no gun or phone, and something had gone wrong. Well, maybe. Cord held out hope that it was just some kind of malfunction even though he knew systems like this had backups for the backups.

"Everybody stay put," the guard ordered, and Cord heard him head toward the door.

"Shane, make sure no one's trying to get in," Dr. Kenney said to the guard.

"Nobody gets through me," the guard assured her. "You just stay where you are."

Cord didn't know this Shane, but he was big, and he was wearing a sidearm. That didn't exactly steady Cord's nerves because Shane could turn out to be dirty. Or someone could just overpower him, but for now Shane was their best bet at putting an end to whatever the hell was happening here.

"I got a really bad feeling about this," Willie Lee whispered. "Undo my restraints, please."

Cord had no intention of doing that, but Karina started fumbling around as if she might. "He's right. Something's going on," she agreed.

Cord was still holding out hope, and he also held on to Karina to stop her. He didn't want Willie Lee untied. Not just yet.

But Cord's hope quickly died when he heard the guard curse.

"The door's locked," the guard said. "It shouldn't be locked. And my communicator's not working, either."

Cord cursed, too. He didn't know the ins and outs of this prison, but the locks often required a code to activate them. No one in the room had done that, so maybe that meant someone had locked it from outside.

Could Sarah have done it?

She didn't seem the sort to be able to negotiate a prison's security system and block a communicator, but if she had indeed managed it, she could be trying to break Willie Lee out of here. Out of some of the scenarios his mind came up with, that was one of the better options. At least he could best Willie Lee and Sarah if it came down to a physical fight.

Shane would be much harder since he had that gun.

"No!" Dr. Kenney said. Not a shout for help. It was more of a muffled whisper, and she could have just been reacting to the fact that the lights hadn't come back on yet.

"Dr. Kenney, are you all right?" Cord asked.

No answer.

He tried again and got the same result.

All right. So, she hadn't just been reacting to the door being locked. Something had gone wrong. But what?

Cord tried to pick through the darkness, but he couldn't

see a darn thing. Even the machines next to Willie Lee's bed had quit working and no longer had the blinking lights. He wanted to go to the doctor, to try to help her if something bad was happening, but that would mean leaving Karina alone.

Since Karina had already been the target of three attacks, Cord had to consider that this might be attempt number four.

"Shane, can you see Dr. Kenney?" Cord asked. He asked the guard that for two reasons. Because he really did want to know if the doctor was okay, but Cord also wanted to know Shane's position. He didn't seem like a man who was light on his feet, but he didn't want Shane or anyone else trying to sneak up on them.

"No. I can't see her." Shane sounded scared.

There was no table next to the bed, but Cord grabbed the metal pole that was holding Willie Lee's IV. Not an ideal weapon, especially since the IV needle was still in Willie Lee's arm. But it was better than nothing.

Cord listened for shouts from outside the door. Maybe someone trying to get to them. But nothing.

Damn.

Was it possible that no one else at the prison knew what was happening in here?

"I'm gonna start pounding on the door," the guard said. "Nobody's out in the hall, but if I pound hard enough, they'll hear me."

However, he had no sooner said that when Cord did hear something. It was some movement coming from the direction where he'd last seen the doctor. He figured it was too much to hope that she'd just fainted and was now regaining consciousness.

"Is someone else in here?" Karina whispered to him.

"Maybe."

And Cord cursed himself for that. There were plenty of beds and machines in this room, and he'd been so focused on getting answers from Willie Lee and Sarah that he hadn't thought to search the place.

Maybe that wouldn't turn out to be a fatal mistake.

"I'm taking off Willie Lee's restraints," Karina said, her voice barely audible. Because her arm was touching his, Cord could feel her shaking.

This time he didn't stop Karina when she reached out for the straps that anchored Willie Lee's arms and legs to the bed. Whoever was in here with them could be there to kill Willie Lee. After all, if Willie Lee was dead, then the real Moonlight Strangler might get away scot-free. Cord wanted to give Willie Lee a fighting chance while at the same time protecting Karina.

That's why Cord worked with her to remove the restraints.

"So help me, if you try to hurt Karina, you're a dead man," Cord warned him. "I don't care if you're my father or not."

"I'd never hurt her," Willie Lee insisted. "Or you."

While the man sounded sincere enough, Cord would decide later if he was telling the truth. After the restraints were off, Cord moved Karina to the side, away from Willie Lee, while putting himself between her and the door.

But Cord had no idea if the threat would even come from the door. It could come from anywhere.

"He could have Sarah," Willie Lee said, his voice frantic now.

True. If the woman wasn't behind this, then the killer could have taken her again. That put a tight vise on his chest, but Cord couldn't borrow trouble. Not when they already had enough of it.

"Dr. Kenney?" Cord asked again.

There were more sounds that came from her direction. Sounds that Cord didn't want to hear.

Some fast clicks. Then a groan, followed by a heavy thud. Someone had fallen to the floor.

KARINA'S FIRST INSTINCT was to run across the room and help the doctor. But Cord held her back.

"It could be a trap," he whispered to her.

Mercy, she hadn't even considered that. Her mind was racing, and it was hard for her to think. But she didn't need to think to know they were in danger.

Again.

What was going on?

"Shane?" Cord called out to the guard.

Nothing. Not at first anyway, but then she heard another groan. Definitely not from a woman. That was a man, and it was likely the guard.

"I think someone hit Shane with a stun gun," Cord said. "Did you hear the clicks?"

Karina had, but she hadn't known what it was. However, she'd had no trouble figuring out that someone had fallen. And that someone was probably Shane.

She tried to rein in her breathing. Her heartbeat, too. Hard to do, though, now that there was proof they were in trouble. Someone had taken out the guard, the biggest threat in the room since Cord wasn't armed.

Had Dr. Kenney done this?

Karina hadn't heard anything from the woman since she'd muttered that *no*, not long after the lights had gone out. But she could have been faking. Could have gotten in a stun gun, as well.

But had she?

Or was she incapacitated like the guard?

"My brother's behind this," Willie Lee whispered.

He'd moved, though Karina hadn't heard him do that. Judging from the sound of his voice, he was no longer on the bed. That was good if he had to fight back, but he wasn't in any shape for fighting. Just the day before, he'd had that seizure.

Well, maybe that's what had happened to him.

She was rethinking that. If Dr. Kenney was helping the Moonlight Strangler, then she could have given Willie Lee something to trigger a seizure or make it look as if he'd had one. If so, that meant the doctor heard everything Willie Lee had said to them. Everything Sarah had said, as well.

"Sarah," Karina whispered. She hadn't meant to say the woman's name aloud, but Sarah had left only seconds before the lights went out. Whoever was behind this could have taken her. She could be in danger.

"He'll kill her if he gets his hands on her." Willie Lee's voice was filled with pain and fear for his wife. "Sarah and I are the ones he wants."

"Well, whoever he is, he's not going to get us," Cord insisted. "Karina, stay close and follow me. I need to get the guard's gun. Willie Lee, stay here, and use this if you have to."

Since her eyes were finally adjusting to the darkness, she saw Cord handing off the IV pole to Willie Lee. That's when she noticed that Willie Lee no longer had the IV needle in his arm.

Cord pulled a fire extinguisher from the wall, and he unpinned his badge and handed it to her. "It's not much, but if you have to, you could maybe stab someone with it."

A sickening thought, especially since she had stabbed a man in that diner. Karina prayed she wouldn't have to do that again. Prayed also that they'd get out of this safely. Certainly by now someone knew something had gone wrong. The Moonlight Strangler couldn't have bought off every single guard and doctor in the place.

She hoped.

Cord and she started moving. Karina did as he said and followed him, staying close while they inched farther and farther away from Willie Lee. Maybe the killer wouldn't use this chance to go after him.

A sound caused Cord and her to freeze. A footstep, maybe. And once again, it'd come from the direction of Dr. Kenney. If she wasn't on the take, maybe she was trying to get to the guard, too. But then, who'd gotten to guard already?

"Get down on the floor," Cord said directly against her ear. "We'll crawl the rest of the way."

Maybe because he thought it would be harder for someone to shoot them that way.

With his badge still gripped in her hand, she went to her knees. Cord, too, and he didn't waste even a second getting them moving again.

The floor was tile. Hard and cold. And even though they were moving quickly, it seemed to take an eternity, but it was probably only a few seconds before they reached him. He was definitely on the floor.

Not moving.

But she could hear him breathing so he was alive. She also heard Cord when he cursed.

"His gun's gone. Someone took it."

No doubt the same person who was responsible for him being unconscious.

Before she could ask Cord what they were going to do next, she heard the clicking sound again. The stun gun. Someone else groaned. But it wasn't Dr. Kenney or the guard this time.

It was Willie Lee.

Oh, mercy.

She looked behind her and saw him fall to the floor. Cord must have seen it, too, because he hauled her behind some of the machines and moved in front of her again.

It took her a moment to see him, but there was a man near him. Someone dressed all in black, and he blended right into the shadows and the darkness.

"Well, well," he said. "We all meet again. Isn't this special?"

God. "That's him," Karina blurted out. "That's the man who attacked me in the barn."

"The man who made the phone calls, too," he proudly admitted. "And sent those texts from God. But I didn't kill you in that barn, did I? No. Because that was just the appetizer. I wanted to finish the job here."

"Who are you?" she asked, her words mostly breath.

"I'm the Moonlight Strangler, of course. And I'm here to settle an old score. A couple of new ones, too."

She shook her head. "That's not the voice of any of our suspects."

The man laughed. "Confusing, huh? Well, I practiced using this voice for a long time, and I only use it for special occasions. Like now. Want to hear my real voice, Karina? How about you, Cord?"

"Yeah," Cord snapped. "I want to hear it. Just quit hiding behind that *voice* and tell me who you are."

He laughed again, stepping over Willie Lee, to move closer. And closer.

Until Karina could see his face.

Chapter Eighteen

Rocky.

Cord knew he shouldn't have been surprised. After all, Rocky was a suspect, but that only added another knot in his gut. Because Rocky had been living right next to Karina for days before he'd attacked her.

And now he was here, obviously ready to make another move.

But what move, exactly, did he plan on making? Or rather trying to make. Because Cord had no intention of letting him get to Karina again. Willie Lee must have thought so, too, because even though he was practically immobile from the stun gun, he was struggling to try to move toward Rocky.

His brother.

Cord could see it now. The resemblance. Something to do with the set of the jaw. Too bad he hadn't noticed it sooner. Maybe then he could have stopped him before it came down to this.

Rocky was armed, a gun in his right hand. The stun gun in his left. And he wasn't alone. Cord cursed again for not having checked out the room. Because a man stepped out from behind some of the machines in the back.

A hired thug, no doubt.

"I'm so sorry," someone said. Dr. Kenney. "I had no choice but to help him. He has my sister. He'll kill her if I don't help."

Well, that explained how Rocky and his henchmen had gotten into the prison with weapons. Or maybe they'd stolen the guns once they were inside.

"Quit your whining," Rocky mocked. "Your sister's fine. We've already released her. The effects of the drugs should wear off soon, and she'll probably call the cops. And if you play nice and don't make a scene, you'll live to see her."

The doctor made a hoarse sob. "You're not going to get any help," she said, and Cord realized she was talking to him. "He has guards on the take, too, and no one will be coming in here to stop this."

Hell. That wasn't what Cord wanted to hear. Of course, Rocky had had a month to set up all of this, and he'd almost certainly covered all the bases. Or at least thought he had. He was probably counting on the doctor to get him and his hired gun out of there when he was finished.

Rocky's plan almost certainly included another murder. His specialty. Since he'd been doing it quite well for decades.

"Doc, you need to get down face-first on the floor, and choose a spot where we can see you," Rocky instructed. "I can't trust that you won't do something to help them."

Judging from her glare, she would have tried to do just that. But the hired gun pointed his weapon at her until she did as Rocky had ordered. Dr. Kenney got on the floor.

Cord kept himself in front of Karina while he stared at this snake. "What do you want?"

Rocky made an isn't-it-obvious? huff. He tipped his head to Willie Lee. "I want him to pay for what he did to me. Because of him, I was locked up in a hellhole mental hospital for two years. Abandoned by our father. And then shuffled into foster care only to end up with idiot parents."

"Parents who gave you the money to do what you're doing now," Cord said.

Rocky shrugged. "There is that. Money allowed me some freedom, and they were happy to pay me off to get rid of me."

"The freedom to hire killers," Karina snapped. "How could you do this? I trusted you."

"Well, Karina-girl," he said, using the Moonlight Strangler's voice, "your trust was misplaced. But if you hadn't hired me, I would have found another way to get close to you. Once I learned you cared for Willie Lee that made you the perfect target. You still are. Because now Willie Lee will get to watch you die."

"Why?" Karina asked.

Because she was pressed against his back, Cord could feel her trembling. Could also feel the fierce hold she still had on his badge. It might come in handy since Rocky would almost certainly want to try to strangle her. That meant coming a lot closer. In a hand-to-hand battle, he could beat this idiot.

But not if his henchmen shot Cord.

That's the reason Cord kept Karina behind the machines and hopefully out of the line of fire. Of course, there was nothing he could do about Willie Lee.

His father.

It wasn't a good time for that to really sink in with Cord, especially since he might lose him before he even got a chance to work out his feelings for him.

It was the same for Karina.

Cord didn't need another reason to get them all out of this alive, but it was part of this.

"Why?" Karina repeated. Not a trembling whisper this time. It was a shout.

"All righty, then." Not the serial killer's voice but it was syrupy sweet. "I'll give each of you one question, just one, and then I get to play. I do like to take my time with that, and I don't want any talking when I start. Screaming is fine, though."

Since the dirtbag had offered it and since Willie Lee couldn't speak for himself, Karina asked the question they all wanted to know. "Did you plant Willie Lee's DNA at that crime scene?"

"No." And it wasn't hard to tell Rocky was irritated about that. "That was all DeWayne's doing, and before I killed him, he said it was to get back at Willie Lee. Of course, he whined and begged a lot before he made that confession."

DeWayne was dead. Cord wanted to believe that was all talk, but he doubted it. The Moonlight Strangler wouldn't have any trouble adding one more body to his list.

"I don't like people using me to get what they want," Rocky added. "And that's why DeWayne's dead."

"And now you want me dead, too," Cord added, "because I'm Willie Lee's son."

Damn. The panic crawled through Cord. *Addie*. Rocky might send one of his thugs after her, too. He prayed his sister was still safe at the ranch.

"You told Addie you wouldn't hurt her," Cord reminded him.

"Oh, and I won't. I'm not really interested in killing my own niece, especially after she managed to get away from me. And you, well, I left you in that bathroom because I didn't want to kill you, either. Of course, that's all water under the bridge now." He glared at Cord. "You've gotten in the way, and you'll pay for that."

Not if Cord could do something to stop it. But what? He still had the fire extinguisher, and he might be able to temporarily blind Rocky and the thug if they got close enough.

Rocky looked at Willie Lee, who was still struggling to move, and he kicked Willie Lee in the ribs.

"Don't you hurt him!" Karina snapped, and she would have bolted toward Willie Lee if Cord hadn't pushed her back.

"Don't make this easier for Rocky by going closer to him," Cord whispered to her. "And if the thug starts shooting, get down on the floor."

If Rocky heard what Cord had said, it didn't get his attention. He was still hovering over Willie Lee.

"Guess you won't get to ask your one question, big brother. So, let me try to guess what you would say if you could speak." Rocky tapped his own chin with the gun. "You want to know how I plan to get away with this. That's what good guys always ask the bad guys. Well, easy peasy. I got plenty of helpers, too, thanks to lots of money and some of the more malleable members of that murder club."

Rocky stopped, shifted his attention to Cord and glared at him. "But I have to say, I'm not happy about you killing so many of them. Good club members are hard to find."

"You got one of them, Scott Chaplin, killed by going back to that barn where you attacked me," Karina snapped. "And you must have had another club member with you that day because there was another shooter."

"Now, now. You've already had your one question, Karina-girl, and Scott was just a necessary casualty. We went there to get those photos and such, but it was too late. The cops had already found them. Besides, Scott was a problem child. You see, he got hurt that night, and it was his blood the CSIs found near the barn. Couldn't have him around after that. Killed the other club guy, too. Can't remember his name, but I didn't want anybody around who might have seen or heard something that day. They didn't know who I really was."

Ironic. The whole time they'd had the real Moonlight Strangler in their midst and didn't know it. And now, they'd died because of it.

Rocky shifted his gaze to Cord. "You got a question for me?" He tossed the stun gun on the bed and pulled a switchblade from his pocket. "Make it fast. I'm getting antsy. I need to cut somebody."

Cord didn't want to ask this piece of slime anything. What he wanted was a way out of this.

And he saw it.

Willie Lee lifted his hand just a fraction. Another inch or two, and he might be able to grab Rocky's foot and distract him. Just enough for Cord to launch himself at Rocky and the thug.

First, though, Cord had to give Willie Lee a few more seconds. He bought him that time with a question.

"How does Harley fit into all of this?"

Rocky pulled back his shoulder as if surprised by the question. "He doesn't. My men chatted with him, and he spewed some nonsense about Willie Lee maybe keeping a journal he wanted to get. Something that had to do with a business they were in a long time ago. I wasn't interested, so when Harley got away from my men, I didn't bother sending them to get him."

That explained why there was blood in Harley's place.

And as for that old business, it was probably the money laundering. The statute of limitations had long run out on that, but Harley could have still wanted to get his hands on Willie Lee's journal if there was something to incriminate him in it.

That wouldn't have set well with Harley's wife and in-laws.

"I'm surprised you didn't ask about the other attack," Rocky said. "The one that happened a month ago where I got *you*." He smiled that sick smile at Cord.

"Didn't need to ask," Cord retorted. "You drugged both Willie Lee and me, cut me and took us to that church. You let me believe Willie Lee had set it all up so I would shoot him."

"Such a clever boy for figuring it all out," Rocky mocked.

Just thinking about that hurt Cord. Hell. He'd shot Willie Lee because that's exactly what Rocky had planned. In Rocky's sick mind that was probably the justice he wanted.

Willie Lee being killed by his own son.

And that had nearly happened. Somehow, Cord would have to learn to live with that. But first, he had to stay alive and get Karina, Willie Lee and Dr. Kenney out of this.

"Q and A is over," Rocky announced, smiling. He flicked open the switchblade and started toward Karina.

However, Rocky didn't make it but a step when Willie Lee latched on to the man's ankle. Willie Lee obviously didn't have much strength yet, but it was just enough to throw Rocky off balance. Rocky made a feral sound of outrage.

And that was Cord's cue to get moving. He hurried toward them.

But he didn't get far.

The thug took aim. And he pulled the trigger.

EVERYTHING HAPPENED SO FAST. One second Karina was standing behind Cord, and the next, he'd pushed her to the floor.

Not a moment too soon, either.

Because the gunman shot at them, and the bullet slammed into the concrete block wall where they'd just been standing. It wasn't a blast like normal shots. More of a swishing sound, which meant he was using a silencer.

Too bad.

Because if it'd been a regular shot, then someone would have heard it, and while Rocky had said he bought off some of the guards, he couldn't have bought off the whole prison.

Her heart was slamming against her chest now, and the sound of her pulse was thundering in her ears, but she had no trouble hearing Rocky's command.

"Kill them all," he shouted to the gunman. "I'll take care of my brother."

Oh, God. Rocky was going after Willie Lee. And Rocky had both a gun and a knife. Willie Lee was in no shape to defend himself, and she had to help him.

But how?

The thug was coming right at them, fast, and he maneuvered around the machines so that he could take direct aim at them.

But instead, Cord took aim at him.

Cord pulled the trigger on the fire extinguisher, the white cloud of chemicals going right in the guy's face. He cursed and staggered back, but still managed to get off another shot.

The shot hit the floor right next to Karina, the bullet tearing into the tile and sending bits of it flying right at her. Karina automatically scrambled away from it, but Cord didn't. He lunged at the thug.

Cord rammed the fire extinguisher into the man's stomach as hard as he could. He rammed his body against him, too, and both Cord and the man crashed to the floor.

Karina hurried toward them. Or rather that's what she tried to do, but another shot came right at her. This one slammed into one of the machines. Metal hitting metal, and the bullet ricocheted, smacking into the wall.

And this shot hadn't come from the thug.

Rocky had fired it at her. And he quickly took aim again.

"Get down," Cord shouted.

Karina did, dropping down next to the machine Rocky's bullet had just hit. She couldn't see Rocky's face now, but she could see Willie Lee. He was bleeding. A cut to his head from the looks of it, and he was still struggling to move.

However, Rocky wasn't struggling.

He made another of those feral sounds and fired another shot. And he didn't stop there. She saw his feet running straight toward her.

God.

There was no place for her to go, and Karina couldn't help but flash back to the other attack in the barn. Rocky had nearly killed her then before she'd managed to get away. Or maybe he'd allowed her to get away. So that he could kill her now in front of Willie Lee. That other attack could have been some sick mind game.

But this one sure wasn't.

Rocky was coming for her.

She got the badge ready, trying to position the sharp edges so she could try to stab him with it. She tried to ready herself, too. Karina brought up her hand. Just as Cord latched on to Rocky.

And Cord pulled him into the fray with the gunman.

Since both Rocky and his man were armed and Rocky had the switchblade, Karina had to do something fast or they'd kill Cord.

The fire extinguisher was on the floor now, but it'd rolled beneath the bed, not far from Willie Lee. There weren't any other weapons around so she hurried to Cord and looked for an opening so she could try to hit or kick Rocky or the thug.

Hard to do, though, with Cord in a fight for his life. Both Rocky and the man were bashing their guns against Cord, and it wouldn't be long before they managed to shoot or stab him.

Karina didn't think. She jumped in, her body landing on Rocky, and in the same motion, she struck him with the badge. He howled in pain and used his gun to back-hand her.

It felt as if her head had exploded.

The pain shot through her, robbing Karina of her breath, but she could still see. And what she saw had her heart nearly stopping. Rocky was standing over her now. His face was bleeding, no doubt from the badge.

"You cut me," he growled, and he lifted his switchblade and came right at her.

Cord stopped him, again, slamming him down to the floor. It stopped Rocky but not the hired gun. He managed to pull the trigger again.

Karina felt a different kind of explosion in her head. And in her heart. God, had Cord been shot? Was he dead?

That got her fighting again. And she wasn't alone. Yelling, Dr. Kenney came off the floor, and she still had that clipboard in her hand. She hurried to the thug and bashed the clipboard against his hand and his gun.

The gun went flying, skittering across the floor, but he punched her, hard, and the doctor went flying backward. Karina could have sworn she heard the sound of bones breaking. However, she couldn't take the time to check on the woman because Karina saw something else that robbed her of what little breath she had.

Rocky was on top of Cord, and he had the knife to Cord's throat. The thug was there, too, bleeding, and while he no longer had his gun, he was big and could help Rocky kill Cord.

"If you move, he dies," Rocky said, glancing back at her.

She believed him. But if she didn't move, then they would all die anyway. Mercy, this was shattering her heart. She couldn't lose Cord. She couldn't.

"I'll go with you," she pleaded, hoping that it would get Rocky to move his knife. "You never wanted to kill Cord anyway, that's why you left him at that gas station."

Rocky's teeth came together. They were bloody, too. The blood had slid down from the cut on his face to his mouth. Ironic. Since the cut was similar to the one he'd given her.

And all his other victims.

Rocky's eyes were cold and flat when he looked at her. "No deal. Cord dies, then you."

He turned, probably ready to finish this, but since Rocky had been looking at her, he probably hadn't seen Cord's fist. Cord knocked the knife from Rocky's hand, and he punched him.

"No!" Rocky yelled. He staggered back, bringing up his gun. And aiming it at Cord.

But there was the swishing sound again. And Rocky froze. For a second or two anyway. Before he clutched his chest, and his gun fell from his hand.

Karina had no idea what'd just happened. Until her gaze slashed to Willie Lee. He was still on the floor, but he'd grabbed the thug's gun from beneath the bed.

And Willie Lee had shot his brother.

Rocky didn't fall, and he turned as if he might lunge at Willie Lee. But Willie Lee didn't let that happen. He pulled the trigger again. And again.

It took four shots before Rocky dropped to his knees and then collapsed.

But that wasn't the end of it. The thug was alive, and he came at Cord. However, he didn't make it. Cord grabbed Rocky's gun, and he fired.

No silencer on this one, so the shot blasted through the air. It was deafening. But effective. The thug dropped like a stone, and Karina only had to glance at him to know he was dead.

Karina hurried to Cord, praying that Rocky hadn't shot him. There was blood, but God, there was blood everywhere. She couldn't tell if it belonged to him, Willie Lee or Rocky.

"Stay back," Cord told her.

Both Willie Lee and he still had their guns aimed at Rocky. And she soon saw why.

Rocky was alive.

He was on his back and was laughing. Or rather that's what he was trying to do. He wasn't making much sound.

"You think this is over," Rocky said. His voice didn't have much sound, either, but it was clear enough that she had no trouble hearing him.

"It's over," Willie Lee assured him.

"Not a chance. Because one of my men has her, you see."

The chill that went through Karina was pure ice. "Her?"

But she already knew the answer, and judging from Willie Lee's groan, so did he.

"Sarah," Rocky confirmed, turning his head to look at Willie Lee. And Rocky used his last breath to finish that. "You'll never get to her in time to save her. Sarah will be my last kill."

Chapter Nineteen

Sarah will be my last kill.

Cord wanted to believe Rocky was lying, but he knew in his heart that the man wasn't. Rocky hated Willie Lee enough to take away something—anything—that he cared about.

And Willie Lee clearly cared about Sarah.

"You have to find her now," Willie Lee insisted. He was still too weak to stand, but that didn't stop him from trying. He caught on to the bed and tried to drag himself to his feet.

Cord glanced at Karina to make sure she was okay, but she was already running for the door. She started pounding on it before he even got there.

"Help us!" she shouted.

The guard that'd been subdued was moving now, too, and he tried to join them. So did the doctor, even though she wasn't 100 percent, either. There was blood on her face, and Cord was pretty sure the thug had broken her nose when he punched her.

Dr. Kenney grabbed the phone from the wall and demanded that someone get there ASAP. Now that she no longer had to worry about her sister, she was obviously doing her part to help.

But he needed a different kind of help from her.

"Rocky probably has Sarah somewhere here in the prison," Cord said to the doctor. "He would have needed a guard or two on his payroll for that."

She nodded. "He paid off two of them, and they should be right outside in the hall. That's where he told them to wait before Karina and you came in."

There was a reinforced glass panel on the door, and Cord looked out. He didn't see Sarah, but there was a guard, and he was backing away from the door while his gaze fired all around. He likely knew from the sound of the gunfire that he didn't have much time before other guards arrived.

Ones who weren't on Rocky's payroll.

Even though it was useless, Cord bashed himself against the door, trying to force it to give way. Sarah was out there somewhere.

His mother.

Rocky almost certainly had left orders for her to be taken away, or worse, if something went wrong. And it had. Rocky was dead. Cord had gotten damn lucky that Karina and Willie Lee were alive, but he might lose his mother before he even got the chance to know her.

He rammed against the door again, the pain from the impact jolting through his shoulder, and this time he heard the click of the lock. Not from anything he'd done. He glanced out into the hall again and saw the other guards storming toward them. One of them had no doubt disengaged the lock.

Cord rushed out into the hall, and one of the guards latched on to him. Only then did he remember he didn't have his badge.

"He's DEA Agent Cord Granger," Karina said, holding up the badge. There was blood on it, but the guard must have seen enough of it to let go of him.

Cord went in search of that guard he'd spotted earlier. He had to find Sarah. He had to get to her in time.

"There's a woman missing," Karina explained. "She's probably somewhere nearby, and her life is in grave danger. You need to help Agent Granger find her."

Even though Cord was making his way up the hall, he heard the doctor step in to help with the explanation. Hopefully, she would help Willie Lee, too. Cord wasn't sure how bad his injuries were. Maybe not enough to kill him.

Hell. He could lose both his parents today.

Cord still had the thug's gun, and he readied it as he threw open the first door he reached. It was an office of some kind, and it was empty.

He refused to believe the guard had managed to get out of there with Sarah, but Karina was taking care of that, too. She was calling out for someone to check the parking lot and to stop anyone from leaving the building. The prison was probably on lockdown now anyway, but that would help in case the guard had already made it that far.

Cord hurried down the hall, checking each room. All empty. Probably Rocky's doing. Dr. Kenney had said Rocky had paid off two guards, and those two had probably made sure the hall and offices were cleared so their psycho boss could go on a killing spree.

"Search each room," Cord told the guards who were trailing along behind him. "And be careful. The two men who have her are guards, too, and they'll both be armed."

Cord reached the next door. Not closed like the others. It was wide-open, but he didn't go barging in there. He stayed to the side of the jamb and peered around it.

Sarah.

She was alive. For now. But there were indeed two guards holding her at gunpoint. The men were having what appeared to be a whispered argument, and Cord could practically smell the panic on them. They obviously hadn't thought things would play out like this.

"If you hurt her, you both die," Cord warned them, and he didn't leave any room for doubt in his voice or the glare he shot at them.

The man on the right cursed, and he threw down his gun, putting his hands in the air. Cord took aim at the other one, and the guy seemed to have a fast debate with himself. Before he, too, surrendered.

Cord hurried to Sarah and pulled her from the room so the guard could go in and restrain Rocky's hired thugs.

"You're hurt," Sarah said, her breath gusting.

He didn't want to be touched by her concern, but he was. And Cord was glad for both her concern and what he was feeling. It felt as if some ice had melted from his heart.

"I'm okay." That was all Cord managed to say before Karina came rushing out of the hospital room.

"It's Willie Lee," she said, motioning for them to come. "Hurry."

KARINA TRIED NOT to look as if she was panicking. There were already enough panicked and worried looks in the waiting room, what with Addie, Sarah and even Cord, and she didn't want to add more. But inside she was definitely panicking.

Before Cord and she had come here today, there had already been so many nightmarish memories in her head, but now she had a new set thanks to Rocky trying to kill them. And Willie Lee collapsing after Cord had gone off to find Sarah. Cord had succeeded, thank God, but Willie Lee might not be so lucky.

Because he'd had another seizure and then collapsed.

Dr. Kenney had been right there to help him and had

called in another doctor as well, but it'd been an hour now with no news.

Cord had used that hour a lot better than she had. He'd gotten the guards to bring him his phone so he could make lots of calls, including one to Addie, and she'd rushed there. She was sitting next to Sarah now. They were holding hands and talking. Not quite looking like mother and daughter.

Not yet anyway.

But as an outsider, Karina could see the new bond forming. Not just between Addie and Sarah, either. Cord was included in that, too. He'd gotten his mother a cup of water and had stayed by her side until Addie arrived.

Of course, he'd kept Karina close.

In a way.

He hadn't really talked to her, but he had wiped some blood off her face. She had no idea whose blood it was, and she'd done the same thing to Cord. They had some more bruises, but that was minor stuff compared to what could have happened.

And what could have happened was that Rocky could have killed them all.

They still might not have come out of this unscathed, though, because Willie Lee might not make it. It sickened her to think that after waiting all these years he might not get to spend any time with his wife and children.

Cord looked up from his call, his gaze connecting with Karina's, and he made his way to her. He dropped down into the seat next to her, ended the call and put his phone away. She figured he was about to ask her the same thing everybody else had asked.

Are you okay?

But he didn't.

He kissed her.

Karina went stiff from the shock. His sister and mother must have been surprised, too, because they quit talking. Or at least Karina thought maybe they had. After the kiss went on for several long moments, Karina wasn't sure she could hear anything.

Mercy, though, she could feel.

Cord eased back, met her eye to eye again. "Better? Because I'm better now."

Karina hadn't thought it possible, but she actually smiled. "Better."

But that feeling of heat and euphoria didn't last nearly long enough. The memories came flooding back. So did the tears, and she tried to blink them away.

"I'm so sorry," Karina said. "This is all my fault. If I hadn't hired Rocky, he—"

"He would have found another way to get to Willie Lee. And you. You heard Rocky. He was crazy and obsessed with getting back at his brother. If you hadn't hired him, he might have just killed you on the spot."

Cord cursed himself when she shuddered at the thought of Rocky getting his hands on her. But Cord was right, and it was something she needed to hear.

Still...

"I wish I'd figured it all out sooner," she said. "If I'd known he was the Moonlight Strangler, I maybe could have stopped him."

Cord frowned. And kissed her again.

"Do you two need to get a room?" Addie teased when the kiss went on a long time.

Cord broke away from her, smiling, but he gave his sister a very brotherly scowl. "I seem to remember seeing Weston and you kiss each other's lights out."

Addie nodded, readily acknowledging that. "My husband and I kiss a lot. And we're just as much in love as you two obviously are."

Cord froze. Karina did, too, but for a different reason. Because for Karina it was the truth. Cord, however, was probably nowhere near the *L* stage. And might never be.

A thought that broke her heart.

Cord, however, didn't get a chance to say anything because his phone rang again, and she saw Jericho's name on the screen. He didn't put it on speaker and instead stepped out into the hall to take the call.

Addie immediately motioned for Karina to join Sarah and her, and while she hated to intrude on a family moment, Karina finally went when Sarah motioned, too.

"I have two very strong, smart and wonderful kids," Sarah said. She also had tears in her eyes again. "I hope I get to make up some lost time with them."

"You will." Addie dropped a kiss on Sarah's cheek, and Karina saw the woman's face practically glow. "And once Willie Lee's fine and out of this place, we can go on a picnic together or something."

It seemed like such a, well, normal thing to do, and Karina wanted to hug Addie just for suggesting it. She didn't know Cord's sister that well, but she hoped she could spend more time with her.

Of course, it was just as likely that Karina would never see her again after today.

The door opened, and the three of them went to the edges of their seats. But it was Cord, not the doctor. Karina went to him in case he'd learned something bad that he was going to have to break to Addie and Sarah.

"It's not bad news," Cord told her right off. "Dr. Kenney's sister is all right. Rocky told the truth about that. She was drugged but wasn't hurt."

That eased some of the pressure in Karina's chest.

"But Rocky also told the truth about DeWayne," Cord added a moment later. He slipped his arm around Karina's waist and moved her several feet away from the other women. "The cops found his body."

So, the man was indeed dead. It was hard for her to feel sorry for the person who'd set Willie Lee up to take the fall, but DeWayne hadn't deserved to die. Instead, he should have been sent to prison for a long, long time.

"And Harley?" she asked.

"Alive," Cord answered. "Jericho's bringing him in for questioning about that money-laundering scheme. Now that the cat's out of the bag on that, there'll be no reason for Harley to try to cover it up."

Which meant there'd be no reason to come after her. Not that he had ever done that. No, Rocky had been responsible for those attacks and heaven knew how many murders.

"The SAPD is tearing apart the Bloody Murder club," Cord went on. "All the members are being arrested as accomplices to murder. That way, they can keep them behind bars until they sort out who was really working for Rocky and who wasn't."

Good. She didn't want any of Rocky's hired thugs on the loose.

Cord turned her so they were facing. "Are you really in love with me like Addie said?"

She nearly got choked on the breath she sucked in, and it took her a moment to realize he was serious, that he wasn't just teasing her.

Karina could only go two ways with this. She could tell the truth or she could give Cord an out. After all, he might feel he had to be with her just because of what they'd been through.

She went with the truth.

"Yes," she said. "I'm in love with you."

She braced herself for any and all reactions. Cord might tell her that she'd lost her mind. But he didn't. That's because the door opened, and this time a doctor came into the room. Not Dr. Kenney. She was likely getting her own medical attention for that broken nose.

"I'm Dr. Litton," the man said.

Addie took hold of Sarah's arm, and the two stood together. Waiting with their breaths held. Karina was doing the same thing.

"Willie Lee did have another seizure," the doctor explained, "but we believe it was a side effect from the drug that the man forced Dr. Kenney to give him. We also had to do some surgery. He'd been stabbed in the side."

Mercy. Karina hadn't even seen that happen, but it was no doubt from Rocky's switchblade.

Sarah touched her hand to her mouth to steady her trembling mouth. "How is he?"

"He'll make it. He just needs some recovery time."

The relief was instant, and Karina found herself in the middle of a sea of hugs. Smiles, too.

"From what I understand," the doctor went on, "the charges against him will be dropped, and when that happens, Willie Lee will be transferred to a civilian hospital. In the meantime, he wants to see all of you. You've got five minutes."

Not much time at all, and Karina considered staying put so that Cord, Sarah and Addie could have a family reunion. But Sarah took hold of her left hand. Cord, her right. And they followed the doctor into a recovery room.

Willie Lee was awake, but like Cord and her, he had some fresh bruises, as well. And of course, that stab wound. If Rocky had had just a few more seconds...

But she cut off that thought.

Rocky hadn't gotten those extra seconds because Cord and then Willie Lee had stopped him.

They went closer to the bed, Willie Lee reaching for each of them. He pulled Sarah closer for a kiss on the cheek. He did the same to Addie. And Cord.

Then her.

"I've always thought of you as one of my own," Willie said, giving Karina's hand a squeeze. "Now, I have two daughters. And a son."

"A grandson, too," Addie reminded him. "You'll get to meet him when you're better."

"I'm already better," Willie Lee assured her. He smiled at his wife. Then, winked at her. The levity was nice, but his expression soon turned serious. "I'm so sorry about all of this."

Cord huffed. "Karina's been apologizing, too. And Sarah…Mom," he amended. The word seemed a little stiff, but the look Cord gave his mother was anything but. Karina was betting within a month, they'd all be a real family.

Well, minus her.

"The doctor said five minutes," Karina reminded them. "I'll wait outside so you can have a few minutes together."

She turned to leave, but she didn't get far.

Cord caught up with her before she could make it to the door.

"Considering you just told me that you loved me," he said, "I think that makes you eligible for family status."

The others nodded, all agreeing. But Karina shook her head. "The love part has to be mutual for that to happen."

"Oh, it's mutual, all right." And he kissed her again.

It was a wow kiss. One of those that she felt from her head all the way down to her toes, which pretty much described any and all kisses that she got from Cord. He left her breathless and wanting a whole lot more.

Including the words that went along with that "it's mutual, all right."

She stared at him so long that he must have figured it out. "I love you, Karina," he said.

Well, that took care of the rest of her breath. So did the other kiss he gave her.

"Please tell me there's a marriage proposal that goes with all that kissing," Addie teased.

Karina had no such expectations. That's why she was stunned with what Cord said.

"We haven't had a date yet," Cord reminded his sister. "But give me a month to wine and dine her." He put his mouth right against Karina's ear and whispered, "And so I can get you in my bed again. After that, it's one knee, a ring and the question—will you marry me. How does that sound?"

Perfect. And Karina managed to say that to him, too. It was all perfect. But Cord made it even more so by pulling her into his arms for a kiss.

* * * * *

USA TODAY *bestselling author*
Delores Fossen's highly popular series
THE LAWMEN OF SILVER CREEK RANCH
returns later this year with LANDON.

"You really do think someone wants to harm me?" Natalie asked. "That it's not my imagination?"

"Isn't that why you hired me?" Clint asked.

She stared into Clint's dark eyes and pressed a hand over her mouth to hide the way her lips trembled. Yes. But why would anyone want to harm her?

Those dark whispers she had tried so hard to close out just before she drifted off to sleep each night these past eight or so weeks nudged her now, echoing deep in her mind. She closed her eyes and let them come. Laughter, soft, feminine... Then the raised voices—a man and a woman. Was it a real memory? Something from before her fall? Something from childhood?

She waited until Clint had parked in front of her home to say, "I don't intend to stay holed up in this house. I can't... do that."

He put his hand on her arm. "Wherever you go, I go."

DARK WHISPERS

BY
DEBRA WEBB

First Published in Great Britain 2016
By Mills & Boon, an imprint of HarperCollins*Publishers*
1 London Bridge Street, London, SE1 9GF

© 2016 Debra Webb

ISBN: 978-0-263-91915-8

46-0916

Our policy is to use papers that are natural, renewable and recyclable products and made from wood grown in sustainable forests. The logging and manufacturing processes conform to the legal environmental regulations of the country of origin.

Printed and bound in Spain
by CPI, Barcelona

Debra Webb is the award-winning *USA TODAY* best-selling author of more than one hundred novels, including reader favorites the *Faces of Evil*, the *Colby Agency* and the *Shades of Death* series. With more than four million books sold in numerous languages and countries, Debra's love of storytelling goes back to childhood on a farm in Alabama. Visit Debra at www.debrawebb.com.

I have met many people in this life but few have proved to be so dear to me as the wonderful Marijane Diodati. Thank you, my friend, for caring so very much for me and for my stories.

I will cherish you always.

Chapter One

Former Deputy Chief Jess Harris Burnett repositioned the nameplate on the new *old* desk in the center of her small office. A matching credenza stood against the wall beneath the window. She had a nice view of the street, unlike her partner whose office window overlooked the not-so-attractive alley at the back of their downtown historic building. She'd offered to toss a coin, but he'd insisted she take the nicer view. Buddy Corlew, her old friend turned business partner, actually preferred the office with the potential *backdoor* escape route. He boasted that he'd worked sufficient cheating spouse cases to appreciate the option of a hasty retreat.

Jess sighed as she surveyed her new office space. A couple of bookcases lined the wall to the right of her desk, while framed accomplishments and accolades dotted the left. Her new office didn't look half bad now that everything was in place. The lingering doubt about the big career change was gone for the most part as were the rumors in the media and even in the department. The people she cared about understood and supported her reasons for change. Though she missed her major crimes team and, to some degree, working in the field, family and friends were what mattered most to her now.

Her closest friends, Detective Lori Wells and Dr. Sylvia Baron, had helped Jess with the decorating as well as the furnishing of the offices. Since the building was one of Birmingham's oldest, they had chosen to go with a casual vintage decor. Jess arranged the two mismatched chairs in front of her desk and stood back to have a look. "Not bad at all."

The baby kicked hard and she jumped. Smiling, Jess rubbed her belly. Her husband Dan insisted this child would play football at the University of Alabama just like his grandfather had back in the day. Jess shook her head. She had no desire to plan her unborn child's college career just yet, much less whether or not he would participate in such a brutal sport. But then, this was Alabama—football was practically a religion. She supposed the idea was no different than her mother-in-law, Katherine, already having Bea, their eighteen-month-old daughter, enrolled in ballet class and baby yoga.

Jess sighed. Her sister, Lily, had warned her that motherhood came with a whole host of new obligations, expectations and no shortage of worries. "And here you are going for round two, Jessie Lee." She rested a hand on her heavy belly. As frustrating and terrifying as being a parent could be, she wouldn't trade it for anything. She wondered if their baby boy would have dark hair and blue eyes like his father? Their little girl had Jess's blond hair and brown eyes.

A bell tinkled in the lobby and Jess wandered out of her office and toward the sound. The private investigation agency she and her old high school friend Buddy Corlew had decided to establish opened on Wednesday with an open house scheduled for next Monday. Had Buddy decided to drop back by or had she left the front door unlocked? Her pulse rate climbed with every step she took toward the entry. She'd spent too many years analyzing and helping to apprehend serial killers to ignore the potential for trouble. Memories of last spring's ordeal with Ted Holmes attempted to emerge but she suppressed them. That nightmare was over. *Don't look back.*

Buddy stood in the lobby appraising the work Jess and her friends had done. She relaxed. "I didn't think you were coming back today."

"Sylvia told me you were still here." Buddy glanced around the lobby and nodded his approval. "Looks great, kid."

Buddy was the only person in the world who had ever called her kid. The fact that he still did reminded her that in many ways he would forever be living in the past. His music taste was pre-1990, his long hair was fastened in a ponytail, and he still strutted around in worn denim and scarred leather the same way he had in high school. Enough said.

"Great might be an overstatement," Jess surveyed the lobby, "but at least we won't be scaring off clients." The exposed brick walls and concrete floors looked less like a dungeon with a few carefully placed upholstered chairs and a couple of tasteful pieces of secondhand art purchased at the most recent fundraiser Dan's mother hosted.

"Did you get your office squared away?"

"I did." Jess braced a hand on her hip and ignored the ache that had started in her lower back. She'd certainly overdone it today. "I was about to call it a day."

Buddy glanced at her round belly and smiled. "I can't wait until Sylvia actually looks pregnant." As hard as it was to believe, Buddy and Sylvia, Jefferson County's medical examiner and the daughter of one of Birmingham's old money families, had married and were now expecting a child.

Jess and Buddy had grown up on the not-so-appealing side of Birmingham and somehow they'd both managed to do okay. Jess had spent most of her law enforcement career with the FBI, first as a field agent and then as a profiler. Just over two years ago she had returned to Birmingham and started a new career with Birmingham PD as deputy chief of Major Crimes. After twenty years separated by their careers and geography, she'd married her high school sweetheart, Daniel Burnett, the chief of police.

Buddy's life had taken a somewhat less direct route to where they were now. A womanizing rebel in high school, he'd ended up spending a tour of duty in the military right out of high school to avoid trouble with the law. Later, several years as a BPD cop and then a detective had ended on a bit of a sour note. Buddy, however, being Buddy, had bounced back. He'd opened a small private investigation shop and done well. Falling for and marrying Sylvia had changed the man as nothing else could have. He could not wait to be a daddy. The change left a large portion of Birmingham's female population bemoaning the loss.

"Don't worry," Jess assured him, "that will happen soon enough." She suspected her old friend didn't have a clue what he was in for. Sylvia would ensure Buddy suffered every moment of discomfort she endured for the next several months.

The bell over the door tinkled again. Jess turned as Clint Hayes strolled in, a box under one arm and a briefcase in his hand. Clint had been a member of Jess's BPD major crimes team. He'd asked if he might come onboard at B&C Investigations when Jess first announced she was leaving the department. She hadn't been able to deny that having an investigator with a law degree as well as several years as a detective under his belt was attractive. No matter, she had discussed the idea with Dan before acting on Clint's request. He had a right to know one of his detectives was considering making the move with her. Dan had been so glad Jess was leaving police work behind, he'd been only too happy to see Clint go with her. That he was handsome and dressed impeccably wouldn't hurt, either.

"I cleaned out my desk at the department," Clint announced in greeting. "I thought I'd get settled here."

Buddy clapped him on the back. "Glad to have you, Hayes."

"We've set up several desks in the large office at the end of the hall," Jess explained. She and Buddy had taken the two smaller offices. The larger one would allow for several investigators to share the space. A third smaller office would serve as a conference space for meeting with clients. Closer to the lobby was a tiny kitchenette with a narrow hall to the only bathroom and a rear exit. "Take your pick."

"Just like old times." Clint flashed Jess a grin and headed that way. Buddy followed, filling him in on the open house planned for a week from today.

For now, Clint was their only investigator. Buddy was working on recruiting. They had interviewed three others so far. Their secretary, Rebecca Scott, who would also serve as a receptionist and occasionally as a babysitter when Lily and Katherine were tied up, was scheduled to start tomorrow. Jess was immensely grateful to find someone willing to wear so many hats and whom she trusted with her child while she met with clients and assigned investigators.

Assessing cases and determining the best way to proceed wouldn't be that different from her profiler days—other than the fact that they wouldn't likely be tracking serial killers and hunting murderers. Then again, through-out her career she always seemed to have a penchant for attracting the faces of evil.

The bell over the door jingled again, drawing Jess from the memory of one serial killer in particular. Four and a half months ago Ted Holmes had done all within his power to reach the highest level of evil by resurrecting the per-sona of Eric Spears and reenacting his obsession with Jess.

Banishing the memories once more, Jess produced a smile for the woman, thirty or so, who stood just inside the door as if she couldn't decide what to do next. She was petite, around Jess's height of five-four. Her black hair was long and lush; she was attractive. Her manner of dress, a soft beige pencil skirt with matching jacket and heels, sug-gested a career woman. Her gaze moved around the lobby, eventually landing on Jess. The fear and hesitation in her expression gave Jess pause.

"I need a private investigator," she said, her voice trem-bling the slightest bit.

Jess was on the verge of telling her they didn't open until the day after tomorrow when the woman added, "I shot a man."

When she swayed, Jess hurried to usher her into the nearest chair. "Why don't you have a seat? I'll get you a bottle of water."

Their first potential client shook her head. "No. Please." She put her hand on Jess's arm. "I need help."

"Let's start with your name." Jess settled into a seat on the opposite side of the reclaimed factory cart that served as a coffee table.

"Natalie Drummond."

"Well, Ms. Drummond, it sounds as if you might need the police rather than our services. I'll be happy to call someone for you." Jess's first thought was to call Lori.

Detective Lori Wells now worked in the Crimes Against Persons division. Jess considered her a dear friend and she was one of the best detectives in the department. It didn't hurt that Lori's husband, Chet Harper, was the ranking detective in the BPD's major crimes team—as well as a good friend.

Drummond shook her head. "You don't understand. I did call the police, but they can't help me."

The woman looked sincere and certainly terrified, but her story didn't quite make sense. "I'm not sure I'm following you. Why can't the police help you?"

Drummond wrung her hands in her lap. "The man I shot is missing. They found no evidence of an intruder in my home...even the gun I used was missing." She shook her head, tears bright in her eyes. "I don't understand how that's possible. I shot him." She looked straight at Jess. "I know I shot him. He fell to the floor. He...he was bleeding. I ran out of the house and waited for the police to arrive." Her eyebrows drew together in a worried frown. "When they arrived he was gone."

"Can you remember the detective's name who came to the scene?" Whatever happened, Ms. Drummond was visibly shaken. That level of fear wasn't easily manufactured.

"Lieutenant Grady Russell."

Jess was acquainted with Russell. He was a detective in the Crimes Against Persons division. Russell was a good cop. "Why don't I give the lieutenant a call and see what I can find out?"

Drummond nodded, visibly relieved. "Thank you."

Jess stood. "Come with me and I'll introduce you to one of our investigators." No reason to mention that he was their only investigator.

Buddy was in his office on the phone as they passed.

Jess escorted Drummond to the end of the hall where Clint was organizing his desk.

"Clint, this is Natalie Drummond."

"Ms. Drummond." Clint gifted her with a nod.

"Ms. Drummond will explain her situation to you while I make a call to Lieutenant Russell."

Clint invited Drummond to have a seat. Rather than go to her office, Jess went to Buddy's and closed the door. When he'd ended his call, she said, "We need a conference call with Russell about our first client. She says she shot a man who is now missing."

Buddy raised his eyebrows as he set the phone to speaker and made the call. "You always did attract the strange ones."

He needn't remind her.

Three rings and Russell answered. Jess quickly explained the situation and asked for any insights the lieutenant could provide.

"We received the call early this morning," Russell confirmed. "I have to tell you, I think maybe the lady is a little wrong in the head."

Jess was immensely grateful for the thick brick walls of the historic building that helped ensure privacy between offices. "What does that mean, Lieutenant?" If the man said Drummond was hormonal or flighty, Jess might just walk the few blocks to the Birmingham Police Department and kick his butt on principal.

"About two years ago Natalie Drummond had a fall down the stairs of that mansion her daddy left her. She was banged up pretty good, but it was the brain injury that left her with big problems. According to her family, she still suffers with the occasional memory lapse and reasoning issue."

"She had a traumatic brain injury?" Jess frowned and

rubbed at the resulting lines spanning her forehead. Even two years later, an injury like that could explain Drummond's uncertainty as to the sequence of recent events.

"That's the story according to her brother, Heath Drummond," Russell confirmed.

Now there was a name Jess recognized. "As in Drummond Industries?"

"The one and only," Russell confirmed. "The brother says she hasn't been the same since the fall. She spent months in rehab. He thinks maybe she's having some kind of relapse. About two months ago, she started insisting that someone was coming into her house at night. Every time she told the story it was a little different. The brother decided she was hallucinating. Apparently that can happen with TBIs. This morning she called 9-1-1 and claimed she'd shot a man. We arrive and there's no body. No blood. No signs of an altercation. Nothing. There was no weapon found on the premises, yet she swears she discharged a .38 at an intruder. She also swears she left him bleeding on the floor."

Jess exchanged a look with Buddy.

"You believe she imagined the whole thing," Buddy said.

"At this point, yeah, that's the only explanation that makes sense."

"Thanks so much, Lieutenant." Before ending the call, Jess assured him she would pass along any information she might discover relevant to the case. To Buddy she said, "Whether she shot anyone or not, it sounds as if Ms. Drummond needs our help."

"I guess we have our first case." Buddy came around to the front of his desk and offered his hand. "I'll leave the logistics to you. I have another investigator to interview over at Cappy's."

Jess took his hand and struggled to her feet. Cappy's Corner Grill was a cop hangout over on 29th that served the best burgers in town. Local cops, private investigators and bounty hunters frequently used Cappy's for unofficial staff meetings.

"Clint is the right investigator for this one," Jess said, the wheels inside her head already turning. She remembered well how cocky the detective had been when he'd first joined her major crimes team, but time had softened his hard edges.

Buddy shot her a wink as they exited his office. "Good thing, since he's our only investigator."

"True." Jess turned to the office at the end of the hall where Clint was interviewing their first client. Whatever troubles Natalie Drummond faced, real or imagined, Jess would see that she received the help she needed.

No one should have to fight her demons alone.

Chapter Two

Clint pulled into the driveway behind Natalie Drummond. He surveyed the place she called home and blew out a long, low whistle. If the lady lived here—the estate looked more like a castle than a home—then she was loaded. He should have realized she was related to *the* Drummonds of Birmingham.

He climbed out of his Audi and strolled up to her BMW as she opened the door. When she emerged her lips tilted the slightest bit with a shaky smile. "I appreciate you being able to start right away. I was afraid it would be days or even weeks before I could retain the services I needed."

"I'll work as quickly as possible to get to the bottom of the trouble, Ms. Drummond. No one should be afraid in their own home." Even if it was large enough to host the next governor's summit.

"You should call me Natalie." She exhaled a big breath and sent a worried glance back at the street.

"Natalie," he repeated. "As long as you call me Clint." She nodded, and then led the way to the front door.

When she fished the keys from her bag, he reached for them. "Why don't I go in first?"

Obviously relieved, she turned over the keys.

As he opened the door the first detail he noted was the lack of a warning from the security system. "You don't arm your system when you leave the house?"

"With all that happened this morning, I suppose I forgot." She closed her eyes and shook her head. "Like I said, I didn't go back in the house after the police left. I couldn't."

He handed the keys back to her, placed a hand at the small of her back and ushered her across the threshold. He surveyed the entry hall. The ceiling soared high above a grand balcony on the second floor. A large painting hung on the broad expanse of wall that flanked the ornate staircase. He recognized Natalie as a child of around ten or twelve in the painting.

"My family," she said, following his gaze. "My parents are both gone now. There's my younger sister, April, and my older brother, Heath. Heath runs the family business and April is a trophy wife who specializes in fundraising." She said the last with something less than pride as she placed her purse and keys on a table near the door. "The kitchen is on the right at the end of the hall. That's where…it happened."

Clint hesitated, the sticky notes on the mirror above the hall table snagging his attention. There were several yellow notes and one pink one. *Leave the keys and your purse here. Lock the door. Arm the security system.* The pink note read *Check the peephole before opening the door.*

"I don't need them as much as I used to," she said with a noticeable resignation in her tone. "My short-term memory gets better every day." She locked the door. "It's certain parts of my long-term memory that still have a few too many holes."

He gestured to the notes. "This was part of the process of getting back into your normal routine?"

She nodded. "I'm not sure anything about my routine will ever be called normal again, but I manage."

"I imagine the journey has been a challenging one." Clint moved toward the kitchen. "Back at the office you said your sister spent a great deal of time helping you get back on your feet?"

"She stayed with me every night for the first year. When she wasn't with me there was a nurse." A weary sigh escaped her lips. "For ten months I was fine on my own, and then…the voices started. April stays the night whenever I need her despite my brother-in-law's insistence that he needs his wife at home."

"Your brother-in-law is…?"

"David Keating, the son of Birmingham's new mayor, who sees himself as governor one day. He's running for state representative and insists that April should be at his side at all times. You haven't seen the billboards plastered all over the city? Vote for Truth and Family Values." Natalie shook her head. "Personally, I believe he's worried that I'm losing my mind and he doesn't want his wife too close to anything unpleasant that might end up attached to his name in the news." She paused. "Sorry. I'm being unkind. In truth, David has been very thoughtful since the fall. Forgive me if I'm a little too blunt at times."

"No apology necessary. Do you and your siblings get along?"

"As well as any I suppose." Her heels clicked on the marble floor as they continued toward the kitchen. "Five years ago, after our father died, I think people expected there to be dissention, but we all felt the terms of the will were remarkably well thought out. Heath inherited the family business, which made perfect sense since he was the only one with any interest in overseeing it. He was Father's right hand. I inherited the house and April was endowed with the largest portion of the family financial trust. Father was well aware of my younger sister's love of spending. The trust pays out slowly over her life so there's no fear of her ever being destitute in the event her marriage to David doesn't work out."

They reached the wide arched entrance to the kitchen and Clint paused. "You're an attorney?"

She stared at the sleek tile floor. "I was. It remains to be seen if I will be again. I feel more like an assistant now. Two years ago I was up for partner at Brenner, Rosen and Taylor. I would have been the youngest partner in the firm's history. Most of the past two years I've been on extended disability leave. I returned to work a few weeks ago. I review other people's cases to see if we're doing all we can for each client. I'm certain the partners fear that giving me a case of my own at this point would be premature, perhaps even detrimental to the firm's reputation. After what happened this morning, who can blame them?"

Her work history was impressive. Brenner, Rosen and Taylor was a small but very prestigious law firm. "Why don't you walk me through exactly what happened this morning."

Natalie drew in a deep breath and squared her shoulders. "I was preparing to go to the office. The security system was apparently unarmed. I could've sworn I set it before I went to bed, but evidently I didn't." She sighed and rubbed at her temple as if a headache had begun there. "I still forget things sometimes and get things out of order, but those instances rarely happen anymore—at least that's what I thought."

"What time did you get up?" Clint moved to the back door. According to the police report, Natalie believed the alleged intruder entered the kitchen through the door leading from the gardens and patio since it had been standing open. All other entry points had been locked when the police arrived, seemingly confirming her allegation. Clint opened the door and crouched down to have a look at the lock and the knob.

"At six," she said in answer to his question. "I remember because the grandfather clock in the entry hall started to chime the hour. It's a habit of mine to count the chimes." She looked away as if the admission embarrassed her. "I've done it since I was a child."

Clint smiled, hoping to help her relax. "I count buttons. Whenever I button my shirt, I count."

Her strained expression softened a bit at his confession. "I guess we all have our eccentricities."

Focusing on his examination of the door, he saw no indication of forced entry. Back at the office, he'd sent a text to Lori Wells requesting a copy of the police report. A quick perusal of the report she'd immediately emailed him had showed the same findings. Clint hadn't really expected to find anything. Still, a second look never hurt. He pushed to his feet. "You were upstairs when you heard an intruder?"

She nodded. "I was dressed and ready to go when I heard a noise down here."

"Describe the noise for me."

She considered the question for a moment. "There was a lot of banging as if whoever was down here was searching for something."

The evidence techs had dusted for prints, but hadn't found any usable ones except Natalie's, which meant the intruder wore gloves and that she had a very dedicated and thorough cleaning staff. Most surfaces in any home were littered with prints. "You came down the stairs," Clint prompted.

"First I came to the landing. I thought maybe Suzanna, my housekeeper, had arrived early." She hugged her arms around herself as if the memories stole the warmth from her body. "I saw him standing at the bottom of the stairs, but I couldn't see his entire face. He was wearing a mask. Like a ski mask where all you can see are the eyes and across the bridge of the nose. I ran back to my room and grabbed my cell phone and my father's handgun from the nightstand. When I came down the stairs I didn't see him anymore. The back door was open so I assumed he'd fled." She took a deep breath. "I came into the kitchen to close the door and suddenly I heard him breathing…behind me. It was as if he'd been waiting for me to come."

"Did he touch you?"

She shook her head. "I spun around and fired the weapon."

Clint closed and locked the back door. "You're certain the intruder was male."

The sound of the door locking or maybe the question snapped her from the silence she'd drifted into. She flinched. "Absolutely. He was tall and strong and he had a scar." She pointed to the spot between her eyebrows.

"He never spoke?"

She shook her head. "He staggered back and then fell to the floor. There was blood on his shirt."

"You ran outside to wait for the police?"

She nodded. "I dropped the gun and ran. I was confused. That still happens when I get overexcited or upset and, quite frankly, I was terrified."

Clint would ask her more about the traumatic brain injury later. According to the police report there was no indication of foul play in the home and no gun was found. Since the detective at the scene had decided the whole event was Drummond's imagination, no test for gunshot residue had been performed. "Did blood splatter on your clothes or your shoes?"

She frowned. "No." Her head moved from side to side. "I suppose there should have been." She closed her eyes for a moment before continuing. "I know what I saw. There was a man here. He wore a black ski mask. I fired the weapon, the sound still echoes inside me whenever I think of that moment."

"You believe," he offered, "while you were waiting for the police the intruder fled, taking the gun with him."

"Yes."

CLINT HAYES DID not believe her.

Natalie didn't have to wonder. She saw the truth in his eyes. There was no evidence to support her story. Nothing. Her brain injury made her an unreliable witness at best. How could she expect anyone to believe her?

Maybe she was losing her mind. Her own brother thought she was imagining things.

"Let's talk about why someone would want to create a situation like the one that played out in your home this morning."

Hope dared to bloom in her chest. "Are you saying you believe me?"

"Yes." He nodded. "I do."

Startled, Natalie fought to gather her wits. She had hoped to find someone who would believe her. Now that she had, she felt weak with relief and overwhelmed with gratitude. "Would you like coffee or tea?"

"No thank you, but don't let me stop you."

"I don't drink coffee after the middle of the afternoon for fear I won't sleep." Her life was quite sad now. What would this handsome, obviously intelligent man think if he knew just how sad? What difference did money and position matter in the end? Very little, she had learned. The years of hard work to reach the pinnacle of her field meant nothing now. She could no more battle an opponent in the courtroom than a ten-year-old could hope to win a presidential debate.

All she had been or ever hoped to be was either gone or broken. Her mother had warned her all-work-and-no-play attitude would come back to haunt her one day. *What kind of life will you have without someone to share it with?* Her mother's words reverberated through her.

A lonely one, Mother. Very lonely.

"Are you taking medication?"

"I have a number of medications, Mr. Hayes." She led the way to an enormous great room where her family had hosted the Who's Who of Birmingham. "There are ones for anxiety and others for sleep—all to be taken as needed. So far I've done all right without them more than six months. I take over-the-counter pain relievers for the headaches that have become fewer and further between."

She settled into her favorite chair. Mr. Hayes took a seat across the coffee table from her. The idea that he might not actually believe her but needed to pad the company's bottom line crossed her mind. The other three agencies she'd contacted this afternoon weren't interested in taking her case. What made this one different? She'd stumbled upon B&C Investigations completely by accident. She'd walked away from the third rejection and noticed the new sign in the window on the way to her car.

"Do you have any personal enemies that you know of?"

She shook her head. "No family issues. No work issues. I can't imagine anyone who would want to do this. Why break into my home? Nothing appears to be missing."

"Let's talk about the people closest to you."

"My sister and I have always made it a point to have

dinner a couple of times a week. Since the fall, she stays the night whenever I need her—or when she decides it's necessary. I don't see my brother as often. He's very busy. There's Suzanna Clark, the housekeeper, and her husband, Leonard, the gardener."

"You said your sister started staying with you at night again because of the voices."

Natalie hated admitting this part, but it was necessary. "About two months ago I started waking up at night and hearing voices—as if someone is in the house. I get up and search every room only to find I'm here alone." If only she could convey how very real the voices sounded. It terrified her that perhaps her brother was right and she was imagining them. "Until this morning."

"What about your colleagues at the office?"

The uneasiness that plagued her when she thought of work seeped into her bones. Since the fall, her professional inadequacy filled her with dread whenever the subject of work came up. She'd once lived for her career.

"I have my assistant, Carol. Art Rosen is the partner I work closest with. I'm well acquainted with everyone on staff. I have no rivals or issues with my colleagues, if that's what you're asking."

"Friends or a boyfriend?"

Ah, now he would learn the truly saddest part. "Before the injury, I had lots of friends, most were associated with work. We lost touch during my recovery." She forced a smile. "There's nothing like tragedy to send the people you thought were your friends running in the other direction. It was partly my fault. I was always so strong and self-reliant. People didn't want to see the weak, needy me. Except for Sadie. She's my psychologist as well as my friend."

"Boyfriend?" he repeated. "Fiancé?"

She drew in a big breath. "There was a boyfriend. He

had asked me to marry him but I kept putting him off. Work was my top priority. About three months into my recovery, he apparently no longer had the stomach for who I'd become."

The dark expression on the investigator's face told her exactly what he thought about such a man.

Natalie shook her head. "Don't blame him, Mr. Hayes. I'm—"

"Clint," he reminded her.

"Clint," she acknowledged.

"If he cared enough to propose," Clint argued, "there's no excuse for his inability to see you through a difficult time."

"He proposed to the woman I used to be." Natalie understood the reasons all too well. Steven Vaughn had ambitious plans that didn't include a potentially disabled wife. "I'm not that person anymore. I doubt I ever will be. Part of me was lost to the injury and now my entire life is different. I don't blame him for not wanting to be a part of it. After all, if you invest in gold, silver is not a suitable substitution."

Clint studied her for a long moment before going on. "No one in your circle would have had reason to want to do you harm at the time of your accident or now?"

Natalie laughed, a self-deprecating sound. "Therein lies the true rub. Though my current short-term memory works well now, everything beyond six months ago is a very different story. So I can't answer that question because I can't remember. To my knowledge I have no enemies. My colleagues and family know of no one who gave me any real trouble in the past."

"How much of your memory did you lose?"

"Perhaps the better word is *misplaced*. The injury jumbled things up. Our lives—our memories—are stored.

Like files in a filing cabinet. Imagine if that cabinet was turned upside down, the drawers would open and those files would spill all over the floor. The contents of the files are still there, but they're hard to retrieve because now they're out of order."

"So you do remember things."

She nodded. "Yes. As my brain healed from the injury, it was like starting over. I had to relearn how to communicate, how to function, mentally as well as physically. As my vocabulary returned, I used the wrong words like saying *hands* when I meant *gloves* or *feet* when I meant *shoes*. Memories came in disorderly fragments. Most often they returned when prompted by some activity or person. It's difficult to say what I've lost when I have no idea what I had. My sister and brother remind me of childhood events and then I recall them vividly. I can look at photographs and recall almost instantly what happened. So, I suppose I've temporarily lost many things. But, so far, the memories return when triggered."

"Then someone may have caused your accident two years ago and you just don't remember."

The dark foreboding that always appeared when she spoke of the fall pressed in on her even as she shook her head. "No. I was here with my sister. There was no one else in the house. My sister and I have been over the details of that night numerous times. If you're suggesting that someone pushed me down the stairs, that isn't what happened."

"All right then, we'll focus our investigation on life since the accident."

She wanted to nod and say that was the proper course of action and yet some feeling or instinct she couldn't name urged her to look back for something she had missed. Frustration had her pushing the idea away. The hardest part of her new reality was not being able to trust her own brain to guide her 100 percent of the time. She also wanted to correct his use of *accident*. She had never been able to see what happened that way. To Natalie it was the *fall*—a moment in time that changed her life forever. A part of her wondered if her inability to see it as an accident was her mind trying to tell her something she needed to remember.

"Since you only recently returned to work, has there been a particular case that may be the root of this new trouble? Maybe someone believes they can scare you into some sort of cooperation."

"I somehow doubt that giving my two cents' worth, so to speak, on the steps that have been missed or that should be taken on other people's cases would garner that sort of attention. Considering what happened today, I doubt I'll have a position at the firm much longer."

Natalie decided that was the part that hurt the most. Losing her friends and even her so-called soul mate hadn't been the end of the world. It was losing her ability to practice law that devastated her completely. Work was the one thing that had never let her down. Being an attorney had defined her.

What did she have now?

This big old house and...not much else.

Her attention settled on the investigator watching her so closely. She hoped he could find something to explain how the man she shot suddenly disappeared other than the possibility that she really was losing her mind.

Chapter Three

Clint's first client as a private detective had been at work for an hour when he decided to make his appearance at the offices of Brenner, Rosen and Taylor.

He'd stayed with Natalie last night until her sister, April, arrived. He'd gone home afterward and done some research on Natalie's career and background. He'd discovered that one of the senior associates at Natalie's firm was Vince Farago, an old school pal of his from Samford. Clint gritted his teeth. He wondered if Natalie was aware that the man could not be trusted in any capacity. Farago was the proverbial snake in the grass.

Clint would stop at Natalie's office and check in with her after he visited with his old *friend*. He had a few questions for Farago, and frankly he intended to enjoy watching the guy squirm.

The moment he entered the posh lobby the receptionist looked up. "Good morning, sir, how may I help you?"

Another receptionist manned the ringing phones, ensuring someone was always available to greet arriving clients. The building spanned from 6th to 29th, filling the corner of the busy intersection much like New York's

Flatiron building. The lobby's glass walls looked out over the hectic pace of downtown Birmingham.

"Clint Hayes," he said. "I need a moment of Mr. Farago's time this morning."

The receptionist made a sad face. "I'm so sorry, Mr. Hayes, but Mr. Farago is completely booked today. May I set up something for you later in the week?"

Clint gave his head a shake. "Let him know I'm here. I trust he'll be able to spare a minute or two." For old time's sake, he opted not to add.

The receptionist, Kendra, ducked her head in acquiescence. "Of course, sir. Would you like a coffee or a latte while you wait?"

"I'm good."

While Kendra made the necessary call, Clint moved toward the wall of fame on the far side of the massive lobby. Dozens of photos of the partners attending various fundraisers and city events adorned the sleek beige wall that served as a canvas. Numerous framed accolades of the firm's accomplishments hung proudly among the photos. Despite his best efforts, bitterness reared its ugly head. Clint rarely allowed that old prick of defeat to needle him anymore. He turned away from the reminders of what he would never have. He was only human; the occasional regression was unavoidable.

He'd done well enough for himself. His law degree had come in handy more than once in his law enforcement career. It gave him an edge in his new venture as a private investigator. If money had been his solitary goal, he would have accepted one of the far more lucrative opportunities he had been offered during his college years.

"Mr. Hayes?"

Clint grinned, then checked the expression as he turned to Kendra. "Yes."

"Mr. Farago will see you now." She gestured to the marble-floored corridor that disappeared into the belly of the enormous building. "Take the elevator to the fourth floor and Darrius, his assistant, will be waiting for you."

With a nod, Clint fastened the top one of the two buttons on his jacket and followed the lady's directions. When he reached the fourth floor the doors slid open with a soft whoosh and revealed a more intimate, but equally luxurious lobby.

Smiling broadly, a young man, twenty-two or -three, met him in the corridor. His slim-fit charcoal-gray suit had the look and style of an Italian label way above his pay grade, suggesting he either came from money or his boss handed out nice bonuses.

"Good morning, Mr. Hayes. My name is Darrius. May I get you a refreshment?"

"No thanks." Clearly Farago's tastes hadn't changed. The assistant, a paralegal most likely, was young, handsome and no doubt hungry. A man did things when he was hungry he might not otherwise do. Clint knew this better than most.

"Very well. This way, sir."

A few steps to the right and Darrius rapped on the first door to the left and then opened it. He gifted Clint with a final smile and disappeared, closing the door behind him.

Farago got to his feet and reached across his desk. "Clint, it's been a while." They exchanged a quick handshake.

"I hear you're scheduled to make partner before the year is out." Clint had nudged a few contacts last night in addition to his internet research. Farago was on his way up at this esteemed firm. Good for him. He'd done his time. Going on eight years now. Still, Clint couldn't help wondering how far his old *friend* had gone this time to ensure his next step up the corporate ladder. He seriously doubted this leopard had changed his spots.

Farago gestured to the chair in front of his desk and settled back into his own. "It's a carrot they dangle when you reach a certain level. Time will tell, I guess."

Clint grunted an acknowledgement.

"So." Farago leaned back in his leather chair. "What brings you to see me after all these years?"

There were many things Clint could have said—payback, for example—but he elected to keep the threats to himself. He had learned that all things come back around in time. Karma truly was a bitch.

As if Farago had read his mind, he fidgeted a bit. Clint could almost swear he saw a sheen of sweat forming on the man's forehead.

"I have a few questions—between old friends—about your colleague, Natalie Drummond."

Farago lifted his head and said, "Ah. I'm certain you're aware, of course, the firm requires we sign confidentiality agreements."

"No doubt." Clint stared straight into his eyes. "I'm equally certain you understand I wouldn't be here if it wasn't essential. So, why don't we cut to the chase? I need information and you *need* to give it to me."

The flush of anger climbed from the collar of Farago's crisp white shirt and quickly spread across his face. "I see."

"I'm glad we understand each other." Clint had no desire to waste time or energy debating the issue.

Farago's glare was lethal. "What is it you want to ask?"

"You've worked with Natalie for the past four or so years. Until her accident had she suffered any professional issues?"

A haughty chuckle and a roll of the eyes warned that whatever Farago had to say it wouldn't be complimentary. "She had a clerkship with one of our esteemed state court justices before coming on board. Some of us had to do our time performing grunt work here at the firm, but not Natalie. The Drummond name and the recommendation of the justice ensured she started with the cream of the crop cases." Another of those unpleasant smirks. "The rumor was, before her accident she was about to become the youngest partner in the firm." He exhaled a big sigh. "I'll never understand why; she wasn't even that good."

Clint clenched his jaw to the count of three to hold his temper, then asked, "Tell me about the cases she worked in the months leading up to her injury."

Farago made a face. "Let's see. The White case—a mercy killing."

Clint remembered the one. An eighty-year-old husband allowed his dying wife to end her suffering with a bottle of the opiates prescribed by her oncologist. The video they made with the wife's iPhone proved the key piece of evidence that turned the tide with the jury. The woman made her own choice, the only thing the husband did was open the bottle since her arthritic hands couldn't manage the feat.

"Other than that one, there was the Thompson versus Rison Medical Center—a medical malpractice case." Farago turned his palms up. "Those are the primary ones I recall without prowling through databases."

Thompson was the case Clint wanted to hear about. The firm represented the medical center. "Thompson versus Rison Medical Center didn't go down the way anyone expected. Your client was damned lucky."

Farago shrugged. "I don't know. Lots of people claim injuries or trouble with medical facilities or their employees; those claims aren't always based on fact. Emotion can become the center of the case, making it doubly difficult for the defendant's attorneys."

"There's no other case that comes to mind?" Clint pressed.

Farago shook his head. "As I recall, those two pretty much took up her time that year. Why all the questions about Natalie? Is she being investigated?"

Clint ignored his questions. "Her accident was a lucky break for you. You took over her spot on the legal team and the win for Rison Medical Center put *you* on the partners' radar."

Another nonchalant shrug lifted Farago's shoulders. "The win would have put anyone involved on the partners' radar. It was a *huge* lawsuit. We performed above expectations and saved our client a fortune."

"The rumor mill had Thompson pegged as the winner until the bitter end," Clint reminded him. Clint recalled well the day the jury returned with the verdict, he'd been damned surprised. It wouldn't be the first time a sharp legal team had pulled a client's fat out of the fire. Whatever his history with Farago, the man was a good attorney. He just wasn't always a good man.

Clint retrieved a business card that provided his name and cell number. "Call me if you think of anything interesting to pass along on the subject."

Farago studied the card. "You aren't with the BPD anymore?"

Clint smiled. "I decided to come to work with my old boss in her private investigations agency. I'm sure you know Jess Harris Burnett." He stood. "We're taking on the cases no one else can solve." He gestured to the door. "Which office is Natalie's?"

The look on Farago's face was priceless. His eyes

bulged. His jaw fell slack. It was almost worth the loss of the career Farago had stolen from Clint a decade ago.

But not quite.

6:50 p.m.

NATALIE WATCHED THE man driving as they moved through the darkening streets. Dusk came a little earlier every day, reminding her that the year was barreling toward an end. It didn't seem possible that she'd lost so much of the past twenty-four months. She didn't want to lose any more. She wanted her life back.

"You don't have to stay with me every minute," she announced to the silence. Neither of them had spoken since leaving the parking garage. She'd worked well beyond the number of hours allowed by her medical release and Clint had insisted on taking her to dinner. "I'm quite capable of taking care of myself, the incident in my kitchen yesterday morning notwithstanding."

Clint smiled. She liked his smile. He was quite attractive for a PI. She'd had her fair share of dealings with private investigators. Most of whom had been older and far less easy on the eyes. In addition to attractive, Clint was well educated and his instincts appeared quite good. He wasn't the only one doing research. She'd done quite a bit herself last night after he left. Clint Hayes possessed a law degree from Samford. He'd graduated with highest honors, but then he'd turned to law enforcement. There was a story there; she just hadn't found it yet. He dressed particularly well. The suit was no off-the-rack light wool ready-for-wear. Neither was the shirt or the shoes. When did private investigators start earning such a high salary?

"Feel free," he glanced at her as he made the turn into the restaurant, "to say whatever is on your mind."

A blush heated her cheeks. She doubted he had any idea of what precisely was on her mind. She might as well see just how good his perceptive powers were. "You went to law school, yet chose a different career path. I wondered what happened to divert your course."

He parked in the crowded lot and shut off the engine. The interior of the car fell into near darkness with nothing more than a distant streetlamp reaching unsuccessfully through the night. When he turned to her it was difficult to read his face, but his voice when he spoke telegraphed a clear message.

"I made the decision I needed to make. I don't think about it and I don't talk about it. Next question?"

The cool tone was so unexpected that Natalie's heart beat a little faster. "I apologize for making you uncomfortable. I was merely curious."

"I'm very good at what I do, Ms. Drummond. Very good. I'll spend every moment with you and on your case until we find the truth. But—"

Her ability to breathe failed her.

"I am not here to satisfy your curiosity about *me*."

Before she could find her voice, he emerged from the car and walked around to her side. Natalie wasn't sure whether to feel incensed or chastised. When he opened the door she finally remembered to unbuckle her seat belt.

She exited the car. He shut the door and, from all appearances, that would have been the end of it.

"Wait."

He turned back to her and with the soft glow of the restaurant lights she could see his expression well enough to know he wasn't angry...it was something else. Had her question injured him somehow? She blinked and wrestled with the best way to handle the situation. Since her injury she rarely grabbed on to the right emotions much less the proper words in a timely manner. She had taught herself to resist emotion and to react with the cool calm for which she had once been known in the courtroom.

"I apologize for asking such a personal question. I'm afraid the injury has left me with far fewer filters than I once possessed. I hope you'll accept my apology."

He nodded, his only consolation to acceptance. "I had dinner here last week. The salmon is incredible."

"Does your expense account cover this restaurant?" The words were out of her mouth before Natalie could stop them. She squeezed her eyes shut and shook her head.

Clint touched her arm and she opened her eyes. "This one is on me," he assured her, his tone the deep, warm one she had grown to associate with him.

Before she could argue about who would pay, he ushered her through the entrance and she decided to stop trying so hard...at least for the next hour or so.

Southwood Road
9:20 p.m.

As HE HAD last evening, Clint insisted on going into the house first. Her sister had phoned to say she was coming to spend the night but she would be late. Natalie wanted to tell her not to bother but she wouldn't pretend she wasn't terrified at the idea of being alone at night after the ordeal with the intruder. The idea made little sense since it had been broad daylight when she shot the man in her kitchen.

You did shoot him...didn't you?

The idea that she was second-guessing herself again after finally, finally reaching the place where she felt she'd regained her confidence made her sick to her stomach.

Clint paused at the bottom of the staircase and she

raised her hand. "No need to check upstairs. The security system was armed. I'm sure it's fine."

"I wouldn't be able to sleep tonight if I wasn't thorough."

Natalie nodded, surrendering. "I probably wouldn't, either," she confessed.

Side by side they moved up the staircase. She was never able to climb or descend the stairs without admiring the painting of her family as it had once been. Life had felt so safe and so happy then. It seemed unfair she'd lost both her parents before she was thirty. Particularly since they had both been healthy and vibrant. If they were still alive, what would they think of Natalie and her sister? Would her father be proud Heath had been so successful following in his footsteps? Certainly April had become every bit the fund-raising and society queen their mother had been. Natalie sometimes regretted that her sister had not chosen a career path, but in truth what she did was immensely important to the community.

"You grew up in this house?" Clint asked as they reached the landing.

She nodded. "My grandfather built it. He and my grandmother lived here until they died. My parents did, as well. I suppose I will, too." She caught herself before she suggested it was her turn for a personal question. Not a good idea. His assignment necessitated the asking of questions.

"My father died when I was at Samford," he said, somehow understanding her need for reciprocity. "My mother remarried and moved to Arizona a few years ago."

"You miss them? I still miss mine."

He checked the first of the half dozen bedrooms as well as each of the en suite baths. Just when she was certain he didn't intend to answer, he said, "I do. My mother calls a couple of times a month, but she rarely gets home anymore. I should visit her more often but I don't think Oscar likes me."

He chuckled and the sound made Natalie smile. He had a nice laugh for a man who preferred not to talk about his early career decisions.

Silence lapsed between them as they moved through room after room. He took extra care with the upstairs den and the balcony that overlooked the rear gardens. The French doors were locked, the security monitor in place. She and her sister had played here as children. In the gardens, too; but not without the nanny. The Drummond name and money had always been a target.

When they reached Natalie's bedroom, she touched his arm. "Please, ignore what you see in my private space."

His dark eyes held hers for a long beat. "I understand the need for personal privacy, Natalie. You can trust me with your secrets."

As foolish as it sounded, she did. Perhaps her need for his understanding was because his academic background was so similar to hers. If he believed her…then maybe she wasn't losing her mind.

The room was neat and freshly cleaned. Suzanna was a perfectionist and perhaps was afflicted with more than a little OCD. On the table next to Natalie's side of the king-size bed were the first of the many notes to herself. Those on the bedside table reminded her to shut off the alarm and to plug and unplug her cell phone as well as to put it into the pocket of whatever jacket, sweater or coat she would wear for the day.

Each drawer of the room's furnishings was labeled with what would be found stored in that space. In the closet her clothes were arranged in groupings so that whatever she needed for the day was together. No rifling through blouses or shoes and trying to match. April helped her keep her wardrobe arranged. The first time Natalie left the house with a mismatched ensemble, her sister was mortified and insisted on ensuring it never happened again. Natalie supposed it was necessary since her appearance reflected on the firm as well as the family name. April reminded Natalie that she'd had impeccable taste before the fall. Natalie still liked the same things, she simply felt confused at times when she attempted to put together an ensemble.

One of many things she missed about her old self. Thankfully the occurrences of confusion were becoming more rare, or they had been until the intruder. Most likely she would be fine without all the notes to remind her. She simply hadn't found the courage to do away with them yet. *Soon*, she promised herself. Her real hesitation was the fear of failure. As long as the notes were there, she didn't have to face her potential inability to work without them.

Though her walk-in closet was quite generously sized, somehow Clint's broad shoulders and tall, lean frame overwhelmed the intimate space. It was then that his aftershave or cologne teased her senses once more. She had noticed the subtle scent in the car. Something earthy and organically spicy as if it were as natural to his body as his smooth, tanned skin. She was immensely grateful she hadn't lost her sense of smell. Many who suffered TBIs weren't so fortunate.

He turned and she jumped. "Sorry." She took a deep breath and followed him into the en suite. There were more notes here. The ones that told her in what order to do her nightly ritual, those that reminded her of where things were stored. Like the others, she didn't rely on them as much as she had before. This time when he turned to her she felt the weight of his sympathy.

There was nothing since the injury that hurt her more— not the ongoing healing, not the physical therapy, not even the endless hours of analyzing by the shrinks—than the looks of pity in the eyes of anyone who learned the full scope of her loss.

"The house is clear. I'll stay until your sister arrives."

She wanted to argue. Damn it, she really did. She wanted to tell him in no uncertain terms that she was perfectly fine and capable of taking care of herself as she always had been. Except...she wasn't so sure of that anymore. "Thank you."

As they descended the stairs, he said, "Coffee would be good."

With monumental effort she smiled. "I am very good with a coffee machine."

He paused before taking the next step down. "I have a feeling you're very good at many things, Natalie."

Whether he truly meant the words or not, she appreciated the effort. No one had given her a compliment in a very long time.

Chapter Four

11:45 p.m.

Natalie woke with a start, her breath coming in short, frantic bursts as the images from her dreams faded. Sweat dampened her skin. She threw back the blanket and shivered as the cool air swept over her damp body.

She tried to make sense of the vivid, broken images. Pages and pages of briefs or reports rifling past…the words flying from the paper, turning to something gray—like ash or smoke. The empty pages fell into a heap and ignited, the flames growing higher and higher, until she could feel the burn.

Natalie sat up on the edge of the bed. She stared at the clock radio on the bedside table, the time mocking her. She hadn't slept soundly through the night without the aid of medication after the fall. Finally, six months ago she'd managed the feat without the pills. Much to her frustration, the dark whispers that started month before last had taken that accomplishment away from her. As if her subconscious was somehow rutted and the wheels of her mind were destined to slide off into that same rut, she woke at this time every night. A scarce few minutes before the grandfather clock downstairs started the deep, familiar dong of the midnight hour.

Had April come in without waking her? Natalie had intended to stay up to make sure her sister arrived safely, but she'd fallen asleep on her bed still dressed in her work clothes. Surely April was here and Clint had gone home. The idea that he might still be sitting in his car on the street made her cringe. The wood floor was cool beneath her bare feet as she crossed the dark room. If her sister was here and asleep there was no need to wake her. Maybe Natalie would be lucky and this would be one of those nights she was able to get a few more hours of sleep before dawn.

The hall outside her door was as dark as her room. She slipped toward the far end to the room her sister had used as a child. Growing up, Natalie had slept in the one directly across the hall. For reasons she couldn't explain, after the fall she no longer felt safe in that room. The nurse and April had moved her into their parents' room. April insisted it was past time they'd stored their parents' things anyway. From her bed, Natalie remembered watching her sister oversee the packing. At the time, Natalie had to be reminded over and over what April was doing. She hadn't been able to hang on to a thought for more than a few minutes. Her memory as well as her ability to function had been in pieces—a part here or there worked, but none operated together.

Downstairs the chiming of the hour began, the deep sound echoing all through the silent house. As Natalie reached her sister's bedroom the sound of voices stopped her. Natalie held her breath and listened. The voices were too low—whispers almost—to understand, but one was definitely April. The tinkling of her soft laugher was unmistakable. The other voice was deeper, definitely male.

Had David decided to stay overnight as well?

Funny, all these weeks she'd been hearing those whispered voices and not once had she been able to identify one of them. Natalie turned and made her way back toward her own room. Though she and David had never really been friends, he had visited Natalie at the hospital and then the rehab facility almost as often as April. Since she'd been home he had ensured the gardener had everything he needed. She supposed she should try and think better of him.

"Not in this lifetime," she muttered. David's arrogance and distance were two things she distinctly remembered about the past.

The incessant beep of the alarm warned that someone had opened the front door. Natalie's pulse stumbled, then started to race. She had locked the door, hadn't she? Obviously she'd set the alarm. Had April remembered to set it when she arrived? Natalie darted toward her bedroom before she remembered the gun was no longer there. It was missing along with the man she shot. Her cell was downstairs in her purse.

Fear burned through her veins.

Laughter followed by April's voice echoed up from the entry hall. "I'm here. Night. Night. I'll be home in the morning."

The sound of the front door closing and the alarm being reset had Natalie turning to stare toward her sister's bedroom. If her sister was downstairs just coming in…

Natalie's heart sank. Heath was right. She was hallucinating again.

Oxmoor Road
Wednesday, September 21, 9:05 a.m.

DR. SADIE MORROW considered the confession long enough without saying anything to have Natalie ready to scream in frustration. Last night was the first time since the voices began that Natalie could unequivocally confirm that she had been dreaming or hallucinating. She had heard April's voice in her room when April couldn't possibly have been there. Was she having some sort of breakdown? Had her decision to return to work prompted a downward spiral? She had no real cases of her own. There was no true pressure related to her work at this point. How could it be too much stress?

Was her career over? The doctors, including the one assessing her right now, had assured Natalie that she would be able to return to work. She might never be exactly the same as she was before, but she would be able to have a life and a career. Emotion burned in her eyes and she wanted to scream.

"Perhaps," Sadie announced, breaking the tension, "you were sleep walking. What you heard may have been a dream."

This was the assessment Sadie had stood by since the first time Natalie mentioned the voices. "It didn't feel like a dream," Natalie argued.

"The vivid ones rarely do. It's very possible you were asleep and the sound of your sister's voice when she came in woke you."

This was the second day this week that Natalie had shown up at Sadie's office for an emergency consultation. Her friend had other patients. Natalie felt guilty taking up her time like this, but the fear that she was losing her mind overrode all other concerns.

"I was doing fine until I went back to work." The conclusion hung like a millstone around her neck. What was she going to do with her life if she couldn't have her career? What client would want to be represented by an attorney struggling with the after effects of a TBI?

"Natalie, you've been a textbook case in success. Every

aspect of your recovery has been the most optimistic of outcomes. This is a bump along the path, that's true. However, I'm confident whatever is triggering these events will pass. I don't think you need to be overly concerned at this point."

Natalie laughed, the sound sad. "You do realize that's my high school BFF talking, don't you?" She shook her head. "I mean, you are the only person who believes there is a medical explanation for the event that happened in my kitchen. I still believe I shot an intruder with my father's gun while the police are convinced I'm a nutcase."

Sadie stood and came around her desk to sit next to Natalie. She took Natalie's hands in hers. "You have to trust me when I say I do not believe you're having a breakdown. Whatever is going on, there is another explanation. New memories may be trying to surface. Your mind may be misinterpreting the memories."

Natalie sighed. "I didn't tell April what happened last night. I just hurried back to my room and pretended to be asleep when she checked on me." The embarrassing emotion she tried so hard to hold back burned like fire in her eyes. She did not want to cry. She needed to be strong. She wanted to move on from this.

"It's not necessary to tell anyone else about this, Natalie. Let's just see how it goes. I'm completely convinced we're dealing with memories. The shooting in your kitchen may be a memory from a case you once worked or studied. What you heard last night could have been a memory from when you and April were teenagers."

Natalie dabbed at her eyes with the back of her hand. "All right. That's the theory I'll operate under for now."

Sadie gave her a hug. "Now, tell me about the man in the lobby. He is incredibly handsome."

"Clint Hayes. He's the PI I hired to figure out what

happened to the guy I shot." The memory of the sound of the bullet discharging from the barrel made her flinch. Had the intruder taken her father's weapon? It was the only explanation. She had the weapon in her hand and she fired it. The .38 had been loaded. Her father had kept it that way. As girls she and April had been lectured many times on how that drawer in her father's bedside table was off limits. Their father had explained over and over the reason he kept the weapon next to his bed and their responsibility for staying away from it. He'd put the fear of God in them at an early age. Neither of them had ever touched the drawer much less the weapon for fear of their father's wrath. As it turned out, the weapon had been outfitted with a trigger guard. It wasn't until after her parents' deaths that Natalie had discovered and removed the guard.

"So, he's your bodyguard, too?"

The twinkle in Sadie's blue eyes was teasing. Natalie managed a smile. "I guess he is. He takes his work very seriously." And he was handsome. He was also nice, though he did apparently have a few skeletons of his own.

"I'm glad you hired him." Sadie patted her hand. "Better to be safe than sorry."

Natalie stood. "I should go so you can get back to your scheduled patients. Your secretary is going to start locking the door when she sees me coming."

Sadie dismissed the idea with a wave of her hand. "Nonsense. Now, I expect to hear from you if there are any more unsettling episodes."

"Count on it." Natalie made her way back to the lobby. As if he sensed her coming, Clint set the magazine he held aside and pushed to his feet.

How was it that she suddenly felt safer just knowing he was waiting for her?

CLINT WALKED NATALIE to her car. Like yesterday, she insisted on driving herself about. Reasonable considering she'd only been cleared to drive again four months ago. No one appreciated the everyday personal freedoms until they were lost. Though he had never suffered an injury like the one Natalie struggled to overcome, he was more than a little familiar with the battle to conquer life's stumbling blocks.

She hit the fob to unlock the doors and he opened the driver's side for her. "You're headed to the office?"

"Yes." She hesitated before settling behind the steering wheel. "Will you be coming as well?"

Clint had planned to meet Lori and Harper for coffee to discuss Natalie's case once she was settled in at her office. Maybe he still would, but the distinct note of hope in her question gave him pause. "I have a meeting, but—"

"Really, you don't need to watch me every moment." She arranged her lips into a smile that failed to reach her eyes. "I'm fairly certain no one is going to attack me at my office. Besides, if the police are correct in their conclusions my concerns are wholly rooted in my imagination."

She turned to get into the car and he touched her arm, stopping her though she didn't face him. "My meeting can wait. Why don't you tell me what happened to bring you here this morning? The appointment wasn't on your calendar."

He'd skimmed her calendar yesterday. Her next scheduled appointment with Dr. Morrow was two weeks away. From the moment she greeted him at her front door this morning he'd recognized something was off.

"Last night I… I think I started hallucinating again." She turned to him and the fear and pain in her expression tugged hard at his protective instincts. "I haven't done that in nearly a year."

"The office can wait. Let's go back to your home. I want you to walk me through exactly what you saw and heard last night."

She squeezed her eyes shut for a moment. "Dr. Morrow said it may have been a dream. But…I can't trust my judgment."

"Your judgment seems fine at work all day and all evening with me. Why is it that all these strange events only occur when you're at home alone?"

Her response was slow in coming. "I don't know. I guess I feel more relaxed at home." She shook her head. "Or because that's where the fall happened. Two psychiatrists as well as Sadie have analyzed me and they all seem to agree on one thing: my brain is trying to recover the pieces and the pieces don't always fall into their proper place leading to misinterpretations. I can't trust…*myself*."

Clint resisted the urge to take her in his arms and comfort her. Not a smart move. The hair on the back of his neck suddenly stood on end. He glanced at the street, surveyed the block. The distinct feeling they were being watched nudged him. "Let's talk about this in a more private setting."

She nodded and climbed into her car. He closed the door and headed back to his Audi. He'd done some reading on TBI patients and he couldn't argue that Natalie might very well be mistaking dreams for reality or hallucinating, but his gut definitely disagreed with the conclusion.

As he followed her onto the street, Clint considered the reasons someone might want to hurt Natalie. Her parents had been gone for more than three years when the fall down the stairs occurred. It seemed unlikely to him that a sibling would have waited so long to take action if the motive was the family estate. No, his money was on her professional life—specifically the Thompson versus Rison Medical Center case.

Until Natalie was hospitalized, the case was leaning toward a win for Thompson, which would certainly have had the firm under serious pressure to turn it around. Once she was out of the picture, the tide quickly turned. Clint had no proof of his working theory but it was far too large a coincidence to ignore. Though he'd had to walk away from the law career he'd expected to have, he'd maintained a few good contacts. He had never been able to resist keeping up with the David and Goliath cases. Seeing the underdog win made him very happy.

Natalie's car suddenly swerved. Tension snapped through Clint. She barreled off the road into the lot of a supermarket, crashing broadside into a parked car.

His pulse hammering, Clint made the turn and skidded to a stop next to her car. He jumped out and rushed to her. Thank God no one was in the other vehicle. Natalie sat upright behind the steering wheel. The deflated air bag sagged from the steering wheel. The injuries she may have sustained from the air bag deploying ticked off in his brain.

He tried to open the door but it was locked. He banged on the window. "Natalie! Are you all right?"

She turned and stared up at him. Her face was flushed red, abrasions already darkening on her skin. His heart rammed mercilessly against his sternum as she slowly hit the unlock button. He yanked the door open and crouched down to get a closer look at her.

"Are you hurt?" he demanded.

"I'm not sure." She took a deep breath as if she'd only just remembered to breathe. "I don't understand what happened. I was driving along and the air bag suddenly burst from the steering wheel." She reached for the steering wheel and then drew back, uncertain what to do with her hands. "I don't understand," she repeated.

"I'm calling for help." Clint made the call to 9-1-1 and then he called his friend, Lieutenant Chet Harper. Every instinct cautioned Clint that Natalie was wrong about not being able to trust herself.

There was someone else—someone very close to her—that she shouldn't trust. He intended to keep her safe until he identified that threat.

Chapter Five

University of Alabama Hospital, 2nd Avenue
1:15 p.m.

"Good news, Ms. Drummond."

The ER doctor who looked ridiculously young to be a doctor and seriously disheveled as if he'd worked a twenty-four-hour shift shuffled into the room with Natalie's chart. She was certainly ready for some good news. Her face and chest were sore from the impact of the damned air bag.

How on earth had this happened?

"You're going to be sore and bruised, but no fractures. Your neuro screening was great. You're a lucky lady."

Natalie knew she should feel lucky, yet she didn't. "Thank you, Doctor. Does that mean I can leave now?"

She had spent more than her fair share of time in hospitals and she had no desire to stay in this one another minute. She picked up her jacket and pulled it on, groaning in the process. He wasn't kidding about her being sore. She felt as if she'd had a collision with...another car. Funny thing was, she had. Except the other car hadn't been moving. She'd read briefs on legal cases related to air bags malfunctioning; she just hadn't expected it to happen to her. Wasn't that the way it always turned out?

"As soon as the nurse brings your release papers, you're

free to go." The doctor flashed her a weary smile as he headed for the door. "Try to keep it between the lines."

"Thank you. I'll do my best." When he'd gone, she blew out a big breath. How was she supposed to keep her car between the lines if the air bag got in her way? She was no mechanic but she understood the air bag deployment wasn't supposed to happen. Events like this morning's were the sort that resulted in lawsuits.

The car had been a gift to herself just a year before the fall. She'd only started driving again four months ago. The vehicle scarcely had ten thousand miles on it. She should call the manufacturer and see about any recalls.

A soft rap on the door drew her attention there as Clint entered the room. "The doctor tells me you're ready to go."

"Beyond ready," she assured him.

He offered his hand. She felt somehow comforted by the small gesture as she placed her hand in his and climbed down from the examining table. Thankfully the nurse arrived with the necessary documents for her escape. As they exited the ER lobby she dug for her sunglasses, but remembered she had been wearing them when she crashed. They were likely still in her car, possibly broken.

"Do you know which towing company took my car?"

Clint opened the front passenger-side door of his car. "I had it towed to the lab."

Natalie held her hand above her eyes to block the sun so she could see his face better. "What lab?"

"The BPD's forensic lab, for testing. We need to understand what caused the air bag to deploy."

A stone-cold certainty settled in the pit of her stomach. "You think someone tampered with it."

"I do."

"My God." She dropped into the passenger seat for fear she'd fall if she remained standing. Could someone have really done such a thing? She had consoled herself with the idea that the intruder in her home was likely there to steal, but deep inside she feared it was more personal. Was it possible that Clint really believed her?

He was sliding behind the steering wheel before she realized he'd moved. "You really do think someone wants to harm me? That it's not my imagination?"

"Isn't that why you hired me?"

She stared into his dark eyes. She'd been so determined to prove she wasn't losing her mind and that she really had shot someone she hadn't stopped to consider what she truly believed about the intruder.

"I don't know." She pressed a hand over her mouth to hide the way her lips trembled. Of course she knew. She was not naive. Of course this was about hurting her—possibly killing her. Why would anyone want to harm her?

Those dark whispers she had tried so hard to close out just before she drifted off to sleep each night these past eight or so weeks nudged her now, echoing deep in her mind. She closed her eyes and let them come. Laughter, soft, feminine…then the raised voices—a man and a woman. She couldn't understand the words or identify the voices. Was it a real memory? Something from before her fall? Something from childhood?

The blare of a car horn snapped her eyes open. Air filled her lungs in a rush before she realized she'd been holding her breath. Natalie blinked a couple of times to clear the fog. The doctors had explained that pieces of memory from different times often tried to blend, making any memories surfacing more confusing than anything else.

God knew she'd heard plenty of arguments. Clients argued. Colleagues argued. This felt more personal. She and Steven had argued. Maybe the voice was hers. She frowned. It could be a memory of one of their arguments.

The laughter could be hers or April's. The sounds reminded her of what she'd heard last night. So maybe the laughter was April from years ago when they'd both lived at home and April had sneaked more than one boyfriend into her bedroom. It was a miracle their parents never caught her. With her sister staying in her old room it was more than possible those old memories had been triggered.

Natalie had never had a boyfriend she liked enough to risk disappointing her father. Then again, perhaps that was why she was alone right now. She pushed away the idea. Feeling sorry for herself wasn't going to solve this mystery and it certainly wouldn't help her recovery.

As Clint made the turn onto Southwood Road, Natalie said, "I should call for a rental car." She had no idea how long her car would be at the lab and then there would be the repairs. Maybe she should just buy a new one. She shuddered at the idea that someone may have tampered with her car.

"You won't need one for a while."

She waited until he'd parked in front of her home to say, "I don't intend to stay holed up in this house. I can't…do that." As big as her home was, the walls had begun to close in on her well before she had been able to return to work. As long as she had half a brain and the ability to walk she was not staying in the house 24/7 ever again.

When she reached for the door, he put his hand on her arm. "Wherever you go, I go, so I might as well drive."

She wanted to argue but some self-preservation instinct prevented her from doing so.

"This is only temporary, Natalie. We'll get to the bottom of the problem and then you'll have your life back."

The roar of an engine and the squealing of tires had them both turning to see who had charged into the driveway.

April.

"I should have called her." Natalie's sister had a way of hearing the news before it was broadcast anywhere.

April emerged from her Mercedes in a huff and stormed across the cobblestone. "What happened? Why didn't you call me?"

"I'm fine, April. Really."

April glared at Clint. "You don't have my number, Mr. Hayes?"

While Clint poured on the charm and added April to his contacts list, Natalie watched her sister. She pretended to be angry that no one had called her, but she was actually terrified. April's slim body trembled and she hugged herself. Natalie bit back the emotions threatening. Her sister was so opposite from her. She'd bleached her dark hair blond when they were teenagers and she'd kept it that way. April had claimed it looked better with her blue eyes. They had the same blue eyes. Before she'd bleached her hair people had often asked if they were twins. Except Natalie had always been the frumpier one. A little heavier and a lot more conservative when it came to fashion. April had always needed to set herself apart.

"Why don't we go inside?" Clint asked when April continued her tirade despite his efforts to calm her.

"Just tell me what it is you're doing to help my sister," April demanded.

"April," Natalie warned.

"As soon as we have the forensic report back on the car we'll know more."

April stared at him in disbelief. "Forensic? What does that mean?"

Natalie reached for her sister but she held up a hand. "No," April insisted, "I want to know what he's talking about."

"I believe," Clint said, drawing her attention back to him, "someone tampered with the air bag."

April swung her stunned glare to Natalie. "Is he serious?"

"Yes." There was no point trying to keep the truth from her sister. "Our current working theory is that the intruder and the accident are connected."

"There was no intruder!" April planted her hands on her hips. "You're only hurting yourself going down this path, Natalie." Her sister shook her head. "I'm calling David. He'll know what to do."

Natalie felt taken aback. "Is that a threat of some sort?" It felt exactly like a threat.

April appeared startled. "Of course it isn't a threat. I'm… I'm just worried about you and I don't trust him." She arrowed a contemptuous look at Clint. "I know about you, Mr. Hayes. My sister may not be herself just now, but she's no fool. She'll see through you soon enough."

With that profound statement April strode away.

Natalie turned to Clint. "What's she talking about?"

"We should go inside."

Numb, Natalie followed him.

If her life felt upside down before, it was totally ripped apart now.

CLINT SAT ON the sofa and waited for Natalie to begin her interrogation. She'd insisted on making tea after he'd done his walk-through of the house. The proverbial wait for the water to boil had felt like forever. Eleven years. He'd put this business behind him more than a decade ago. He'd made up his mind he didn't care and he'd walked away. He'd applied to the police academy and moved on. All those years as a detective had driven home the point that stuff happened and sometimes good people got the short end of the stick.

Natalie returned her cup to its dainty little saucer. The delicate china with its pink rose pattern reminded him of her vulnerability. The cup would shatter if dropped despite its ability to withstand being fired at thousands of degrees. Natalie Drummond might be tough as nails but she had her breaking point and someone was pushing her further and further in that direction.

"What did April mean when she said she knew about you?"

There were some secrets a man couldn't keep forever no matter how hard he tried. No matter how badly he didn't want to look back. The only surprising part was that April had discovered his secret. There were only a handful of people who knew that part of his history. Farago, the bastard, had likely put in a call to the sister. One of these days he was going to get his. Clint hoped he was around to watch.

"It has something to do with why you chose not to pursue a career as an attorney," Natalie suggested.

She'd asked him about that before and he'd done what he always did, he'd brushed her off. Making that leap now was the reasonable route to take. "It does."

"Is it relevant to my case?"

"No." Was she offering a way out of this discussion?

She nodded. "I see. Well." Shoulders squared, she picked up her cup. "I don't see any reason to discuss the matter."

He wanted to be relieved but he understood this would not be the last time the issue came back to haunt him. "Why put off the inevitable? April feels the issue is relevant to my trustworthiness."

Natalie lifted her chin. "But I don't. Despite recent events, my sister is not my keeper."

The seed of doubt had been planted. Clint was well aware how this worked. The subject might feel irrelevant at the moment but in the middle of the night when she couldn't sleep it would nag at her.

"My father worked in a factory," he began. "My mother operated a daycare in our house for the neighborhood children. Together they made enough to keep a roof over our heads and to fall above the income level for any sort of government aid. There was no money for college, much less law school." He resisted the urge to stand and pace. "I was a smart kid. I didn't get the kind of scholarships the athletes received, but it was enough to get me in the door. The rest, however, was up to me."

"So you worked your way through school," Natalie offered. "There's no shame in hard work. College is expensive. Law school is even more costly."

She couldn't hide the automatic guilt she clearly felt for growing up rich when she heard stories like his. No matter, when she heard the rest that guilt would shift into outrage and disgust. What the hell?

"I worked as an *escort*." He figured she would comprehend the full implications of the statement without him going into graphic detail.

She sipped her tea, cleared her throat and took a breath. "Do you mean—?"

"I mean exactly what you think I mean. The Alabama State Bar used its morals clause to preclude my admission to the bar based on my character and that was that."

"You did this for...?"

If she blinked too hard the frozen expression on her face would no doubt shatter. Clint almost laughed. He was a damned good investigator. Whether he'd delivered pizza or pleasure during college should be of no consequence to the job he had to do now. "Five years."

The duration of his early career startled her and the dainty cup almost slipped from her slim fingers. "I see."

No. She didn't see at all. There were other things he could tell her, like the fact that he earned more in his first year than the average attorney did in his first four. He'd had a high-end operation, not a street corner. His clients had been the rich and famous of Alabama. By the time he hit law school he had invested widely and wisely. He could retire now, if he chose, on the investments he'd made. None of that would matter. He saw the horror and disbelief in her eyes.

He stood, fury and frustration beating in his pulse, and buttoned his jacket. "You have my number. Let me know if you still require my services. If not, I'll ask the boss to send someone else."

"Sit down, Clint."

Whatever hesitation she'd felt before, there was none in her blue eyes now. He, on the other hand, hesitated. He wasn't apologizing for his past.

"Please," she added.

He ripped the jacket button loose once more and sat. His boss, he still had to work at reminding himself not to call Jess chief, would be the first one to say he didn't care for taking orders. He preferred giving them. That said, he wanted this new venture to work out for all concerned— including the lady staring at him right now. Whether she realized it or not, she needed him.

"I don't care what you did to survive in college. We all did things we might not have done at any other time in our lives." She smiled. "Kudos to you. Law school was tough as hell and still you made it. The State Bar's decision was unfair and antiquated in my opinion. If you ever decide to fight that decision, I would be more than happy to represent you."

Clint did laugh then. "I appreciate the offer, but I'm completely satisfied with my current career."

She drew in a deep breath and immediately pressed a hand to her chest. He imagined she'd be damned sore for a few days. Did she understand she could have been killed in that crash? She could have killed someone else?

"What do we do now? You said my car is at the lab."

"Ricky Vernon, one of the forensic guys at the lab, is sort of a computer geek. He's the best. He'll be able to tell us why the air bag launched prematurely. If the perp left prints or any other evidence, he'll find that, too. If we find evidence a crime was committed, Lieutenant Harper—he leads the BPD's major crimes unit—will give us the full support of his team."

"How long will the lab take?"

"Harper put a rush on the analysis. Vernon will probably work all night if necessary." Clint had seen the guy pull an all-nighter more than once. Damn he missed the team, but working with Jess was where he wanted to be.

A knock on the open door drew Clint's attention there. Suzanna, the housekeeper, stood in the open doorway, her bag draped over her shoulder. "Ms. Natalie, Leonard and I are done for the day unless you need anything else."

Natalie smiled, clearly fond of the older lady. "We're fine, thank you."

"I left chicken salad in the fridge." She turned to Clint. "You take good care of her."

He smiled. Suzanna and her husband had worked for the Drummond family for three decades. "You can count on it, ma'am."

When the housekeeper was gone, Natalie stood. "We should eat."

Clint pushed to his feet. "You go ahead. I'd like to have a look at the garage."

Someone who had access to her home was screwing with Natalie's life. No matter how long the housekeeper and her gardener husband had worked for the family, everyone was a suspect. Even Natalie's sister.

Especially her sister.

Chapter Six

Athens-Flatts Building, 2nd Avenue
7:30 p.m.

The elevator door opened and Natalie's jaw dropped. "Wow. What a view."

Before Clint even invited her to step out of the elevator that opened into the foyer of his condo, she was already walking toward the incredible wall of glass that looked out over downtown Birmingham.

She turned to the man watching her so closely as if he feared her disapproval. "This is the penthouse." She shook her head. "I've always wondered who lived here." She laughed. "Just wow." The view was absolutely amazing.

"It came up for sale last year. The couple who owned it were getting divorced and neither wanted the other to end up with the best party spot in the city."

Natalie lifted her gaze to his. "You bought it for having parties?" She'd spent the past four hours struggling not to think about him having sex with all those women...

Don't think about him that way.

"I've been to my share of parties, but I rarely play the role of host."

She turned back to the view, certain she didn't want him to see the trouble she was having keeping his past occupation out of her head. Had she ever known a man who provided personal services?

No. No, she had not.

"Well, it's a lovely home." There. A perfectly benign statement of the truth.

"I can't take credit for the decorating. I bought the place, furniture and artwork included."

"The previous owners had good taste." She tugged at the collar of her blouse, feeling warm. She'd changed into casual slacks and a blouse and still she felt constricted and... *hot*. "Is it all right if I see the rest of the place?" She had to do something besides stand here and make small talk.

"Of course. I'll grab a few things."

They came to his home so he could pack the clothes and other essentials he would need to stay with her for a few days. The idea of having him right down the hall had abruptly taken on a whole new connotation considering his confession. She refused to linger on the subject. She needed help finding the truth. Clint was helping. End of story.

Natalie waited until he'd disappeared into the master suite, and then she moved in the opposite direction. The main living space was one massive room with that breathtaking view. Lots of gleaming hardwood, sleek granite and stainless steel. The furnishings were a tasteful blend of leather, wood and upholstered pieces. The ceiling soared high overhead where metal pipes and ductwork lent an urban feel. The few art pieces on the muted gray walls were stark and yet somehow compelling. The one that drew her in was the artist's rendering of a city street disappearing into the night. She thought of the way so many pieces of her life had slipped into the darkness. How many more pieces were missing?

Dismissing the worry, she wandered into a short hall

that led to a well-appointed bedroom with an en suite. What she decided was the guest room had a similarly spectacular view. The glimpse of her reflection she caught in the mirror over the bathroom vanity made her groan. No black eyes, but her left cheek was bruised. Her chin was scraped. Her chest felt as if the bare skin had been slapped over and over. Was it possible someone close to her had caused the accident? Clint had suggested as much.

"Not possible."

Natalie turned away from the mirror and wandered back into the main living area. She perused the kitchen with its restaurant-quality style. Checked out his wine selection and then rifled through the magazines on the coffee table. She noted the coat closet and the powder room near the elevator.

She roamed back to the sofa. "What now?" she muttered to herself.

"You doing okay out there?"

His deep voice drifted through the space making it seem somehow smaller.

She cleared her throat. "Yes." Natalie rolled her eyes. Evidently the proper etiquette for visiting a friend's home was another of those missing pieces.

"I'm almost finished."

Before she could come up with a good enough reason not to, she strolled in the direction of his voice. A short walk down the hall off the kitchen side of the condo led into the master suite. A jacket landed on the king-size bed. Again there was that stunning view. The city was the first thing he would see when he woke in the morning. She pictured him lying in that enormous bed and—

He appeared from the door to her right, a couple of shirts in hand. "I'll get these in the bag and I'm ready."

She peeked beyond the door to the walk-in closet. The

only place she'd ever seen that many suits was at a men's clothing store. Her father had owned his share of suits, but not even her pompous brother-in-law owned so many. She wandered into the closet, allowed her fingers to drift over the fabrics as she walked past. The suits were arranged according to color and fabric, she realized. Dozens of pairs of shoes. She raised her hand as she reached the starched shirts, her fingers slipping over the smooth fabric. Most were white. There were a few others in pastels and a couple of gray ones. And, sweet Jesus, the silk ties. All hanging neatly behind glass doors.

When she turned around he waited in the doorway, one shoulder braced against the doorframe. "Clothes are an addiction of mine."

Her mouth felt dry. She moistened her lips and managed a smile. "I see that."

He watched her as she turned all the way around for one last look. The idea that he was watching her made her heart beat faster.

"I don't see any jeans or plain old get-my-hands-dirty shirts."

"I have a few."

She laughed, couldn't help herself. "Somehow I can't see you getting your hands dirty under the hood of a car or in the yard."

"You'd be surprised at all the ways I've had my hands dirty."

There was a warning in his words. She heard it clearly and still she dared to move closer. After all, he stood in the doorway. If she intended to escape she had to move past him. "Would I?"

He studied her for another long moment, and then he straightened away from the door. "We should go."

She watched as he grabbed the garment bag and the

duffle from the bed. "You have a truly beautiful home." Had she said that already?

He nodded and walked away. She followed. He didn't speak again. Perhaps it was best he didn't. Natalie admired the view one last time before the elevator doors closed.

She squeezed her eyes shut and examined the feelings swirling inside her. There was another piece she'd lost. It startled her a little to suddenly remember it now.

How long had it been since she'd actually been attracted to a man?

Why in the world did her libido have to show up now?

Southwood Road
11:45 p.m.

WHISPERS ROUSED NATALIE. The sound seemed to slide over her skin. Her heart beat faster; her skin tingled. Pages and pages of briefs drifted downward, the words sifting from the paper and falling into a pile. The pages faded into darkness. She was walking…walking toward the light, her fingers sweeping along the soft fabric of suits, rows and rows of suits.

Her eyes opened, she blinked and stared into the darkness for a moment before rolling onto her side. *11:45 p.m.* She came a little more awake, her mind grappling for some sense of the dream.

It was the same every time.

Except this time there had been the suits. It didn't take a degree in psychology to know the suits were about her visit to Clint's home this evening. She pulled the sheet closer and thought about the man who somehow managed to invade her dreams when no one—not even her ex-boy-friend—had done so.

April was furious that Natalie had asked Clint to stay

here with her. Her sister wouldn't be back, she'd warned, as long as he was here. David was coming to speak with her tomorrow. Natalie sighed. She had lost all control over her life. On some level she understood her sister's concerns. The brain injury had made a mess of Natalie's ability to function and think for herself—that was true. But the worst was behind her and she continued to get better…the intruder episode aside. She refused to consider last night's hallucinations. Sadie was probably right. Natalie had been dreaming. Dreaming and sleepwalking.

Tinkling laughter floated through the air.

Natalie stilled. Had April changed her mind? She threw back the covers and sat up, dropping her feet to the cool floor. Her sister had sounded quite adamant when she'd called about nine thirty. Maybe guilt had gotten the better of her.

Running her fingers through her hair, Natalie moved soundlessly toward the door. When she reached the hall, she listened. Those soft whispers reached out to her. The sound was definitely coming from her sister's room. She continued toward the sound. The laugh was April's. There was that deeper voice again. Natalie frowned. David hadn't ever spent the night to the best of Natalie's recollection.

Natalie stopped and took a moment to confirm that she was indeed awake.

If she was awake, that meant her sister was in this house, in her old room. Natalie walked to the door of April's childhood room and reached for the knob. She curled her fingers around it, the whispers wrapping around her like a swarm of bees, and turned the knob. She pushed the door inward and reached for the light, the sound of the whispers growing louder and louder.

The bright light made her squint. April's bed was made…the room was empty. The voices vanished.

Natalie closed her eyes and fought the urge to cry. Why did this keep happening?

She turned off the light and closed the door. Maybe she couldn't stop the voices, but she could prevent the incidents from shaking her up so badly. Whatever the voices meant, since they clearly weren't a dream as Sadie had suggested, there was something she needed to remember. Her mind was struggling to bring something to the surface. Fine. She could live with that. Maybe.

She stood in the hall trying to decide what to do next. She could go back to bed and toss and turn for the next couple of hours or she could admit defeat and go downstairs for a glass of wine. Since coming home from the rehabilitation center she had avoided all alcohol. She'd wanted to keep a clear head. Tonight she needed something and she despised the idea of taking the medication again. To reach for the sleeping pills felt like going backward.

She descended the stairs slowly, taking special care to be quiet. Clint had insisted on sleeping on the sofa. He'd put his things in one of the spare bedrooms but he maintained that it was better if he was downstairs. Natalie wasn't sure if that was because downstairs was the most likely entry point for an intruder or if he was trying to protect her reputation.

She felt reasonably certain the part of her reputation that mattered to her, her professional one, was forever damaged already by the TBI. She genuinely appreciated the firm allowing her to return to work, but it was painfully obvious they had no intention of assigning her a case anytime soon.

The lamp on the hall table provided a warm glow in the darkness. The lamp had been turned on each night for as long as she could remember. Neither she nor her siblings had been afraid of the dark, but her mother had insisted there be enough light to get safely down the stairs even in the middle of the night.

As difficult as it was not to peek in at her protector, she managed. He wouldn't appreciate his privacy being invaded. She turned on a light in the kitchen and headed to the wine fridge. She selected a bottle of her favorite white wine, something light and sweet with a slight fizz. A few moments were required to open the bottle. When she'd managed to release the cork, she found a glass and poured a healthy serving.

As she sipped the sweet drink, she stored the bottle in the fridge. She wouldn't risk a second glass. Out of habit she checked the back door before turning out the light and padding back to the staircase. She paused at the bottom, tempted again to peek into the great room.

Instead, she reached for the bannister and started up the stairs. If she was lucky the wine would help her get back to sleep.

"Having trouble sleeping?"

The sound of his deep voice trapped her breath behind her breastbone. Good thing she had a tight hold on the wine glass. Smile pinned in place, she turned to face him. "I thought I'd try something new." She held up the glass of wine.

"Understandable."

It wasn't until that moment that she allowed her gaze to take in the whole of him. Her attention drifted down from his face to his bare chest. Smooth skin, ripped muscles. His trousers hung low on his hips. For the first time since the fall she tried to remember how long it had been since she'd been kissed by a man—not the I'm-so-sorry pecks from her family. A passionate kiss...the real thing. She couldn't remember. She had no idea when she'd been held, much less kissed. Years. At least two years.

She should never have asked him what April had alluded to about his past. She hadn't needed to know... She hadn't thought about sex in so long. How was it she couldn't banish it from her mind now?

"Good night," he said, interrupting her silent discourse.

She managed a nod. "Good night."

Somehow she turned her back and resumed her climb up the staircase. Her chest ached but it was from the air bag and not from the loneliness. A frown furrowed her forehead. When had she become so obsessed with being alone?

For the first time she wondered if she would ever have a sex life again. She'd wondered plenty of times if her life would ever be normal but she hadn't afforded any time on the subject of sex. Sadly, it took only one handsome man under the same roof with her to remind her of all that she was missing. Most women her age were married and had a child already.

Before she climbed back into bed she downed the remainder of the wine. Curling up beneath the covers, she sighed and closed her eyes. She sifted through the day's events. She replayed the moments in the car before the air bag hit her in the face and then the hours at the ER. The unpleasant scene in the driveway with her sister and the examination of the garage for signs of foul play. But the last thought tugging at her before she slipped into the darkness was of the man downstairs and how grateful she was to have him here.

She didn't want to be alone.

Chapter Seven

Ricky Vernon passed the report he held to Clint. "Whoever did this knew what he was doing. This was no amateur job. The new sensor was set to engage the air bag as soon as she reached a speed of sixty miles per hour."

Clint glanced at Natalie's BMW. The vehicle would have to be towed to the dealer for repair. All sensors would need to be checked. They couldn't be sure of the true extent of the damage to the electronic systems.

Vernon brushed his brown hair back from his face and adjusted his glasses. His button-down shirt was wrinkled with the sleeves rolled up to his elbows. The trousers bore the same telltale signs of a long day in the lab that had extended through the night and into the next day. Some women considered the rumpled geeky look sexy. Clint wondered if Natalie would prefer Vernon's type.

She'd seemed nervous last night when he interrupted her return to her room with a glass of wine. Had she forgotten he was in the house? Or had she wandered down the stairs wearing a nightgown and no robe on purpose? One narrow strap of the gown had fallen off her shoulder but the way the hem hit midthigh was the most surprising. She spent her days in those fashionably conservative suits that hardly showed her great body. Last night she'd looked young and innocent, vulnerable. Not the kind of woman who would want a man like him.

Vernon spoke again, drawing Clint's wayward attention. "I'm sorry, what did you say?"

"This isn't the first time this vehicle has been tampered with," the forensic expert repeated. "The main brake line has been repaired. It appears to have been damaged at one time, but the damage was a straight cut, which I find indicative of tampering versus some sort of normal wear and tear. At some point later it was repaired."

"Would this have been recent?" A new kind of tension rippled through Clint.

Vernon shook his head. "Since the vehicle has been garaged for the better part of two years, it would be difficult to guess based solely on the road film and breakdown from routine exposure to the elements. But according to the maintenance log in the glove box, the brakes were repaired twenty-six months ago."

Two months before her fall down the stairs.

"Thanks, Vernon. I owe you one."

"Anytime. Lieutenant Harper said someone's life depended on the findings." Vernon glanced beyond the glass wall that divided the lab from his office on the other side where Natalie waited. Harper and Cook had arrived and were talking to her. "It's nice for a change to be able to help someone before the worst happens."

Far too often by the time evidence like this made it to the lab someone was dead.

Clint was very glad Natalie was unharmed for the most part. He intended to do whatever necessary to see that she stayed that way.

Clint assured Vernon he would get the BMW out of

his way as quickly as possible before heading into the office to join Natalie and the detectives. He wasn't looking forward to explaining the details to her. It was difficult enough when a person could accurately assess the threat around them, but for Natalie, there was no way to be certain. There were too many holes in her memory and too many questions she couldn't answer. She had no idea who would want to harm her or for what reason. There was no way at this point to get a fix on the threat.

Harper and Detective Chad Cook had already introduced themselves to Natalie by the time Clint left Vernon to his next task. Harper and Cook were the only two remaining original members of the department's Major Crimes Special Problems Unit. Harper was in command for now. He'd made lieutenant last year. Clint respected both men, called them friends. For him, that was high praise. Clint didn't play well with others.

Harper gave Clint a nod. "Vernon says we got foul play here."

Clint glanced at Natalie who looked even more worried than when they had arrived. "No question."

"I confirmed that the mechanic who repaired the brake line is still employed at the Irondale dealership," Cook explained. "His name's Beckett. His rap sheet is clean other than a DUI back in high school. Harper and I are heading there now to interview him."

Natalie's worry turned to confusion. "I don't understand. What's going on with the brakes?"

"I'll explain the full report to you," Clint promised. To Harper he said, "I'd like to talk to the mechanic first. I don't think we should tip our hand just yet as to police involvement. I'd prefer for whoever is behind this to feel safe for now."

Harper didn't look convinced. "I can give you twenty-four hours, but we can't risk this guy posing a threat to anyone else. You know as well as I do that if he'd do it for a dollar once he'll do it for a dollar again."

Clint couldn't argue his reasoning. "Twenty-four hours is all I need."

"How is this possible?" Natalie turned to Clint. "I haven't taken my car in for service recently. How could he have gained access to it? The only people…"

Her voice drifted off as realization struck her hard. There were very few people with access to her home and unfortunately she was extremely close to those few.

Clint could think of at least four people who were close enough, but which one was motivated enough to commit murder?

It was too much.

Natalie couldn't reconcile what the lab's analysis meant. The only people who had access to the house were Suzanna and Leonard, and April, of course. David had a key but he rarely came to the house unless Leonard called him.

Except, how could she be certain?

Before her fall she had worked long hours at the firm. Afterward she'd been in the hospital and then in rehab for months. In the past two months she had spent several hours a day at the office. How could she say for sure who had come and gone? Had Suzanna or Leonard given a key to anyone else? The pest-control service? A plumber or electrician? What about the painters? The house had been given a fresh coat throughout while she was in rehab. The rugs had been cleaned and the floors polished. April had thought it would make Natalie feel better to come home to a fresh start.

Any one of those people coming in and out of the house may have picked up a key.

Or perhaps it was easier to believe a stranger was the culprit rather than someone close to her.

"Harper will check the security cameras at the parking garage next to your office."

Clint's voice startled her back to the present. "I appreciate the department's efforts."

What was the likelihood that someone had come into the garage where she parked while at work and tampered with her car?

None of this made sense.

"You're in a difficult position."

His voice was gentler this time, as if he understood her inability to comprehend the magnitude of what was happening.

"The worst part is I don't know why." She blinked back the tears that burned her eyes. When had she become so emotional? How could she forget? The brain injury had changed some aspects of her personality that might or might not return to normal at some point. "How can I not remember someone who wants to hurt me?"

"Sometimes we remember what we feel comfortable remembering."

The man had done his research. Sadie and the other doctors had said the same thing. The pieces she felt more comfortable with would fall into place first. If she'd had a confrontation or received a threat of some kind, those details might not return until her mind felt ready to accept the burden.

As long as she didn't get murdered first, no problem.

The Irondale dealership wasn't crowded the way it had been three years ago when she'd bought her new BMW. A salesman trailed a couple strolling the lot. Inside, sparsely furnished cubicles where salespersons were either making phone calls or finalizing deals with customers lined one wall. The large customer-service desk stood against the opposite wall while the center of the showroom was occupied by the current models of the carmaker's most popular series. After the formal introductions, the manager, Adam Wheeler, was only too happy to see Natalie and Clint in his private office.

"You must be ready for an upgrade, Ms. Drummond." He smiled broadly as they took their seats. "Mr. Drummond was here just a few days ago to order a new car for his lovely wife."

Her brother hadn't mentioned a new car to Natalie. She wasn't surprised at the omission and it certainly didn't trigger any alarms in her opinion. Like their father, Heath was focused on the business. Other than Thanksgiving and Christmas, the man was generally unavailable.

"Maybe another time," Natalie assured him. "We're actually here about one of your employees. My friend, Mr. Hayes, has a few questions he'd like to ask."

"Of course. I am always happy to brag about my employees. We take great pride in the service we provide." He turned his attention to Clint. "How may I help you, Mr. Hayes?"

"Your mechanic, Mike Beckett, what can you tell us about him?"

"He's a very reliable employee. He has been for the past four years. Always on time and rarely missed a day. We haven't had the first complaint about his work."

"Is he here today?" Clint asked.

"He called in on Monday. Said he needed to get to Denver. Something about his mother being ill."

"Did he indicate when he would return?"

"He did not. His absence left a big hole in our service schedule. We've been rescheduling appointments all week."

Clint stood. "Thank you, Mr. Wheeler."

Natalie promised to call Wheeler soon about a new car. Considering the damage to her current vehicle, he might be hearing from her sooner than either of them anticipated. She waited until they were back in Clint's car to ask, "What now?"

"Now we talk to your housekeeper and gardener."

"I don't think it's necessary to question Suzanna and Leonard." The idea was ludicrous. She wanted no part of offending them with pointless questions.

"I'm not accusing them of wrongdoing, Natalie," Clint glanced at her as he spoke. "I'm suggesting they may have seen something or someone without realizing it mattered enough to mention. You need to trust me, I know how to handle the situation without stepping on toes or injuring feelings unnecessarily."

He was right. She had no reason to doubt him. "Fine. Just be extra nice, okay?"

The smile he flashed in her direction interrupted the rhythm of her heart in a good way. She thought about the way he'd looked last night only half dressed and standing in that doorway. Her throat went dry. Why was it her sexuality had to reawaken at the worst possible time?

What difference did it make? She had enough trouble at the moment without getting involved romantically with anyone, much less the man who needed to remain focused on finding the source of whatever the hell was going on in her life. Just now, neither he nor she could afford to be distracted.

Natalie leaned back in the seat and closed her eyes. Now was not a good time for getting involved. She cringed at the ludicrous thought and reminded herself that it was difficult to get involved without someone to get involved with. Clint Hayes was the investigator she had hired not her friend or her potential boyfriend.

He was a professional providing a service…

Her fingers tightened on the armrest when she thought of the service he had provided other women during his college days. She wondered what his girlfriend—assuming he had one and she couldn't imagine he didn't—thought of his colorful work history.

Clint received a call on his cell. Natalie tried to gather the gist of the call based on his side of the conversation. He repeated an address that wasn't familiar to her. He thanked the caller then dropped his phone back into his jacket pocket.

She found herself holding her breath as she waited for him to tell her what the call was about. It might have nothing to do with her case.

"That was Harper. Beckett's girlfriend found him at his residence. From the looks of things he had been packing to leave town, but he never made it."

Her heart sank. "He's dead?"

"He is. Has been for at least a day. One gunshot to the chest."

Natalie stopped the rush of thoughts whirling in her head and forced herself to focus. "Is there any way to determine if he tampered with my car or if his murder has anything to do with…me?"

"Harper and Cook are two of the best detectives in the department. If anyone can determine what Beckett was up to the final days and hours of his life, they can."

"I don't understand." Why was this happening? She'd gone to bed one night with nothing more to worry about than the case she was assigned and when she woke up her world had changed. She didn't remember getting up or falling down the stairs. Her first memory was waking up in the hospital with April asleep in the chair next to her bed. At that point Natalie had been in a coma for ten days. "What does this mean?"

"I don't know," Clint admitted as he made the turn onto her street. "But I will find out."

"The whole situation is simply insane." Natalie shook her head, stunned, horrified and frustrated. She didn't realize she'd braced her hand against the console until he wrapped his fingers around hers. He didn't say a word, simply gave her hand a quick, gentle squeeze and then let go. Somehow that basic touch calmed her, made her dare to hope.

Natalie kept her chin up the rest of the drive. Clint pulled into the driveway to find Suzanna and Leonard packing up their SUV. At first Natalie thought perhaps they were merely leaving a little early today, but the back of the SUV was loaded with boxes.

"What on earth?" Natalie climbed out of the car.

Leonard closed the tailgate and moved around to the driver's door without uttering as much as a hello.

"Suzanna, what's going on?"

The older woman faced Natalie, her expression cluttered with dread. "We can't do this anymore, Natalie. It's past time we retired anyway. I left you a letter explaining our feelings."

Natalie shook her head. "I don't understand. You can't do what? Has something happened you haven't told me about?"

"Suzanna!"

The older woman glanced at the SUV. "He doesn't want me to get tangled up in this mess."

"Tangled up in what mess?" They couldn't possibly know about her air bag fiasco or the murder of the mechanic who may have tampered with it. "What in the world are you talking about?"

Suzanna glanced toward her husband once more, but then leaned forward and whispered for Natalie's ears only, "I found the bloody clothes and the gun hidden in your room, Miss Natalie. I don't know what it means, but I can't protect you anymore."

"Suzanna, wait!"

Natalie's words fell on deaf ears. The couple who had taken care of her family's home for three decades loaded up and drove away while she stood helplessly watching.

"What was that all about?"

Natalie looked up at Clint, possibly the last person on the planet who believed in her. "I have no idea."

The mechanic, Beckett, had been shot... Suzanna had found bloody clothes and a gun in Natalie's room.

Could she...no, no, she could never have gone to his home and killed him...but she had shot someone.

Was Mike Beckett the intruder she shot in her kitchen? Why would she have changed clothes and hidden them and the gun before the police came? How could she have moved the body? She hadn't even known his name, much less where he lived. Dear God, had she killed a man?

Chapter Eight

8:59 p.m.

Natalie closed her bedroom door and sagged against it. From the moment Suzanna whispered those horrifying words to her, Natalie had been trying to think of a way to go to bed early without Clint asking questions.

He had almost managed to distract her from her thoughts by making dinner. Like any good hostess, she had tried to help but her fingers had fumbled at every turn. Finally, he'd told her to sit and keep him company. She'd tried to pay attention to the conversation but her mind had whirled with memories and those dark whispers... and fear. Had the man she shot been Mike Beckett? The threat of tears forced her eyes to squeeze shut. The sound of the gun discharging made her jump.

She straightened away from the door and took a deep breath. Suzanna said the gun and the clothes were hidden in Natalie's room. Shoring up her courage with another deep breath, she began the slow, methodical search of her room, the bathroom and then the closet.

Nothing looked as if it had been moved. What had Suzanna been doing prowling around in here anyway? And wouldn't bloody clothes smell?

Natalie pushed her hanging clothes aside and checked

behind them. She searched every shelf and drawer. Then she turned to the white wicker laundry hamper. She removed the lid and at first thought it was empty, but when she leaned down for a closer inspection she realized there was a white garbage bag at the bottom. Hand shaking, she closed her fingers in the plastic and pulled it from the hamper.

Heavy…too heavy to be only clothes.

Her heart started to pound and she sank to the floor.

She opened the bag and the smell of blood made her gag. Covering her mouth and nose with her hand she peered at the contents. A pastel blue suit Natalie didn't readily recognize as her own was wadded up inside. Blood splatter dotted the fabric. Crushed against the suit was a handgun…a .38 exactly like the one her father had kept in his bedside drawer. Just like the one Natalie had used on the intruder.

Natalie scrambled up, stuffed the bag back into the hamper, and ran to the bathroom just in time to lose the wonderful dinner she had forced herself to eat. She washed her face and stared at her reflection in the mirror. Why would she change clothes and hide them and the gun?

Did the bloody clothes have something to do with what Suzanna meant when she said she couldn't protect Natalie any longer?

Protect her from what? Or whom?

Herself?

She should call Clint up here right now and show him what she'd found. He would call his friend Lieutenant Harper…

Natalie bit her trembling lips together. Why couldn't she remember? Had she blacked out between the shooting and the time she actually called for help?

Right now she needed to think and to calm herself.

First she had to get the stench of blood from her lungs. She turned on the shower and stripped off her clothes. She climbed in and let the hot water beat down on her. She scrubbed her hair and her body, wincing as her hands moved over the bruises made by the air bag. When she'd finished, she scrubbed her skin so roughly with the towel that it stung. She didn't care. By the time she dragged on a nightshirt, she was too exhausted to think. Her mind had had enough.

Hair still wet, she climbed beneath the covers and let the exhaustion consume her, dragging her into the darkness where the whispers she didn't understand waited.

SHE WAS RUNNING… Where was she? In the hall outside her room. Why was she running? The dark whispers followed her… April's voice, her laughter… The man whispering. Who was the man? David? Suddenly screams filled her ears. Who was screaming? Natalie was falling, falling, falling, and then her world went black.

Natalie bolted upright. Her frantic panting was the only sound in the darkness. More dreams. God. She pushed her still damp hair back from her face. Would this nightmare never end? The memory of the bloodstained clothes and the gun in her hamper slammed into her like a battering ram.

Soft laughter filled her mind…the whispers. April?

Knowing full well she was hearing things but unable to resist, Natalie threw back the covers and stormed out of the room, her anger and frustration building with every step. She marched straight to her sister's room and opened the door. The voices stopped the instant her gaze took in the empty room.

Natalie closed her eyes, took a deep breath and exhaled slowly. What was happening to her? She was supposed to be getting better and stronger everyday.

A scream ripped through her ragged thoughts.

She ran to the staircase and stared down at the cold, unforgiving marble floor below...the place where she'd landed.

The screams...*her* screams...played over and over in her head making her dizzy.

Natalie hung on to the banister and lowered onto the top step. She pressed her hands to her ears and tried to quiet the screams. She couldn't bear it...didn't want to see.

"Natalie."

Someone was calling her name.

Hands clasped hers and pulled them away from her ears. Natalie opened her eyes. Clint stood over her, searching her face, his clouded with worry.

"You're okay. I'm here." He sat down beside her.

Tears spilled past her lashes despite her best efforts to hold them back. "I can't make it stop." He drew her into his arms. The feel of his warm skin and his strong arms ripped away the last of her defenses. "Please help me."

For a long moment he just held her. She cried against his shoulder, relished his warmth and strength. He drew her more firmly against him and stood. She wanted to protest as he carried her to her room. She could take care of herself. She'd always taken care of herself but somehow she had lost the ability. She needed help...she needed *him*.

He drew the covers back and lowered her to the bed and climbed in next to her. He pulled her against him and held her tight. He stroked her hair and whispered promises to her.

"I'll keep you safe. No one's going to hurt you now. I'm right here with you."

But how long would he stay when he learned her secret?

Friday, September 23, 6:30 a.m.

NATALIE'S EYES DRIFTED open and she turned her head to check the time. She had to get up. Get ready for work. Did she have court today?

Wait…memories came rushing back.

No court. She didn't even have a case. Not since the fall. Everything was different now.

Clint.

Heart starting to pound, she turned to check the other side of the bed. Empty. She smoothed her hand over the pillow, then pulled the sheet closer. The sheet still smelled like him. Warmth stirred deep inside her, but the sweet feeling was short-lived. She'd made a fool of herself last night with her nightmares and hallucinations.

When would they stop? She'd felt her life was finally hers again until two months ago—when she started back to work. Was the pressure of merely showing up at the firm too much?

She didn't want to consider what kind of breakdown she would have if she dared to set foot in a courtroom.

"Stop." Natalie shook her head. She'd done the self-deprecating thing enough during her initial recovery. Going down that path now would be a big step backward. She had to stay focused on moving forward.

The memory of the bloody clothes and the gun jolted her.

She couldn't deal with that right now. At some point she would have to tell Clint, just not now. She couldn't do it yet. She couldn't bear the idea of him turning against her, too.

Moving quickly she selected a suit and the necessary underthings and hurried from the closet. Even with the bag closed up in the hamper the smell of blood seemed to assault her.

"It's only your imagination, Nat. Not real."

But the bloody clothes and the gun were all too real.

She stared at her reflection in the mirror. "You are a mess." Her hair was the most pressing matter at the moment. Going to bed with it wet was always a bad idea. Her chin still sported a red spot from the air bag. The bruising across her chest was a deeper blue. At least she was alive.

A snippet of memory—her frantically clutching at the railing and then falling. She swallowed back the fear and uncertainty that crowded into her throat. "Don't go there."

Half an hour later she looked reasonably calm and composed. Now for the hard part—facing Clint. She imagined he'd already decided she was in serious need of meds and more counseling. She'd fought so hard to get past that place. One step at a time she'd mastered the requirements for getting through a typical day. From dressing herself to making coffee and even driving again.

Was her brain determined to go in reverse now?

The smell of coffee had her forgetting her worries for a moment as she descended the stairs. In the kitchen she found Clint pouring freshly brewed coffee into two cups. His suit jacket hung over the back of a chair. The gray shirt and dark trousers fit his body as if they'd been tailored just for him. Judging by the man's closet she suspected that might very well be the case.

She summoned her courage and joined him at the counter to add cream to her coffee. "Good morning."

He glanced at her as he picked up his steaming mug. "Morning. You look well for a woman who battled an air bag just yesterday."

Not to mention her demons. She was grateful he didn't mention that part. Sadly, one of them had to clear the air. "I'm sorry about last night." She stared at her cup, watching the cream swirl into the dark Colombian roast.

"Did you remember something new?"

She shook her head and dared to meet his eyes. "I was dreaming, I suppose, about that night. The voices woke me and then I was at the stairs…falling."

"You screamed."

She looked away, embarrassed. "Sorry. They tell me I came out of the coma screaming. For months I would wake up screaming. I haven't done that in a really long time. Until…"

"Until you returned to work."

She nodded. "I guess Vince was right."

"Right about what?" he asked, his tone suddenly sharp.

Natalie searched Clint's face but he schooled his emotions before she could define what she saw. "When I first returned to the office he mentioned being worried that I was trying too much too soon."

"Don't trust him, Natalie. Take my word for it."

She wanted to ask if there was a personal history between the two of them but a call on his cell interrupted. Natalie took her coffee and wandered to the French doors that overlooked the gardens. She hoped it wasn't his friend Lieutenant Harper calling to tell Clint that he needed to arrest his new client for murder.

Natalie closed her eyes and sipped her coffee. Maybe she had imagined the bloody clothes. Except Suzanna had seen them, too. She should talk to Suzanna. How was she going to take care of this big old house without them? Granted she could understand they might truly want to retire, but she didn't want whatever was going on with her to be the reason.

This—whatever it was—had to stop.

When the call ended, she held her breath waiting for the news. From the corner of her eye she watched Clint sip his coffee. He wasn't looking forward to telling her the news. That much was clear.

Why didn't he just say it? They suspected her of shooting Beckett?

She opened her mouth to blurt the question but he spoke first. "The parking garage cameras didn't give us anything. We do know the gun used on Beckett was a .38."

"Like your father's," he didn't say. But she knew. Soon they would all know.

There was something terribly wrong with Natalie. The fall down those stairs had done far more damage than they had realized.

"I should get to the office."

She set her cup on the counter and walked out of the kitchen. She would be okay at the office. Work was the one thing that had never let her down—at least not that she could remember.

Richard Arrington Boulevard and 6th Avenue

NATALIE SAT FROZEN in the chair. Russ Brenner, Art Rosen and Peter Taylor sat on the other side of the conference table. Mr. Brenner's secretary had called Natalie into the conference room as soon as she arrived in the building. Clint had taken her briefcase and gone to wait in her office.

Brenner had kicked off the impromptu meeting with a lengthy monologue regarding Natalie's superior standing at the firm. Rosen had picked up from there, waxing on about how important the relationship with clients was to the continued success of the firm. Now, Taylor had taken his turn and launched into how the firm was like one big family. Somewhere along the way understanding had dawned on Natalie.

She was about to be fired.

"We care deeply for each member of our staff, especially our associates," Taylor went on. "However, we cannot afford the slightest risk to our clients. Our security protocols can never be anything less than impeccable."

"I do apologize," Natalie spoke up before he could continue, "but, with all due respect, I'm afraid I'm quite lost as to the point of this meeting."

The three exchanged a look. She wanted to pound her fist on the table and tell them to get to the damned point.

"Natalie," Rosen offered, "there has been a very serious breach in security. This morning we were informed that this breach originated from the computer in your office."

Horror tightened its grip around her throat. "Are you suggesting I had something to do with a security breach?" The idea was preposterous, but that was exactly what they were saying.

"We aren't accusing you of anything," Brenner put in quickly. "We are only saying that perhaps you aren't up to the stressors of the workplace. Perhaps you need more time off."

She was flabbergasted. "I don't know what to say. I thought my work since I returned had proven useful. I had hoped to be taking cases soon." She should have known better. Rather than her mental faculties improving, she was falling apart.

"You will always have a place here, Natalie," Rosen assured her. "We're suggesting that you take some more time and let's reevaluate in a few months."

"Months?" The rush of hurt and anger burned in her veins but Natalie refused to cause a scene. "Very well. If you believe that's best for the firm, then what else is there to say?" She stood. "Thank you so much. I'll make the necessary preparations for an extension of my leave."

"Give us a moment," Rosen said to the others.

Brenner and Taylor stood and shook her hand in turn.

When the room was theirs, Rosen came around to her side of the table and leaned against it. "Natalie, we've been through a lot together."

Every ounce of strength she possessed was required to hold back the words she wanted to hurl at him.

"You're well aware that you've always been my favorite."

Oh she was very well aware. *Deep breath, Nat.*

"But I have a responsibility to the other partners, to our clients and to the rest of the firm. You are not yourself. The accident changed you. When you're back to your old self, we'll make this right."

He dared to touch her, just a gentle brush of his cool fingers against her cheek. "Take care of yourself, Natalie. I'm going to miss you."

Shaking with fury, Natalie walked straight to her office, feeling as if all eyes were on her. Clint stood as she entered the room. He took one look at her and opted not to ask the question she knew full well was poised on the tip of his tongue.

Rather than leave him in suspense, she said, "I've been asked to extend my leave from the firm. Apparently," she started to shove personal items into her briefcase, "there has been a security breach that originated from my computer and I've been deemed unreliable or untrustworthy— maybe both." She jammed in a few more items. "So, I'm on leave for a few more months."

He took the briefcase before she could attempt to stuff anything else into it, ensuring it never closed. "I'm certain it's only temporary."

"Maybe."

They exited her office. "Let's take the stairs." She had

no desire to walk back down the hall past all those other office doors to reach the elevator.

Natalie held her tongue as they descended the stairs. She refused to be caught on the security cameras venting, which would only make bad matters worse.

"Natalie!"

Vince Farago hurried to catch up.

Natalie stopped and turned back to see what he had to say. She imagined he'd been gloating all morning. He was likely the first to hear the news.

"Are you all right?" he asked as he looked her up and down and then glanced at Clint. "We're all very worried about you."

"I'm fine, Vince. I'll be taking a little more time off. There's no need for you to be concerned."

He glanced at Clint again. "I am concerned, Natalie. You haven't been yourself all week and…frankly, I have serious reservations about your involvement with Clint."

"I'll wait outside," Clint offered.

Natalie held up a hand. "No need." She lifted her gaze to Vince where he stood a few steps up. "I am fully aware of Clint's history and I have complete confidence in his ability. So, don't waste your time and energy worrying about me, Vince. I'm in very capable hands."

The bastard had the audacity to smirk. "I can't say I'm surprised. How long has it been since Steven dumped you? They say women get desperate after—"

Clint was nose to nose with him before Natalie realized he had moved.

"That's enough, Farago."

Vince held up his hands and backed away, almost stumbling on the step behind him. "Just telling it like I see it."

Clint turned his back on him and headed down the stairs, guiding Natalie along with him. The feel of his hand at the small of her back gave her a sense of reassurance she hadn't felt in a very long time.

Once they reached the parking garage, she paused before getting into the passenger seat of his Audi. "Thank you for backing me up."

The slow smile that released across his lips made her pulse flutter. "I'm the one who should thank you."

He had no idea. His only indiscretion was giving women what they wanted…she, on the other hand, had quite possibly killed a man.

She suddenly felt sick.

He squeezed her arm. "Don't worry. We've got this under control."

Natalie nodded and settled into the passenger seat. She should tell him what she'd found before he discovered the truth some other way. Her heart lurched. If she told him and he stopped believing in her, what would she do? Who could she trust?

The one thing she understood with complete certainty was that she could not do this alone.

Chapter Nine

Southwood Road
10:50 a.m.

Clint placed the last box on the dining room table. "Last one."

Rather than allow Natalie to stew over the injustice of the morning, he had decided to lay out his suspicions about her fall. In his opinion, it was someone from her professional life that had set out to harm or to kill her. If he'd had any doubts, the so-called security breaches on her computer at the firm had banished those.

Fortunately, Natalie kept copies of her work files at home. Going through those files, he decided, was a step in the right direction. Not to mention, he needed something more to do than to focus solely on the woman.

"Thanks." Natalie reached for the lid on the box. "This should be everything I need." She scanned the contents of the box before lifting her gaze back to his. "You really think what happened to me has something to do with the Thompson case?"

His fingers itched to reach out and brush those dark bangs back from her blue eyes. She had amazing blue eyes. Clear and inquisitive. Instead, he reached up and pulled the tie he'd already loosened free of his collar. His jacket lay across the sofa in the great room. He wished now that he'd brought something a bit more comfortable.

He cleared his head of any thoughts of getting more comfortable. He recognized the line to which he was edging far too close. "It's the only scenario that makes sense. Your accident took you off the defense team and suddenly the case does an about-face based on new evidence. Rison Medical gets the win and your colleague gets his long awaited spot in the limelight."

One hand on her hip, she rubbed her forehead with the other. "Vince isn't capable of…" Her voice trailed off. She turned to Clint. "Is he capable of pushing me down the stairs?"

"You were pushed?" Clint cocked an eyebrow at her question. He'd read all the reports related to her injury and never once did she or anyone else mention the possibility of her being pushed.

She shook her head and sighed. "I don't think so." She reached for a file. "Truth?"

He read the uncertainty in her eyes. "Nothing else will do."

"I don't know if I was pushed." She moistened her lips, drawing his hungry eyes there. "In my dreams, sometimes it feels like I'm being pushed, but it was dark and I just don't know for sure." She shook her head again. "The concept is ridiculous. No one was here with me except my sister. There is no way April pushed me."

The way she pretended to focus on the pages in the file belied her words. "You keep dreaming of hearing your sister in her room with a man. Are you sure her husband wasn't with her that night?"

"No, David was in Montgomery for a meeting. April said she called him from the hospital and let him know what happened."

It was time to take off the kid gloves. "Was she involved with someone else?"

"What?" Natalie's brow furrowed with a frown. "Of course not. April would never cheat on David."

Clint pulled out a chair and took a seat at the table. "Could Heath have been here with another woman that night?"

"Absolutely not." She tossed the file aside and moved on to the next one. "Heath is the quintessential good guy. He married his high school sweetheart. They go to church every Sunday and support every charity in Alabama. Their first child is on the way. No. Heath has always been the one who made April and me look like the bad children."

She assessed Clint for a moment. "Why all the questions about my siblings? I thought we cleared up any potential involvement by them when we first spoke?"

"You answer my questions and we won't go there again."

Her hesitation warned she wasn't happy. Still, she pulled out a chair and sat. Like his, her jacket was somewhere in the great room. Her heels were somewhere between here and there. If he'd been a stronger man he might not have watched her skirt slide up her thigh as she sat down, but he wasn't. He'd never wanted to be that strong.

"Fire away." She lifted her chin and waited for his first shot.

"What does either your sister or your brother have to gain if you were to die or be mentally incapacitated?"

She laughed, it was the first real laugh he'd heard from her. He liked it. The sound came from deep inside, making it rich and sweet.

"Well, that's easy." She lifted her arms wide apart. "This lovely old home that costs a mint to maintain. Fair market value is somewhere in the two- to three-million-dollar range. Since both my siblings have assets worth far more than the value of this estate, I highly doubt they're in any hurry to take it from me."

"Life insurance?"

She deliberated on her answer for a moment. "I have a healthy policy. Five million. Half of which goes to my siblings as long as I remain unmarried and the other half goes to my chosen charities."

Clint still wasn't convinced. "Are you protecting any family secrets?"

Natalie looked away. "I'm not sure what you mean."

So, she was covering up something. He leaned forward, braced his forearms on the table. "Do you have knowledge that could create problems for either of your siblings?"

"I do not." She grabbed another of the folders. "I thought we were going to discuss the Thompson case."

He would come back to this because the lady was definitely hiding something. "Walk me through the case."

"Walter Thompson entered the Rison Medical Center for a fairly routine procedure," Natalie began. "The complaint alleged that after his procedure the next morning, a nurse, Imogen Stuart, wheeled him back to his room and helped him to the bathroom, where he fell and hit his head. According to Stuart, Mr. Thompson did not fall until *after* she had settled him into his bed. Stuart claimed that as she was leaving the room he attempted to climb out of the bed to look for his wife and that was when he fell. The wife returned to the room as Stuart was helping him back into bed. So there were no witnesses to what actually happened. However it occured, the fall fractured his skull, causing an acute subdural hematoma that went undiagnosed until the onset of symptoms. He was rushed to surgery, but they were unable to save him. The wife insisted that her husband told her repeatedly that he'd fallen in the bathroom and that the nurse had been on her cell phone in the corridor instead of helping him."

"The nurse," Clint said, recalling the rumors he'd heard about the case, "stuck to her story that she never left Mr. Thompson's side until he was in the bed with the rails raised. Still, Rison offered to settle quietly but Thompson's wife insisted on a public admission of liability."

Natalie nodded. "She requested a jury trial. Except for her testimony, there was no evidence to support her allegations. An eleventh hour search of Mr. Thompson's health records—which had already been submitted as evidence— found a single incident of him falling down the garage steps when he knew better than to try going outside the house without assistance suggested a pattern that seemed to confirm Stuart's story and won the case."

"No one had noticed this incident before," Clint countered. Very convenient, in his opinion.

"It happens. You read files a hundred times and you miss a little something here or there. We were working night and day. It goes with the territory in a big case."

"There were rumors about a witness who confirmed the wife's allegations," Clint reminded her.

"Yes." Natalie reached for another folder in one of the boxes and took a moment to review it. "Just before trial Stuart claimed that her original statement was a mistake, but later she recanted that allegation." Natalie shook her head. "I don't remember any rumors about actual evidence."

"The timing of the rumors was around the same time you were recovering from your own fall."

"So that's why you asked about Vince." Natalie shrugged. "I can't see him going that far for a case—especially one that wasn't even his. You're thinking that if I hadn't fallen,

I would have come forward with any evidence that might have damned my own client."

"Winning is more important than truth?"

She held up her hands stop-sign fashion. "You know as well as I do that I was bound by attorney-client privilege."

"As true as that is, I have a feeling you would never have ignored the truth."

She turned back to the files. "I appreciate your high opinion of me, but you must have forgotten the first rule of being an attorney."

"Never say never," he finished for her.

"It'll come back to bite you every time." Her lips lifted the slightest bit. "Most attorneys learn that lesson fast."

"What about your almost fiancé, Steven?" Clint had checked out the guy. Steven Vaughn was another politician. He'd been elected state representative the year before Natalie's accident. Vaughn and Keating, Natalie's brother-in-law, appeared to be close. If Clint's sources were accurate, Vaughn wanted to end up as lieutenant governor when Keating was elected to the state's highest position. Clint found it strange that Vaughn hadn't stuck by Natalie under the circumstances. Why hadn't Keating disassociated himself with Vaughn after he deserted Natalie? April had been all too happy to show her concern for her sister's association with Clint. Yet, she had no trouble with her husband maintaining close ties to the man who dumped her sister at the worst time in her life. It didn't sit right with Clint.

When Natalie continued to ignore the question, he nudged her again. "Was he in any way connected to the case?"

Natalie looked up. "I'm sorry. What was the question?"

"Never mind." Her distraction with one of the files from the box was more intriguing to him than anything she would likely tell him about the fiancé. "What're you reading?"

She frowned and turned her attention back to the file. "Stuart's statement is missing." She reached for the next file. "It's in here somewhere. I reviewed it with her before trial."

"Let's take it step by step." Clint surveyed the boxes he'd stacked on the table. "Where do we begin?"

"The day Rosen called me and two paralegals into the conference room." She pushed back her chair and went to one of the boxes stacked on the floor. "All we had was the incident report filled out by the hospital's head of security."

Clint moved to where she was opening the box. She lifted the first of several binders from the box. "Start here. I'll make tea."

He took the binder from her and watched her walk away.

Eventually she was going to have to share her secret with him.

NATALIE PLACED THE teakettle on the stove and adjusted the flame. She refused to think about the fact that she was now officially unemployed—no matter that the partners had insisted she would always have a place at the firm. She knew better. She needed to call Sadie and tell her.

Should she tell her about the gun and the bloody clothes, too?

Her hands shook and she almost dropped one of her grandmother's prized teacups. No. She wasn't telling anyone about that until she remembered why she had done such a thing.

"Like that's going to happen," she grumbled. She had no recall of blood on her clothes much less of changing and stashing the evidence. She'd been warned that unpleasant memories were the slowest to return.

She placed the cups and saucers on the counter and then reached for spoons. Clint made her want to trust him with that dark secret, but she wasn't sure she could even trust herself. How good were her instincts? Not very good now or before, she decided.

Steven had waited until she was out of the hospital and in rehab to break up with her. She'd wanted to be devastated, but she hadn't been. In all honesty, she hadn't been in love with him. At thirty years old she'd been more enamored with the idea of being engaged because all her friends were either engaged or married. April had kept pushing her to give Steven a chance.

Had she only committed to a serious relationship for appearances' sake or to make her sister and Steven happy?

Maybe so. From the time she was a young girl she'd wanted desperately to make the people around her happy. Her mother had scolded her time and again about being true to herself. Somehow it never took.

The kettle started to squeal, prompting her to gather tea bags.

Pounding from the front door reverberated in the entry hall. Natalie dropped the tea bags on the counter and started in that direction. Clint was already at the door and opening it.

Fear launched inside her. What if it was his police friends? Had they discovered the truth…that maybe she killed the mechanic?

Heath walked in, giving Clint a long, hard look as he passed him. "Nat, what the hell is going on here?"

She should have called her brother. April had obviously done so. "This is Clint Hayes." She accepted a kiss on the cheek from Heath. "Clint, this is my brother, Heath." Heath was older than she by one year and taller by about a foot.

He was a big, broad-shouldered guy and he'd always considered himself the protector of his sisters.

The two men shook hands, but the gesture was quick and visibly unfriendly.

"Clint is the private investigator helping me sort out the strange happenings of late."

Heath stared at Clint, openly skeptical. "April said he was some kind of gigolo out for your money."

Natalie laughed, couldn't help herself. "Trust me, big brother, Clint doesn't need my money."

Clint's stony features warned that he wasn't amused.

Heath grinned. "April's always been a drama queen. Besides," he looked Clint up and down, "if he makes you happy I don't care what he is. I never liked Steven, he had his nose too far up David's—"

"I know what you think of Steven," Natalie cut in. "We were about to have tea. Would you like some?"

"Tea's for old ladies," Heath grumbled as they moved into the kitchen.

"Be nice," Natalie warned. Heath had snubbed his nose at college, choosing instead to immerse himself in the family business. Who needed a college degree to know how to manufacture steel, he'd said. So proud of his only son, their father had indulged him for a little while. Eventually he and Heath had struck a deal. Heath continued at the plant by day and attended college classes in the evening. An MBA hadn't changed her brother much. He was still the man who was as happy working alongside a manual laborer as he was behind a desk. The degree, however, had made their father very happy. Natalie inserted a pod into the coffee machine to brew her brother a cup.

"You were a cop before becoming a PI?" Heath asked as he and Clint settled at the breakfast table.

"That's right," Clint confirmed.

Heath grunted. "You went to law school, too, I hear."

"I did."

"Heath," Natalie sent him a warning look as she poured the tea, "do not embarrass me or yourself."

"I don't blame him for changing his mind. Lawyers—" he glanced at his sister "—my sister not included, are a pain in the butt."

She placed the cup of coffee in front of him and sent him a disapproving look.

"They are a different breed," Clint agreed.

With tea and coffee served, Natalie joined them at the table.

"April says Suzanna and Leonard quit."

Suzanna's words echoed inside Natalie. "I suppose it was time they retired."

"Seems strange to me."

"I find it strange," Clint said, "that you were at the BMW dealership this week and a mechanic there, Mike Beckett, tampered with Natalie's car."

Natalie started to demand what Clint was thinking when Heath looked from Clint to her. "Is he serious?"

"I am," Clint answered. "Someone tampered with the air bag in Natalie's car. She could have been killed in the crash."

"You crashed your car?" Heath threw up his hands. "Nobody ever tells me anything."

She and Clint would talk later. For now Natalie kept her temper in check. "The air bag launched and I crashed into a car in a parking lot. No one was hurt. Other than the few bruises and a couple of abrasions I sustained."

Heath shifted his attention back to Clint. "You're sure it wasn't just a factory malfunction."

"It was no malfunction."

Heath scrubbed a hand over his face. "Well, then, I

guess I should have paid more attention to the bastard is all I can say."

"What do you mean?" Natalie's heart nearly stopped. How could Heath know anything about this?

"The knucklehead called me a few days ago and said you were going to get hurt but he could stop it from happening for the right price."

"That's why you went to see him?" Clint pressed.

Heath nodded. "Only he wasn't there. The shop foreman said Beckett had been off all week. Some kind of family emergency. I thought he was a nutcase but I wasn't going to risk Nat's safety so I went to see him, yeah. Did the cops arrest him?"

Natalie couldn't breathe. She clasped her hands in her lap so no one could see them shake.

"He was found at home yesterday," Clint told him. "Murdered."

"Damn." Heath turned to Natalie again. "What's going on, Nat? Why the hell didn't you tell me about this?"

She shook her head, not trusting her voice.

"We believe," Clint said, drawing his attention, "someone hired Beckett to tamper with the air bag and then maybe that same person silenced him."

"This doesn't make sense." Heath pushed away his coffee. "Who would want to hurt you? You haven't been getting those threatening letters again, have you?"

Shock radiated through Natalie. "What?"

"Remember? About two weeks before your accident you started getting these letters. You know," he glanced at Clint, "the kind done with words cut out of a magazine or newspaper and then glued on the page. I was here when you opened the second one. You promised to call the cops, but I don't think you did. Then everything happened and I forgot about it until just now. You made me promise not to tell anyone. You thought it was about that damned case."

"Thompson versus Rison Medical?" Clint asked.

"Yeah, that's the one."

The image of a page with cut and pasted words swam before her eyes. *I know the truth, do you?* A few days later a second one had come. *Are you really going to let this happen?*

"I never got the chance to call the police." The words were scarcely a whisper. She had been very upset by the letters because she knew what they meant...she had known something then that eluded her now.

Why couldn't she remember what it meant? What truth?

Clint's voice as he answered his cell dragged her away from the troubling thoughts.

"I understand." He ended the call and put his phone away. "We need to speak privately."

Heath stood. "I have to get back to the plant."

Natalie managed to get to her feet without swaying. "I'm glad you came by." She loved her family. She wished they had more time together. Though April had spent most nights with her for months, they never really talked the way they used to.

After she had assured Heath she would keep him informed and shown him out, she turned to the man waiting in the middle of the entry hall. Judging by the grim face he wore, the news wasn't good.

"Beckett's girlfriend claims he was blackmailing someone about *you*. The morning he was murdered he was supposed to meet with that person. Harper and Cook are on their way here. Is there anything you want to tell me before they arrive?"

Ice chilled Natalie's veins. "There's something in my closet you need to see."

Chapter Ten

Clint waited at the door while Natalie crossed to the far side of her walk-in closet. She stared at a wicker laundry hamper for a moment before opening it. The little gasp that followed had him moving toward her.

She reached into the hamper and then drew back, her expression somewhere between shock and fear. "It's gone."

"What's gone?" He peered into the empty hamper.

"The gun." She met his gaze. "Yesterday Suzanna told me she'd found a gun and bloody clothes in my room and that she couldn't protect me anymore. I had no idea what she meant, and then last night I found a white garbage bag in the hamper." She closed her eyes and shook her head.

"You're thinking the clothes and gun were from when you shot the intruder."

"Except the gun disappeared along with the intruder." She stared into the empty hamper again. "How could I not remember changing clothes and hiding the gun before calling the police? My brain tells me that I ran out of the house and called 9-1-1."

The doorbell rang, echoing through the house. Natalie looked stricken.

"Is there anything else you haven't told me? Anything at all?" Clint might be a sucker but he believed her. She needed to be straight with him. Any secrets she held back could create serious problems going forward. With a man dead, this was no time to hold back.

"I think my sister *was* having an affair." Natalie let go a shaky breath. "My brain keeps replaying these voices and this soft laugher. One of the voices belongs to April, the other to a man. The voices wake me up and I follow the sounds to April's bedroom—the one she slept in growing up and uses whenever she stays the night. For the past several weeks it's happened every night. No one's there, of course, but it has to mean something. Once the voices wake me up, I go to the stairs and I remember snippets of my fall."

Clint braced his hands on his hips and contemplated the possibilities. "Why do you think that means she's having an affair? Maybe her husband was here with her."

Natalie hugged her arms around herself. "I've tried to convince myself the male voice was her husband's, but in my heart I know that's not true. David and I were never really friends. He certainly wouldn't have spent the night here. Frankly, at the time, April wouldn't have either unless she and David had quarreled."

Clint nodded. "All right."

The doorbell sounded again. She flinched.

"For now we keep this between us." No need to put her through the kind of interrogation associated with being a suspect in a homicide until they sorted out what the hell was going on around here.

"It's bad enough that I've impeded the investigation into the intruder I'm certain I shot," she protested. "I can't have you breaking the law for me by doing the same in a homicide investigation. This has gone too far already, Clint."

"Let me worry about the homicide investigation." He had no intention of hindering anything. "We shouldn't keep them waiting."

The doorbell launched into its classic tune a third time before Clint reached the door. Natalie waited in the great room. She needed a moment to pull herself together. He sure as hell hoped she wasn't holding back anything else.

He opened the door as Harper was calling his cell. Harper ended the call and dropped his phone back into the pocket of his suit jacket. "Everything okay?"

Anytime a person of interest knew the police were en route and took his time getting to the door it created suspicion.

"Besides a dead mechanic who tampered with my client's car?" Clint gestured for the two detectives to enter. "Everything is just peachy."

Harper sent him a sidelong glance. "Where's Ms. Drummond?"

Clint ignored Harper's skeptical tone. The man was always overly suspicious when it came to murder. "This way."

As they joined her in the great room, Natalie summoned a faint smile. Clint wished he could take some of the worry off her shoulders. So far he was batting zero where her peace of mind was concerned.

"Lieutenant Harper and Detective Cook are here about the mechanic who may have tampered with your car," Clint explained.

"Ms. Drummond." Harper nodded as he took a seat on the sofa across from where she sat. "I'm sorry to bother you with more questions, but unfortunately it's necessary."

"I understand."

Natalie was nervous. Harper would notice. Natalie had tried a number of high-profile cases. The idea of the woman who'd come so close to being the youngest partner in such a prestigious firm being nervous under any circumstances was completely out of character.

Spending as much time with her as he had the past few days, Clint got it. The brain injury had done a number on her and her confidence in herself. A great deal of what an attorney did relied completely upon the ability to recall and analyze the facts as well as the law. The injury had taken away, at least to some degree, her ability to recall facts as well as the sequence of past events. How could she assess the problem if parts were missing or out of order? She had every right to be nervous and uncertain. Someone was taking advantage of her vulnerability.

As Harper started his questions, Cook took his cue from Clint and opted to stand. The young detective had chosen Clint as his role model. Clint had tried repeatedly to discourage him, but he was one determined guy. Clint liked him, as well. Shortly after joining the BPD's Special Problems Unit, he'd helped Cook prepare for the detective's exam. They'd been friends since.

The team had formed a strong bond—one carried beyond the job. They were like family.

"Ma'am, you stated that when the intruder entered your home you took the .38 that belonged to your father and fired it at him."

Clint's attention shifted back to Natalie. She nodded. "That's correct."

"You dropped the weapon, left the intruder wounded and ran from the house to call the police?"

"Yes. I might have reacted differently in the past," she admitted. "The TBI altered certain things about my personality, at least for now."

"You believe the intruder took the weapon and left while you were waiting outside for the police?"

"I do, yes."

She relaxed a bit. Clint did the same.

"Where on your property did you wait? Were you near the house?" Harper asked.

"No." She shook her head emphatically. "I waited in the street. I was terrified. I even knocked on the front door of my closest neighbor, but no one was home."

Clint had read the report. She hadn't mentioned going to the neighbor's house in her initial statement. If she was remembering more details, that was a good thing. If she was confusing the facts, that was not. He hoped the former was the case. If Harper didn't mention the point, Clint would. Later.

Harper flipped back through the pages of his notepad. Clearly he'd picked up on the discrepancy. "You didn't mention going to the neighbor's house in your statement."

Natalie frowned. "I was upset. I must have forgotten to mention it. No one was home so it wasn't relevant."

Harper scratched a few words on his notepad. "Your father owned a Smith & Wesson .38. That's the weapon you used on the intruder?"

"Yes. My father owned it for as long as I can remember. I suppose I should have registered it in my name after his death. I simply never got around to it."

"Had you fired the weapon before?"

"No." She glanced at Clint for the first time. Her tension rising again. "I took a course on weapon safety after I inherited the house and the gun, but other than the course and the intruder, I've never fired any weapon."

"Ma'am, did Lieutenant Russell have someone swab your hand for gun powder residue?"

"No. He didn't believe there had been an intruder or a gun. I didn't think of that myself until days later or I would have insisted the test be done."

Tension nudging him, Clint moved to stand behind Natalie. "Where is this going, Harper?"

"The slug removed from Beckett's chest was a .38," Harper said, his face somber. "The ballistics was an exact match to the slug we recovered from the trash in his bathroom where he'd tended his first gunshot wound. The one we believe he sustained here."

Natalie's hand went to her throat as she looked over her shoulder at Clint.

"I thought Beckett died from a single gunshot wound to the chest," Clint argued. "How did you miss the second gunshot?"

"The shot to the chest is what killed him," Harper said. "He'd already patched up the other wound and changed clothes. We didn't know about it until we found the evidence of the cleanup in the bathroom. I called the ME's office and got confirmation about the second wound."

Natalie said, "Wait, are you saying the weapon taken from my home was used to kill him?"

"Yes, ma'am."

"Did you recover the weapon?" Clint asked, his own tension ramping up. If the housekeeper found the .38 here and Natalie saw it just last night, how the hell could it be the same weapon?

Harper shook his head. "The shooter took it with him… or *her*."

"The ME estimated time of death at what time?" Clint knew damn well Harper had that piece of information. For whatever reason he'd chosen not to share it up front.

"Between nine and midnight on Wednesday night." Harper turned his attention back to Natalie. "Ma'am, have you ever had any dealings with Beckett beyond having your personal vehicle serviced at the shop where he worked?"

She shook her head. "I didn't know his name before this… and to my knowledge I never met him."

"Does anyone else in your family or a close friend use that dealership?"

"The manager said my brother had bought a car there for his wife. I'm not aware of anyone else using it. My sister and her husband prefer Mercedes."

Harper closed his notepad and stuffed it back into his jacket pocket. "Ma'am, if you think of anything else that might help our investigation, Hayes knows how to reach me."

The pointless meeting ended and Clint escorted the two detectives to the door. "You could have asked those questions when you called."

Harper shrugged. "Then I wouldn't have seen her reaction. She's hiding something, my friend. And you know it."

"Since I was here with her all night Wednesday night, we know she's not your shooter."

"I never thought she was," Harper admitted. "But this guy had a connection to her or to someone close to her."

"Did you find evidence at the scene or are you going solely on the girlfriend's testimony? We both know emotional witnesses are rarely good ones."

"Watch your back, Hayes," Harper warned. "Something's up with this family."

Cook kept his head down as he followed the senior detective out the door.

Yeah, well, Clint was well aware that the Drummonds had more secrets than they wanted to share.

Who didn't have secrets?

NATALIE STOOD AT the window watching the two detectives leave. The man she'd shot was dead. Her father's gun had been used to shoot him a second time. The same blood-stained gun she had seen in her laundry hamper last night.

Clint joined her at the window. "I was here with you

when Beckett was murdered. Whatever you're thinking, you had nothing to do with his death."

"Someone close to me did." Emotion swelled into her throat. How could she believe her sister or her brother had done this? April was the one behaving so irrationally, but it was Heath who had gone to the dealership looking for Beckett. He was the one Beckett had contacted with a blackmail threat.

She closed her eyes. Why would Beckett or anyone else want to hurt her? What had she done to make anyone that angry?

"I can think of only two reasons anyone would want you out of the way, Natalie. You're either standing in the way of something or you know something they want to hide."

He said the words softly but there was nothing soft about the meaning. "I know. I just can't remember what it is."

"We will find the answer."

"I don't want anyone else to end up dead." She turned to face him. "If my sister or my brother are somehow involved or if they're targets, too…" She closed her eyes and struggled to slow the emotions whirling inside her. Somewhere on this journey she lost the ability to keep her wits about her.

Warm fingers brushed her cheek, stealing her breath and at the same time soothing her frayed nerves. She opened her eyes and searched his as he spoke. "We should have a meeting with your family and warn them about the situation."

She forced the softer emotions aside and gave him a skeptical look. "Warn them or assess their reaction to what we know so far?"

"Both. We should talk to Suzanna and Leonard, as well. Suzanna may know more than she's told you."

"She said she couldn't protect me anymore. I don't know what that means."

"We'll find out. I'm certain you're skilled in how to approach a hostile witness."

Natalie thought of the way April had behaved and then Suzanna's abrupt departure. And even Heath's unexpected visit. "I guess I never expected the hostile witness to be a member of my family."

"Sometimes family is the most hostile of all."

She searched his face. As silly as it was, she had memorized every line and angle. His eyes were the part that tugged at her the most, so very dark and tempting. His eyes made her want to be closer...to know him more intimately. If only she dared permit herself to indulge in those feelings again. A relationship required trust. She didn't trust herself—how could she expect anyone else to have faith in her?

"You don't doubt me, do you?" she asked. His answer was suddenly, inexplicably important to her.

"I believe you've told me everything you feel is relevant."

"You're evading the question, counselor." She wanted him to trust her. No, she needed him to...at least on some level.

"You hold back what you're unsure about. I need you to trust me with your darkest secrets, Natalie. You're aware of how important full disclosure is to any case."

There was certainly no denying that charge. "The only things I haven't told you are the vague images I see in my dreams or hallucinations. At first it was nothing more than pages of briefs or reports. The words fall from the pages into a pile before igniting. It wasn't until after Heath mentioned the threatening letters that I remembered receiving them. Typically that's the way it works. If a memory is triggered it comes to the surface. Otherwise it just stays buried somewhere in my gray matter."

"You remembered nothing about the cut-and-paste letters until your brother mentioned them?"

"Nothing." She wanted to scream in frustration. "As soon as he mentioned them pieces of memories returned. I could see the letters. One said something like 'I know the truth, do you?' There was another that demanded how I was going to let this happen. If there's more, I can't remember them."

He held her gaze but said nothing. What was there to say? Her dreams made no sense. The way the memories returned was unreliable at best.

Finally she had to look away. "I don't know how I thought I could practice law again." She closed her eyes and shook her head, then took a breath and dared to meet his steady gaze once more. "Sorry. I'm usually a little stronger than this."

"You're plenty strong, Natalie."

Why oh why did he have to look at her that way? As if he appreciated what he saw...as if he wanted more than to talk.

"Would you just..." Good grief, what was she thinking? She looked away.

He took her face in his hands and turned her eyes to his. "I would."

Her next breath deserted her as his lips lowered to hers. He brushed her mouth with his so very softly once, twice and then he kissed her slow, deep and deeper still. She leaned against him, relishing the feel of his warm body.

His fingers delved into her hair, angling her head just so to deepen the kiss.

And then he stopped. Every part of her protested. He pressed his forehead to hers. "We have work to do."

She licked her lips, savored the taste of him. "Yes."

For once, she wished he was wrong.

Chapter Eleven

Wenonah Road
2:00 p.m.

Clint parked at the curb in front of the house belonging to Imogene Stuart. "You do understand this is crossing a line. The firm will fire you for a move like this."

She nodded. "For all intents and purposes, they've already fired me."

"There will be damage to your professional reputation," he reminded her.

She turned to him. "I have to do this. I *need* to know."

He nodded. "I can do this part without you. You don't have to—"

Natalie placed her hand on his arm. "I need to do this."

Clint emerged from the car and went around to the passenger side to meet her. His instincts moved to the next level. He took a long look around the neighborhood. He didn't see anything that looked out of place, but he felt it.

They were being watched.

Narrowing his focus, he scanned for any sign of a dog. The home was a small bungalow from the first quarter of the last century, bordered by a neat yard and a picket fence in need of a fresh coat of paint. A quick search had shown that Imogene's husband passed away less than a week before the Thompson-Rison Medical trial. The twenty-year-old Dodge parked on the street was registered to the owner of the house, which hopefully meant she was home.

He climbed the steps behind Natalie, keeping an eye out for whoever was watching them as well as for a dog. He liked dogs but they often didn't like him. As a cop he'd run into more than his share of unfriendly ones. There was always the chance that perps trained their dogs to dislike cops on sight. Maybe he'd have better luck as a private investigator.

Natalie opened the wooden screen door and knocked.

Television noise suggested someone was at home. The curtain in the window to the left of the door moved just enough for the occupant to have a look. It paid to be careful these days, particularly for a woman at home alone.

The door opened a crack. "No solicitors." Female. Brown hair streaked with gray and a pair of glasses that shielded accusing eyes glared at them.

Clint gifted the lady with a smile. "We're not solicitors, ma'am. We need a few minutes of your time to—"

"I have my own church, so just take it on next door. The heathens who live there could do with a sermon."

Natalie said, "Mrs. Stuart, my name is—"

"Wait." The door opened a fraction farther. The older woman scrutinized Natalie a bit more closely. "I know who you are." Her lips tightened in anger, then she said, "I have nothing else to stay to you."

When the door would have closed, Natalie braced a hand against it and stuck her foot in its way. "Please, Mrs. Stuart. This is very important."

Whether the lady of the house allowed them in or not, Clint was impressed. This was the side of Natalie Drummond that had gone dormant with the brain injury. He was glad to see a glimmer of the fighter she used to be.

The door opened wide. "I'll hear what you have to say

because I'm a Christian. Come on in." Stuart turned her back and shuffled to the sofa.

Natalie exchanged a look with him before going inside. Clint followed, closing the door behind him.

"Thank you, Mrs. Stuart. This is—"

"Clint Hayes." He extended his hand to the lady. "It's a pleasure to meet you, ma'am."

Openly suspicious, she accepted the offered hand and gave it a shake. "We'll see about that."

He smiled. "I suppose we will."

"Take a seat." She reached for the remote and muted the television.

Clint waited for Natalie to be seated first, and then he took the remaining chair.

"Mrs. Stuart, I'd like to ask you a few questions about the Thompson case."

Stuart had a kind face but there was nothing kind about the fury that contorted her features just then. "Why would you come back here now? It's done. I told you all I had to say the last time we talked."

Clint watched Natalie's face. She seemed surprised at the woman's words.

"I was on the legal team for your employer, I'm sure we spoke many times, Mrs. Stuart."

Stuart's gaze narrowed behind her glasses. "I'm talking about the private conversation we had. The one where I answered a certain question you had asked me."

"I don't understand," Natalie pressed. "What private conversation?"

Stuart got to her feet. "I don't know what you think you're doing, but I'm not going to jail for what I was forced to do by your firm so you just get out of my house right now."

"Please," Natalie kept her seat, "let me explain."

Clint kept quiet. If he got involved at this point Stuart would likely feel pressured.

Openly reluctant, Stuart took her seat once more.

"Before the trial I was injured." Natalie gestured to her head. "A brain injury. I was in the hospital for weeks and then in rehab for months after that. I've only recently started to work again."

Gaze still narrowed in suspicion, Stuart asked, "Is that why I didn't see you at the trial? I kept expecting you to do something. But I never saw you again after we talked."

A cold, sick feeling twisted in Clint's gut.

"Yes. I was in the hospital fighting for my life."

Stuart's face softened. "I didn't know. I just figured they shut you up the way they did the rest of us."

Natalie glanced at Clint. The worry on her face told him all he needed to know. She wasn't sure what was coming and she was terrified it would be news she didn't want to hear.

"Can you tell me what question I asked?"

"Don't see why I can't." Stuart took a big breath. "You asked if anyone instructed me to change my story about what happened in Mr. Thompson's room that morning."

Natalie waited for a long moment before she responded. "Will you share your answer with me again?"

Stuart shook her head. "No way. They made me sign one of those papers that says I can never talk about it again." She frowned. "You can't remember?"

Natalie shook her head. "I'm sorry. I don't remember."

Stuart nodded. "That's a real shame." She stood once more. "I wish I could help you, but I'm all alone now. As you know I lost my husband to cancer. His treatments took a lot of money. My retirement from Rison Medical is all I got. I can't risk losing it or having them come after me if a lawsuit." She took a big breath as if trying to shore up her courage. "You should leave now and don't come back."

Natalie stood. Clint did the same. Stuart was afraid to talk and he got that. Anything she did or said posed great risk to her livelihood. If his theory about what happened to Natalie was correct, Stuart's life could be in danger, as well.

Natalie hesitated at the door. "Mrs. Stuart, is there anything at all you can say that might guide me in my search for what really happened."

Stuart hesitated for only a few seconds. "Look at the evidence you have. That will tell you all you need to know. You had it before the trial, maybe you still do."

"I don't have any evidence beyond what you saw presented at trial."

"Yes you do. I gave it to you." She shook her head, "I tried to tell you with those anonymous letters warning you to do something, and then I called. After that we met in person and I gave you what you needed to make things right. I did all I could do two years ago. I can't help you now."

Stuart ushered them onto the porch and closed her door.

"At least now we know who sent the cut-and-paste letters," Natalie said wearily.

"That's something." Clint scanned the street. Coming here may have been a mistake. If this was where Natalie had come just before her fall…then whatever it was she'd been told at the time was why she ended up at the bottom of those stairs.

Moss Rose Lane
Hoover
5:15 p.m.

"This is too risky."

Natalie reached for patience. Clint wanted her to stay

at his office with Jess but she couldn't do that. "We can't be sure she'll even talk to me," she argued. "I won't risk scaring her off with a stranger."

Clint stared out the windshield of his Audi, his profile turning to stone. He'd told her he suspected they were being watched but he hadn't spotted a tail since leaving the Stuart home. Natalie wanted to hope he'd been wrong about their being watched, but she felt confident his instincts were far too good for such a mistake.

"No memories were triggered when I was at Mrs. Stuart's home," she urged when he remained silent. "That's not a good sign, Clint. It means those memories may be lost forever. If there's no chance of my recalling what she's talking about, I have to find it another way. This—Mrs. Thompson—is the way. Maybe the only way."

He turned to her, his dark eyes nearly black with frustration or something on that order. "They are watching us."

"You can't be sure. You said you hadn't seen—"

"You worked at your firm for four years before your injury, you are well aware of how smart and cunning those guys are. Whether we spot their eyes or not, they *are* watching us."

He was right. There was no point in denying the assertion or his perceptive skills. She supposed she should be afraid but somehow she wasn't. She was out of a job anyway, but if anyone at her firm was responsible for her fall...

Natalie couldn't assimilate the concept just now. Seeing this investigation through required all her cognitive skills. "Let's give them something to worry about."

Before he could argue, she opened the door and got out. She surveyed the street, giving whoever was watching a perfect view of her face no matter where they were hiding. Clint slammed his door, darting a hard look in her direction. He recognized exactly what she'd done.

Mrs. Thompson lived in the same home she had shared with her husband. A classic brick ranch with a big yard and perfectly manicured shrubs. Natalie was halfway up the sidewalk when a big dog raced around the corner of the house, barking for all it was worth.

She froze. Clint stepped in front of her. "Good boy."

The dog obviously didn't feel the same. He growled.

Clint crouched down and offered his hand, palm down.

"Do you think that's a good idea?" Natalie held her breath as the dog she now recognized as a golden retriever eased closer to Clint.

"You're just protecting your kingdom, aren't you boy?"

"Jasper!"

Natalie looked up. Mrs. Thompson stood at the front door. She produced the biggest smile she could manage and waved to the woman. "Mrs. Thompson, it's Natalie Drummond."

The dog trotted up the two steps onto the porch. Clint pushed to his feet and started that way. Natalie moved up beside him, hoping Thompson wouldn't shut the door in their faces.

Watching their approach, Thompson scratched Jasper behind the ears. "I remember you. You're one of those lawyers who cheated me and my family out of what we deserved."

Natalie would have preferred to deny the charge. Instead, she crossed the porch and stood before her accuser. "I guess I am. This is Clint Hayes, my associate." Natalie didn't want to frighten her by mentioning the term *private investigator*.

Thompson glanced at Clint. "What do you want?"

As if a gust of cold wind had swept through her soul, Natalie remembered the devastated wife during her deposition. The images and the voices poured through her, stealing her breath and at the same time sending her heart pounding. She and her husband had been married for twenty-five years. Being a wife and mother was all she had ever known. She had three children in college at the time, ranging from a freshman to a senior. The whole family had been devastated. Natalie felt ill at the idea that she may have been a party to compounding that devastation.

Summoning her wits, Natalie said, "I want to know what really happened in that hospital room."

Rather than startle Thompson as Natalie had thought the statement would, it seemed to enrage her. "How dare you come back here after two years and stir that pot again. I told you the last time you stood on my porch what really happened and you promised to make sure the truth came out in that courtroom." She shook her head. "I don't know what your game is, lady, but I want you off my property. Now."

Natalie's knees felt weak. "You're saying I came to your home before the trial and discussed the case with you?" That alone was a career-killing move.

"You damned sure did."

As if sensing the shift in the tension, Jasper growled. His mistress called him down.

"Mrs. Thompson, can you tell me the exact date I came to your home?" Natalie's pulse raced, her heart pounded so hard she could scarcely hear herself think over the roar of her own blood.

Thompson's gaze narrowed. "Something happened to you, didn't it? I remember seeing you on the news."

Natalie nodded. "I was in the hospital for a long time." She had no desire to discuss her injury a second time today.

Thompson ushered her dog inside. "Come on in and I'll look it up." She went on as they followed her into the house, "I think it was the day before the trial. I even tol my lawyer but I don't think he believed me since you never returned any of his calls."

She gestured to the sofa. "Sit. I'll get my calendar."

Natalie and Clint settled on the sofa. He appeared focused on taking in the details of the room. Mrs. Thompson's walls were filled with family photos. A portrait of her husband was centered on the wall above the television. A cross hung on one side of the portrait and an angel hung on the other. Natalie's heart pressed harder against her sternum, threatening to burst from her chest.

"Here we go." Thompson came back into the room carrying a standard wall calendar. She sat down in what Natalie suspected was her favorite chair and flipped through the pages. "So…" She studied the page. "You came on Sunday around five o'clock the evening before the trial."

She passed the calendar across the coffee table. Natalie, hand trembling, accepted it. She looked over the page and all the notes Thompson had scribbled on the blocks that represented days in that month. Her throat tightened when she read her name penciled in as Thompson had said.

With monumental effort, Natalie returned the calendar to its owner.

"Will you tell us what you and Ms. Drummond discussed that day?"

Thompson shifted her suspicious gaze to Clint. "She wanted me to repeat what happened to my husband. I told her, same thing I told everyone who asked because it was the truth. After his procedure, I stopped by the cafeteria for coffee and a breakfast sandwich. The nurse was supposed to be taking care of my husband. She was supposed to get him back to the room and into bed."

She paused a moment, the memories visibly painful. "My husband said he told her he needed to go to the bathroom. She helped him to the toilet but then she got a call on her cell. He kept waiting for her to come back but she didn't so he got up and tried to get to bed on his own. He fell in the bathroom and hit his head on the shower curb. I guess she must have heard him because she rushed in there and helped him up and to the bed. When I walked in he was talking and seemed to be okay so the nurse didn't act worried."

The lucid interval. The death of actor Liam Neeson's wife had made the term a household one. Thompson had repeatedly mentioned what she'd seen on television and read in magazines and, she claimed, the staff ignored her.

"They killed him. Not only did the nurse let him fall, they ignored my concerns about checking his head with an MRI or something until it was too late."

"Mrs. Thompson, did I say anything to you the day I came to your home that made you believe I possessed knowledge or evidence that confirmed your allegations?"

Clint sent Natalie a questioning look. He didn't have to say a word. With that question she had crossed the point of no return. She had just implicated herself in a possible fraudulent act—not to mention she'd broken attorney-client privilege.

"You said for me not to worry, you were going to make it right."

And that night she had fallen down the stairs.

Chapter Twelve

Lori Wells joined them at the dining room table. "Sorry about that, guys. Layla should sleep for a while now."

"Your little girl is beautiful," Natalie said.

Lori beamed. "Thank you. We think so."

"I hear you're still working too many hours," Clint said as Lori grabbed her beer.

"Don't get him started." Lori darted a look at her husband.

Harper had made lieutenant only a few months ago. With Jess and Clint gone, Harper was the senior detective in SPU, the major crimes team. Lori had moved over to Crimes Against Persons.

Chet Harper grunted as he glanced up from the report he was reviewing. "Her mom takes good care of Layla when we're at work."

Lori grinned. "Sounds like someone's trying to stay on my good side tonight."

Clint laughed. "The joys of married life."

"And how would you know, Mr. I'm-staying-single-forever?" Lori teased.

Clint held up his hands surrender style. "You've got me there."

Lori turned to Natalie. "I do have wine if you'd prefer."

Natalie had accepted the offer of a beer but she'd hardly touched it. "No thanks. The beer is fine." She lifted the bottle to her lips as if to confirm her words.

Harper closed the folder in front of him and reached for another. "The case reads pretty cut-and-dried." He glanced up at Clint. "It boiled down to the word of the nurse against the wife."

"Why didn't she take the settlement they offered instead of going to trial?" Lori asked. "Seems like that would have saved her a lot of grief."

"Mrs. Thompson really wanted the world to know what Rison had done," Natalie spoke up. "Her attorney was adamant that the only way to do that was a trial. I'm sure you're aware the settlement offer would have come with a confidentiality agreement."

Lori made a face. "Wow. She risked everything to try to get justice for her husband."

Natalie nodded slowly. "Others would see it as an attempt to get more money."

"Lawyers." Harper looked from Natalie to Clint and back. "No offense, ma'am. Sometimes I wonder…"

"If we have hearts?" she finished for him. "Sometimes it feels as if we don't, but everyone has a job to do. Keep in mind there are plenty of unethical people out there who file lawsuits based on false claims."

Lori rolled her eyes. "Forgive my husband. He sometimes speaks before thinking."

Clint laughed. "I thought I was the one who had that problem."

"You are," Harper assured him.

They all had a good laugh, but the amusement died quickly.

"Natalie," Lori broached the bottom line first, "it's pretty clear from an investigator's point of view that your accident was no accident. I'm with Clint on this one. I think it has to do with the Thompson case, which means someone at your firm could very well be responsible."

Clint wished there were a different answer, but he couldn't see any other scenario. He added, "You know the only alternative."

Natalie inhaled a deep breath. "My family." She moved her head from side to side. "For all our imperfections, we love each other. I don't believe my family was involved."

"The firm won't let this go," Clint reminded her. "I'm certain they have someone watching us."

"Unfortunately," Natalie confessed, "I have to agree."

"Our next step is to determine who has the most to lose if you recall whatever it was Stuart confided in you." Lori scooted the files over to one side and unearthed a sheet of poster board. She grabbed a marker. "Where would you start?"

"Vince Farago," Clint answered for her. "He wanted to be partner. Natalie was under consideration before her fall. He stepped into her spot on the team defending Rison."

Natalie didn't disagree with him. Maybe she finally recognized Farago for what he was—a shark with a straightforward motto: eat, sleep, kill.

Lori added his name to the board. "Anyone else?"

Natalie leaned forward and braced her arms on the table. "There's one other person we need to add to that list."

Tension rippled through Clint. Had she recalled something new or was this the thing he'd sensed she was holding back?

"Art Rosen." She moistened her lips and stared at the

bottle of beer for a moment. "He and I had a brief affair when I first came on board at the firm. I've never told anyone about it, but…I said I'd be completely truthful." She glanced at Clint. "This is deeply personal and, frankly, I'm ashamed I allowed it to happen."

Clint wanted to reach out and touch her, to let her know he understood, but this wasn't the time. "We all have our uncomfortable secrets."

"Some more than others," Harper said with a pointed look at Clint. He tipped his beer up and had a long swallow.

"I have a secret," Lori said.

Harper's expression fell.

Lori laughed and held up her beer. "Don't worry, I'm not pregnant. I wouldn't be having a beer." She punched her husband on the shoulder.

"Don't get me wrong." Harper held up his hands. "I want more babies. But first we need a bigger house. When Chester is here, it gets pretty tight."

Chester was Chet's son with his first wife. The kid started kindergarten this year. Chet was already certain his son was the next Einstein. The kid was damned smart. That was another thing about his friends, Clint realized. Moments like this, they made him yearn for his own family.

"Cook is planning to pop the question to Addi," Lori said.

Harper made a face. "How do you know this and I don't?"

"Because he showed me the ring he was planning to buy. He wanted a woman's opinion."

"Addi's a catch." Clint was glad the relationship had worked out for the two despite Cook's prior relationship with Dr. Sylvia Baron who also happened to be Addi's biological mother. It wasn't until Addi came to Birmingham in search of her biological mother that Addi and Cook met.

"I'm sorry," Harper spoke up, "but that relationship is going to take some therapy if you ask me."

"It was complicated," Lori explained for Natalie's benefit. "Cook and Addi's mother had a relationship a couple of years ago. They've worked it all out and I'm thrilled for them."

Harper shrugged. "Me, too. Addi's hot."

Lori's jaw dropped and even Natalie laughed at Harper's remark.

"Sylvia's sister Nina is planning the engagement party," Lori warned. "Jess says it will be the event of the year. You'll have to wear a suit."

Harper groaned and the women laughed again.

Clint was grateful for the *normal* chatter. Natalie needed a dose of normalcy. He had a good idea that it had been a long time since she'd felt that way. He hated to be the one who drew her back to the painful reality of the present. "Would you have shared your misgivings about the Thompson case with Rosen?"

Natalie considered the question for a moment. "Our affair ended two years before that case. He was my mentor and friend. Nothing more," she added as if she sensed he needed to understand. "I have no recall of going to him with any concerns."

"But," Clint countered, "he's the one you would have gone to."

She met his gaze, uncertainty in hers. "Yes."

"Art Rosen," Lori said as she wrote the name on the makeshift case board. She drew a line from his name to Farago's and inserted the firm's name between them.

"Beckett is a wild card," Harper said. "We don't know who hired him. Chances are it was Farago. I don't see a senior partner getting his hands that dirty."

"Agreed," Clint said. "We should add any private investigators the firm hired on the case."

"There was only one," Natalie said. "Donald Murray."

"I think he retired," Harper noted.

"As long as he didn't move to some exotic island finding him shouldn't be a problem." Clint wasn't familiar with the man, but he would find him.

"Let me run his name in the morning," Lori offered. "Save you some time."

"I appreciate that." Clint might not admit it out loud, but he missed these brainstorming sessions with the team. He suspected that Jess did, as well.

Layla woke from her nap and demanded her mother's attention while Harper saw them out. When they reached Clint's car, Natalie hesitated before getting in. "Your friends are nice. I can see why you made such a good team."

"We got off to a bumpy start, but we pulled it together." She settled into the passenger seat and Clint closed her door. He rounded the hood to the driver's side. When he'd first been assigned to SPU, he'd been on a mission. Chief of Police Burnett had asked Clint to keep an eye on Jess since the serial killer obsessed with her was still on the loose at the time. It hadn't taken then Chief Jess Harris long to figure out what Clint was up to. Thankfully, the team accepted him anyway.

Lori, Harper and Cook were the first people he'd let this close to him. He intended to keep them close.

Lately he'd been feeling the urge for something he'd sworn he would never want again. He stole a glance at the woman next to him. He knew better than to trust those feelings.

The sooner he wrapped up this investigation, the better for all involved.

11:45 p.m.

THE WHISPERS WOKE HER.

Natalie threw back the covers and sat up, dropping her feet to the cool floor. She closed her eyes and allowed the sounds to envelop her.

No...laughter—April's laughter. *We can't...she might hear us. If David found out...*

She won't tell—the man's deep voice. *I need a drink. Didn't you say the liquor cabinet is in your father's study? Come on...*

Natalie's eyes opened. Her father's study. She used his study as an office. Could she have hidden something there? Was that what the dark whispers were trying to help her remember?

Heart thundering, she hurried to the stairs. For a moment she stood there, recalling that fateful night. She'd come out of her room. Why would she come out of her room at that time of night?

Her body trembling, she grasped the bannister and closed her eyes, trying harder to recall the events. *Relax, let the memories come. No fear. No resistance.*

The sound of secret laughter, so soft it was barely audible swept past her. Her breath caught as if her sister's very presence had just touched her.

Come on, the man whispered. *Nat will kill me*, April protested. *Shhh...we won't wake her*, the man promised. April and the man had gone downstairs.

Natalie opened her eyes. Her sister's laughter had awakened her that night. Natalie held very still, allowed the memories to surface. She remembered climbing out of bed, dragging on her robe, and padding to the stairs. Then...

She was falling.

This is your fault.

Natalie clung to the bannister, her lungs struggling for air. Who had said those words? *This is your fault.* Male, for sure. Harsh, deep…a growl. The voice was at once familiar and at the same time completely alien. Had a man pushed her? The man with April? Not David, it seemed.

The night of Natalie's fall her sister had claimed she was angry with David, which was the reason she'd decided to come to her childhood home and spend the night. Had April lied just to have a secret rendezvous with her lover? But why would a man Natalie didn't know try to hurt her?

Could April's lover have been Vince? Natalie couldn't see that match under any circumstances.

Where had the secret lover been when the ambulance arrived? Had he taken off, leaving April alone with her gravely injured sister?

"You always did know how to pick them," Natalie muttered.

She steadied herself and descended the stairs. At least she hadn't awakened Clint. She resisted the urge to look in on him. As much as she would love a glimpse of his bare chest, there was something else she had to do right now.

Holding her breath she eased apart the pocket doors of what she would always call her father's study. Though she had years ago packed his files and stored them away, many of the things that made the room his space remained. She turned on the light and went to the liquor cabinet. She opened the doors and surveyed the variety of liquors her father had prided himself on collecting. Most were decades old and unopened. Her father had rarely partaken, but he'd felt the need to have a variety available for guests. She opened a door and touched the rich wood of the humidor that still held his special occasion cigars.

She smiled. Whenever she opened that humidor the scent of fine tobacco made her think of her father. She closed the doors and tension banded around her chest. The air fled her lungs.

The sound of doors and drawers slamming echoed in her ears. She closed her eyes and told herself to relax. She had hurried from her bedroom…saw the intruder at the bottom of the stairs.

She frowned and took a moment to sort the memories. This new one wasn't from the night of her fall, it was from Monday morning when she'd shot an intruder.

Wait. Natalie opened her eyes. The intruder—Beckett, she reminded herself—hadn't been facing the stairs as if he were looking upward. He had been facing the direction of the great room, his back to…

This room. Her father's study. Her office.

Natalie turned around, surveying the room she had loved her whole life. It made her feel close to her father.

The intruder had been *here*…looking for something.

It's in your hands now.

Natalie tried to breathe.

You're the only one who can make it right.

Imogene Stuart's voice whispered through Natalie's mind. Imogene had given her something. A new statement about what happened in that hospital room. Stuart had been in the corridor on the phone. She'd just found out her husband was dying with cancer. She was upset. She couldn't even afford to take a day off to be with him. The treatments were incredibly expensive. Her insurance wouldn't cover everything.

She'd lied to secure her early retirement and for the money Rison Medical offered her. Money she needed for her husband's treatments, but neither the money nor the treatments had saved him. He died anyway. On his deathbed he'd begged her to tell the truth. She had called Natalie. They'd met at the funeral home. She'd given Natalie the amended statement. That was the reason Natalie hadn't remembered any of this when she was at her house today. She and Stuart had met at the funeral home where the poor woman had been picking out her husband's coffin.

Natalie gasped for air.

The evidence was here. *Somewhere.*

If she had to take this room apart she would find it. She started with the desk. She removed drawers, dumping their contents on top of the desk, and then looking on the underside as well as in the cavity. When every single drawer in the room had been emptied, she moved on to the shelves and cabinets.

"What're we looking for?"

Natalie dropped the books she'd moved from the shelf. Her heart launched into her throat. "Good Lord, you scared the hell out of me."

Clint was at her side, retrieving the books before she could get a breath past the band around her chest. She might have helped him with the books if she hadn't gotten lost staring at his naked torso.

"Where do you want these?"

Just watching his muscles bunch and flex as he reached and grabbed and then straightened made her wish for a long cool drink.

"What?"

"The books?" He held up two handfuls.

"Look through them for any document I might have hidden." *Focus, Natalie.* "Then put them in the stack over by the chair."

She turned back to the bookshelves. *Keep your wits.* This was too important to be thinking about anything else.

As they rifled through book after book, looked on top of and under every item in the room, she explained her most recent memories.

"I don't understand." She braced her hip against the desk and rubbed her temples with her fingertips. The inability to find what she absolutely knew she had possessed was so damned maddening. "It has to be here."

He turned the leather executive chair upside down as if it weighed nothing at all and made sure nothing was taped on the under side. "At least now you know you had evidence."

"If I can get Mrs. Stuart to talk, I won't need the evidence. Her husband urged her to tell the truth. I can use his final wish as leverage."

Clint placed the chair back on its wheels. "It's been two years. His dying wish may not carry as much weight now." He threaded the fingers of one hand through his hair.

Natalie so needed something to relieve her dry throat. "True. I guess when I failed to follow through she decided to put it all behind her. Now her life is about self-preservation. I can understand that."

He came around to her side of the desk. "You should go back to bed."

This close, his scent enveloped her, made her want to lean into him. Memories of the way he'd kissed her had her knees growing weak.

"Don't look at me that way, Natalie."

"I don't know what you mean," she lied.

"You're just getting your life back and you still have a long way to go. You don't need a man like me."

She dared to touch him, the slightest brush of her fingertips across his contoured chest. His skin felt hot and so smooth. "What kind of man are you?"

Those dark brown eyes blackened. "A man with a not-so-appealing history that too often comes back to haunt him."

"That part of your past is irrelevant to me." Her heart

pounding, she reached up and touched his lean jaw, trailed her fingers along the sharp angle and traced the softer, fuller ridge of his lips. She trembled while he stood stone still. "You aren't attracted to me? Your kiss said differently."

He curled his fingers around her wrist and pulled her hand away from his face. "The kiss was a mistake. A lapse in judgment. You hired me to help you solve this case. Have you changed your mind? Maybe you've decided you want to hire the man I used to be."

She watched his lips move as he spoke and she wanted to feel them against hers again more than she wanted to draw in her next breath.

He backed her against the desk and pressed her down onto the cluttered surface, his face not an inch from hers, his body crushed intimately against hers. "Are you sure this is what you want?" He brushed his lips across hers. "I can pleasure you like no one else ever has." He tasted her mouth again. "I can touch you so intimately you won't ever think of sex the same way. Is that what you want?"

She couldn't speak…she whimpered.

"Tell me that's what you want. That you want me to do this now. Here. And I'll do it."

Anger flared in his eyes.

He didn't want this.

He didn't want her.

She flattened her hands against his chest. "Get off me."

"I thought this was what you wanted," he growled.

"No."

He moved off her so fast, she lost her balance just lifting herself up.

He stood at the window staring out into the darkness. His arms folded over his chest. The rigid set of his shoulders told her he was furious.

Part of her wanted to apologize but the other part, the needy woman inside, wanted to demand why he didn't want her. She'd thought he did when he kissed her that once.

She chose the coward's way out. "Good night."

He said nothing as she left the room.

Tomorrow morning she was going back to see Imogene Stuart. And then she was getting justice for the Thompson family.

Chapter Thirteen

Clint poured the remainder of his second cup of coffee down the drain. He rinsed the cup and set it on the counter. He should apologize for his behavior last night. Natalie was not speaking to him this morning. She'd taken her coffee into her home office and closed the doors.

He'd walked past the door half a dozen times. From the sounds on the other side she was either still searching for the evidence Stuart had given her or she was attempting to organize the mess she'd made last night. He should offer to help.

No. He plowed his fingers through his hair. Spending too much time in a confined space with her was a bad idea. He braced his hands on the sink and stared out the window. His freshman year in college he'd learned to disengage emotionally with the blink of an eye. The call came and he stepped into character. It was that simple. In the beginning the need to disengage was about survival. He turned off his emotions and turned on the charm along with his physical prowess. He'd done his research, learned how to give what his client wanted even if the client didn't know how to articulate the desire. The human body had all sorts of pleasure points. He learned how to manipulate each one.

He hadn't gone looking for the work that had changed his life. Supply and demand—that had been the name of the game. He hadn't been naive. He'd recognized his looks were his most readily marketable asset. So he wrangled a fake driver's license that said he was twenty-one and hit the classier bars in hopes of landing a bartender position. He knew how to work a crowd and he was banking on good tips keeping his rent paid.

Regrettably for him, that year it seemed every damned body wanted to tend bar. After the tenth rejection he'd basically given up. An older man, probably Clint's age now, had stopped him as he left the last ill-fated interview. Clint remembered being impressed with his suit and the Rolex he wore. The man had explained how Clint could earn all the money he would ever need. Women with only money to keep them company would gladly take care of him for a little attention. Of course he'd resisted the idea at first. When an eviction notice landed on his apartment door, he did what he had to do.

He refused to regret his decision or the time he'd spent giving his clients pleasure whether it was nothing more than an escort to a dinner party or it was a no-holds-barred all-nighter.

In all these years since he'd left that part of his life behind, he hadn't been able to teach himself to engage emotionally. Relationships never lasted. Until he'd joined the SPU he'd even avoided maintaining friendships. He had spent his entire adult life dodging emotional entanglements. Period. The problem was the past two years working with Jess and the team had undone most of his hard-earned indifference and desire for solitude.

He watched the people he considered friends form permanent bonds and have children and suddenly he felt the building need to have those things, as well. It was the proverbial want what you can't have syndrome. Or, in his case, it was what he didn't know how to have.

"I'd like to apologize."

Clint turned around, surprised that Natalie had managed to get as close as the kitchen doorway without him sensing her approach. "Apologize for what?"

Her shoulders stiffened ever so slightly. He liked the soft blue sweater she wore. It matched her eyes. The jeans did a stellar job of reminding him of all those lush curves he'd felt beneath him last night. Desire stirred at the memory. *Very bad move.*

She brought her cup to the sink. He stepped aside. She rinsed the cup as he had and placed it on the counter. "I've allowed the stress and uncertainty to cloud my judgment. I haven't been thinking clearly." She met his gaze. "Rest assured it will not happen again. I'd like to pay another visit to Imogene Stuart. Since I can't find the evidence she gave me, perhaps I can convince her to cooperate."

He was supposed to be happy to hear this news. She'd just taken full responsibility for his misstep. Instead, he wanted to kiss her until she admitted she wanted him as desperately right now as she clearly had last night. The concept that touching her or kissing her might not happen again was unacceptable, yet she was right. It could not happen again.

His cell vibrated, preventing him from repeating last night's stupidity. He answered without checking the screen, which would have required he take his eyes off hers and for some ridiculous reason he couldn't do that. "Hayes."

"It's Lori. Imogene Stuart is dead."

Clint looked away from the concern gathering in Natalie's eyes. He didn't want her to see the defeat in his own.

This was a major setback. Potentially, Stuart was the only person who could confirm what Natalie remembered about the Thompson case. "What happened?"

"Her daughter came to pick her up for a weekend trip they had planned. When she didn't answer the door she went inside and found her still in bed. She thought she'd had a heart attack or maybe a stroke, but the ME says she was suffocated. We think the perp used her pillow. Sometime between midnight and three this morning."

Damn. "Was anything taken from the house?"

"There's no indication of forced entry. Nothing out of place. The daughter doesn't believe anything is missing, but she's pretty upset."

Clint blew out a disgusted breath. "They took the only thing that mattered." Stuart was dead, her life stolen. The truth snatched again from the Thompson family. Natalie would be left with regret for putting her in the line of fire with yesterday's visit. She would shoulder the responsibility for the woman's murder. "Let me know if you find anything or if the family knows anything at all about our case."

"Will do," Lori assured him.

Clint thanked her and ended the call. "That was Lori. Imogene Stuart is dead."

"Was she…?"

He nodded.

Natalie pressed her hand over her mouth. Tears brimmed on her lashes.

"There doesn't appear to be anything missing in her home. If she kept a copy of the evidence she gave you, it could be hidden there somewhere or in a bank deposit box. Lori will give us a hand on that end by searching thoroughly and questioning the family. At this point, that's about all we can do."

Natalie hugged her arms around her chest. "I want to talk to April, in person, and then I intend to talk to Vince."

She was distraught and definitely not thinking clearly. "Do you think it's a good idea to tip our hand since there's a good chance Farago is involved on some level?" Natalie's safety was Clint's primary concern. As badly as he wanted to nail these bastards, he would not sacrifice her security.

"I intend to finish this before anyone else dies."

When she would have walked out, he stopped her with a hand on her arm. The contact was like grabbing a live wire. The heat and energy rushed through his body. "It's my job to finish this," he reminded her, "but more important it's my job to protect you."

"Don't worry." She drew away from his touch. "I'm well aware of what you're here to do."

He supposed it was better for her to be angry with him than to keep testing the boundaries he struggled to maintain. His focus could not be divided—as tempting as taking what she'd offered was. The brain injury she'd suffered made her even more vulnerable. As foolish as the idea was, he didn't want her to want him only to get through this hard time in her life. It was an irrational idea, but as hard as he worked not to be, he was only human.

Before entering the garage, he scanned for signs of entry during the night and then he checked his car for any indication of tampering. He'd learned the ways to protect himself from that kind of surprise. Alarm systems could be bypassed but there were other measures. Like the tape he'd put in strategic locations around the hood as well as the doors. He checked for loss of fluids and damage to the tires.

When he felt confident there were no surprises, he opened the passenger door for her and then climbed behind the wheel. She was focused inward, likely beating herself up for yesterday's visit to Stuart.

He backed out of the garage. When the overhead door had closed, he rolled out onto the street and drove in the direction of her sister's house. "This isn't your fault, Natalie."

"It is my fault. You mentioned that someone might be watching us and I disregarded that warning."

He glanced at her, wished he could touch her. Damn him, last night had been the straw that broke the camel's back. Beyond that one kiss, he'd managed fairly well to restrain his desire for her—his need to touch her—and then he'd gone stupid and tried to scare her off. All he'd actually done was push himself over the edge he'd been avoiding for years.

"The people responsible for this want you to feel that way. Don't give them the satisfaction, Natalie. They did this. You tried to stop them once and they almost killed you. Now you're back, fighting for justice again."

She shook her head. "If we can't find proof of what really happened in the Thompson case, they'll get away with it. Mrs. Stuart will have died for nothing. If my brain would work right...maybe..."

He spared her a glance, the worry in her eyes making his gut clench. "We won't let that happen."

She stared straight ahead. "You're right. We have to find the truth. The Thompson family and the Stuart family deserve justice and I want my life back."

He wished he could promise her the kind of outcome she and those families deserved. Unfortunately, even if they found the evidence she needed, he suspected some things would never be the same again. Too many of the people she cared about were involved and the TBI would always have an impact on her life.

There were some things that couldn't be undone. They

would know soon enough if her sister had played a part that couldn't be taken back. Certainly Vince Farago had. His actions may have been with the full knowledge of Rosen. How often did such a big case get turned around at the last moment without the involvement of the upper echelon of the hierarchy?

Never.

18th Avenue South, Five Points
10:20 a.m.

NATALIE STARED AT her cell. "April never goes anywhere without her cell. I don't understand why she hasn't called me back or at least responded to my text."

"Maybe she's at the spa." Clint hoped her sister was just out spending her husband's money. "You sure about this?" He glanced at the craftsman-style cottage that sat on a postage-stamp-size lot in one of the city's most highly sought after neighborhoods. Vince Farago had good taste if nothing else. Bastard.

Natalie followed his gaze. "I'm sure. I'm only a couple of years late."

Clint wasn't so certain. A confrontation with Farago or maybe even Natalie's trust in him likely had set the events of two years ago in motion. Someone at the firm had learned what she was doing and taken steps to stop her. Whatever Farago or one of his cronies had done then, he wouldn't have the opportunity to do it this time.

They exited the car and walked up the cobblestone path leading to the sprawling front porch that was larger than the front lawn. Farago wasn't married but that didn't mean he didn't have a companion inside. Proceeding with caution was necessary. Until this was over, the last thing they needed was word to get out that Natalie Drummond was delving into the Thompson-Rison Medical case. There were far too many legal issues that might put a stop to their investigation.

Clint rang the bell and waited. Farago showed up at the door wearing jeans and nothing else. He stared at them for a moment before opening the door as if he understood he wasn't going to like the purpose of their visit and certainly didn't want the neighbors overhearing.

"What an unexpected surprise," Farago said, his tone as well as his posture suggesting their visit was no surprise at all. "I was just about to have coffee," he went on. "Come in. Join me." He glanced at Clint, but his gaze lingered on Natalie the longest.

Clint wondered if the two had shared more than a working relationship. Not that he could blame Farago. Natalie was a beautiful, smart, sophisticated woman. She deserved a hell of a lot better than either of the two men staring at her just now.

"We need to talk," Natalie told him, her voice cold.

Farago ignored her icy tone and closed the door behind them. Beyond the entry hall, the living space had been opened up into one large room that looked out over downtown Birmingham.

"Nice view," Clint commented.

"I hear yours is better." Farago picked up a glass and downed the orange juice.

"I wasn't aware you kept up with my real estate ventures."

"Only the ones that involve the most valuable residential real estate downtown." He set the glass aside and reached for a mug. "You're sure you won't have coffee?"

"No thank you," Natalie said with a firm shake of her head.

When Farago looked to Clint, Clint shook his head, as well.

"So." Farago filled his cup. "What do the two of you want to discuss this morning? Frankly, I'm surprised to see you after the unpleasant exchange we had yesterday." He looked from one to the other. "Don't be shy, have a seat." He gestured to the stools flanking the island.

Ignoring his invitation, Natalie demanded, "Tell me why you ignored the truth in the Thompson-Rison Medical case?"

Farago looked at her for a long moment then shrugged. "What truth are you referring to? We all have our own versions of the truth, after all."

"The day before I ended up in the hospital fighting for my life, I learned the only truth that mattered in the case." She moved closer to the island. "But I think you already knew that."

He grabbed a piece of browned bread from the toaster and tore off a bite. "I have no idea what you're talking about," he said between chews.

"Imogene Stuart told me everything." Natalie shook her head. "She told me all about the cover-up. Even gave me the evidence I needed to prove it. But then I took that untimely dive down the stairs."

Farago tossed the bread onto the counter. "What cover-up are you talking about?" He shot Clint a glance. "Has she had her meds this morning?"

Clint faked a smile. "You have no idea how badly I want to hurt you, Farago, so I would suggest that you watch your mouth."

Farago rolled his eyes. "Cut to the chase, Nat. What evidence?"

"Stuart left Mr. Thompson unattended and he fell. The resulting head injury that went ignored for hours cost him his life."

A real smile tilted Clint's lips as he watched Natalie in

action. One of these days, when she was fully recovered, he wanted to watch her in the courtroom.

Another of those indifferent shrugs lifted Farago's arrogant shoulders. "If that's true, why didn't Stuart say so two years ago?"

"Because she was paid to keep quiet. Are you the one who took the offer to her?"

He held up his hands. "I have no idea what you're talking about. You do realize that what you're doing is—"

"I know exactly what I'm doing," Natalie assured him. "I'm fully aware of the ramifications for a number of people, including me. I would have done this two years ago except someone stopped me. So I'm doing it now," she warned.

Farago continued to appear unfazed. "Then why don't you and Stuart take this theory you have to a judge. Why beat around the bush?"

"Stuart is dead," Clint informed him. "She was murdered in her home last night. Where were you this morning between midnight and three?"

"I was with friends at the Rare Martini over on Seventh until midnight. Then I came home. Alone."

"So you don't have an alibi." Clint wasn't sure Farago had the guts to kill anyone, but that didn't mean he wasn't responsible for the woman's death. If Rosen told him to get it done, Farago would have found a way.

"I'm afraid not and you don't have a badge." He turned his attention back to Natalie. "Really, Nat, you and your sidekick need to practice your good cop–bad cop routine. I'm not unsettled in the least."

"I'm happy for you, Vince," Natalie said, her voice empty. "Because I feel responsible for her death. If I hadn't gone to see her yesterday, she would still be alive. She's dead because of my actions."

"I guess that's one you'll have to live with, huh?" Farago sipped his coffee. "Life is hard that way sometimes."

Natalie smiled. "Oh, wait, there's one other thing, I failed to mention. I have the evidence, Vince."

Farago's posture changed so subtly Clint would have missed it had he not been watching him so closely. Natalie had hit a nerve. Clint wanted to tell her to slow it down, but he had a feeling her intention was to bait Farago. Bad idea. Farago would go straight to Rosen.

"Like I said," Vince tossed back, "take it to a judge."

Natalie laughed. "You think I'm bluffing."

Farago flattened his hands on the marble counter top. "I *know* you're bluffing."

And there it was. Fury charged through Clint. He wanted to beat the hell out of the guy. The bastard was somehow involved in what had happened to Natalie, there was no denying it. He couldn't possibly know the evidence was missing unless he'd been a party to taking it.

"I thought you might," Natalie said. "Thank you, Vince. That's all I needed to know."

His face paled as he realized his faux pas. "Wait a minute, I—"

"Goodbye, Vince." Natalie turned and headed for the door.

Clint gave his old nemesis a nod and followed the same route.

"Natalie, wait!" Farago rushed to catch up with them. "You really need to think about this. You're throwing away your career. What firm is going to want you after this?"

She stopped at the door and glared at him. "I think that's already been done for me, wouldn't you say?"

"You don't know what they're capable of," Farago warned.

"Who?" Natalie demanded. "*You* and who else?"

"It's Rosen," Farago said quickly when Natalie reached for the door once more. "He'll do anything to stay on top. *Anything*. If that woman is dead, he'll be the one who ordered it."

"Are you willing to help stop him?" Clint asked. "I'm confident a plea deal could be reached if you were involved in Beckett's or Stuart's murder. Maybe even immunity."

Farago shook his head. "You don't understand. None of us will live long enough to care."

Chapter Fourteen

11:10 a.m.

"Did your sister say what she wanted to talk about?"

Natalie forced her fingers to relax before they cracked her cell phone. No sooner than they'd left Vince, April had returned Natalie's call. She was waiting for Natalie at the house. "She didn't tell me. She only said that it was urgent."

Clint drove a little faster. Natalie's heart seemed intent to do the same. Vince's words were still ringing in her ears. How could she have worked at the firm all those years and not understood what Rosen and Vince were capable of? She was no neophyte. She was well aware of the ways of the world. Her law school professors had made it clear the kinds of evil their students would encounter in their future careers. Maybe she'd still worn the rose-colored glasses just the same. She had considered herself and Vince part of the good guys. Rosen had been her mentor. She'd thought he was the perfect example of an upstanding attorney.

She had been wrong.

April's Mercedes waited in the driveway as Clint made the turn. He tapped the garage door opener they'd taken from Natalie's crashed car and waited for the door to lift, and then he rolled into the space where her BMW usually sat. At some point she needed to get a new car. She wasn't sure she would ever feel safe again in the old one. For now, she felt safest with Clint.

Don't do this, Natalie.

Her last relationship had ended nearly two years ago. She hadn't really had time to feel alone considering her entire focus had been on recovery. April had been at her side. Suzanna and Leonard had been with her every day after she came home.

Now the sting of loneliness burned deep. She was thirty-two years old, almost thirty-three, and she had no one except her sister and brother. Suzanna and Leonard had quit. Her colleagues wanted nothing else to do with her—the feeling was mutual. Clint turned off the engine and closed the overhead door.

The two of them were very similar except he had more friends. She suspected Clint's single status was by choice. Had his early career ruined him for relationships? She imagined many of the women he had…attended to…had husbands who ignored them. Natalie's only excuse was that she had always been too focused on work.

And just look where that has gotten you, Nat.

"There's something you want to ask?"

His question startled her. She hadn't realized she was staring at him. "Sorry. I was just thinking."

"About?"

"It's nothing." She reached for the door. "April's waiting."

Clint stopped her with a hand on her arm. Her body reacted instantly to his touch, aching for far more. She dared to meet his eyes.

"You are an amazing woman, Natalie. You don't need the firm or anyone else. Once this is over, put it all behind you and embrace the life you deserve with someone who deserves you."

He let her go and emerged from the car. Natalie drew in a shaky breath and steadied herself. When this was done, she and Clint were going to have a long talk. He didn't give himself enough credit.

April stood in the middle of the great room. Her face was red from crying. She glanced at Clint. "We have to talk privately, Nat."

Natalie sat down on the sofa. "Whatever you have to say, you can say it in front of Clint. He's here to help us."

April collapsed into the closest chair. "Us?"

Clint drifted to the other side of the room, giving them space. Natalie appreciated his effort to make April more comfortable. She nodded in answer to her sister's question. "He'll help us figure out whatever has to be done."

A frown furrowed April's brow. "I don't think you understand."

"You were here the night I fell down the stairs. You said you and David had a fight."

April's eyes widened slightly. "We did."

"You had a man here with you," Natalie went on, "someone with whom you were having an affair."

Her sister's face paled. "I didn't think you remembered."

"I wasn't completely sure the details were accurate until you confirmed them just now." She drew in a deep breath. "You were laughing. I woke up. When I realized you were in your old room with someone who wasn't David, I decided to go downstairs for coffee and to think."

April's face crumpled. Tears flowed down her cheeks. "I'm so sorry. I'm the reason you fell. If I hadn't gotten involved with that bastard, you... Oh my God." She buried her face in her hands.

Natalie held her emotions in check. She had to know

everything before she allowed herself to feel. Whatever April had done or had allowed to happen, the truth had to come out. There was no more time for games, too many people had suffered already. "Did you or your friend leave your room before you heard me scream?"

Scrubbing at her tears, April's frown deepened. "What? No. We heard you scream. I jumped up and pulled on my gown. He was still dragging on his jeans when I ran out of the room." Realization dawned and her expression turned guarded. "Why do you ask?"

"Someone may have pushed me, April."

"You think I did that?" She shot to her feet, her arms going instinctively around her thin body. "I can't believe you would think that. We're sisters, Nat. I would never hurt you."

"What about your friend?" Natalie refused to look away even when her sister's trembling tore at her heart.

"I told you he was still in the room when I ran out. You were at the bottom of the stairs when I found you. He couldn't have pushed you." She dropped back into her chair. "Oh my God. This just gets worse."

"Then someone else was in the house."

April shook her head. "I never saw anyone else. The jerk took off while I was calling 9-1-1. There was no one else, Natalie. I swear. It was just the three of us until he took off and help arrived."

For a moment Natalie started to doubt her theory. Had she tripped, rather than been pushed? Was the feeling in that one memory one that had been planted by all the deceit she had uncovered?

"I know he didn't push you," April said, drawing Natalie back to the present, "but he was the one who tampered with your air bag."

"How do you know this?" Clint came up behind Natalie. He braced his hands on the sofa.

April swiped her eyes. "When you told the police the intruder had a scar, I knew it was him." She touched her forehead between her eyebrows. "I couldn't believe it. Other people could have scars there, too, but then I remembered the stuff he told me."

"What stuff?" Clint pressed.

Natalie was glad Clint asked. Her mouth felt full of cotton, her chest so tight she couldn't possibly hope to breathe.

"He worked for the dealership." She dropped her gaze to the floor. "The one where you bought your car. Before your accident, David was looking at BMWs and this man who worked there was looking at me. He was everything David wasn't. Drop dead gorgeous with lots of muscle. I was desperate for attention so we started seeing each other." She pressed her fingers to her lips before going on. "At first it was just great sex, then he started telling me stories about how easy it was to cause brake failure and all sorts of other problems. He bragged about how he could control the people who hired him to do that kind of work. He said that once some low-level dirtbag hired him to do something to a brake line. Then when the guy didn't pay up, he repaired it before the owner of the car even had a clue what had happened. He laughed and said people turned over their key rings when they had their cars serviced. The dealership has one of those machines that make copies of keys. He went on and on about how security systems are jokes."

Natalie exchanged a look with Clint.

"His name," Natalie said, her voice taut, "was Mike Beckett."

April gasped. "How did you know?"

"The police lab found evidence of her brakes having

been tampered with previously and then repaired," Clint explained. "It wasn't difficult to trace the activity back to the dealership."

"He did that to you?" April's face darkened to a deep shade of furious red. "I swear I didn't know. Bastard."

"Were you still involved with him after my injury?" Natalie felt numb now. Beckett had used April to get to her. Now the most important step was determining who hired him.

April shook her head. "Not after that night." Her watery gaze settled on Natalie. "After you were hurt. I never even thought of him again until you crashed your car. It was easy to put together the intruder with the air bag tampering." Her voice sounded so hollow, her gaze distant. "The scar was too much of a coincidence considering what he had told me before."

Suddenly Natalie understood. The bottom dropped from her stomach. "What did you do, April?"

April glanced at Clint briefly and then settled her gaze on Natalie. "I went to his house and demanded to know if he was the one who broke into your house and messed with your car."

She fell silent for a long moment before she continued. "He said he didn't have to break in. He'd made a copy of your key the last time you had your car serviced. I slapped him and he tried to push me away. He said he would have killed you when you caught him in your house, but you shot him first."

Silence lapsed again while Natalie's heart continued to break.

"Then he told me to leave. He said if I told anyone they would kill you and Heath. I tried my best to get him to tell me who paid him to do this and he wouldn't say."

"April," Natalie began but her sister held up a hand to stop her.

"That's when I saw the gun."

Natalie's heart surged into her throat. "April, don't say anything else."

Her sister shook her head, tears flowing down her cheeks. "I killed him."

Natalie's hand went to her mouth to hold back a sob.

"I grabbed the gun and pointed it at him. I told him he'd better stay away from my family and he just laughed." She shrugged. "He said he would put a bullet in my head and make it look as if you shot me. He tried to take the gun from me and somehow during the struggle it went off."

"You came here and changed," Clint suggested.

April nodded. "I was in your closet getting something to put on when Suzanna came into the room. I hid the clothes and the gun in a trash bag in your clothes hamper so Suzanna wouldn't see."

"You came back for…them." Natalie was so relieved that she hadn't imagined the whole thing that she felt lightheaded.

"Yes. I put them in a trash bin downtown."

"Where exactly?" Clint demanded.

April looked taken aback.

"It's all right," Natalie assured her. "It was self-defense. Beckett threatened you. But we have to let the police know what happened."

"Oh God. David doesn't know. If he finds out… I'm so sorry, Nat. I wasn't thinking of anything except how it was my fault. I had to try and make him stop."

Natalie refused to let her emotions get the better of her. "David is a smart man. He'll forgive you and stand by you if he wants to be governor one day." Maybe if he hadn't been so interested in running for office he wouldn't have left April vulnerable to an affair. Perhaps that was a stretch but blood was thicker than water. "I know you were trying to help and that means a great deal to me, but a man is dead and we have to do this by the book."

April reluctantly gave Clint the address and he called his friends in the BPD.

Natalie and April hugged. Her sister had been there for Natalie through her darkest days; Natalie had to be here for her now. They needed each other.

One thing nagged at her though. Suzanna had known April was in Natalie's closet. What else did Suzanna know that she hadn't told Natalie?

3:15 p.m.

NATALIE SAT ON the sofa on one side of April and her husband, David, sat on the other while Lieutenant Harper took her statement. Detective Cook had recovered the trash bag from the trash bin and called the BPD's evidence collection team.

"Will she be arrested?" David asked, his somber tone uncharacteristically quiet.

"Not at this time, sir," Harper explained. "When we sort this all out, we'll see how it stacks up. For now, it certainly sounds as if Mrs. Keating felt her life was in danger and acted in self-defense."

"I hope we can keep this out of the media," David urged.

"I can't promise that." Harper put his notepad and handheld recorder away. "But the department has no reason to talk to the media regarding the details we've just learned." He stood. "I have everything I need for now."

"Thank you, Lieutenant." Natalie was grateful Clint's friends in SPU had the case considering it was now a homicide investigation. She felt confident Harper would do all he could to protect April.

Clint showed the detective to the door.

David stood and held out his hand to his wife. "I think we should go home now." He smiled at Natalie, but the expression fell short of his eyes. "I'm certain you're exhausted. This has been a harrowing week for you."

Natalie rose. "I love my sister, David. I hope you're not holding back on my account. She's suffered enough over this. I would hate to hear that you caused her any additional distress."

He nodded his understanding as he drew April into the shelter of his arms. "You're a good sister, Natalie, even after you've been through so much yourself. You have my word that April and I are fine. She's the love of my life. We've both made mistakes. It's where we go from here that matters."

Though her brother-in-law's speech sounded less than passionate, Natalie nodded. "We'll all get through this."

Clint had just closed the front door as they moved into the entry hall.

"Until we know," he said to David, "who hired Beckett to hurt your family, I would advise you to keep April close. Watch each other's backs."

"With the election coming up next year, competition is heating up," David explained. "I've already contacted a security service about around-the-clock protection for both of us." David looked from Clint to Natalie. "I can have my contact there meet with you if you're interested in hiring someone, Nat." He glanced at Clint. "It might not be a bad idea moving forward."

"Thank you, David. I'll let you know." Natalie and April shared another hug before the couple left.

"Well, that went better than I expected," Clint said, echoing her thoughts.

Natalie watched through the leaded glass of the front door as her brother-in-law opened the car door for her sister. "David is a politician through and through. If it's best for his campaign, then he's on board. I just wish I knew what was in his heart."

"I take it you and your brother-in-law aren't the best of friends."

Natalie thought about the question for a moment. "We've never had any real disagreements beyond our differences on political issues. I suppose I always felt that he married April because she was a Drummond. I've never felt close to him, but he has reached out repeatedly since my fall."

Clint's gaze narrowed. "So you felt he wasn't good enough for your sister? He didn't meet the financial criteria or was it something else that made you feel that way?"

The question surprised her. "It wasn't about the money or that he wasn't *good* enough. The Keating family is quite well to do. They moved here about twenty years ago. He and I went to high school together. What I meant about the Drummond name was his impression that the Drummonds were among the founders of the city. I believe that was important to his political aspirations, but it's possible I'm wrong."

Clint looked away. "We should talk to Mr. and Mrs. Clark."

Confused by his odd question, Natalie took a moment to weigh his recommendation. She didn't want to believe that Suzanna might be hiding something from her, but her abrupt departure suggested otherwise.

"If you're up to it," he amended, obviously taking her hesitation for something else.

Natalie squared her shoulders. "Of course." She smoothed the hem of her sweater. "I'm ready."

Two people were dead...because of her. She couldn't think of resting until she found the truth.

Chapter Fifteen

Crestwood Circle
Birmingham
5:45 p.m.

Clint knocked on the door a second time just in case the doorbell wasn't working. Natalie surveyed the yard. She looked nervous. Considering what she'd remembered last night and what she learned from her sister this morning, apprehension was understandable.

Her life had been twisted into a few dozen knots the past couple of years. She deserved a break. He wanted to help her get her life back. He wanted it badly. Maybe more than he'd wanted anything in a long time. He was still kicking himself for questioning her thoughts on David Keating. His feelings of inferiority had nothing to do with her and he had no right dragging her into it.

The door opened and Suzanna Clark schooled her startled expression as she looked from Natalie to Clint and back. "I've said all I have to say."

Clint had a feeling pressure tactics wouldn't work with the older woman. Not even he would give a lady who reminded him far too much of his mother a hard time. Still, the situation was urgent. Time was not an available luxury at the moment. "Mrs. Clark, I feel compelled to warn you that if you don't cooperate with us, the police will be knocking on your door."

Her face paled. "Leonard!"

Clint winced at the fear he heard in Mrs. Clark's voice.

Natalie reached out to the woman she had known most of her life. "Suzanna, please. I need your help. Please, help me."

"What're you doing here?" Leonard demanded as he bellied up to the door.

"I just want the truth," Natalie pleaded. "I'm certain the two of you have done nothing wrong. This is—"

"Just stop." Suzanna put a hand to her chest. "Come inside."

Leonard sent her a look that spoke loudly of his disapproval.

"Let's just get this over with," Suzanna argued, defeat in her voice. "The police can help them sort it out but we're not helping anyone by remaining silent."

Clint never understood anyone's desire to keep secrets as a means to protect the innocent. The innocent did just fine when secrets were revealed. It was the guilty who didn't fare so well.

Leonard stepped back and Suzanna led them into their home. The brick rancher had a larger than expected living room. Clint sat next to Natalie. Leonard settled into his well-worn recliner next to the matching one his wife chose. He made no bones about how unhappy he was they had appeared at his door. He'd washed his hands of the situation and wanted nothing more to do with Natalie's troubles.

After a lengthy and somewhat awkward silence, Suzanna spoke. "It started a few months before your accident."

Leonard shook his head. "Your folks raised you girls better, but somehow it didn't take as well with April as it did with you."

"April told me about the affair," Natalie spoke up. "The man she was seeing lured her into the relationship. He's the same man who came into my house and tampered with my car."

The couple exchanged another one of those looks. "We," Suzanna said, "suspected he was not a nice man."

Clint was as surprised by the statement as Natalie appeared to be.

"You met him?" Natalie asked.

Suzanna nodded. "She brought him to the house four—"

"Five." Leonard held up one hand, fingers spread wide. "Five times."

"Five," Suzanna amended. "While you were at work. April said they were working on a surprise for you."

"For me?" Natalie shook her head. "What sort of surprise?"

Leonard harrumphed. "The first couple of times they *worked* in your daddy's study. Then they moved their *work* upstairs."

Damn. Clint had hoped April was as innocent in all this as she claimed. "This work," he asked, "was it something more than sex?"

Suzanna's cheeks flamed. Leonard's jaws puffed. "I don't believe so," Suzanna said. "I never found any evidence of anything else."

Leonard shook his head. "The girl should have known she would get caught."

"Wait," Natalie leaned forward a bit, "did you say she got caught? By David?"

"Well," Suzanna hedged, "I can't say that they had any kind of confrontation, but there—"

"He had to know," Leonard protested.

"Why do you think so?" Clint asked. "Was Keating watching the house?"

"He was doing more than that," Leonard said. "He brought some fellow to the house with him. A security technician or so he said. Claimed there was something wrong with the security system."

"That's preposterous," Natalie argued.

"I'm just telling you what he said. I knew he wasn't exactly telling it like it was because the technician only worked in the entry hall and upstairs."

"In April's old bedroom," Suzanna put in. "I was changing the sheets in your room when they went in there."

"So David suspected." Natalie clasped her hands in her lap. "What else did he do that I don't know about?"

The edge of frustration in her voice told all present that she was not happy to learn there had been so many goings and comings in her home without her knowledge. Clint could see how the Clarks didn't feel comfortable reporting April's activities since she, too, was a Drummond and had grown up in the house. Natalie had likely never given them reason to believe she didn't want her sister on the premises when she wasn't home.

"As far as I know," Suzanna said, "David wasn't in the house again until you came home from the hospital."

"There was that one time," Leonard reminded his wife. "He said he had to get clothes for Natalie."

"I was at the hospital," Suzanna said. "You were in bad shape."

Natalie blinked a couple of times but not before Clint saw the shine of emotion there. Reliving those days was hard enough on her, but to hear that her own family was somehow using her added insult to injury.

"He went upstairs and then he piddled around in the entry hall." Leonard reached for the sweating glass of iced tea on the table next to his chair. "I imagine he was taking out the cameras and such he'd had his *technician* install."

"April came through, though," Suzanna offered. "She and David have tried their best to help since you were hurt. I was hoping everything would be all right now."

Leonard nodded. "He called me or came by every week or two to see if there was anything I needed. Being a husband, I figured he had a right to know what his wife was doing so I put the whole business behind me and tried not to hold his behavior against him. A Christian should never hold bad thoughts against another."

"Me, too." Suzanna looked to her husband. "Until I found the bloody clothes and the gun."

"When Suzanna told me," Leonard said, "I told her we were done. We couldn't be involved with the likes of that. It was bad enough Suzanna could have been there alone when that intruder broke in." Leonard nodded toward Natalie. "I knew you were telling the truth no matter what the police thought. You've never lied or made up nonsense in your life."

Clint resisted the urge to take Natalie's hand in his. She listened patiently but he could feel her tension mounting.

"We're getting older," Suzanna said gently. "It was just too much."

"April said you were there the day she left the gun and the bloody clothes," Natalie ventured.

"We'd been to the grocery store. Leonard always drives me," Suzanna explained. "When we came back her car was in the drive and she was in your shower. I knew she was the one."

"I didn't even want to know what she'd gotten herself into," Leonard admitted. "It was best that we just walked away."

"I wanted to tell you all of it," Suzanna said, "but Leonard didn't want me to get in the middle of it."

"I understand," Natalie assured her. "Please know that you're welcome to come back and I guarantee none of this will happen again. April and her husband have spoken to the police about what happened with the gun and the bloody clothes. There will be an investigation but it has nothing to do with either of you. She and David are standing together on this. He, as you know, is focused on winning this election as a stepping stone to bigger things. He's not going to risk that goal with a nasty divorce."

The couple seemed to consider her offer for a moment. "It's time we retired," Suzanna confessed. "We need to spend more time with our grandchildren."

"I can't blame you." Natalie stood. "Thank you for telling me. If you think of anything else, please don't hesitate to let me know. When I spoke to the police, I didn't mention your names in relation to the gun or the bloody clothes. They have no idea you saw it," she said to Suzanna. "They won't bother you."

Clint had to give her credit, Natalie held it together exceptionally well until they were out of the house and in his car. Even then he wouldn't have known how very upset she was if not for the tears sliding down her cheeks.

"We're taking the evening off," he said. "You need a break."

"What I need is a plane ticket to take me far away from here."

"I'll see what I can do."

He hoped that was a promise he could keep.

Athens-Flatts Building, 2nd Avenue
8:30 p.m.

NATALIE STOOD IN the darkness and watched the lights of downtown Birmingham twinkle. She did love this view from Clint's penthouse. She'd come out onto the grand terrace to feel the cool breeze and to inhale the night air. He senses came alive just standing here, soaking in the atmosphere. Maybe it was time she sold the house and moved into something more manageable.

Would her parents have wanted her to keep the house if they'd known how much heartache she would suffer there? But then her parents had left her the home because, of their three children, they had known she would be the least likely to sell it or allow it to fall into disrepair. She thought of all the happy years the family had shared in the home. Endless Christmases and birthdays. So many happy memories…and a few devastating ones, as well.

She was not in a good place for making that kind of decision. The aches she felt went deep. Her sister had used Natalie's home and her trust. Her brother-in-law had done the same. Sadly, those were only the beginning of the injustices. The firm, the colleagues she had trusted and supported with every part of her mind and spirit, had let her down so egregiously that she could scarcely permit the thought without feeling sick to her stomach.

How had she surrounded herself with those so filled with greed and selfishness? She hadn't known these people at all. She laughed. Clearly, she scarcely knew her own sister. What did that say about her?

How had she been so oblivious to the deceit? Her father had once said that her need to see the best in people would be her downfall. Regrettably, his sage words had seen fruition. As difficult a pill as it was to swallow, she had learned a great lesson. She would not be so gullible moving forward.

The silver lining amid all the darkness was that her memories continued to return and she felt far less confused and uncertain. She had reason to believe a great deal of the uncertainty and confusion she had felt in the past several months had been about those around her attempting to hide their treachery. The interference hadn't permitted her mind to properly put the pieces back together.

She could see clearly now.

Clint joined her. "Aren't you cold?"

The breeze had picked up but she'd ignored it. Now that he mentioned it, she shivered. "A little."

"Dinner's ready."

She smiled. "I smelled the ginger and something else, maybe garlic."

"It's one of my favorite entrees from Belinda's." He handed her a glass of wine, and then sipped his own.

"I've heard about that shop. She does gourmet meals for you to take home and heat up at your leisure."

"That's the one."

Natalie sipped her wine. It was fresh and sweet on her tongue, bubbly in her throat. "Thank you for bringing me here. I don't think I could have gone home tonight."

"Sometimes home isn't where we need to be." He leaned forward and braced his forearms on the steel railing. "Sometimes we just need to disappear from all that we know."

"Do you ever do that?" She downed a swallow of wine, needing courage. "Disappear, I mean?" She leaned against the railing.

"Sometimes."

She thought of the elegant home just beyond those disappearing doors that allowed for an unobstructed extension of the main living space onto this amazing terrace. Clint Hayes had an enviable home, a wardrobe that would make the most impeccably dressed man jealous and he was incredibly handsome. Yet, Natalie recognized a sadness in him. Maybe even a little loneliness. She almost laughed out loud at the idea. He could have any woman he desired. His relationship with his detective friends was proof that he possessed the ability to develop and maintain relationships.

"Why are you alone?" Her breath caught. She hadn't meant to say the words.

He straightened, downed the rest of his wine and took the two steps to a table to place his glass there. "The same reason as you, I suppose." He moved back to where she stood frozen, desperate to hear more. "Wouldn't you say?"

He felt so close standing out here with only the city lights and the stars to chase away the darkness. She drained her glass. More courage, she told herself as she placed it next to his. "How can you compare your choices to my reactions to events over which I had no control?"

He waited until she returned to stand next to him. "Your recovery has been nothing short of miraculous. Despite recent events, you've come through amazingly well. So what's stopping you now?"

His deep voice and the intensity in his eyes made her shiver. "Do you mean right now? This very moment?"

"Why not?"

Heat seared through her body. Was he inviting her to be with him? He'd certainly had a different attitude last night. "Is that why you brought me here? I thought—"

He touched her hair. Her voice deserted her as he let his fingers glide through the length of it.

"I don't want to want you." He reached up, traced her lips with the pad of his thumb. "I don't want to lie awake at night thinking about how it would feel to be deep inside you."

Her thighs trembled. "I...don't know what to say."

"Don't say anything." His mouth swooped down and claimed hers. "Let's just do this before I lose my mind."

He picked her up and carried her to his bedroom. He lowered her to her feet, his hands sliding up her torso, drawing her sweater up and off. He stared at her breasts for a long moment before dropping to his knees and removing the sandals she wore. When his fingers unfastened her jeans, she gasped. He leaned forward and kissed her belly button and heat funneled beneath it. The whirlwind was so ferocious she could scarcely breathe.

She sank her fingers into his dark hair, relishing the silky feel. He dragged her jeans down her legs, and she stepped out of them one foot at a time and kicked them aside. He stood and spun her around. His fingers trailed up her spine leaving a path of pure fire in their wake. He unfastened her bra and pushed it off her arms. His lips followed the path of fire he'd ignited, all the way down to her bottom where he teased her relentlessly, tugging down her panties with his teeth. He kissed and licked and tantalized his way back up her legs and then along her spine, taking extra time at her neck. She was burning up, need building so fast she wanted to beg for mercy, but her lips wouldn't form the words.

He turned her around and the instant he took her nipple into his mouth she lost all control. She pushed him away and tugged at the buttons of his shirt. He joined her, tearing at his buttons, pulling loose the shirttail. Her fingers tangled in his fly, slipping loose the button and lowering the zipper. The trousers and the boxer briefs came off in one quick sweep.

He lifted her onto the bed and lowered his body next to hers. She vaguely remembered the last time she'd made love, but this was something far stronger, wilder…soul awakening. He kissed every inch of her, made her come so many times she was certain her mind and body couldn't possibly bear one more moment.

"Please," she pleaded, "I can't take any more."

"Just let go, baby…lose yourself." He trailed his tongu

down her belly and lavished her in the most intimate and carnal ways a man could pleasure a woman.

Gasping for breath, she took his advice and threw off all her inhibitions. No rules, no worries, just the incredible pleasure coursing through her veins. Feeling fearless now, she turned the tables on him. She wanted to taste all of him. She wanted to touch him in ways she had never touched anyone. She wanted to drown in the sensation of his voice whispering against her skin…of his body moving against hers.

She wanted him…all of him. And then she wanted more.

Chapter Sixteen

Sunday, September 25, 6:50 a.m.

Clint watched the woman sleeping next to him. He tried to convince himself that last night had been about having ignored his physical needs for far too long, but that wasn't true. He wasn't a fool and he hadn't survived this long by lying to himself.

Last night had been about desire. The basic, naked longing to have something or someone you wanted so desperately. Yes, last night had been about desperation. Complete, utter desperation several degrees above primal craving. He wanted Natalie Drummond for far more than her body. He wanted her mind and spirit. He longed to touch her heart. No…he yearned to own her heart.

More terrifying, he wanted to give himself to her without reservation. This was a place he had never been before. He didn't want to be here now. He wasn't the sort of man she would want to spend her life with.

He freed himself from the tangle of silk sheets and moved away from the bed. The rising sun filtered through the floor-to-ceiling windows, stretching its glow across the white rumpled linens, touching her face. Her long dark hair fanned over her pillow making him want to run his fingers through it. He had learned every part of her…tasted every inch of her. And he wanted more.

His body stirred with need. How easy it would be to slide between those sheets and take her again this morning. She had shown him over and over with her soft whispers and urgent whimpers that she wanted him with equal ferocity. With her touch, her kiss, and the way her body opened and accepted him so completely. The trouble was, he understood that what she had needed—what he had needed—last night was only temporary.

Natalie was in a vulnerable place right now. She was desperate for the truth and equally terrified to trust. He was the anchor she clung to in these turbulent waters. Though she was recovering exceedingly well, the TBI would continue to impact her life on some level. When the case was closed and her life was hers again, she would realize her mistake. She wouldn't look at him the same way and that was the part that terrified him the most.

Clint shook his head. He was a fool. He hit the shower and washed away the evidence of just how big a fool he'd been. He would get his act together and finish the job. He'd never been anything less than completely reliable. He wouldn't fall down on the job now.

CLINT WAS HAVING his second cup of coffee in the morning sun when she found him. She smiled and his chest tightened.

"Coffee's great." She sat down at the table with him and set her cup there. "What a perfect way to spend the morning." She admired the city view. "I love everything about this place."

Despite his best efforts he couldn't help inventorying every detail he adored about her. She had showered and dried her long hair. Though she wore the same sweater and jeans as yesterday, she looked fresh and soft. The urge to carry her back to his bed and block out the rest of the world for a few more days was a palpable force.

"You want breakfast?" Last night they had devoured dinner between lovemaking sessions. Still, he was ravenous this morning. Unfortunately his appetite went well beyond mere food.

She shook her head. "I'm not hungry." She stared at her cup and traced a slow circle around the rim. "I didn't dream last night. At least nothing I remember."

"Is that unusual?" He directed his thoughts to the case. She'd come to him for help and here he was feeling sorry for himself for developing these feelings. Not to mention his selfish need to make love to her again and again.

"In the beginning I took something to help me sleep. It was crucial. My brain seemed to forget when to shut itself down. To heal, it needed rest. When I stopped the sleep aids, the dreams became more vivid and intense. It didn't bother me at first. I was warned that some memories would return that way. You know, hard and fast and complete. Sometimes the dreams were just jumbled pieces of my life. But they were always there, every night. Except last night."

"The wine," he proposed. "I slept like a rock myself."

Her gaze held his, the same desire he felt was crystal clear in those blue depths. "I think it was more than the wine."

"I should get you home." If she stayed and kept looking at him that way he would end up carrying her back to his bed post haste. Not a good idea.

"I called my friend Sadie for an appointment."

"Dr. Morrow?" He searched her face. "Are you feeling all right?" He hadn't thought of anyone but himself last night. He should have realized sex would have a major impact on her emotions for a whole host of reasons.

"Yes." She nodded. "I feel great. Better than I have in a long time."

Now he was confused. "Then why do you need to see your psychologist?"

"I don't want to waste any more time. People are dying. I can't keep waiting for the memories to come back to me. We know Rosen and Vince withheld evidence—or worse. The only witness who can prove what really happened is dead. I must find that evidence. Sadie can help me. She can take me back to the day before the…fall."

"You want to use hypnosis. Have you done that before? Is it safe under the circumstances?" He wasn't comfortable with this. If hypnosis was the answer, surely one of her doctors would have suggested it before now.

"There are always risks when toying with the mind," she confessed. "I'd rather take that risk than to sit around waiting for the next attempt on my life. By now Rosen is aware that I know his secret."

He couldn't have said it better himself, but that didn't mean he liked her plan one bit. He could protect her from outside threats. What she was proposing took her beyond his reach. "We'll talk to Dr. Morrow. If the risk is too great," he shook his head, "we'll find another way."

Natalie scooted back her chair and stood. "I appreciate your concern, but I've spent the better part of two years having people tell me what's best for me. I think it's time I made a few decisions of my own."

Knowing a brick wall when he hit one, Clint gathered their cups. "You're the boss."

He left the cups in the sink and headed for his closet. He secured his handgun at his belt. Since turning in his badge he rarely carried. With recent events, being armed

was warranted. He selected a jacket and a tie. As he secured the silk fabric around his neck, he studied his reflection. At thirty-six he thought his life was on track.
Financially secure, a satisfying career, no family obligations other than the occasional call to his mom. Why the
abrupt urgent need for more?

He already knew the answer. Everyone he counted as
a friend, including his boss, was either getting married or
having babies. He wanted that, too.

"Ridiculous." He dismissed the restless feeling and purposely kept his gaze away from the rumpled sheets as he
left his bedroom.

Natalie waited near the elevator. She looked him up
and down, and then her lips spread into a smile. His gut
tightened at the sheer beauty of that smile. His feelings
weren't about marriage or having babies—they were about
this woman.

Oh yeah. He was in trouble here.

Oxmoor Road
9:40 a.m.

"WE'VE DISCUSSED THIS BEFORE," Natalie insisted. "There's
no other way. I have to do it."

Sadie wasn't convinced. "Dr. Cromeans is not a fan of
regression therapy. He prefers to allow the memories to
return in their own time. Since he's the physician of record
on your case, I would need—"

Natalie expected her to resist. "Two people are dead,"
she reminded her old friend. "There have been at least
two, potentially three, attempts on my life. I need to be
proactive."

Sadie considered her reasoning for a moment. "You

seem more like your old self today. Are you feeling stronger? More confident?"

"Yes." Natalie nodded. "In spite of the trouble cropping up around me, I don't feel out of control." In fact, she felt as if she could take on the world. She felt strong.

"This is very good news, Nat. So many patients who've been through a TBI never fully regain their confidence in self, which is so essential to moving forward with their lives. I am immensely pleased with your progress."

Natalie wanted to tell her about last night, but she couldn't share it just yet. Her pulse reacted to the idea that Clint waited just outside the room. She had no idea how she would ever convince him to stay once the case was closed. Somehow she would find a way. She didn't want to let him go. The idea might be foolish but her father had taught her to go for what she wanted and to never let go.

She wanted Clint Hayes in her life.

"Do this for me, Sadie," she urged. "I'll sign whatever sort of release is needed. I can't afford not to try and I certainly can't wait another day."

Sadie sighed. "I really wish you would reconsider."

"I won't," Natalie warned. "I have to know where I hid the evidence."

"Though I don't know all the details, I can understand how time is your enemy in this."

Natalie could feel her old friend's resistance weakening. She couldn't make Sadie a target by sharing the tragic truth with her just yet. When this was over and those responsible were brought to justice she would tell her friend everything.

"All right, if you're sure this is what you want."

"I'm sure."

"Let's move to the session seating."

Natalie relocated to the chaise lounge. She sank into the butter-soft leather and closed her eyes.

"Find a comfortable position and just breathe. Deep and slow. Notice how your body relaxes as the air slowly leaves your lungs. Breathe. In…out. Deeper. Slower. Feel how your body is relaxing. Each breath you release purges your body of the stress and worry. It's going…going…all gone."

Natalie felt so light she could be floating. *Breathe… deep and slow.*

"Imagine you're walking along the street where you live. You can see your house but it's far, far away. As I slowly count you're going closer to home. Each number takes you closer and closer. One…you are so relaxed and your body is just floating toward home. Two…"

Natalie floated along, closer and closer to the home where she'd grown up…where she'd lived her whole life.

"Natalie, it's September eighth two years ago. You wake up that morning feeling relaxed and happy."

Natalie threw the covers back and stepped out of bed. "No," she murmured, fear creeping into her bones.

"It's all right, Natalie, you can see but nothing from that day can hurt you now. Where are you going?"

"I have a meeting at the funeral home with Mrs. Stuart. She has something to show me. She says it's important. I'm worried that it's a setup, but my instincts won't let me ignore her." Natalie's heart started to pound. Her body felt stiff and her lungs burned as if she'd been running. "I shouldn't go, but I have to. Whoever sent the letters knows something I need to know…"

"Where are you, Natalie?"

Sadie's voice touched her in the darkness like a soothing whisper. Natalie moved toward the sound. She felt calmer now. She could do this. "I have the evidence. I don't know what to do. This is going to change everything." She moved her head side to side. "This is bad…so bad."

"Where are you taking the evidence, Natalie? Do you need to hide it?"

"Yes." In her mind, Natalie opened the pocket doors of her father's study. "It's late. I'll turn it over to the judge in the morning." She needed a safe place to hide it. Natalie searched the room that served as her home office. A really good place where no one would think to look. She went through the drawers and the shelves. Where did she hide it? Her attention landed on the liquor cabinet. "There."

"Where, Natalie?"

"The liquor cabinet." She opened the lower doors and found the beautiful carved wooden case that contained a fifth of Jack Daniels sipping whiskey. It had been a gift to her father from one of his friends. Natalie removed the bottle and set it aside. She carefully folded the two documents and placed them in the box so the bottle would cover them. Then she closed the box and tucked it safely in the farthest corner of the cabinet. "It'll be safe here."

"Where are you going now, Natalie?"

The sound of Sadie's voice was farther and farther away. Natalie stood in the entry hall and gazed up to the second-story landing. It was late. She should get some sleep. Tomorrow she was going to jeopardize her career by doing the right thing. She must be out of her mind. No. No. It was the right thing to do. Poor Mrs. Thompson deserved justice for her family. How could the firm have allowed Rison Medical to get away with what they'd done?

Not fair.

She took the first step up.

"Natalie, you can wake up now."

Sadie's voice was so far away she could hardly hear her. Natalie climbed the stairs and went to her room. She was so tired. She slid into the bed and closed her eyes. She needed to sleep.

"Natalie!"

Natalie opened her eyes. Where was she? At home in bed. What day was it? She had to hurry. She threw back the covers and sat up.

Laugher floated to her.

Whispers brushed her senses. More laughter. April? What was her sister doing here?

Natalie moved into the hall. More whispers, a man's voice this time, drifted in the air. April was in her room with someone. Had she and David come here for some reason? Why didn't they wake her? No, wait. She remembered. April and David had a fight. Had they made up?

What time was it? A single dong sounded downstairs. She wandered in that direction. She reached the landing. Below, the entry hall was dark and yet somehow the grandfather clock stood in a pool of light. *Eleven forty-five.*

Good grief. It wasn't even midnight. She should go back to bed. Her stomach rumbled. Had she forgotten to eat? After the meeting with Mrs. Stuart she'd had no appetite. She could eat now. A sandwich maybe. Coffee would be good. Maybe not. She might not be able to go back to sleep.

"Natalie!"

She frowned. Was that Sadie calling her name? What was she doing here?

Natalie started down the stairs and suddenly her body bowed forward as if something had struck her in the back. She was tumbling down the stairs. Screams surrounded her, rising up in the air until her head slammed into the marble floor.

Darkness.

Whispering voices.

"Natalie!"

Clint burst into the office. Sadie was shaking Natalie. The screams abruptly stopped and Natalie sat up.

Clint rubbed his neck and swore. "What the hell happened?"

Sadie shook her head. "I'm not sure. She stopped listening to my voice and went off on her own journey. Are you all right, Nat?"

Natalie nodded and then stared at Sadie for a long moment before lifting her gaze to Clint. He held his breath as she spoke. "I know where the evidence is."

Sadie refused to permit them to leave until she was convinced Natalie was calm and feeling balanced. Clint navigated after-church and lunchtime traffic while keeping one eye on his passenger. She hadn't said much since they left her friend's office.

"Did you remember anything else?"

"Just the impact of being pushed…and falling. My head slamming against the floor and then the darkness."

"What about the whispers and the laughter? Could you hear those up till the moment you were pushed?"

She took a few moments to answer. "Yes." She turned to him. "They were still whispering and laughing in April's room."

"I think," Clint said carefully, "in that case we can rule out April and Beckett. If they were still in the bedroom, they were nowhere near you."

"We can also rule out Suzanna and Leonard and certainly David." She laughed, a sound that held no humor. "April wouldn't have brought her lover to the house if there was a chance David might join them."

"Farago." Maybe Clint just wanted it to be him. He couldn't deny a sense of giddy anticipation at the possibility of seeing the guy go down.

"Or someone he or Rosen hired." She stared out the window. "It's hard to imagine my colleagues as enemies but I know it's true of at least two or three of those closest to me."

He told himself not to do it, but he might as well have been talking to the wall. He placed his hand over hers on the console. "I can't promise this will sharpen your powers of perception to the point you'll never have to worry about being deceived this way again, but I can guarantee you it won't hurt as much next time."

"I suppose that's something."

Clint parked his Audi in her garage. "As soon as we find the documents, we'll take them to the office, make a copy and put them in the safe. We don't want to risk losing the only copy."

"Good idea," Natalie agreed. "I'll call the one attorney in Birmingham I know won't be swayed by the influence of Rosen."

Clint unlocked the door to the kitchen. "Are you sure he's an attorney?"

"He's the best," she assured him.

She smiled and he felt better just seeing those blue eyes sparkle.

Clint stepped ahead of her as they entered the house. He frowned at the idea that they'd failed to set the alarm when they left yesterday. While he surveyed the great room she headed straight to her office. The hair on his neck stood on end. "Natalie, wait."

The doors glided apart with the groan of metal on metal and she hurried in.

"It's about time."

Clint reached for his weapon. Too late. David Keating stood in front of Natalie's desk with a .9 millimeter aimed at her.

"Why don't you close the doors, Mr. Hayes?"

"David, I don't understand. What're you doing?"

Natalie sounded calm but Clint saw the fear in her eyes. He settled his full attention on the man. "Put the gun down and we'll talk about this, Keating."

"I'm not playing games here, Hayes. Do exactly as I say or I will pull this trigger. Take off your jacket," he ordered.

Clint was not giving up his weapon. Grunting and groaning sounded behind them. Someone else was in the room.

"I told you to shut up!" Keating screamed.

Clint couldn't see who was behind them. He didn't dare take his eyes off the bastard with the gun. "Think about what you're doing, Keating. If you hurt her, you won't make it out of here alive. You have my word on that."

"Take off the jacket!" Keating's face was red with fury now.

Clint took his time shrugging off his jacket.

"Toss it on the chair and put your weapon there."

This was it. There would be no going back once he gave up his weapon. Clint met Natalie's gaze, urging her to understand that he had to make a move. She nodded ever so slightly.

Clint tossed his jacket and reached for his weapon.

Keating's attention fixed firmly on him, watching for any sudden moves.

Natalie dropped to the floor.

Keating snapped his attention to her.

Clint fired one shot, aiming for the right shoulder. The bullet hit its target and the weapon dropped from Keating's hand. He howled in pain.

Clint was on him before he had a chance to recover from the shock of being shot. "You okay?" he called to Natalie.

"Yes." She scrambled to her feet.

He slammed Keating down into the nearest chair. Natalie had gone around the desk and was preparing to release Keating's other hostage. *Vince Farago.*

"Leave him," Clint ordered. "We don't know why he's here."

Natalie looked uncertain but she did as Clint said. "Is the duct tape he used on Farago lying around somewhere?"

Natalie grabbed the roll and brought it to him. She grimaced at Keating's continued howling. "I'll call 9-1-1."

"Then call Harper."

While Natalie made the calls, Clint secured Keating, starting with his mouth. "You'll live," he warned. Clint imagined he would wish for death many times before he was out of prison.

Clint left Keating and moved on to the other man. He ripped the duct tape off Farago's mouth, garnering another yelp. "By my estimates you have maybe ten minutes before the police arrive, Farago. Why don't you give me your version of what's going on and maybe I can put in a word for you."

"He came to my house and told me that Natalie wanted to make a deal with us."

"A deal for what?" Clint demanded.

Farago glared at him. "You know what."

Clint glanced over at the liquor cabinet where Natalie was checking for the documents she had hidden there two years ago. She shook her head. Damn it.

"He took them," Farago said.

Clint frowned. "Who took what?"

Keating started making all sorts of grunting and groaning sounds. Natalie tore the tape from his mouth.

"Tell me what you did, David. Tell me now."

"I planted cameras," he said between gasps. "I knew

April was having an affair." He glared at Farago. "That bastard paid Beckett to seduce her."

"Beckett said I didn't have to pay him. She wanted him," Farago hurled back.

Clint grabbed the bastard by the chin. "Shut up."

"I saw you," Keating said, his gaze on Natalie. "I was watching from my computer at home and I saw you hide the documents. I heard you talking to him." He glared at Farago. "You told him you had the evidence and you were taking it to the judge the next morning."

"What did any of this have to do with you?" Natalie demanded, fury sparking from her eyes.

"I wanted a political career. I needed leverage to get the kind of backing required. I knew it had to be something big so I drove over here, waited until you were in bed, and came inside. Imagine my surprise when that slut wife of mine showed up with her lover."

Natalie slapped him.

He sneered at her. "I found your evidence and I knew it was my ticket to where I wanted to be. Art Rosen had the kind of influence I needed. I called Vince and asked him what it was worth."

"Tell her what you did," Farago shouted as sirens sounded outside.

"He told me it wouldn't matter because you were going to the judge and rock the boat. Even without the documentation, you could ruin everything."

"He pushed you down the stairs," Farago shouted.

"And now you'll never have your evidence," Keating said. "All this was for nothing because Stuart can't back you up."

Natalie's face paled.

Clint strode over to Keating, ripped off another length of tape, slapped it over the man's mouth, and then he slammed his fist into his face. Keating's muffled howls made Clint feel just a little better.

"I need that evidence," Natalie said to Clint, the pain in her voice a raw ache inside him.

He turned to Farago. "Actually, I don't think you need it. You have an eye witness to the whole fiasco."

Farago shook his head. "No way. As long as I keep my mouth shut, Rosen will protect me."

Clint walked back to where Farago sat on the floor. He crouched down and looked him straight in the eye. "By the time Keating gets through singing for a plea deal, the firm won't even look at you much less protect you." He leaned even closer. "I was a cop for a long time, Farago. I have contacts in prison. Do I need to spell out how miserable I can make it for you in the tank? You sure you want to take your chances with Rosen?"

"I would listen to him if I were you," Natalie recommended. "Between Keating's testimony and mine, you're screwed, Farago. You and Rosen are going down."

Farago's eyes widened as the sound of sirens grew louder.

"The way I see it," Clint added, "you have one option. Make a deal fast—before Keating. I guarantee you will not like prison."

"How can I be sure my rolling over on Rosen about this case will be enough?" he whined.

"That depends," Clint offered. "Did you kill Imogene Stuart?"

"No! That was Keating!"

Keating made more of those urgent, muffled sounds. Clint ignored him.

Natalie looked even more stricken. "He's right, Vince. You should hurry, otherwise David may get a deal from the DA first."

"Okay, okay! I'll talk to the DA." Farago glanced at Keating. "Right now! I can give him enough to send Rosen away for a very long time." He sneered at Natalie. "While you were busy with all those cream-of-the-crop cases, I was the one doing his dirty work on the cases you never hear about in staff meetings. Call the DA now."

Natalie smiled, the expression weary but triumphant. "I think I can arrange that for you."

It was done. Natalie could have her life back. Clint wanted to feel relieved, to be happy for her. Instead, he felt lost.

Chapter Seventeen

4th Avenue North
Birmingham
Monday, September 26, 5:00 p.m.

The lobby was overflowing. Jess brimmed with pride. The open house had started at two and there had been a steady flow of visitors since. Buddy cut free from the crowd and joined her.

"Looks like we're a success, kid."

Jess gave him a nod. "We are."

The new mayor and every department head at Birmingham PD had passed through this afternoon. Of course, Jess was pretty sure Dan had something to do with that. Her smile widened as she watched him work the crowd. She had been in love with him since she was seventeen years old and he was still the most handsome man she had ever seen. As if to punctuate the thought, the baby kicked. She pressed her hand to her belly and sighed. Life was good.

"Both the new recruits are here," Buddy said. "All we need now are some new cases."

"Those will come," Jess assured him. "There's never a shortage of people who need the kind of help we can offer." Sad but true.

Jess watched the two new hires. Owen Welsh was an excellent choice. Sean Douglas she still had reservations about. He was a far-too-cocky guy. His background as a bodyguard to the stars made his resume desirable, but there was something more than his one failed assignment that nudged at her. Jess couldn't put her finger on it just yet. Before he went out on a case she would know everything about the brazen young man.

"No frowning allowed. Your open house is a smash hit."

She glanced up at Dan and smiled. "I was just thinking."

He leaned down and whispered in her ear. "I was thinking I might take my gorgeous wife home early."

She shivered and tugged on his tie. "Look. Lori and Chet are here. And Sylvia."

Dan groaned. "One more hour and I'm taking you home, Mrs. Burnett."

"Whatever you say, Chief."

Jess glanced around the room. Where were Clint and Natalie? She'd seen them just a moment ago. Natalie was still stunned that her brother-in-law had committed such atrocities. Jess was rarely surprised by what one human could do to another. All too often the face of evil was one the victim knew too well.

"I swear," Sylvia Baron grabbed Jess and gave her a hug, "if I throw up one more time during an autopsy I'm going to belt my husband."

Jess laughed. "The morning sickness will pass."

Sylvia groaned. "Not soon enough," she grumbled. "Did I tell you Nina is planning Addi's engagement party?"

"You did," Jess said. Nina continued to do exceedingly well on her new medication. Jess could not be happier for the Baron family. Now that she had a child of her own, she understood more so than ever how hard it was to see a child—even an adult child—suffer.

As if another wave of nausea had hit, Sylvia pressed a hand to her belly and made a face. "Why do women do this?"

Jess laughed. She had never seen the medical examiner get even a little queasy at the most gruesome scene. "When the baby arrives you'll understand."

"Who's that gorgeous young man over there?" Sylvia nodded in the direction of Sean Douglas.

"Trouble, I fear."

Sylvia patted her arm. "Nothing you can't handle, I'm confident."

Jess relaxed. Her friend was right. Jess had taken down more than her share of serial killers. A cocky guy like Douglas would be a piece of cake. As if he felt her scrutiny, Douglas's gaze collided with hers. He nodded in that enigmatic way of his.

She would be keeping a close eye on him.

"You wanted to talk?" Clint shut the conference room door, closing out the sound of the open house.

Natalie shored up her courage and launched into her practiced speech. "April was such a mess last night, you and I didn't get to talk after the police left."

Her sister had shown up right after the police. David had drugged her coffee. He'd hoped to keep her down for the count until he accomplished his mission. He'd intended to kill Natalie and Clint and then Vince, staging the scene as if Vince had committed the murders and been mortally wounded in the process. David had even coerced Vince into picking him up so no one would see his car at the house. Her brother-in-law had been that greedy for power.

David had been one of those unexpected faces of evil

Jess Burnett had told her about. Eventually the wounds he'd caused would heal.

"What do you want to talk about?" Clint asked, nudging Natalie from the troubling thoughts.

She smiled. "I wanted to thank you for all you did. I wouldn't have been able to do this without you. Mrs. Thompson and her family will finally have the vindication they deserve."

"No thanks necessary. I provided a service. You paid the fee."

He wanted to sound indifferent but she knew he didn't feel that way. And she was not going to let him pretend nothing had happened between them. "Actually, I was interested in an additional service."

His gaze narrowed. "I don't want to play games with you, Natalie."

With a deep breath, she took the leap. She put her arms around him and stared deeply into those dark eyes. "I want to explore the feelings I have for you. The feelings," she said when he would have loosened her grip on him, "I know you feel, too."

"I'm not the right man for you."

"You're the only man for me." She went up on tiptoe and pressed her lips to his. He resisted at first, but then he surrendered. And then he took control of the kiss.

"I'm not what you need," he murmured against her lips.

"You're everything I want," she whispered back. "And more."

His fingers threaded into her hair and he kissed her for so long her knees went weak. "Fair warning, once you're mine, I won't let you go."

"I'm counting on it," she whispered.

He flashed her a grin before lowering his lips to hers. Despite all the things she wanted to say about the wonderful future they were going to have together, Natalie lost herself to the promise of his kiss.

They had the rest of their lives and she would never take a single moment of it for granted.

* * * * *

MILLS & BOON®

INTRIGUE
Romantic Suspense

A SEDUCTIVE COMBINATION OF DANGER AND DESIRE

A sneak peek at next month's titles...

In stores from 8th September 2016:

Just can't wait?
Buy our books online a month before they hit the shops!
www.millsandboon.co.uk

Also available as eBooks.